THE
FIREMAN'S
SON

THE FIREMAN'S SON

A Post-War Anthology

DANIEL F. POWELL

ARCHWAY PUBLISHING

This is a work of fiction. All of the characters, names, incidents, organizations, and dialogue in this novel are either the products of the author's imagination or are used fictitiously.

Archway Publishing books may be ordered through booksellers or by contacting:

Archway Publishing
1663 Liberty Drive
Bloomington, IN 47403
www.archwaypublishing.com
1 (888) 242-5904

Because of the dynamic nature of the Internet, any web addresses or links contained in this book may have changed since publication and may no longer be valid. The views expressed in this work are solely those of the author and do not necessarily reflect the views of the publisher, and the publisher hereby disclaims any responsibility for them.

Any people depicted in stock imagery provided by Getty Images are models, and such images are being used for illustrative purposes only. Certain stock imagery © Getty Images.

Scripture quotations are taken from the King James Version of the Bible.

ISBN: 978-1-4808-8422-9 (sc)
ISBN: 978-1-4808-8423-6 (e)

Library of Congress Control Number: 2019916869

Print information available on the last page.

Archway Publishing rev. date: 11/19/2019

Thanks, unbounded for my husband Ted's support.
A very sincere "thank you" to Jacqueline Busterna.
A heartfelt "Thank you" to Christy Lynn Weidman

.

PROLOGUE

"It is very difficult finding someone to share a room with you, Chief. Mr. Reynolds asked to be reassigned. He was afraid the room was going explode when you lit your cigar," Nurse Logan, (the local Nurse Ratchett) complained. She knew that his room always had a pungent earthy odor due to the Chief's flatulence.

The old man disgusted his previous roommates; he now hoped he would be left alone. Cursing, farting, and smoking cheap cigars chased the others away. Only a person out of touch with reality could tolerate sharing this room.

"The Chief" (a former fire chief), as he was known to all (and not affectionately), was, in medical jargon, a 94-year-old male Caucasian. His favorite hobbies, smoking and drinking, enabled diabetes to invade his body. His hobbies said "Hello" by way of causing five heart bypasses; their "Good-bye" was the loss of both legs below the knee. He had become a pain in the ass to everyone, including himself.

In early life, he bragged he would shoot himself before he became a burden to anyone. In later life he was quick to brag, "Lead poisoning doesn't run in my family." Here he was, still alive, and in a hospice.

As the nurse discussed the room situation with the Chief, she knew just what she was going to do.

A transfer patient was arriving today; he was going to become the Chief's new roommate.

"Not expected to live much longer?" she cynically thought. "Well, this will either push him along or bring him back to the living." She was going to punish the ornery old man by putting the new arrival in this room.

CHAPTER ONE

LEE LARUE WAS A FIFTY-NINE-YEAR-OLD man found unconscious lying on a sidewalk in Philadelphia. His chart was blank regarding medical history or family information. The medicine found in his pocket indicated he was an AIDS patient.

The hospital staff weren't sure if he could understand them. If these patients are off their medicine and not receiving proper care, their communication skills may be impaired. AIDS patients are known to float in and out of reality as their body functions start to shut down entering the last stages of life.

He was adamantly clear when he told the staff, "I don't want any care! Dope me up and let me die! I do not want to be resuscitated! I want to go home to the mountains to die."

Lee's social worker filled out the paper work to send him to Mountain View Manor. Located in the beautiful Seven Mountains, this was as close as they could place him to his hometown of Lewistown. Since Mountain View Manor received federal funds, they had to take some AIDS patients even though they didn't want to. Lee was sent there.

In this centrally located part of the state, the inhabitants were stuck in the old mire of race and religion. You were not accepted unless you were heterosexual and Anglo-Saxon. A "dark tan" was even suspect.

You could be screwing your neighbor's husband or wife. Your children could be kicking the shit out of less fortunate kids. The seriousness of the event would depend on who, what, and race. Punishment was meted out and someone was prosecuted or everyone looked the other way.

Fate ultimately brought Lee to his final home, to this bed. He was already tormented mentally. His last trial would be sharing a room with his ill-mannered roommate

"Mr. Larue? Can you hear me? Please try to wake up! You are in your room at Mountain View Manor; just outside of Lewistown." Nurse Logan raised her voice and started, "This is Mister…" but realized that the patient wasn't receptive. "Oh, just call him 'Chief'; everyone else does. I will let you rest and look in on you later," Nurse Logan said, over her shoulder, as she moved to the other bed.

"Chief, this is Lee Larue, your new roommate. Please try not to bother him. He's just arrived from Philadelphia.

"The city of 'queer ' brotherly love!" the Chief snarled.

"Clean that mouth up! You know that kind of talk isn't welcome here." Emily Anderson admonished the Chief. "Well, Nurse Logan, I see your patient is as fit as ever!"

"Yes, he's in fine fettle. Good luck! Sorry you have to be subjected to him again, Mother Anderson." The nurse apologized as she left the room and went back to her routine.

Because she was known to "mother" her patients, Emily was often referred to as "Mother." She took it in stride because she was also called "Mother" by some of the ladies at her church.

When Emily retired, she found she had too much time on her hands and too much energy to stay home. She could spend time with her friends lunching… Alternatively, she could sit around speculating which pill to take for her arthritis. But she decided to make "Arthur Itis" run along with her if he was going to keep her company.

At seventy years young, she began a prison ministry. But she switched to volunteering at Mountain View Manor's Hospice after too many narrow escapes from belligerent inmates. Since Mountain View was notoriously shorthanded, they were glad for the likes of this sweet old lady.

Five two and a little bit of a thing, she was a force to be reckoned with when she got a bee in her tiny bonnet (and all her hats were lined with a pile of tissue paper because her head was so small.) Being the daughter of a Baptist preacher, Emily broached no nonsense.

She had mocha colored skin, dark piercing eyes and a smile that would brighten a city blackout. Her only jewelry was her wedding band, as she refused to adorn herself with earthly trappings.

Her wardrobe consisted of high necked, long sleeved dresses suitable for someone coming out of deep mourning. She chose only sensible, "old lady" lace shoes and heavy cotton stockings showing frequent darning. She wore a sweater year-round. If the weather was _very_ hot, the sweater would be in the carryall bag she lugged along with her everywhere she went. The carryall bag, besides holding her purse, had anything Emily might need to do her ministering: crackers, a piece of fruit, a bottle of water, writing materials, safety pins, extra Kleenex, body lotion, a couple of new magazines and her constant companion, the Bible.

More than once, she left the Bible in her bag untouched – not so, since she met the Chief. He did not like anyone who wasn't from English or German extraction. He didn't want _this woman_ anywhere near him.

She was often tempted to chastise him with scripture from the Bible but she pulled herself up short. She was taught better than that! She realized the Bible was not to be used to empower yourself; it was wrong to pick and choose gospel words and hurl them like rocks to hurt someone. Emily knew these words were given to the world to use as guide, to show us how we are to live and treat others.

She lived by the Golden Rule: walking it and talking it, not just repeating it. One of her favorite Bible quotes was to forgive and turn the other cheek, seven times seventy. She'd lost count with the Chief.

She met him just as she was now meeting Larue. Some of the chores she did were helping people unpack, settle in and familiarize them with facility routines; be their "patient advocate."

Like many old women, Emily had an active curiosity, wanting to know all she could about someone new. By handling someone's belongings, she could intuitively get a feeling about the person. In this case Larue only had a small valise when he collapsed on the sidewalk in Philadelphia.

Inside she found a few changes of outerwear, some underwear, socks, and a well-worn red paper covered edition of the New Testament from a Billy Graham Crusade. Inside the book were various cards, letters and inspirational verses by Helen Steiner Rice. Emily was delighted with the book's contents; she felt they expressed romance, sentimentality and spiritually. The mementoes told her this was someone who had lived a full life and had been loved. Emily hoped she could get through to this man and help him make his peace with God before he died.

As she was leaving the room, the Chief assailed her as usual. "Take your incense and feathers and get the hell out of here, old woman!" he shouted.

"God still loves you!" Emily shouted so he could hear her. Under her breath she would have been heard muttering, "You old heathen! God forgive me."

As Emily walked away, she remembered when the Chief's wife had found Emily unpacking for her husband and quickly chased her away saying, "I'll take care of my husband!"

Edie, the Chief's wife, had certainly tried to "take care of her husband" at home. She told her girlfriends she hoped he would pass away at home so he wouldn't have to go to one of those dreadful places where "nobody cares."

When the doctor revealed the Chief was borderline diabetic, she bought him Tasty Cakes by the six-pack. When he wanted his whiskey, she gave it to him in a water glass and then handed him the bottle.

When the Chief's son asked why she did these things, Edie replied, "He asked for them! It saved me giving him one at a time and he can put them by his chair and have 'em whenever he wants. It's bad enough I have to fetch his beer in a cold mug."

The Chief's last abode prior to Mountain View was a one floor bungalow close to her son. Although the home he raised his family in was much nicer, his second wife would not live in the first wife's shadow.

When asked why they moved, Edie would respond, "Because both of us were having trouble doing the stairs." Their former neighbors thought of other reasons. The Chief's wife didn't want witnesses. The

Chief's legs had become unsteady and he would often fall. The neighbors could see Edie sitting on the back-porch swing, berating him because he had fallen in the yard. It was increasingly harder for him to get up by himself.

She would call out to him, "Get your fat ass up. Roll over on your stomach and push yourself up."

The neighbors would call out to her, "You better help your husband get up or call an ambulance, or we're going to call the police!

The Veterans' Association renovated their bathroom to accommodate his wheelchair. They gave him a bed lift to help him get from his chair to the bed.

Caretakers don't know if it is age or laziness that makes someone forget what they had known all their lives. Peeing in his television chair and defecating in his bed became a ritual convincing wife number two it was "time for him to go."

Neighbors, relatives and intimate friends knew he had made a mistake marrying this woman. It was obvious to everyone that wife number two was nothing in character like his first wife. This woman was unpolished, crude and from the wrong side of town.

It was no shame to have been a farm girl who had to work hard and was unable to finish high school. Edie learned two talents at home: sewing and cooking. She started working at a young age to help support her family. From the experience of working in many restaurants as a kitchen helper, she became a popular cook. Realizing she had a talent for cooking, she also supervised her family's small grocery business.

She had several children.

Her pregnancies were the results of sweaty workouts on the floor, up against a basement appliance, on top of a spare table, or on that musty stained mattress in the basement of a current employers' restaurant.

Gossip mongers speculated about who could possibly be the fathers of her children. It appeared that she would become pregnant and then leave her job. After the child was born, she would take another position. Within a short time, she would become pregnant again. It became a pattern: leaving a job, having another baby, finding another job. This woman was no Monica Lewinski! She was such a good cook that she could have been the first female Chef in the White House.

Edie was working in a kitchen the first time she met the Chief. He had stopped at his favorite bar to have his nightly nerve pill, a shot and a beer chaser. The bartender called out, "Edie come and take the Chief's order." Edie was forty-five years young at the time. She wore glasses, and had short, almost mannish salt and pepper hair. As with many rural women, she had no interest in skin care. She was a friendly, jovial woman who wanted a secure future.

She smoked, drank, cursed and could tell a dirty story with the best of the boys. But this middle-aged woman was still a little girl; looking to be rescued from the smoky kitchens she had to toil in by her Prince Charming. And that night her prince rescued her.

For being seventy-two years young when they met, the Chief was an active, physically virile man. He was only five feet eight, having a stocky, muscular build that many younger men envied. He had bravado enough to tell any man, "I'll knock you on your ass if you get in my way!"

His frame was topped off by a full head of silver white hair. He told everyone that his half inch part "is where a bullet grazed my head in World War II." He had large twinkling blue eyes and a politician's smile. As far as attitude and charisma, you would think Norman Lear patterned Archie Bunker after him.

Being a widower for over a year the Chief had heard about Edie and thought, "What the Hell, she likes sex and I need some." Edie wanted security and thought, "What the Hell, social security is still security!"

Everyone knew the man had no time for anyone unless he or she was as bigoted as he was. He was not someone who would be sought out to make up a card party. Quite the opposite - people made it a point to keep away from his foul mouth and bad temper.

The Chief had few visitors at Mountain View. Edie cut back on the frequency of her visits. She took umbrage of the fact he called her by his first wife's' name too often. He had one true friend who still came to visit. It was Cornpopper – although his real name was Bob Comprost, the Chief had somehow turned the name around.

On Bob's next visit the Chief asked him, "See that guy over there? A real three-dollar bill; never thought I would be in bed next to one of them!"

Trying to soothe the agitated Chief, Bob explained, "Aw, shucks, nowadays being gay is no more than being a Democrat or Republican. In the big cities, nobody cares who sleeps with who."

"That's politics! This is bullshit! I didn't lose half of my face in the storming of Normandy for the likes of him!" the Chief raged.

CHAPTER TWO

THE CHIEF HAD BEEN FIGHTING FOR SUR-
vival all his life. He was born into a family whose ancestors came from
Europe in 1850.

A wealthy local family had sent letters to friends in England inquiring if anyone knew of a Christian, English-speaking woman who would
want to travel to America and be a nanny for their family. Prospects
being bleak in Cheltenham, England at the time, a brave mother decided her daughter should apply for the position in the new country.
The young lady, daughter of a poor but respectable seamstress and a
farm laborer, traveled to America.

At the same time, the Reverend of the local Episcopal Church sent
a similar notice to his former church in Swansea, Wales. He let them
know the church needed a young strong Christian man to help him as
sexton of the church and caretaker of the cemetery.

The two young people met after church one Sunday. They courted,
dated and were married in that same church on Christmas day, 1850.
The parish provided a small cottage on the cemetery grounds for them
to live in. It was their destiny to raise a family that would give the
church a hundred years of service. Father and son were sextons for the
church. The women of the family baked the bread that was used in
communion. They were instrumental in developing the activities of
the women of the church, the Altar Guild and the Monday Club. This
couple were the great-grandparents of The Chief.

The Chiefs' mother, Edna, was a granddaughter of the family
whose roots were centered in the Church. Her family raised their children to be proper pious Christians who lived their lives by the Bible's
standards, without impropriety.

The Chiefs' family had origins in England also, good, quiet, unremarkable people. His father Richard, who was called "Dick," was a fine example of the saying, "You can raise your children well; you cannot control them once they are grown." He was ruggedly handsome, a 'man's' man." He impressed people with his straightforwardness, and his ability in fisticuffs. No one was going to 'kick the shit' out of him; he would do the kicking.

Edna's' parents, the Jacksons, did not approve of Dick. He was employed but did not hide the fact he liked to drink and enjoyed his reputation as a womanizer. Without approval, but within the church's guidelines, Edna married the rakish Dick Powell. She went into the marriage knowing he drank too much and was reluctant to give up his philandering. She loved him with all her heart and knew he would settle down.

He worked in a steel foundry that manufactured railroad parts. Everything seemed to go well for the young family until Dick had problems on the job. Edna explained to her children, "Your father invented the switch that railroads use to switch trains from track to track. The company stole his idea and cheated your father out of the patent rights."

He never forgave the company nor himself for losing his chance at success. He could only find solace in the numbness that liquor gave him. He turned into a bully at the bars. He would pick a fight with anyone; pity a newcomer who didn't know of his reputation.

No one wanted to hire a drunk. The only jobs he could get were strictly brute force labor, often quarry work or breaking large stones on the highway. This helped use up some of his anger so there were a few periods of calm for his wife. When rejected by his wife during his drunken binges he would look for a warm bosom anywhere.

Edna had sympathy for Dick, because she knew how hard he had worked on the train track switching project. This sensitivity and great love enabled her to withstand his wandering ways with the women. Edna's' parents were worried that the worry and stress would injure her frail health. Influenzas of epidemic proportions was ravaging towns and thousands were dying.

Dick couldn't fight steady work and took to staying away from home for days at a time. He rode his motorcycle all over the state as witnessed by the many cards and perfumed letters that arrived at their home. Edna loved her husband and wanted to give him time to deal with his anger; that she believed stemmed from his being cheated out of his rightful due. She was willing to wait for him.

Dick did not "deal with his emotional problems" before her death. Edna died in the great influenza epidemic of 1920, leaving a family of five. Edna's mother had her husband Michael; her children Dorothy, John and his wife Tress living at home. What could she do? She had to take care of her grandchildren!

Dick came home for his wife's funeral but disappeared later that day. Everyone guessed he was facing his demons and dealing with the shame of how he treated his wife. Bereavement was not a cloak he would ever wear.

His solace was getting back to having fun. He wanted the company of a healthy young woman. He wanted someone to take care of his children.

Some weeks later, he sputtered up to the house on Hale Street, in a puff of smoke and a calliope of noise. The family peeking out between the lace curtains was very surprised.

No one was quite ready for the caricature of Mae West on his arm. The voluptuous Lottie appeared in a brightly flowered dress replete with rows of ruffles. A large hat, with a jaunty feather bouncing in time to her full hips, announced her arrival.

As Mr. Jackson opened the door to a cloud of cheap perfume, he was instantly aware why Dick had claimed this beautiful creature. A full bursting bosom and luscious red lips foretold of many nights of pleasure.

When Mrs. Jackson greeted her son-in-law, she was quickly taken back by his young bride's obvious youth. "She has no experience with children - she's only a child herself," she mused. "She will have all she can do to keep track of Dick."

Mrs. Jackson saw the look of concern on Lottie's face the minute the children appeared. A stunned 'haalloo' and her twitchy demeanor as she accepted a chair revealed her uneasiness with the situation. Dick attempted to introduce their new mother to his children. Wanting to greet and hug his children they moved away from his reach. The baby, called Bubby, pushed forward and yelled; "You're not my mommy!" Dick's children were aloof and distant to the drunk of a father they remembered.

Lottie had been told she was being taken home to "meet the family." Dick neglected to tell her he had five children aged five to seventeen. The nubile Lottie was all of twenty years old.

As Dick and Lottie left the Jackson family, that day, all parties involved were thinking of what to do with Edna's orphans.

Mother Jackson decided she was not relinquishing the well-being of her grandchildren to "that man" and his child bride. Seeing his children's faces reminded Dick of Edna, a ghost he would like to forget. And the image of raising some dead woman's family is not what Lottie envisioned as a lusty newlywed.

When they met the next day, Mother Jackson shared her plan. She was very fond of Ken, the youngest ("Bubby"); she would keep him. The oldest boy, Fred, could stay because he was working and helped the household. The second oldest, Marguerite, would have to stay with her grandmother because she tended to be wild and needed a stern hand. There were childless farm families from the church who were anxious to adopt children. Those families would welcome the middle girls, Velma, Evelyn and Frances.

Bubby was a scamp, but he could do no wrong. He was his grandmother's favorite, even over her husband. He would taunt Aunt Tress then run and hide behind the big coal stove in the kitchen where she could not reach him. When she moved away, he took his slingshot and shot coal at her.

He watched and timed it so when certain people would go to the outhouse they would sit on a coating of lard. Some people found out the hard way that someone had rubbed sand onto the paper in the outhouse. There was more than the usual amount of missing and lost items in the house, attributed to Bubby.

Marguerite, on the other hand, became the favorite target of her Aunt Dord (Dorothy). Dord was engaged and would soon be leaving her Hale Street home. She intended to teach Marguerite how to be a help to her Grandmother. According to her, Marguerite *would* learn how to clean and keep a house. This included taking rugs up to beat, dusting, scrubbing, (floors, woodwork and walls,) AND the laundry, which included how to wash those lace curtains that needed extra starch and dried on stretchers.

On one occasion, Dord asked her niece to go upstairs and straighten up. Marguerite, being completely uninterested in cleaning, decided to ignore the request. Working downstairs Dord heard the Bissell vacuum moving. It seemed to be concentrated on one spot. Going upstairs to see how her niece was progressing; she found Marguerite lying across a bed with a novel in one hand, pushing the vacuum back and forth over the same spot time after time. Her Aunt, full of youthful exuberance herself, jumped on top of her niece whaling her until her niece called for her grandmother.

Fred was working at the local ice plant, bringing money home to Grandma. On a cold night, he was late getting home, breaking the curfew of the house. The doors were locked and he had to stay in the cold outer shanty all night. They hadn't known he had fallen into the water at the ice plant and caught a chill. He developed a cold that turned into pneumonia, dying at the early age of nineteen.

When Grandfather Jackson died in 1925 Grandma and Bubby were alone. Bubby was becoming more than his grandmother could handle. Tress and John decided Grandma was too old to live alone and take care of Bubby. They came one day and packed Grandma, Bubby, and everything in the house and moved them, lock stock and barrel, to their home on Montgomery Avenue.

Now that they were living in Tress's house, things would be done Tress's way. When Grandma tried to help around the house, her way of doing things was not "how things were done" here! Meal times varied in this house; they were not set in stone. Laundry was not done as carefully, or on the 'traditional' day. Grandmother Jackson thought the way this house was run was a little slip-shod.

Tress and John had children of their own now and they really did not want Bubby in their household. For Grandma's sake, they gave him a home; not a family, only a roof over his head. He was to have a cot in the basement by the furnace.

Every time the kids got a chance, they would add seasoning to the food so that Bubby would not eat, making the adults of the house think Bubby was pouting. After a dinner, where the kids poured vinegar all over the fried potatoes, and mustard on the meat course, Bubby was again caught in a fight with Tress's sons.

His grandmother, not knowing all the behind-the-scenes shenanigans of the other children, started to have her doubts regarding Bubby's conduct.

When he saw he'd lost her favor, he decided to leave. He planned and knew what he would do to get back at them. On the final night he would be in his uncle's house, his revenge developed a life of its own.

That night, when everyone went to bed, he snuck into the bedroom of the oldest boy. That boy was older than Bubby, but taken one at a time, Bubby was stronger than either of the boys. He crept into the room and looped a rope around the bedpost entwining his cousin's arms and legs. The leader of the bullies opened his mouth to say "What the hell!" as Bubby jumped on his chest and stuck his dirty socks in his mouth.

Bubby used some of the old cans from the garage to 'paint' his victim. He finished his 'artwork' by dumping sooty ashes on top of the paint.

Being an old house, the family was used to creaking noises during the night. Grandma always slept soundly and Tress and John were entertaining each other again, so no one was aware of Bubby's nocturnal machinations.

When he jumped on top of the younger boy, he was so surprised that Bubby had no trouble tying a gag around his mouth and hog-tying him. More paint, ashes; Bubby was done with the boys.

Their younger sister lay asleep in her bed. She was lucky she did not have to suffer the smell of paint like the boys. Bubby neatly cut her pigtails off as they lay on her pillow. He took the prized pigtails and placed them neatly out of sight in her small clothes that were waiting to be put on the next morning. He hoped they would fall out to the floor giving her a good scare, as if maybe a rat had been in her clothes. His last prank before he left that night was to dump some blue ink on the white clothes Tress was soaking in the summer kitchen. Unafraid, he went out into the calm June night never to return to the house on Montgomery Street.

He was going to live with the "MoDockers," a gang of kids from the south side who were territorial. They discouraged other groups of children who might have wanted a presence in the neighborhoods.

Being a group of variously aged boys, with the only commonality being homelessness, they had taken up refuge in an old mansion called Greenlawn, the former Greens estate. The large once grandiose property stood surrounded by a wrought iron fence.

Behind the fence was a profusion of flowering shrubs and bushes that all but hid the house from view. Large once graceful trees lined the double driveway that meandered up to the house and returned to the front padlocked gate. Tall pillars ran up to the second floor supporting the broad expanse of balcony that the boys slept on during warm weather. Some of the rooms boasted ceiling with holes that let you view the stars even if you slept indoors. On the walls were large dark rings pointing out where elegant family portraits had once been displayed. The proud staircase still boasted a sturdy railing to support young revelers sliding down from the second floor.

Grand rooms once host to elegant soirees were now a playground for kick the wicket and marbles, not a home an ordinary family would live in; but to the MoDockers, it was Heaven. It was large enough to accommodate many more than were there now; it provided a shelter from the weather, and was well away from prying eyes.

This group of unrelated boys knew they had to depend on each other. They became as close as blood brothers, looking out for one another. If one of them were picked on, they reacted as one. Everyone who knew of the MoDockers tried to look the other way to avoid a larger problem.

They lived by "borrowing" bread from Mr. Stuey's bakery cart, vegetables from the local gardens, chickens from Mrs. Brown's hen house, and milk from a parked milk truck or from someone's front porch. They would rotate turns supplying the various needs. That way it was always a different face seizing an item, hoping the "lending" party would be caught off guard.

Claire Ulrich was always a ready ally for the boys if they needed something and could not get it. She was a second cousin to Bubby who lived a block from where Grandma Jackson lived on Hale Street. She was a late-in-life baby to very well-to-do parents, who had a nurse for their baby. The nurse fell down the stairs while carrying her charge. In the accident, Claire's back was broken. Although it healed so she could walk, she remained a hunchback all her life.

As a young child, she had suffered the ridicule and taunts of young children at a boarding school who did not understand her physical deformity. She made such a ruckus her parents brought her home and hired tutors for her. Nurse, tutor, nanny (now chaperone), all learned quickly what Miss Ulrich wants, Miss Ulrich gets. Her parents threw their hands in the air and gave up; anything to keep Claire happy. By early adulthood she developed quite the personality. She had beautiful silky long red hair and the proverbial temper of a redhead to match.

She spent many afternoons on the side porch watching the activity at the Ice Plant. She heard the conversations between the workmen and rowdy tradespeople. The employees of the ice plant would notice Claire and wave, calling "Hello" and "Good Morning."

When she became accustomed to the men, and they less timid of Miss Ulrich, they would go over to Claire's porch and visit with her. Having grown up quicker than many of her peer group, she was known for having the mouth of a sailor.

Everyone toadied to Claire but Bubby. Early on he told her, "You're just a spoiled little hunchback who only gets her way because she was dropped down the stairs!"

Still, he and Claire came to get along fabulously and shared confidences. She called him by his given name Ken. Bubby was too babyish.

She didn't feel Ken should have to live with homeless boys. He was a Jackson!

During the hot summer dog days, the boys would go down to the river and skinny dip. Being one of the youngest, Bubby was embarrassed by his small amount of manliness. Others with hairy chests would strut like peacocks. These sessions were the beginning of Bubby's sex education. Some of the bigger boys would tease him, making fun of his small "pecker." Often a few of them would handle themselves until they made stuff squirt from their pee hole. This was the first-time Bubby found out a boy could do this; he didn't know if it hurt - it must because how could this happen? The guys doing it would yell and moan; when it was over, they were awfully happy.

When playing in the water it was obvious some of the boys grabbed at each other and later rolled playfully on the grass.

These same boys slept together many nights where Bubby saw them moving around not understanding what they were doing. One hot muggy July evening some of the boys were getting a little rowdy. Some started pushing and shoving and soon were wrestling near Bubby. During the closeness of the playful fighting some of the boys were becoming aroused.

As he lay trying to ignore the interaction, Bubby felt someone's hot breath and droplets of sweat on his back. A dark-skinned boy they'd reluctantly let join their group had jumped on his back. He jumped up slugging at anything near him. The boy backed off pulling up his pants shoving the "missile" he was going to use on Bubby back into his pants.

Bubby gathered his belongings and ran from Woodlawn. Scared, remembering that glistening black boy trying to "pound his fudge," he took refuge in the unused summer kitchen behind Claire's home. The next morning, he waited for her chaperone to bring Claire out to the side porch for her breakfast. He told Claire of being accosted; she, a little older, understood a lot more. She told him to sleep in the summer kitchen at night until she could figure out what to do.

That afternoon Miss Ulrich took the family by surprise. Because of her deformity, she never went out to shop; trades people brought clothes to her home. Today, she told her family and chaperone she wanted to get dressed and go uptown.

Happy to see her show some interest in going out, her chaperone got her into her rolling chair and they set off for the shopping district. Claire only had one stop to make; she knew where Ken's sister Marguerite worked. She was going to convince her to find a solution to her brother's need of a clean place to sleep and decent meals. She was going to take up the task of making sure Ken had what he needed and attended school.

She wanted him to have the "normal life" she didn't.

CHAPTER THREE

As Cornpopper was leaving he said to the Chief, "Tell me one of your stories before I go."

The Chief thought and thought, and then he said, "Well, there were these two big-wig officers sitting at a sidewalk cafe in Paris after the liberation relaxing over a victory drink. They spied a lowly PFC with a beautiful mademoiselle nearby. They wrote a note and sent it to the PFC saying, 'We believe we recognize you, I from having studied with you at Princeton; my colleague thinks he studied with you at Cambridge. Please come over and straighten us out.'"

The Chief continued. "The private send back a note saying, 'I didn't study at either school - I went to a college of taxidermy and I'm mounting and stuffing this bird myself.'"

Cornpopper laughed! He grasped the old Chief's hand and said, "You always could tell a story. Take care of yourself, old man."

"The hell with you!" the Chief roared as his old friend chuckled and left the room.

"Why are you always saying 'hell' when I hear you?" Mother Anderson asked the Chief as she came into the room.

"Christ sakes you back?" the Chief shot off to her.

"You know, you have a reckoning coming, don't you? We all do! You had better get ready for yours if you know what is good for you!" Emily preached.

"Oh, just pull the curtain so I can have some peace and you do your mumbo jumbo," the Chief loudly sputtered.

As Emily pulled the curtain out from the wall to the bottom of the beds, the hard glare in her eye for the Chief changed to a soft look of compassion for the soul she came to minister to.

Her new charge had spent two days in his bed and Emily was now positioned to attack and see if she could stir him out of his cocoon. She thought she might have caught him sneaking a peek as she pulled the curtains between the two beds.

She went to the pillow where a noble head once covered with thick dark hair was now barely covered by a few gray strands.

Bending close she whispered, "Good morning - I am Mrs. Emily Anderson. Please, make an old woman happy and open your eyes."

Listening to her musically lilted voice he was reminded of his grandmother. When he looked up, he found himself to be the object of soft inquiring eyes, and a face whose wrinkles had wrinkles. Obviously old, but so sweet looking. He thought, "She smells of lilacs," a scent he remembered from childhood. It was his mother's favorite scent. She kept lilac soap in her dresser drawers so all her clothes had a lilac scent lingering on them, and the fragrance enveloped her children as she hugged them.

Lee couldn't remember wanting to talk to anyone for a long time, and he said, "You smell very nice."

"Why thank you." Mother Anderson said. "You have been in this bed for quite a while. Don't you think it's time we get you up into a chair?" she asked.

He felt weak, but the old woman was so nice. "All right." He decided he would try.

When Emily saw him start to stir, she said, "Now just a minute, let me get some help." She went out to the nurse's station, "Mr. Larue would like to get out of bed and into a chair - could someone please help me do that?"

"We are awfully busy right now, we'll be back later," a woman at the desk said.

"Later? That phone call doesn't sound that important, and you can do that crossword later - or do I have to go down to the office?" Mother Anderson asked.

The people at the desk rolled their eyes at each other and two orderlies begrudgingly got up. They would rather help her now then hear

Emily had gone to the office to complain. They followed her down the hall and made ready to get Lee out of bed.

"Wait," she said. "You need to put a pillow on that chair - he needs some padding."

"He had an ass! What did he do with it?" the taller of the two men said. "He didn't use it right or he'd still have it!" the other laughed.

Mother Anderson let the slur pass and watched as they moved the patient from the bed to the chair. All they did was put him in the chair and leave quickly. It was up to her to cover him and put a pillow behind his head.

A lunch tray came and she decided to try to get him to eat something. The dietary department had sent him a soft diet tray. The food did not look very appetizing but she wanted him to have some nourishment.

He said, "That doesn't look good. Besides, I don't think anything will stay down. I'll just drink the juice." At his stage, AIDS patients can usually only take liquids, so she was not surprised at his response to the food. As he was sipping his juice she went back out to the nurse's station. "Excuse me," again interrupting private phone calls and magazine reading.

"Could you find out if Mr. Larue would be allowed to have Ensure?"

The staff looked at each other and one of them asked, "Why? You do know he came here to die? Why give him something to prolong the inevitable?" the man who made the slur sassed.

With that, Emily turned and headed for the elevators. She was so disgusted with the staff member for saying those words. "When God is ready, He will decide the time," she announced. Until then she would do what she could to see that Lee had the proper care.

She proceeded to the office and gave the administrator her opinion. "What kind of people do you have working here?"

Sadly, the administrator acknowledged her remark. "The people hired today are not like the people of yesterday. Years ago, people took pride in their work! Those who worked in patient care, be it in a doctor's office, hospital, or home, did it because they wanted to help people.

They cared about their patients. But nowadays, it's just a paycheck. Eight hours!

"It used to be that the first thing people would want to know when they came back to work the next day was, 'How is Mr. So-and-So? How is Mrs. So-and-So? Did So-and-So make it through the night? Did you reach So-and-So's children or parents?' Not today! The only thing they want to know is, where am I working, and who is going to relieve me for breaks and lunch. No, it's not right - and I will make sure that man is written up and counseled. I apologize." The administrator offered.

With that, Emily went back to Lee's room.

She found him in his chair with his eyes closed. He has had enough of shut-eye, she thought. Perhaps now we can talk.

"Mr. Larue, is Lee Larue an adopted name? I found notes and letters in your belongings that I put away that were addressed to another person. Do the things I unpacked not belong to you or are you playing incognito?"

Startled out of his daydreaming he opened his eyes and thought, "My God, what am I in for?" In Philadelphia, the hospital staff was content to let him alone to slip away into sleep.

"I know you must be a lovely lady, but I'm just here to die."

"I don't think so! No one is *just* here to die!" she said emphatically. "Do you believe in God?" she questioned.

"Yes, I do, but I told God he could go about his business and I would see him soon," he said facetiously.

"How soon is His business! And my business is His business! Now unless you tell me to get out of your room, I am here to do my job for Him. Now I asked you, is Lee Larue your given name? Please answer me."

"Lee Larue is my stage name, for professional purposes," he said.

Taken aback, Emily sputtered, "Sounds like a woman's name."

"It's a long story; I really don't feel like telling right now. A lot of my friends and I had feminine nicknames. Like Superman's girlfriend's names: Lana Lang, Lois Lane... I wanted a name that began with the same letter, so I chose Lesley Larue. They shortened mine to just Lee when we were around straight people. The last time I had friends they called me Lee. So, I'd be happy if you could call me Lee, Mrs. Anderson - if you don't mind."

Glad to have a dialogue going with her new charge, she thought to herself, "We should pick our wars and battles wisely. Let him win the skirmish now - at least he's talking to me."

"Well then! You must call me Emily. That is what my friends call me and I intend for you to be my friend. I will certainly be your friend! I believe that God has put us all on this earth for a purpose. Some of us are lucky and fall right into that purpose. Others may not; and some may never find their purpose."

Moving close to him, lifting his wan hand in hers and holding it tightly she explained, "I think our lives are like tapestries. You never see the beauty of a tapestry while it is being woven. One must wait until it is done!

"You must turn it over, stepping back away from it somewhat, to see the entire story. You must look at it from side to side to see the entire story revealed in the mural type artwork. Such are our lives on Earth. We are weaving our tapestry.

"How we live our lives, what worthwhile things we do or make happen, give our tapestry its story. The people we meet give our tapestry its color. Our errors of judgment and whatever good deeds we may do affect the tightness of the weave. We meet everyone, good and bad, for a reason. There are no chance encounters in God's world. We may see them that way, but only because we were not wise enough to accept God's plan for us. And sometimes, we make mistakes in our lives that muddy up our tapestry.

"There is no good or bad luck! Only God's way. We only label something good or bad depending on if it is convenient for us. God is always there to help us start weaving the right colors into our tapestry again, and no one is lost to the Lord. We can turn our backs, but He does not turn His back - He is always there. He will always try to show us a way to find Him, to do the right thing, and to end our tapestry well. When we are done in this life, He views our work and helps us walk away so we too can see the beautiful creation we have made with His help. I am making it my job to see you finish your tapestry well."

As Emily finished speaking, the man was overcome with emotion. It had been so long since anyone spoke to him with such love. The muscles in his throat constricted, his eyes spilled over with bitter tears that should have been purged ages ago. He was so filled up with emotion his head felt like it would burst. He wanted to cry out loudly but his chest was too near collapsing to bear his shouts of sorrow. Emily took him to her bosom, patted his moist brow, and let him quietly weep until he was spent.

CHAPTER FOUR

"Somebody over there read their death notice?" the Chief called out.

To keep his hearing disability from being other people's hearing problem, the staff had given him a pair of earphones to wear. When the Chief did not have visitors, the old man passed his time with them on, listening to country music or watching old war movies.

"Quiet, you old heathen, and put your headset on," Emily told the Chief.

Emily continued speaking to Lee. "There, there, you know we still don't know that much about you. Tell me about your family," Emily softly said.

Lee slowly started to talk to her. "I came from a very poor family, all sons, all born at home. We lived in a building that was originally a large one family house. When you opened the front door, you entered a long hallway that led to the front door of our apartment. Right inside the entrance to the house was a coat tree with a mirror and a seat to sit down on to remove your wet shoes. I remember my father's sister, Aunt Peggy, coming to visit, only to disappear to the seat by the door.

"My mother told me that Aunt Peggy would spend hours sitting in the hall, on that seat, looking out onto the street through the sheer front door curtain. She'd met a good-looking man when she was out dancing one night. She discovered his family lived at the top of the alley, across the street from our apartment. Every time she visited us, she sat in the hall on that small coat rack seat, hoping to see him leave his house so she could start across the street to meet him. One day she was lucky enough to catch him, enabling her to create a 'serendipitous' meeting.

She yelled and when my mother went to see what she was yelling about, Aunt Peggy had turned into a wind-up jumping toy.

"She jumped up from her sitting position, flounced her curls, pinched her cheeks and licked a finger, brushing it over her eyebrows. All the time she was primping she turned her face from side to side, pursing her lips together in the mirror making sure she looked her best.

"Out the door she rushed across the street exclaiming, 'Why Sherm! Imagine meeting you! I was just visiting my brother across the street.' She hooked her arm in his and off they walked. Her pre-meditated 'chance' encounter worked out, and fortune smiled on her. They began dating seriously, marrying a few months later.

"When I was very young my father bought a car. My family said there was no way I could remember it since I was only three years old, but I did. We figured out the date because that was the only time, he had a 'new' car. Someone had been holding me and laid me down on the front room floor to allow them to go outside and look at his pride and joy.

"The reason my father could buy the car was that he had selfishly purchased it with an insurance settlement from an auto accident. We had been the victims of a hit and run drunk driver. My mother was a good-looking woman and the injury she sustained marked her face for life. The monetary award was because of her facial damage.

"Wanting to show off his new toy, my father decided we were going for a ride. Someone came back and got me ready to go along. They took me out to the car and handed me to my grandmother in the back seat.

"I was fascinated by something about the door. I had my fingers in the door jamb playing with the button that went in and out, to turn the light on/off when the door was shut. My father shut the door and my fingers were smashed in the doorframe. My father angrily blamed my mother's mother, Mom-Mom, for being careless and stupid.

"My mother's people were of Pennsylvania Dutch extraction, and my grandmother had a heavy Pennsylvania Dutch accent. My grand-mother had been a 'bound girl,' a title given to a girl whose impoverished parents had 'bound her over' to another family as a household servant. When poor parents could not afford another mouth to feed, an agreement was reached between the parents and a usually wealthier family. That family would take the child to raise, and in return, the child would become a servant in their household. Such children would be given a roof over their heads and adequate food, and would be taught very basic reading and math skills by the mistress. A female child would be expected to master the domestic duties of taking care of a house and family. Since my grandmother had no formal education, her Pennsylvania Dutch accent was still very strong.

"My mother was born late in my grandmother's life. She told me her mother, Mom-Mom had very little interest in anything at home. Mom-Mom did not want another child, since all her other children were grown; Mom-Mom preferred to spend her afternoons at the local movie matinees.

"My mother's older sister Ruth took the place of her movie-struck mother. Between Ruth and their father, they raised my mother. After Mom-Mom died my mother told me she'd heard rumors that her mother would meet men in the theatre and take them up to the balcony for a 'good time.'

"My mother realized early on that her mother found her older husband dull, and certainly not manly enough for her. After my mother died, my father's aunt confided to me, 'I heard your mother's father might not have been your grandmother's husband. He could have been Homer Searer, one of the men she had a dalliance with at the movies.' Homer was the father of the young man my Aunt Peggy married.

"I never met my mother's father; he died before I was born, while my father was overseas in the war. My mother said he had been a handsome mountain man with dark hair and deep blue eyes. She told me her mother saw him when he came into town one day and pursued him until they got married.

"My mother loved her father very much. Whether it was because his wife ignored him or because my mother was the youngest child, he babied her more than he had his other four children.

"There were times she would not like what was served for supper.

He would give her a nickel or dime and tell her go to the corner store to buy something to eat. She told me she would usually buy dried beef, candy, or potato chips.

"As a child, her father would take her by the hand and say, 'Come, it is time to tame the lions.' They would go out in the fields and pick dandelion. When they got home, he would clean the greens and let my mother sell them to the neighbors for use in their salads. He would allow her to keep the change for pocket money.

"My parents met when they were in high school. My mother was in ninth grade and my father was in eleventh. From my very first memories, my father always told me, 'I saw that Dutch ass wiggle down the street and that was enough for me!'

"My mothers' version was, 'Your father followed me around in the halls every chance he got. He would follow me home after school. Every time he found out that a boy had talked to me or he knew of a boy I talked with, he would threaten the young man and tell them not to talk to me or he would give them a beating. Soon no other boys would talk to me or have anything to do with me. My girlfriends were impressed by his cave man attitude. I did not find it cute but he finally won me over by his constant flattery and attention. He started waiting outside my front door in the morning and would walk me to school. He carried my books for me and bought me candy and little gifts.

"My parents liked your father and often invited him to stay for supper. My mother even washed some of his clothes for him because he had so few. She would wash his socks and he would go home without them. They would dry overnight on the stovepipe and he would pick them up when he came to walk me to school the next morning.'"

"My mother quit school after the ninth grade because she was embarrassed," Lee continued. "One of her teachers sent her to the school nurse where she was asked if she was pregnant. She told them she wasn't! She knew she had gained weight from eating all the candy my father had been giving her. She was so mad she didn't want to go back to school. Her mother hadn't had an education so she didn't care.

"I remember a story about one night when Mom-Mom invited

my father to dinner. After my mother's parents went to bed she and my father started making out in the front room. Afraid they would do something to the sofa they moved to the floor. In the morning, her father came down to get ready for work and found them sleeping, lying on the floor naked. He pulled the afghan off the couch, covered them up and went into the kitchen. He made his breakfast, left for work, never speaking of the incident.

"Mother Anderson," Nurse Logan interrupted, "there is a phone call for you."

"Excuse me Lee, let me go see what it is. I'll be right back." He watched the remnants of the once stately woman leave the room.

Lee had found comfort in the old lady's bosom; it took him back to his infancy. He fondly remembered.... It was his father who would get up trying to calm and sooth the cries that broke the silence of the early morning.

When his mother delivered her baby boy, the doctor assisting had to cut the tissue under her vaginal canal. The incision never healed correctly and caused recurring abscesses between the vaginal area and her rectum. After the birth she had bouts of constipation and poor appetite. With no insurance she could not afford to see a doctor, let alone go to the hospital.

His father's relatives were great supporters of, F. W. Black Hospital. Dr. Black knew his father and through the influence of his family my mother was accepted as a charity patient at Blacks hospital.

There were rampant rumors of the good doctor having a sobriety problem and philandering with the nursing staff. In fact, it was said that Dr. Johnson caught him using the operating room table for his own "operatering."

Within a week the operation site was oozing pus and was odiferous. They were fortunate to know the interns working the emergency room at the Lewistown Hospital, who were willing to come to the house. The recurring sicknesses were blamed on the extra cutting during the birth.

Although the visit from the interns took care of the operation site problem created by Dr. Black, his mother was losing weight and not able to keep food down. His father met a doctor, new to town, and he said, "Bring your wife to see me and let me examine her."

He diagnosed she had a growth in her stomach and said we'll have to take her to the hospital and do an exploratory procedure on her. My father walked the halls waiting for an answer. The doctor came out excitingly saying, "Your wife has a lump on the right side of her chest. We have to operate." And he rushed back to surgery.

Within minutes he rushed back out! My father knew something happened to his wife. "I am so sorry," the doctor continued, (my fathers' heart dropping down to his feet) "Her heart is on her right side. It wasn't a mass. However, we did see some ileitis. It is related to ulcerative colitis, characterized by provocative infection of the colon and rectum."

Hours later Doc came out to where my father had fallen asleep in a chair. "Ken your wife is out of surgery. The Ileitis was more aggressive than we knew going in. Her intestines were full of disease. The only thing I could do was cut it all out; connecting her bowels to her colon. I am afraid she is going to continue losing weight and have digestive problems, I'm sorry.

"Hell, how can she live like that?" his father roared.

The doctor looked at the man in front of him. "Take her home and treat her well."

His father took care of night time baby needs so his wife might get a good nights' rest.

His father would sit in the old wide and sturdy mission style rocker; holding his baby close on his chest he cooed, "Hung Ka, Fung Kaa, Chick da Lick a Yung Kaa... that means I love you." (H.K.F.K.C.L.Y.K. These were the initials he wrote on the flap of the letters he sent home to his wife during the war)

Lee's father tried to stay involved in taking care of his children. After the evening meal his mother would clean the kitchen and he would help with the boys. As his father took his bath, he would bathe his sons. Oldest to youngest each had their bath with their Dad. That was a fun time for him. He loved the soaping up; he and his father would do to each other. It made him feel tingly all over. His Dad and he would play hide the soap.

Lee often found the soap but as much as he tugged on it, he could not pull it out of the water. His father always washed Lee's backside especially well, tickling him by inserting something to make sure he was clean.

Emily came back to Lee's room, so he picked up his tale where he left off.

"My parents decided since I was such a handful to give me to a childless family, the Machamers. They packed my clothing and toys and took me to the second-floor apartment on Third Street where my new family lived.

"In later life my mother told me, 'It was heart-breaking. I was so sick and knew I would not be around to care for you. The wrenching knowledge that someone else would raise my child was almost too much for me to think about in my condition. My heart was pounding and I thought my head was going to explode that day I had to leave you. Your father was beside himself. He felt for your own good that it was the best solution. You would have two healthy parents to love you and they would have only one child to raise. You would have it made. Your father thought he would have all he could do just raising the other boys alone."

As sick, weak and upset as she was, my father started berating her the minute they drove away from the Third street apartment. He yelled at her, "Your father spoiled you! You have always been a fussy eater. Maybe if you had eaten a better diet; more variety, more vegetables, less sweets, maybe you would not be sick. You should have taken better care of yourself, now I am going to be stuck with the kids alone, by myself."

A few days after taking me to my new home, my mother and father received a phone call from a Doctor Tumen in Philadelphia. The doctor who operated on her in the local hospital had consulted his former teacher regarding my mothers' condition.

Doctor Tumen told my mother, "If you would consent to be a guinea pig; entering the hospital as a charity patient; we will try to help you. All the services of the medical and surgical departments would be at our disposal to diagnose your situation and find a remedy. You must understand we are a teaching hospital; your procedures will be performed in an Amphitheatre. Many doctors will be involved because they are here to learn. We will do our utmost to preserve your modesty and dignity as a human being. There will be extensive tests and surgical probing procedures. We do believe we can help you! You have my word!"

They listened to the phone call together, both with tears in their eyes. What could they do? They knew they could never afford the doctors' bill, let alone the hospital bills if she was not treated as a charity patient.

My mother was scared. She thought, "Are they going to cut me open just to see what is going on? Can they really help me? What if I die on the table and never get back home? Tests! Surgical probing! No guarantee! I will be alone two hundred miles from home. She realized there would be no one there to hold her hand, no one to comfort her. Go to a strange city far away, lay on a table, say, go ahead cut me open, do what you will. Can I do this alone? Do I have a choice?" These are questions my thirty-four-year-old mother asked herself.

"What was the name of the hospital where your mother was admitted?"

"The Graduate Hospital," Lee responded.

"Why, *that* is the hospital where I studied nursing," Emily replied. "What year did you say she was there?"

Lee replied, "From 1953 until 1958."

"I was twenty-four and working as a med-surg nurse." Emily said.

With that, Lee pulled a locket up from around his neck and opened it for the old woman to look at.

In the locket, there was a picture on each side: a man on the left and the profile of a very pretty, dark-haired woman on the right. Emily would like to have been able to say, "Yes I remember her, she was a sweet lady." She looked like a sweet woman, but she didn't remember seeing her.

There were so many people coming and going it was hard to remember faces of people she had seen back then. Yet she said, "I do think
I may have helped with her care. There is some familiarity."

Lee continued. "My mother had never been out of our small hometown. My Father told her, "the city is full of black people; all black
people hate white people and would stick a knife in you as soon as look
at you. They are all lazy and never do their job right.""

Even though these were not Lee's thoughts but those of his father,
Emily was quickly taken back to the memory of her own life in the
fifties. A time when a black man was relegated to jobs at the corner
filling station or stocking groceries and delivering them. Occasionally a
black man would get a chance to advance from washing the cars to the
status of mechanic. He was good enough to work on the white man's
car, but only a white man could talk to the car's owner

An attractive "light skinned" black woman may be "lucky" enough
to get a job doing day work. Any climbing Jewish mother would have
her own black "girl." She would arrive by the back door, go to the
basement, iron and put on her uniform. She had to look perfect when
answering the front door for the rich white lady. When she was done
for the day, she returned to the basement, and washed her uniform for
the next day.

Some of the "fine featured" black women who were both good
looking and well-spoken were fortunate to be employed by the better
department stores. They looked down on their "sisters" who were doing
day work for the white man. Day work; humiliating, yes - but it helped
pay the household bills.

At that time blacks were not the only minority. The same bigoted
people who believed in calling a black person the 'N' word also called
the Italians wops or dagos; the Polish were Polacks, and the Jews were
kikes. The thought of that day about the Greeks was . . . well they
know how to cook, *and* run a good restaurant; but, too dark and curly
haired to be white.

Like the black people of the period, each ethnicity had its own
geographical section of town to live in. But it was only the blacks who

had their own Laundromat. At that time, blacks were not even allowed to wash their clothes in the same washing machines white people used. A black person could work in a "whites only" laundry but could not use those machines to *do* their laundry.

In the small country towns entertainment revolved around fraternal organizations such as the Elks, the Owls and the Moose. Dues were cheap and for a paltry sum you could get dressed up and go out. Whites would dine, dance and drink in a gracious atmosphere of shiny tile floors, mirrored walls, plush cushioned seats and great food from the club's kitchen. The clubs would have live music on Friday and Saturday nights by the local Joe Blow Trio. It was accepted that the musical groups might have black performers. The only blacks allowed in the clubs were either smokin' hot in the band or bangin' out the food.

In every community, there were those elitists who want to be above everyone else; they belonged to The Country Club. Yearly membership cost a lot more than the common clubs for working class people. The Country Club presented even greater atmosphere and amenities such as a golf course and pool. The ONLY blacks allowed in The Country Club worked in the kitchen or on the grounds or performed in the musical group. It did not matter if you were a doctor or lawyer. If you were black, the country club was off limits; it was upper class whites only."

Hearing voices, caught Lee and Emily's' attention. They had not noticed that Cornpopper had wheeled the Chief back to his room and that Edie was there.

"Edie! We didn't know you were here; didn't anyone tell you we were in the Sunroom?

In a slow voice Edie responded, "Oh I was just tidying up for my husband."

That got Emily's attention. "Odd," she thought; she hadn't heard anyone's presence or known Ede to have visited recently.

"Oh, yes, your poor mother - what did she do?"

"She had been trying to decide about going to Philadelphia when the Machamers called to say, 'We're bringing your child back! He is not happy here. He cries all the time. He will not do what we tell him.

He rips his clothes off. He is constantly throwing his toys around. We cannot take him knocking the plates of food we give him on to the floor any longer!'"

"My mother said, 'My heart skipped a beat - I was never so happy to hear you were misbehaving.' Her decision was made. She was going to Philadelphia.

"As a popular captain of the Fire Company, my father could use his company's vehicles to transport my mother to Philadelphia. His friend Junior Ulsh also helped him do the driving back and forth.

"And when the ambulance came to pick up my mother for the trip to Philadelphia, she asked my father, 'Can I have my baby ride with me for company?' Every time she went to the hospital, I went to the hospital too.

When her medical condition was discussed, it was always said that everything started with my birth. Between that and not wanting to stay at the Machamers I always felt to blame for so many of the family problems.

She was my mother but making me ride in the back of the ambulance in a very confined, uncomfortable space made me feel like I was being punished. I was scared because it was like a little hospital room with oxygen tanks and emergency medical equipment. There was nothing to do and my mother slept all the way to the hospital. I sat there in that sterile, antiseptic smelling area listening to my father reminding me, 'Don't touch anything!'

Over the next several years, I had five trips like that. I was always the last person she kissed as my father and I left to drive home, leaving her alone in a strange city. The only good memories I have of the trips back and forth to Philadelphia were when we stopped to eat at Howard Johnson's.

It was a different world, exciting. I had never been in a restaurant before. It was a whirlwind of activity; people everywhere, moving between the gas station, restrooms and the restaurant. There was a bank of vending machines along the wall, the first time I saw candy dispensed from machines. The restaurant would always be filled with wonderfully strange looking people. Sometimes there would be other languages being spoken in the restaurant and different styles of dress.

That was the first time I heard my father talk about painted women (women who wore more than Tangee natural lipstick and Lady Esther translucent face powder). He never noticed his sister was one of those ladies. These are the only two products my mother ever used on her face: a touch of color, a puff of powder, and a pinky swiped across a wet tongue picking up just enough moisture to glisten her eyebrows.

Of all the times, she was admitted to the hospital in Philadelphia my father never once went to visit her. He would only go back when she was discharged to go home. He hated that city so much!

When my mother came home from Philly after the first harrowing hospital stay, she gathered her sons together. My father wasn't home at the time.

My mother said, 'I want to tell you when you meet someone you don't know, regardless of how different they are from you, don't prejudge them. Many of the staff at the hospital were black. Department heads, doctors and nurses alike. Everyone who took care of me when I was too weak to take care of myself was black. I would not be here today if it had not been for the wonderful staff and personal care ladies. They gently washed me. When I wouldn't eat the hospital food, they brought me food from their own kitchens that I could eat. I only had two nighties and they washed those for me and provided a couple more so I would always be clean. There was someone with me twenty-four seven, around the clock, I was never scared or lonely. Dr. Tumen and Dr. Ferguson promised me the best of care and those ladies did more than I could have ever expected.'"

Lee reminded Emily, "My mother went through eleven operations altogether between 1949 and 1958. Then she started having the nervous breakdowns."

As Emily Anderson listened to Lee tell his story she thought, "I have raised my family. Dear God, give me wisdom and strength to help this man find his peace."

CHAPTER FIVE

EMILY ASKED, "HOW DID YOUR FATHER cope with his children while your mother was away?"

We were all well-liked by our relatives. Somehow our choice of who we would like to stay with was the same relative who would have requested each of us. Aunt Ruth took me. She had no children at home and enjoyed having me. She would play the organ and we would sing together.

As I got to know the people who lived in her neighborhood, she sent me up to Martha Habershon; she raised chickens to sell and sold eggs. I expected to pick up a dead chicken wrapped in paper. IT WAS ALIVE! I had to carry this squawking flapping chicken back to Aunt Ruth's. She had told me to return by the side door that led to the cellar. I barely made it in the door before the bird wiggled out of my gasp and flew down the cellar steps. There it was walking around the basement big as you please.

Aunt Ruth came out from the kitchen with a small axe and asked me, "Where is the chicken?"

Scared, I pointed down into the cellar. "Come on," she said. "We got to kill it for supper."

I could not believe she was going to kill the chicken herself. She expected me to hold the bird across a block, stretching its neck while she whacked the head off. I couldn't do it. Somehow, she managed to hold it *and* swing the ax. Next thing I knew the bird jumped up, with no head, ran around and dropped over.

She and her husband, "Uncle Smittie," had a cottage in a church camp meeting ground. In the summer time, they would take me along when they went to the cottage. It was way back a narrow winding road trailing deep into the forest. At the end of the road was a circle of maybe eighteen cottages.

There were two large buildings; each positioned half way around the circle, one of the buildings was the tabernacle. The other building was a community hall where there were weekly community suppers and Bingo games.

There was a special little corner stand only open in the evenings. It had a walk-up window where someone sold candy, ice cream, newspapers and comic books. That was the first time I had ever seen ice cream sandwiches. The only sandwiches I ever knew of were buttered bread with cheese or bologna. It was so nifty to have two cookies with ice cream between them.

The cottages were very small, only a story and a half, maybe 16 square feet. One large room and a small kitchen on the first floor and one big open bedroom on the second floor. No one furnished these cottages like they did their homes.

This is where your cast off, slightly soiled, worn furniture was used; mismatched kitchen utensils, paper window shades, no cloth curtains unless they were very simple. Think of something hanging on a tight string, and the string stretched like a worn-out rubber band. This was the original shabby chic of Home and Garden Television.

There was no indoor plumbing; you used a chamber pot and slop jar to go to the bathroom. For those who did not want to squat or miss the pot when peeing there were outhouses here and there around the camp.

When you wanted water, you had to take your pail and walk to one of two communal pumps and be ready to exercise. I can still see Aunt Ruth using a big silver dipper to transfer water out of the bucket when she wanted it. The only cooking source in the cottage was a small oil fired two-burner stove. The water was heated on that to wash the dishes or if you wanted, hot water to bathe with. Of course, you know that was a standup quick wipe off. Modern day PTA (Pits-Tits-Ass).

The only way to keep perishable items cold was an old wooden ice refrigerator (now a highly desirable piece of antique furniture!). In the early evening, we would visit with the neighbors as we sat on the small front porches. The music from the revival service would float around the cottages as the katydids sang along.

I found there was a footpath that led from the cottages to a swimming hole. It was the proverbial storybook kind where an old tire hung by rope from a tree on the pond's edge. The guys would use it to swing out over the water then jump off. I guess it was propriety that made it a "men only" thing. You could not have young men and young women partially undressed swimming together.

Many older boys swam there. It seemed the older they were, the more likely they were to remove their bathing suits. Whenever those of the male sex are "skinny dippin" there are always those guys who flaunt their manhood. They would go out of their way to call attention to their endowment. Big! Small! Whatever! Like theirs was the only one. They just seemed to be so overtly proud!

"Me oh my," Emily exclaimed, "That was more information then I needed!"

"If you think that's something, you have not heard the best part." Lee said. "It was at the church campground that I was really impressed."

"I beg your pardon?" Emily sourly grimaced.

"One morning I woke up and found that while I had been sleeping my uncle had come down to the cottage. He did not have vacation time; he was working and driving back and forth to visit when he could. He had climbed in bed with my aunt; laying on his side, with his back to me. All he was wearing was a T-shirt. As I awoke, I saw he had tucked his manhood between his legs, (she probably didn't want him rubbing up against her). It was drooping out between his legs, down over the curve of his thigh muscle and lying on the bed sheet behind him. It looked to me like a very large worm with a huge evil eye, watching me!

"Around Christmas, they took me to an evening of barbershop music at a local high school. I had to go to the bathroom so Aunt Ruth told Smittie to do the honors. We went to the bathroom; I think that was the first time I had ever been in a public toilet. He took me up to this wall of urinals.

"He looked at me and said, "Here this is what you do. He unzipped his fly, pulled out that monster, and just let it hang; the end in the swirling water; that was how long it was. When he was done, he announced, 'That is how I wash it,' grinning at me the whole time. When I went home after visiting with Aunt Ruth and Uncle Smittie, I happened to see my father naked. I was watching him and he asked, "What do you want?"

I told him about how big Uncle Smitties' pee-pee was, I asked him, "Why do some men have big ones and others have small ones?"

"It all depends what you are born with" He answered.

I asked him, "Why are there different sizes?"

Well," he said, "Aunt Ruth is a large lady so he has a large one." With that he turned me around, pushed me out of the bathroom and shut the door.

Uncle Smitties' "big one" got him in trouble when he sneaked around with one of the girls in Buttermilk Alley. In our town, all the black people lived in one area called "Coons Diamond." In the center of the triangular shaped community was a short thoroughfare called "Buttermilk Alley" (supposedly because all the girls who "worked" there had skin the color of buttermilk).

The alley was home to the very poor and known to be a place where a white man would go slumming for some "strange stuff." He would lower himself to solicit sex from a girl of the alley but would never acknowledge her in public. God forbid, if a black girl forgot her place and tried to make a white man acknowledge her in public. She would soon be a victim of a bone breaking accident.

One night when my father was at one of his meetings, Aunt Ruth came to the house around eleven o'clock. My mother woke up my oldest brother and had him get dressed and go somewhere with Aunt Ruth. We heard in bits and pieces that Aunt Ruth found out her husband was visiting someone in Buttermilk Alley. She asked my brother to take her where my uncle had parked his car, so she could drive it away. She did not take it home, she hid it. We never heard anything else about that night. My aunt and uncle did happen to adopt an infant baby girl, months after that night. My mother always thought it was Smittie's bastard from an affair with an alley girl.

From then on I could not stay at Ruth and Smitties' when my mother was sick. They sent me to my Aunt Peggy's. What they did not know, was that her husband Uncle Sherm would be responsible for starting me on the road to transvestitism.

Needing a respite, "I believe I am going to get some coffee," Emily softy murmured, "Can I bring you something?" she asked Lee.

"You wouldn't bring me what I'd normally tell someone to bring me, and I couldn't do anything with it anyway. So, the answer is no thank you. "

Lee remembered when his Aunt Peggy went to play Bingo and his uncle would baby sit. Lee found himself fingering and handling the things on her dresser. He didn't know why, but he would open the compacts, dusting his face with the billowy puffs. He was attracted by the lipsticks' shiny containers, and he would screw them up out of their case and quickly wind them back in. Sherm saw that his nephew enjoyed playing with his wife's face products. He encouraged him to put them on as he saw his Aunt apply her makeup.

Sherm then gave him some of her clothes to wear; rolling sleeves up, rolling waist bands over. He then put one of her wigs on his head and took him to the neighbors' houses and rang the doorbells. He would hide somewhere close, but out of sight, so he could see the reaction when the door was opened. He would roar with laughter when the people reacted to a boy in women's clothing. That little boy never understood why his uncle did that.

In later life, he would reflect to those days wondering if that was the beginning of his liking to shock or, should we, say surprise people.

When she came back to the room with a bracing cup of black coffee, Emily questioned, "Why do you talk such smut?"

"Smut!" Lee archly asked.

"Yes smut! We all know what the human body parts are and what they do. Why is it that so much of your conversation contains lurid descriptive references? "Emily countered.

"Have you ever known a gay person? Had one as a friend?" Lee asked.

Emily replied with fervor, "Well if I have ever known anyone who was 'different', they must have been good enough friends to keep it to themselves! We do not need to know such stuff about people! There are men in the church that may seem a little too flashy, gushy or move their hands too much. Maybe some women dress a little too tailored, severe. Maybe there are those who wear a too mannish haircut, too few frills. So, what? They don't talk this trash."

"Are you saying you have never been in the church and heard someone saying about a man, he has a little sugar in his shoes?" Lee shot back. "You think you know me! Did you think I drank it in the water? The way they used to try and say nuns became pregnant. Are you getting a little judgmental? Never hear the words dick or balls before? Is that kind of talk making you wet, Emily?"

"If I wasn't a Christian woman, I'd slap the white off your face," Emily said a little louder than she liked to speak. No, she was here for a purpose. She had to realize the **Devil** had his hand on this child of God.

"Why are you so angry? Did I insult you so badly because I said you talk smut?" She quizzed.

Lee replied, "You don't understand. To many people, any gay person is worse than smut. Do you have any idea what it is like to be gay?"

"When I was young and my mother was able, she would play bingo as a diversion to take her mind off her problems. My father would park outside the Knights of Columbus Hall, waiting to take my mother home form bingo.

"We would watch all the people pass by on the sidewalk. As a woman went by on the sidewalk he would say, 'She's got a nice ass!' No one would have a problem with that, would they? No, because he is a man and that's expected. They would not think it unusual if he commented on her tits. "Wow – what a nice rack!" That is how men talk.

"I would be looking at the men. Not their ass, nothing in particular, just the men. I watched to see how normal men behaved with each other. I did not know why; I enjoyed watching the men.

My brother and I would sleep together in the same bed; my parents told us how cute we looked as we slept because we were often hugging each other. Later we started to play doctor and look at what we each had in our underwear. Why? I do not know. We were curious.

One day my best friend and I went to the local swimming pool. We were in the water and he asked me, "How hairy are you?"

I was stunned; I asked him, "What do you mean?"

He said, "Around your nuts. I'll bet you have a big bat." This was a little out of my league. At the time, I was still naïve; for a couple more hours at least.

When we went in to change our clothes, he asked me to follow him back to a far corner of the room and told me, "Hold this big towel up for me to change behind." Skinning off his suit I said, "You're the one with the big hammer." I did not know why he wanted to hide it. I learned immediately how ashamed and embarrassed boys with small dicks could be around those who are well endowed. When we were playing in the attic around Halloween, he put on a robot costume made out of cardboard boxes. He took my hand and put it around something under his costume. It scared me; I did not recognize what I was feeling. It was hard but felt like rubber, warm, I yanked my hand back and asked, "What was that? Let me see it." He took off the costume and showed me his big protrusion. I was fascinated that something that had been much smaller had grown to this size and changed from soft to hard. Looking at him gave me an arousal. "Immediately I realized I was somewhat embarrassed and ashamed of my size."

When I was in eighth grade, I was sitting in my homeroom drumming my fingers on the rails of my chair back.

The kid beside me asked, "Are you practicing?"

"Practicing what?" I asked.

"Jerking off," he whispered. I had heard the term in older boys' conversations. I did not know what it was. When I went home, I looked for the proverbial preacher's son who lived next door. He was a year older than me and I thought probably more knowledgeable

I asked him, "Do you know what jerking off is?"

Looking at me, he asked, "Yeah, are you being a smart ass?"

I explained why I was asking him and he said, " Come on, I'll show you." No one was home at his house. He took me into the kitchen and we sat down at the kitchen table. The chairs were straight ladder back and his chair screeched against the floor as he dragged it over beside me.

He said, "Take down your pants. This is how my older brother showed me."

The thing is Emily, how do boys learn about masturbation? Do you think a father shows a son? Of course not! It is human nature that a male child learns from other male children. Nevertheless, grown men do it. Do they admit it to their friends? I doubt it.

The difference is that some male children stop learning from boys and start learning with girls. However, it is acceptable to learn with girls. You can like a girl, be seen with her in public, pet with a girl, get fresh with a girl, date a girl, and kiss her. Do you see what I am saying?

What about gay boys? When I was growing up my friends and I had to sneak around lying to our parents about what we were doing. When we played together, we had to play in the attic or a dirt basement so we could get away with what we wanted to do. We could not do this in the front room or dining room. We had to hide our exploration of each other. We would go up to the ridge and lay on the ground in the bushes.

We would go to the public library, pretending to have an interest in the books. Observing who might be watching us we would eventually make our way back to the rear of the building to the restrooms. We would both go in a bathroom meant for one person and explore each other. We would go to the movies and sit in the very back with heavy coats on our laps, hiding our interaction.

It sounds sordid and dirty doesn't it? That is how we felt - sordid and dirty - having to sneak around and hide these feelings all the time.

Do you have any idea how difficult it is for a gay boy when he reaches the part of his schooling when he has Physical Education? The teachers expect to help teach you hygiene by having everybody partic-ipate in community showering. For a gay boy it is a huge confusion of emotion. First, you already feel there is something wrong with you. Not different, wrong! By this time, you are aware that your parents, older people in general (society) and even the kids your age are acknowledging that there are men who are *queer*.

Think about it. How often did you hear as a youngster or young adult about a female being queer? It is a man thing. For a boy who knows he is attracted to boys; to have to get naked and shower side by side with the same kind of sexual beings you desire to be with. It is hell! A real case of don't look and don't touch. No, it is not a smorgasbord of free looks or cheap thrills. It is not like a kid in a candy store, a kid in a candy store can buy candy. As a gay boy in the showers you think, "What if he sees me looking at his penis?" I do not know if times have changed that much, but when I was in high school a gay boy could not tell people he was gay or act out in any manner that may cause someone to suspect he was "queer."

I am sure you have heard some tale of a gay boy getting beat up by straight boys. Think of how many more beatings there would be if all gay boys were known in the junior and senior high school levels.

I am sure you have heard that football and baseball teams do not want a gay man on their team. Why? Because they are showering together. Why are they afraid? Is it going to wash off on to them? Are they afraid of letting a gay man look at them naked?

If so why? When I was in tenth grade, I remember several of the boys going into the shower and things were normal. When the same guys came out of the showers there had been a physical change. I was toweling off and one of them saw me watching them. Our eyes met and he grinned. I could see their arousal dwindling and realized they had expended their energy in the shower.

Another time everyone was done showering except two guys. When they came out of the shower, their towels were not hanging where they left them. They yelled, "Come on, where's my towel?" Whoever took the towels hid them for a long time. Everyone else was almost dressed and the naked guys stood in the center of the dressing room asking for their towels.

One had his thrown to him. The other said, "All right, I'm down on my knees, can I please have my towel?" As he sank to his knees, it was evident he was becoming aroused. Not until then did the perpetrator throw him his towel. I looked to see who threw the towel, a 'friend' franticly excited quickly put his shorts on. To this day, I think about that scene and wonder about the psychology of the incident between the two.

Not to say I was an angel. By eleventh, twelfth grade, I was getting a little braver. When I was in senior high school, I worked in the school library and opened it an hour before school started. One morning I came in early and went to the restroom before unlocking the library. One of the school janitors who had been my bus driver since 3rd grade came in after I had. I fantasized many times of laying my head on his hairy chest. He saw me looking at him, while I zipped up. The next day I went to the restroom before the library and the same janitor walked in and unzipped loosening a hard-on. Again, I was embarrassed by my lack of size.

In senior high school, I had an English teacher who mesmerized me. He had very craggy looks. I remembered him from when I was in ninth grade when he was a 23-year-old student teacher. He had then and still had a way of perching on the corner of his desk when leading the class. The corner of the desk would have been right under his bottom pushing his crotch out. I just knew I could see the outline, length and shape of what he had as he sat on the edge of the desk. Rotating to my math class one afternoon, I had gone to the boy's room. He came in and stood right beside me on my left side. Well, I thought I was finally going to see the object of my fascination. I did not care if the bell was about to ring, meaning I would be late for my class; I was going to wait him out.

He had a briefcase in his left hand as he tried to get into his underwear with just the right hand. He had difficulty. The right hand stopped moving. He tried to put the briefcase up behind the urinal head with just his left hand, right hand still in trouser opening. He could not do that with one hand either. He removed his right hand from his fly and with both hands placed the briefcase up out of the way. I thought it must be a monster because he dove in with both hands. He must have had very small, tight jockeys on. One hand pulled this way. The other hand pulled that way. The first hand dug down to pull out what I expected to be a whopper. By the time, he was done fumbling all I got to see was what looked like a very stretched out something and a small nub jutting out from a big hand. Talk about disappointment.

Emily was thinking the same thing as she said, "I am an old woman. I do not have much time left. When I think of all the chances someone, your age had and how you have squandered them, I am disappointed in you. I do not know you, but I am sure I am right when I say, you did not do the best you could with your life. Such a vulgar, stifling existence! I am truly sorry but I am going to leave now."

"When I come back tomorrow, I will make sure someone else is assigned form the hospice care group to be your advocate for the rest of your stay here. Before I leave the building, I will have the orderlies come back and help you into bed."

"Hmm, I did not think I would have any company here, so what. Who needs an old Bible thumper around?"

As Emily gathered her bag making ready to go, she heard a very small voice in pain mumble, "Thank you for listening. Good-bye."

. Alone with his thoughts, he thought of the old phrase, "If you can't stand the heat, get out of the kitchen." There are people who commit terrible crimes, far worse than my disregard for who I'm talking to. I talk smut, what about the killers, rapists, pedophiles serial murderers. She thought I was so bad. I did not coerce, force or make anyone do anything against his or her will

I gave people what they wanted. Like when my knob was polished the first time. I was playing with my friend Paul, in the yard by the alley, when Gary Hopple came down through the alley and called out, "You better be careful, he likes lollipops!"

I asked Paul, "What is that about?"

I do not remember the next few minutes. Although it was not very long until we were running up the two steps onto the porch into the old summer kitchen. The screen door was slapping shut by the time Paul and I were wrestling on the floor.

The experience didn't last long. Things happened so fast and I felt strange. I thought something bad had happened. I jumped up, scared and rushed out of the room. Running to the porch swing I sat down before I fell over from fainting. I was afraid I was hurt; I would have to tell my parents. I left Paul on the floor in a messy disarray from the adventure.

Thankful to have these happy memories to enjoy as his days dwindled down, he slipped off to slumber through the night.

Emily tossed and turned all night. Having had the benefits of being raised in a Christian family and living with a God sent man of a husband for more than fifty years, Emily could not reconcile the lifestyle Lee had chosen. Her daughters were perfect, never a moment of worry. Her son was a mother's joy. All true, but her conscience plagued her. What if her son had turned out like Lee? Could a son from her womb turn out to be like him? What would she do? How would she cope? Am I a snob? Am I wearing my coat of Godliness so tight a chilling call of woe and despair cannot warm my heart?

She prayed for guidance, but none was forthcoming. She did not expect it to come knocking on her door but she looked for some spiritual inspiration. Feeling worn, she went to sleep resigned to ask to be relieved of this new charge.

Lee awoke the next morning to the clatter of a food tray slapped down beside his bed. He saw the orange juice and sipped at that. Soft, pureed diets are not known for their visual appeal and they did nothing for his appetite. He closed his eyes and hoped his memory bank might play back another fond souvenir of times past.

As Emily dashed between the cars in the parking lot, trying to avoid each drop of rain, she realized her mood was as bleak as it was at that rainy-day funeral last month. Finally reaching the entrance she rushed inside shaking the rain off her umbrella and removed her plastic rain bonnet. Stomping her shoes lightly to remove the last traces of wetness she took the elevator to Lee's floor.

As she was going to the nurses' station, she thought she saw someone going into the Chief and Larue's room; "Good Morning everyone! Great day for fishermen....the rain brings the worms to the surface. My husband, God rest his soul, always did say worms are the best fishing bait. Everyone bright eyed and bushy tailed?" Emily chattered to the crowd at the nurses' station.

Never an energetic staff, still taking report, no one appreciated the sunshine trying to blind them. A mumbled "Morning" and sour faces sipping coffee was the only greeting Emily received in return.

Not to be daunted Emily quizzed, "Did I see people going into the Chiefs' and Mr. Larue's room just now?"

One of the group offered up, "Oh. They went to get some clothes for the Chief. He managed to sneak out on his electric wheelchair this morning, neglecting to dress himself. The Police called and said they picked him up after a jogger reported seeing him pass by with only boxer shorts and a T-shirt on. Since it is raining cats and dogs, his clothes were plastered to him, and his fly was open and everything was hanging out."

As Emily turned to find her supervisor regarding her replacement for Lee's advocacy, a voice in the back offered, "They are also doing a procedure on Mr. Larue."

That stopped Emily in her tracks. Eyebrows raised, she asked, "What procedure?"

"Why a feeding tube. He is not eating," came the response that before it was finished was floating on empty airspace as Emily rushed down to Lee's room.

As she approached the room, she could hear the commotion. With labored breath he prayed to God, *"Please let me die, let me go!"* "My God" she thought, they are stuffing that tube down his throat against his wishes. As she entered the doorway, two men were holding the weakened Lee down while another was attempting to thread the plastic feeding tube through his nostril.

With arthritic gnarled hands, Emily reached out to comfort his shaking body. "He has in writing what he wants and does not want,

and he does not want anything to prolong his life! That is his right! Get out of here, have you no humanity? I do not know your names, but I will find out who you are. The administrator will hear of this!" Emily scolded.

Mother Anderson held Lee and rocked him like a baby. As the trembling eased, she excused herself. "I need to find the Administrator and settle in for the day. I'll be back as soon as possible."

His bravado about who needs a Bible thumper haunted him. What would have happened had she not appeared when she did? He had to expressed how glad he was that she returned.

"I need to thank you for your return! May I request a favor? When the time comes, I want to listen to Donna Summers' record Last Dance. I am sure there is a record player somewhere around here for the patients. I think I had some cash on me. If not, I will give you the phone number of a friend not far from here who would bring me the record. Would you do that please?" Lee asked.

CHAPTER SIX

SHE MAY BE OLD BUT HER YOUTHFUL MIND grabbed on to that information like a Venus fly trap on a fly.

Lee asked Emily for his Billy Graham Bible; pulling out of it a very worn piece of paper, he handed it to Emily. "Actually, there are two names you could call."

Emily tucked the small shred of paper in her purse. She had hope now that someone from his past may yet give him a glimmer of happiness.

"Of course, I will be very happy to take care of that for you. It is not as if you are asking me to cook you a big Christmas dinner. I stopped those years ago. My son usually cooks the holiday dinner; he is a much better cook than his sisters. He has a great friend who always helps him." the old woman chortled.

"Now let us sit back and relax and you can tell me a little more about yourself."

"I was in ninth grade when my mom-mom passed away. There was the usual bickering about the deceased's possessions. My mother knew mom-mom made a will in her favor; dividing everything in percentages. Her sister Ruth convinced the eldest sibling Sam to set the will aside and sell everything. My mother received a check representing her part of the proceeds of the insurance and receipts for the auction of household goods, but not what she expected.

She cried, complaining, "I have nothing that belonged to my Mother!" She was unhappy because she had not received what she expected from her Mother's estate. Instead she received some old knick knacks: odds and ends of small glass items of a blue color and some with gold decorations.

Because I knew I was "different' and uncomfortable around people my age I developed a rapport with older people. My father would have myself and brothers sell ambulance club memberships. We also came in handy going around our neighborhood handling out his election cards. The interaction with the older age group created my gift of gab. I was always out on my bike meeting all kind of people.

One summer evening on my way home I saw colored light, similar to Christmas decorations up the alley on the ridge behind Valley Street. You could see the glow of whatever it was from the front of our first home, scene of the magical meeting of Aunt Peg and Uncle Sherm.

The first chance I got I took my bicycle and went exploring. The short alley ended in front of a big Victorian style home on the end of 4th Street. There was little more than a wide foot path that went away from the house to the right. The foot path led onto a rough dirt road that went up the side of the property over the ridge to the reservoir. Veering to the right the road created a hair pin curve which was another alley that ran behind Pine Street. Captured in the road's arc was a white clapboard cottage. Working among flowers, growing along the road, was a short stooped over lady. It was not a "garden" that you would define as a garden. You would have thought the flowers grew there by themselves it looked so natural. Living in the cottage alongside the alley, with no available ground to have a garden, she decided to beautify the area with plants and flowers.

She said, "Hello. What are you doing?"

I told her about seeing the glow of lights at night and was trying to find out what it came from.

"A kindly old gentleman, Homer Searer and his sister Esther live in that house on East Fourth Street. He has created a little fantasy village in his backyard. The lights you see at night are lights in his village. He enjoys working with his hands and creates those little houses out of odds and ends using broken jewelry, china, mirrors, colored glass, bottle caps, and anything else he comes across. He likes people looking and admiring his handiwork. There's a small white gate at the side of the house that leads back into the yard. He has created a series of small steps that wind up through his houses so you can walk through his village."

He tells people, "I build the houses for the wood fairies to live in."

"The path meanders back and forth eventually, leaving his property, taking you out along the alley up where the flowers stop. Along the way, he has built a small bridge over a man-made pond that he puts goldfish in for the children to enjoy. It must be a labor of love. Adults and children come from all over to visit 'Fairyland.' You must come back at night when the lights are turned on. It really is quite beautiful when the light reflects through the small windows and open doors."

"If it had not been for 'Fairyland', I may have never met Mr. and Mrs. Smith. They were both raised on plantation homes in Maryland and went on to become schoolteachers. Mrs. Smith retired from school teaching when her son Marshall was born. Mr. Smith was still teaching high school business mathematics when I met them.

Mrs. Smith loved her gardening along the side of her house and met many of the neighborhood children while doing this. She would be quick to confide she did not care much for girls; she liked the boys best. At a young age, she thought girls too frivolous and had no time to deal with their interest in dolls and such.

I became one of her "regular boys." Mrs. Smith encouraged several areas of interest in me. Every time she had a flower or plant over growing its boundaries and crowding other plants; she would give me the "throw-away." In time, I had a lovely garden from her throw-a ways.

She taught me to recite, "The kiss of the sun for pardon, the song of the bird for mirth. One is closest to God in a garden, then anywhere else on Earth."

Whenever I would visit, she would tell me about her plants and rock collection. As I got older, she encouraged me to be an individual and read better literature. She would talk to me of writers, painters, philosophers, politics and geography. And antiques! I was drawn to her family heirlooms and a lithograph by Currier and Ives, titled 'Little Daisy." She encouraged me to read books on theology, philosophy, poetry and Shakespeare and then discuss them with her.

She also touched on my education with the opposite sex. "If you marry, marry a woman above you in class." Her reason was, "A woman if she is smart, can always make a man want to achieve more and do better. Because of that 'gift' she has. If a man marries below him, he can never make a woman rise above the level she was born to. A woman must already possess that in her personality, because a man does not have that same Cleopatra gift that a woman does."

Lee promised Mrs. Smith, "I will only marry someone who will be a good housekeeper; one who can cook and sew, to make her own clothes, if she wants to.

She exuded warmth and was very animated. Her husband was the opposite, withdrawn and would seem to be measuring every word when he said something, and every word he heard.

If anyone said they lived "frugally," they would be insulted. They gave the term penny pinching a new meaning. They would pinch a penny until it yelled Uncle! And Aunt!

Mrs. Smith told me, "When we were young, we both wanted to have money. I mean big money! Not little money. Money in six figures!"

Their home was furnished with lovely antiques, a Hepplewhite tray, a Chippendale table, a painted Pennsylvania Dutch dining room suite, a Boston rocker, a Victorian settee, an old tavern table, cherry stands, a Currier and Ives lithograph, and a lot of "shabby chic." The antiques were inherited. The rest of the furniture was gathered from here and there, some other peoples' castoffs.

Until the mid-1960s their refrigerator was an old wooden icebox. They cooked on an old two-burner coal oil stove. Mrs. Smith baked her delicious Boston Brown Bread on that glorious antique and had me asking for more when she made molasses cookies and sugar cookies with her signature two raisins.

The corner cupboard was filled to over-flowing with beautiful glassware, china, and knick-knacks. The top of the Chippendale table was decorated with patina-hued old silver. Their bedroom was furnished with miscellaneous items from several bedroom sets. Their son's room had a very Spartan metal cot for his bed, and the simplest of dresser drawers. I do not remember there being anything present to give the illusion that a child, let alone a teenager growing into a young man ever lived in that room.

Mrs. Smith told me, "We didn't believe in giving Franklin toys when he was a child; other parents gave toys and playthings that got broken and thrown away. He didn't even have a baby-rattle. If he was restless, his father or I would hold him, if we thought he needed it. Otherwise we would let him lie in his crib or on the floor and cry it out. On any occasion that people would normally give a child a gift, Franklin received a good book."

Tablecloths and bed linens were patched on top of patches. In this house, the toilet was only flushed when someone made a bowel movement. If you went to visit after dark, you would think no one was home because they would sit in the dark listening to the radio. There never was, nor would there ever be, a television in that house. Mrs. Smith enjoyed reading very much; there was a forty-watt light bulb beside her chair. I know there were other lights in the house but I never saw any others turned on.

They owned a dark green 1937 Chrysler, bought new, only driven for their summer vacations to the White Mountains in New England. After vacation, the tires and battery were removed; the car put up on jacks and covered until the following summer. All local traveling to the grocery store and to the high school, regardless of the weather, was by "shoe leather express."

Several years before Roger died, they made a couple trips to Europe traveling on the Holland American Cruise Line. They both loved those trips. They shared tales of their adventures: a French cabaret girl from the Follies Bergere giving her husband a French kiss; an effete Spanish tour guide wowing all the ladies of the group with beautiful manners; her blowing one of those large horns in the Swiss Alps; attending bull fights in Spain and describing the statue of 'Pi' in Brussels. They would always take time to send me postcards from every place they traveled. They instilled in me the desire to travel Europe and I vowed I would get there before I was forty.

When Roger died he left an estate of $300.000. In 1965 that was a large amount of money. The only jewelry between the two of them was a small "fleur de lis" pin Mrs. Smith inherited from her French grandmother. It was decorated with a few dangly pearls under a cluster of small round rubies. After Roger died, Mrs. Smith mourned irreconcilably. A phone was put in the house in case of emergency. She did not want the phone but the lawyer and her executor demanded it.

Having known both of them as long as I did and being aware of their metaphysical beliefs it did not strike me as odd when Mrs. Smith would say, "My Roger is with me. He is sitting right there in his Boston rocker. I am never alone. We talk all the time."

She expressed this view to the wrong person resulting in a call from her lawyer. He and the banker were coming to see her. The morning of the day they were to visit I cleaned her house and tried to make it look a little cleaner and neater. I told her not to tell the two men of her conversations with Roger or how he was still sitting in his rocker. She did not listen and they thought she was off *her* rocker. From a neighbor's house, I watched as the two men, one on each arm directed Mrs. Smith out of her home, her French grandmother's "fleur de lis" at the neckline of her blouse.

She was a great influence on me. Over the years when I visited Mrs. Smith, in the William Penn nursing home, I could see the bank made sure the home took very good care of the lady.

The Smiths had told me how they had planned their estate with everything going to benefit a boy's college, leaving Franklin nothing. I talked to the bankers when they were having public sale of Mrs. Smith's household goods. It gladdened my heart when the banker said he had contacted Franklin to tell him of his mother's situation, they allowed him to remove what he wanted from his parents' home. He chose wisely and took the Chippendale and Hepplewhite items along with a few other choice items.

It was very sad that the Smiths never reconciled to their son's marriage. Mrs. Smith told me stories about her son and his childhood, and of his adolescent problems. I think it must have been very hard growing up having two so very different people as parents. As far as I know he never heard all the wonderful stories about their lives and travels that I was lucky enough to hear. I remember Mrs. Smith crying when I visited her because she regretted she and her son were not closer. She loved her son very much saving every letter he ever wrote her. The letters were for her eyes only; her husband no longer had a son.

The Smiths went to their graves thinking their son was a disappointment. While serving in World War Il he met a Japanese girl. When the war ended, he brought home a Japanese wife they could not accept. To think their son would settle for being a **photographer** *and* marry a Japanese, with his natural intellect and heritage, was just too painful for the couple to accept. She thought he was unable to adjust to their unique lifestyle.

She did instill an interest in money. I liked having it to spend; but I didn't have enough! I needed to earn more. I started a part-time job at G. C. Murphy's 5&10. I told my relatives I was looking for work, and I put a notice in the paper for odd jobs.

My aunt had me wash her walls and ceilings and clean out the attic. Another relative told her hairdresser, and I was asked to clean her house. Her daughter liked what she saw at her mother's and asked me to do her home. I unloaded boxcars of lumber, helped farmers in their fields and dug gardens. You name it - I would earn that money.

My hometown was very small; everybody knew everybody. Being my father's son and always listening, I was always good for gossip about someone or something. Some of those I visited would give me money just for dropping in and saying hello. Knowing I could get money that easily, I had a schedule of who, where and when.

My Aunt Peg had me come downtown every Saturday afternoon to have lunch with her at the Rea & Derick drug store. On the way, I would stop in to see my dad while he was working. His boss, Mr. Olskey, took a liking to me. He would ruff my hair, pull my ear and give me a quarter. Off I would go to secure counter seats for Peg's and my free lunch. With Murphy's pay, odd job money, and collecting alms from everyone I could, I had money to spend. Realizing my success, my mother informed me I could buy my own shoes.

One of my many odd jobs was for Mrs. Klum. After working several hours, taking wood from outside her house down to the cellar and stacking it, she offered me lunch. While I was sitting at her kitchen table, I looked up and saw these beautiful old cut glass dishes in her cupboard. "The dishes on the top shelf are valuable antiques." I told her.

She said, "Ah, those old things, I got them as wedding gifts, I never did like them. Do you want them? You can have them dust catchers."

"I would think your daughters would want them," I replied.

"My daughters don't do anything for me. You want them, you can have them."

I told her I would take them instead of money. She thought I was foolish for wanting those old dishes rather than money. When her oldest daughter found out, she was furious. She called me and said, "I want those old dishes you took from my mother."

I told her, "I will call your mother and ask her if she wants me to return them. If she does, I certainly will." I called the old woman and asked her, "Do you want me to return the glassware to you? Your daughter called and she is very upset and wants me to give her the glassware.

"She said, "No, I want you to have them. My children never do anything for me."

We kept a "friendship" for a while, it did bother me somewhat to find out that the mother and daughter did not talk for quite a while after that because of my 'getting' the glassware. I always cherished what she gave me and thought of Mrs. Klum often.

I developed a passion for old dishes and glassware. In my travels I saw a sign 'Antiques' on a private home and knocked at the door. An older grandmotherly dressed lady opened the door. "Yes?

I responded that I had seen her sign and would like to see what she had. She looked at me for a minute, tilting her head to take my measure because she was blind in one eye. I suspected she was dubious of some kid wanting to come in her house.

"What are you looking for?" she asked. I told her I liked colored glass and gold trimmed glass.

Stepping back, opening the door she asked me in. I had been in many shops by that time and most looked like rummage sale merchandise. This lady had "'Bee U Tee full" collectibles. I admired many of her pieces. She asked me who I was and I told her who my parents were. "Are you Ken and Lena's son?" I told her I was.

"My Lord, I know your parents I was at their wedding; I gave them towels for a gift."

That was the beginning of a long relationship. If I didn't have enough money, she would let me pay a little each week until the item was paid in full.

One day my mother asked me," Why are you bringing all this junk home?"

I told her, "I bought the dishes and china for you because you were so upset when you didn't get any of the old dishes that belonged to your Mother.

"I don't like old dishes! I just wanted them because they belonged to my mother!" was her acid response.

Sometimes I bought things and sold them to other people before I even left the sale site. I was making money on that alone. When I visited neighbors and relatives, I would admire things I saw sitting around or in the china closet and ask them where they got them. Soon they were giving me things they did not want any more. To them the old stuff was junk; to me it was found treasure.

Relatives started giving me keepsakes that had been in the family. My great-aunt gave me a three-legged bowl in carnival glass. My mother lamented, "I told her *I* wanted that when they got rid of the cottage." She did not understand why it was given to me.

The same aunt later gave me a Tiffany-style table lamp that she received as a wedding gift in nineteen twenty. A cousin gave me a complete washbowl and pitcher set in perfect condition. I received quite a few items from my relatives.

When my mother realized how many things relatives were giving me and learned the value, she got jealous. "They should have given those things to me. You are just a kid; I am an adult. I am a closer relative then you." My aunts told me that the reason they gave me those things was that my mother wasted money and didn't take care of her household possessions, even though most of our dishes and furnishing were their hand-me-downs.

While I was collecting and learning, I realized my mother had a carnival wine glass and a carnival glass punch cup.

I asked her, "Can I have them?"

She said, "No you cannot have everything, your brother should have one of them."

I said, "Everything? Why? He is not interested in old stuff." Just the same, she was going to give him one. I could have my pick.

I told her, "Okay - and since I can't have it. I will buy the other one from you." I paid her three dollars for the cup. When I went to bed both items were sitting on the dining room table. In the morning, the one I paid for was broken; no one knew how it got broken, and she kept my money.

I saw a neighbor woman put a small bookcase out on the sidewalk for the trash men to takeaway. I asked her if I could have it. She said yes. I took it home; my mother loved to read and had a large collection of books. When she saw the bookcase, she wanted that too. I put it in my bedroom but her books went into it.

My mother did have issues. I came home from school one day and my mother said, "There is some money on the table for you."

I asked her. "Where did it come from?"

She said, "A man was here today and bought two of your dishes."

"What man?" I asked.

She said, "I don't know. He said he met you and talked to you about buying them from you when he saw you at a sale." I gave my mother as much hell as a kid could at that age for letting some stranger take my possessions for whatever sum he decided. In later years (looking back) I think she probably was telling our insurance man (a budding antique dealer himself), about dishes I bought and he asked to see them. I firmly believe she let him buy them not realizing I would know their worth, leaving her think he was generous.

My complexion was really giving me problems when I was going thru junior and senior high school. I bought Clearasil and other acne products to no avail. My mother bought me special soaps, nothing worked. My neighbor told me to dissolve a cake of yeast in orange juice and drink that...!

My father told me to lie on the bed. He covered his fingertips with Kleenex and squeezed all over my face breaking pimples. My face looked like the proverbial fruitcake that had exploded in the oven. I had to argue with him about how bad it was for my skin to get him to stop popping the pimples. I think he liked hurting me. After all that, I found Propa pH. Thank you, Jesus! You know, Emily, I do know God.

When I was eight years old my father and mother had us join my father's family church. Again, their thinking being to attract more attention from my father's relatives, in the hope we would ingratiate ourselves into their wills.

What better? Have us join the Acolyte Guild? Before we went to the meeting to learn how to become altar boys our father told us he had heard of some bullies in the church. He reminded us that there were three of us and not to let anyone else be mean to one of the others. We were to stick together and gang up on anyone who picked or one of us.

"After all, when your mother and I are gone there will only be the three of you. You have to stick together and take care of each other, helping each other when one of you needs help."

We were taught to march out on the same foot, be careful to bow our heads in unison at the altar. When lighting the altar candles, we had to watch so we moved in unison lighting the candles on each side of the cross exactly together. We had to time our crossing so we blended together in the center. My brothers and I became the precision acolyte and crucifer drill team. During the processional and recessional, we were taught to keep our eyes cast down, no peeping into the congregation.

We were also told of the previous ministers who drank too much and of the ministers who were too friendly with the young altar boys.

"If Father touches you, you know what to do, hit him in the balls and run."

Yes, I was introduced to God in his own House. I felt He knew me well and heard my prayers. He heard me as well as he heard anyone. There was a time when our relationship was better.

I also believe there is a Devil. I do not mean a red suited horror movie inspired villainous type. I think we create our own devil that influences our life. Just as we cultivate the God-like part of ourselves which help us succeed. I believe there is certain behavior that corrupts the human personality so slowly we do not even realize it happens. It is so insidious it starts with the parents. Parents should teach the difference between right and wrong. Unfortunately, many parents today cannot teach it because they did not experience it themselves.

The Devil slowly appears when you are unaware of the responsibility you have, to have, for your actions and words. It is how you treat your fellow towns-people, your co-workers, and people you live beside every day. It grows when you have impatience, lack of regard or interest in anyone else's life and how they manage to live.

When, in your day-to-day life, you cannot stop to let an old person, a less physically able person, a mentally challenged, handicapped person, have a speck of consideration, but instead run over them, as if they were not there, that's when you are letting the Devil in your soul.

These people are just trying to fit in, and have a life, but your snide actions and behavior towards them can squash their joy.

When you do things that you consider trivial; throwing waste paper on the ground or out your open car window, dump your grass clippings on someone's else's property, throw that banana peel you ate as you were walking down on the sidewalk, going on someone else's property and picking a flower, letting your dog relieve itself on someone's property, seeing someone else going for the same grocery check-out and quickly speed up to get ahead, running a red light and making someone else slam on their brakes so you can be first.

When you look at people on the street and decide (without hearing them say a word), they must be below you, less intelligent, not worthy of making eye contact with, let alone saying "Hello" to. Is it their dress? Level of cleanliness? Level of grooming? None of us knows what transpired for that individual to be manifesting whatever you find wrong. You need to remember! *There but for the Grace of God, go I.*

Misfortune happens in a second! These actions are those, by which we create our own Devil which is "mean spiritedness." Me first! Who are you? Where did you come from? This kind of thinking makes that negative outlook. Which of these actions, characteristics or behaviors is positive?

Yes, these people sometimes do become successes and financially well off. It is the old tale of Scrooge, how many ghosts have we left behind to reach the pinnacle of individual happiness and contentment. You cannot take anything with you when you close your eyes for the last time. You can only hope to leave pleasant memories of chance encounters and times shared with others you liked and loved.

Maybe there just haven't been enough strong mentoring people out there in everyone's lives to affect the desire in people to do better. Or is it a sign of the world we live in that human nature heals our grieving of the loss of loved ones so quickly?

Why is it that we forget or no longer think or care what they would say of our actions? How is it that personality and behavior can change so much that we could cause our loved ones to roll over in their graves? Yet that behavior never happened when the person was still alive, influencing our desire to do good; be honest, be loyal, trustworthy be dependable law-abiding citizens. People talk of "bad actors"; hell, the world must be full of terrific "actors" when so many people are hiding their true natures from their loved ones.

Emily told Lee, "You know, I think you may have some sense in you yet." Realizing Lee was getting tired Emily said her good-byes.

CHAPTER SEVEN

THE NEXT MORNING EMILY AGAIN TRIED to decipher what the thread was in Lee's narrative so she could help him understand his life and make his transition easier.

Just as Lee was about to say something to Emily, there was some commotion on the Chief's side of the room. Lee saw the back of a woman as she left the room with the Chief. Apparently, they decided to roll the chief to the day room for a little distraction.

Emily took note that the Chief's wife was visiting more than usual. She also observed the juice glass on Lee's bedside table, thinking she might want to mention to dietary that the juices' taste wasn't quite right.

"What did your father do for a living? I think I remember you said he was an ambulance driver?"

My father had been working two part-time jobs to pay the bills. Since he'd come home from the war, he tended bar at his favorite firehouse and drove truck. My aunts knew a fellow church woman, Mrs. Emma McClinton, who owned the local newspaper. They approached her about using her pull as major stockholder to secure my father a position in the G. I. Training program. She did, and every Thanksgiving until her death they sent her flowers on Thanksgiving Day.

Being very active in the fire company gained my father recognition among the townspeople. He was approached by the Republican committeeman to run for councilman.

He was successful and was soon hobnobbing with some of the town's wheeler-dealers. His days became very busy; he was working for a living and juggling his fire house meetings with his various borough council committee meetings. The local steel mill maintained a fancy banquet hall, "Birch Hill," which they hired out for private functions.

There was a clique of town business people who had private parties of their own at the old Boy Scout camp in the Seven Mountains. My father told my mother they had parties of a "different" type. Those parties were places where men and women met to "party" with someone other than their spouses.

Coming home back over the mountains the mistress, of a married lawyer was very drunk, and drove down the mountain on the wrong side of the road. She hit a car head-on, and that driver was killed. Because of the names of the people at the party there was another cover-up. The mistress was driven home by a friend, also a lawyer. Because of the close friendships among emergency crews and the police departments the accident was re-staged to eliminate another car.

It was becoming routine to hear my father tell my mother, "Won't be home for dinner tonight. Having dinner out at Birch Hill."

Eleanor Stimely was Borough Secretary and was a great ally and friend to my father. When he attended his first dinner at the club he was sat beside the lady and she helped him get through the evening without making etiquette guffaws. She wanted him to understand how local government worked and how to work it to get what you want.

With steady work and his monthly pension my parents decided to move into a bigger house. They moved a block up and to the other side of the street. We were four doors away from the City Hook and Ladder Fire Company.

The government was cracking down on firehouses having slot machines. My father took the three from his fire company and put them in our attic. It was fun to pull the levers and watch the wheels go around and have three cherries line up to make it spit coins.

When my brother and his wife broke up the first time my parents were scared, she would report my father for having the machines. My father had a good friend on the City Council, who owned a junk yard. In the middle of the night my father took the machines to his scrap yard. He was supposed to destroy the machines but my father said, "Being Jewish he probably sold them on the sly."

Our neighboring fire company was expanding at the time, and they bought Bob Peters' corner store to build a new addition. My father said they took their machines and put them up on the steel beams that were supporting the roof of the new addition.

He told me, "Only two officers of the company and me know about building the machines into the ceiling." One of the officers worked for the construction company; he's the one who built them into the construction. The idea being, when slot machines became legal, they would take them from their hiding place and use them. Everyone associated with the scheme is dead now. Are they still there? Does anyone else know? Am I the last person to know this secret? Will it become an urban legend? Who knows?

Mini-markets such as the 7/11 were coming into vogue, and a developer bought our property to build one. It was then that my parents bought the last home they lived in together.

One summer evening a family get-together was held for them to tell us they wanted to buy a house but needed financial help. It was explained an insurance policy had been taken out for each of us when we were born. It was meant to give each of us a thousand dollars when we reached eighteen, to go to school. They asked each of us if we were willing to surrender the policies. They wanted to sell them and use the money towards the expenses of buying our new home. Their logic being we would all benefit from it and when they were dead, we would get the money back.

My father's sister gave them two thousand for a down payment, paid the lawyers' fees, moving expenses and bought an Alexander Smith carpet for the front room. My father's mother's aunt bought Venetian blinds for the front of the house (they felt it made a nice impression!). My father's aunt bought them a new living room suite. Everyone pitched in to help make my father's dream of owning his own home come true.

The home was on Pannebaker Avenue; an arthritic widow could

no longer live alone and had to sell the property. She lived next door with her three sisters-in-law who were her full-time care givers. Just as we meet bedeviled people in our daily lives, if there are angels walking among us, these three women must have qualified.

The widow's name was Martha. The three sisters were Annie, Lula, and Rhoda. Rhoda was sixty-four, Lula sixty-eight, and Annie was seventy. Martha had married their oldest brother, John, who was the "fair-haired child." A younger brother Clarke also lived with them.

Martha had rheumatoid arthritis so bad she could not walk. I first met them when they were trying to carry Martha back and forth from the house to their car. I saw their struggle and offered to help.

Martha protested, "No, he's too young - he'll hurt me!" The sisters assured her, "We'll be right here making sure you're not hurt and that he doesn't drop you."

I carried Martha into the house. After that, I would stop in and visit with everyone. I learned to know their routine. In the morning, the sisters would bathe and dress Martha and carry her downstairs to the dining room where she would "hold court" from a dining room chair with a pile of cushions. She could barely feed herself. Her finger joints had popped out of their sockets, they locked into a curved scoop position. Her spine and hips locked into a permanent sitting pose. Her elbows locked into a 'holding a book position', her legs locked at the knees and were permanently bent. She could grasp a pen placed in her fingers; or hold a light missal for daily devotions. With a hankie tucked between the long parts of the thumb and first finger, she could swipe across her nose. The girls (as they referred to themselves), would have to hold a hankie for her if she wanted to blow her nose.

By their sitting her in the dining room, they kept her involved with the household. They would share a lunch together and listen to Paul Harvey on the radio. If I was going to visit, that is when I would visit. Martha loved to share his comments and opinions with me, young as I was. Sometimes they would place a crochet hook in her fingers and encourage her to do light doily repairs.   I was fascinated by the lace like work and asked her to teach me how to do it. Although she could not move her fingers as nimbly as she would have liked she taught me with verbal directions how to crochet and later knit.

When my only nephew was born, I crocheted a receiving blanket for him. The sisters lined it with bridal satin then 'tufted' it on the satin side to make a better presentation. When I gave it to my sister-in- law, I got the distinct impression that she did not appreciate the gift, or the work that went into making it. She seemed somehow dismayed that crocheting was one of my talents.

The sisters and brother still maintained a full garden and canned everything they could and made as much grape wine as their vines would produce. No longer having a butcher house, they still butchered meat in the garage at the end of the lot, and smoked hams on the third floor.

They had another brother, Porter, who was married. "The boys," as the sisters referred to them, still enjoyed hunting. They were very lucky at hunting, and all the squirrel, rabbit, and deer went to good use in their home.

As Martha's condition worsened, they moved her downstairs to their front parlor and made her bedroom there. They still gave her all the care they could, and then even more.

Because both boys had bad backs, the ladies would often ask me to go with them to visit relatives so the boys didn't have to strain their backs. I would transfer Martha from the car to a wheelchair and see she got in and out of the house all right. Martha had a grown married daughter, a schoolteacher who had two young children. The sisters told me that her husband was a very successful insurance man, a 'Shirk' from Mifflintown, who could give his family the best of everything.

To my young eyes, they both looked down their nose at me. I always felt they had a questioning look of, "Why are you around my relatives?" Her aunts and uncles doted on her, and she could do no wrong; they were so proud of her success.

Annie was the first sibling to pass away. Still the sisters took care of their sister-in-law. I could not help wondering; why the daughter let her elderly aunts work so hard, so long? Taking care of her mother?

Eventually Lula passed away and the daughter finally took her mother to a nursing home close to where she lived. It had been all right for the elderly sisters to do all that work but the young daughter was not going to do it.

Those women were *saints* to me.

CHAPTER EIGHT

ALONG WITH THE NEW HOME CAME ARGU-
ments about money and how much time my father's council and fire
department activities demanded of him. To get away from their squab-
bling I began to spend more of my time involved with after school
activities. Volunteering in the library gave me something to do so I
wouldn't have to go straight home from school.

Tired of hearing the arguments about money, I got a job delivering
newspapers. To further increase my income, I kept some of the money
I collected from selling refreshments at my father's firehouse's bingo
games. The man in charge of the refreshments told my father, and I
was severely beat with a razor strap.

My father was running for re-election to council, and to get back
in his good graces, I handed out political leaflets for him door to door.
I met Mrs. I. V. Walters, who liked me and introduced me to her
grandson so he would have a nice "Christian boy" to play with when
he came to town.

When he was graduating from high school his family invited me
to come to Bradford for his graduation party. I asked my parents if I
could go and they were reluctant. I would be expected to give a gift
and I would need some pocket money, and they did not want to give
me money for either.

I asked my mother, "Can I go if have my own money?"

She asked, "How would you get your own money?"

I told her, "I will sell some of my glassware!" And that is what I did!
I had met a lady at the public sales I attended who collected Carnival
Glass. I sold a large carnival glass bowl to her. I took a gold edged water
pitcher set with six glasses to an antique dealer, Mr. Schontz on Valley

Street and sold that to him for twenty-five dollars. I was very happy knowing I did not need their help

In tenth grade a group called The Spurlows came to town and did a free concert at the school. They were a Christian group who performed popular religious music. I went to their concert that evening at a local hall and during the evening was "saved"; that is where I got that worn red New Testament. Some of Martha's cards are still saved inside the pages.

I was at the age when all boys are horny. It was very difficult. During particularly boring high school classes, I started to notice other boys squirming in their seats they would start to shift things to a more comfortable position. Temptation was everywhere. I had to go to the Physical Education teacher's office after school one day to have him grade a paper I did for his Health class. He had me wait at the door to the office, went to the back of the room, and sat down at his desk. Halfway down the room was my History teacher; He was standing in a partial open doorway talking to someone. In a few minutes he backed out of the door way and the young hunky Junior High School Physical Education teacher walked out toweling off his naked body.

I did not know that the doorway my history teacher was standing in was the doorway of a shower-room. I immediately looked at my teacher, my eyes asking the question, "Was that the reason your hand was so busy jiggling something in your pocket while you were talking?" I did not think he was playing with his coins. He likewise gave me an odd look, and I think he knew what I was thinking, because I looked at that naked ass and then looked at him. Just then, for some reason the naked teacher turned around gave me a quick "Hello" and moved to the end of the room as he dried his back.

He attended the same church as my family. That Sunday as he walked his two little boys to church; we met at the crosswalk, he looked at me not remembering where he had seen me. We exchanged hellos. For once, I had no lascivious afterthoughts.

I began to wonder if teachers could tell which of their students were "different." After the time in the men's room with the janitor, a new janitor was assigned to clean the library where I worked before school. I immediately thought the janitor, who I exposed myself to, might have said something to someone else about how he exposed himself to me. Why was the change made? He had cleaned the library for years. The next janitor avoided me like the plague. Of course, it could have been my imagination.

Another incident happened to make me even more paranoid. I went to an out of the way restroom in the basement after classes ended. As I went down the hall, I passed the teachers' lounge. The English teacher with the briefcase who followed me into the bathroom was sitting inside the open doorway talking to another male teacher.

I had no sooner gone into the bathroom and that other teacher followed me in and stood close to me. It seemed to be too much of a coincidence. I remember he was tall, short hair, square face, attractive, and wearing a dark green corduroy suit.

He said, 'hi' and made some other small talk which I didn't hear. He had no problem unzipping his fly, putting his hand in his pants, bringing it out, pissing, doing a combination shaking/stretching/squeezing, putting it away and zipping, all with one hand. Compared to the "briefcase" teacher, this guy did a quick slam-dunk.... get in, get out. He must have worn loose boxers. I do not remember anything more than the tuft of light golden hair above the shaft that had my full attention.

This kind of situation is everywhere for a young gay boy.

When Joey, my older friend from Bradford, Pennsylvania, came to visit he would take his grandma's old 1948 Dodge and drive us over to Greenwood Furnace, a popular swimming destination. On this occasion he wore his suit so he did not have to go to the bath-house to change. I went into the rest room side of the bath-house first to pee. While I was taking care of business, a voice says to me "Nice day. The water looks inviting". The chat took me by surprise and I mumbled something and I went to the other side to change into my swim shorts.

Shortly thereafter a man about twenty-two, walked in and said, "Hello"; I recognized the voice from the restroom. Even at that young age when I looked at a man I would decide right away if I found him attractive. He passed the test. Facing me, he unzipped his pants and undid his belt. As he slid his trousers down and raised his leg to lift his foot out of the pant-leg, the front opening of his boxer shorts gaped open revealing a plume of black hair. He repeated this with the other leg and the plume again waved at me.

He turned around away from me and I was relieved because I thought the show was over. Slowly he bent forward at the waist, placed his thumbs in the band of his boxer shorts, and slid them down his hips revealing a lovely ass covered with black down. He raised one leg to lift his foot out of the boxers and as he did his large hairy sac dropped down into view. The scene was repeated as he lifted the other foot. He certainly had my attention. He turned around full front. As he held his boxers against his chest, hand-ironing them flat to fold them he inquired, "Do you think I should take my undershirt off here, or wait until I get to the beach?"

Duh, do it now, sure, I was stammering in my mind. I had not moved my eyes, which betrayed my interest in what I was watching, his body, that mass of black hair. (I so wished I could have a masculine body like his.) Instead I blabbered, "Well, they do not wear shoes on the beach." With that he sat down, and everything he had was dangling in front of the wood bench. I thought to myself, "Yeow!!! Splinters!!"

He removed his shoes and socks and stood up asking, "Should I take anything else off?" I silently shook my head as he reached for his jock strap. He shook out the folds and did a lovely shake-wiggle as he maneuvered each leg into it. He pulled it up to his waist covering everything but the frame of black fluttering hair. After he straightened the broad band around his waist, he did one more hand gesture of stretching the waistband out at his waist. He slowly inserted his hand all the way down, cupping the fingertips under his balls and bringing everything up into the cup to rest comfortably. I almost needed smelling salts!

Looking back, I wonder what he must have thought about the kid he entertained. Had I looked like I had been moonstruck? Later I realized he knew exactly what he was doing and probably was having a bad day and needed his ego stroked; too bad he only got admiration and rave reviews for a show well done.

With all the temptations I faced, I could talk to Martha about my feelings and sexuality. She tried to understand and counseled me saying it was just a phase. She advised me to read my Bible and when the Devil tries to lead me astray to substitute prayers for my sinful thoughts. She did her best to reassure me that the teachers did not suspect I was gay. She was sure no one thought of me as abnormal. I did read my Bible back and forth twice and for two years was able to restrain myself from lusting and having any physical contact with other boys. What I don't think people in general understand is that straight kids are programmed from the beginning on how they should think and behave and what sexual feelings and behavior is usual for them.

What guidance is there for kids who are not straight? We know somehow, we feel differently, think differently. Where are the older parental mentoring role models who can verbally tell us it is all right to have the different feelings, attractions and desires?

NOWHERE! Contrarily we are told we are sick, perverse, and abnormal, an object of God's loathing.

CHAPTER NINE

IT WAS AFTER WE MOVED THAT MY MOTHer's mental health problems manifested. We do not know for sure when they started. Dr. Marthouse, our family doctor, later said he was not all that surprised she had a nervous breakdown. He said all those surgeries over the years would have had an effect on anyone's nervous system.

On a Friday in late October,1959, when I normally would have been in school, I was home sick. My father came home for lunch, as always, at exactly eleven forty-five. He would eat quickly then lay down for a nap until exactly twelve forty-five, then get up and go back to work. Fridays were paydays. This particular Friday when my mother opened my father's pay envelope while he ate lunch, she found out there was not the amount of money in it she had expected.

My father said he knew the envelope was short. Jane Grubb had forgotten to put the overtime pay in this week's envelope, but it would be in next week's envelope.

My mother budgeted very closely, and because of her medical expenses, there were always outstanding bills to pay. But although we were poor, we did not do without.

I thought we were pretty well off the way we lived. Nice home equal to my friends and relatives. My father got cars and guns when he wanted.

There were weeks when my mother played bingo every night. Nights she won big she would get home at ten thirty. She would wake us up to treats of milkshakes, hamburgers, and French fries she had bought us at the Royale Dairy store. There was enough money for clothes and shoes and always plenty of food.

Then she and my father had a very bad argument. My father went back to work early without his nap and my mother rushed upstairs. I could tell by the footsteps she had gone to her bedroom.

I thought I heard her on the phone, then her bedroom door opened and she ran over to the bathroom. After she was in the bathroom the phone rang and it was my Aunt Ruth saying, "Lee, go get your mother! She's in the bathroom. She got a gun - she's going to shoot herself!"

I ran up the stairs, knocked on the door and called to my mother, "Come out, I need to talk to you!

"No, go away!" she said.

"What are you doing in there? Open the door!" I begged.

"Get away or I'll shoot you too!"

I was beside myself. I heard a car screeching to a stop. It was my father. He came rushing up the stairs and banged on the bathroom door.

"Lene open the door. Goddamn it Lene, open the door." She had pulled the trigger. I heard the hammer fall. "Back up, we have to break the door down," my father yelled.

Emily's heart began to ache as Lee's eyes filled with tears. He could not go on. The room was starkly silent except for a few moments of soft sniffling. Emily could not imagine how a memory so old could still manifest so much pain.

He felt like his head was going to explode; his tears were painful silent tears, the kind that do not make a sound. They only draw your chest muscles tight from the constricting of your throat as your eyes and nose both turn into water works.

To watch a person hurt this much and know there is no way to rip that horrible memory out, was almost unbearable for Emily. To think a mother did this to her child is intolerable.

The pain of the memory subsided, leaving a dull headache. Lee continued. "My father and I backed up and rammed the door. When we broke down the door, I slid to my knees, landing in a heap by the bathtub watching as if I were miles away unrelated to this scene.

My mother was lying on the bathroom floor on her back, the .357 magnum in her mouth. My father took the gun and laid it aside and gathered my crying, shaking mother up off the floor cradling her like a baby, saying, "Holy Christ Arlene, you scared the shit out of me."

The front door slammed and my Aunt Ruth came up the stairs as fast as she could.My mother's sister pushed into the bathroom, saying, "Is she all right? Did she shoot the gun?"

I was still on my knees as Aunt Ruth and my father took my mother to her bedroom. I got up off the floor, and laid down on my bed, my mind going blank. I was angry and confused, and I felt rejected. I heard them discuss my mother as people sometimes do; as if they are not in the room.

They called our family doctor and he came to the house. He went into my mother and said," Jesus Christ! Lene, what is the matter?"

I am sure more was said between the doctor and the others, but I cannot remember. As they were passing my bedroom, I heard the doctor say to my father, "How is the boy?"

My father said," He is all right, it is her."

How is he? How should I be? I just witnessed my father break into the bathroom; wrestle a gun from my mother's mouth and then her hands. She threatened to kill me! I crawled up off the floor and went to my bed. No one said anything to me or asked me anything.

"Well," the doctor says, "I think we better take her to the hospital. You need to call an ambulance."

"No, Doc, I can take her in the car," my father said.

"No, you cannot, I won't allow it! She may try to wreck the car. She needs strapped down until we find out what is going on," Doc said.

My father turned to the house and called out, "Lee! Come on! Your mother's going to the hospital."

To add to her misery, the ambulance attendants did indeed strap her down to transport her to the hospital. The entire neighborhood saw my mother removed from her home strapped to a gurney. The doctor traveled with her, and because she was now considered a mental patient, she was admitted directly to a room.

After she was put in a bed, my father was at the nurse's station talking with the doctor. My Aunt Ruth and I were in my mother's room. Aunt Ruth was talking to my mother; I do not know exactly what was said. I heard my mother say, "Christ, Ruth, if I still wanted to kill myself, I could jump out the window or tie the electric cord around my neck and strangle myself."

Aunt Ruth ran out of the room straight up to the nurses' station. "She said she could jump out the window or hang herself with the light cord!" That sealed her fate; she was immediately transferred to the State Hospital on McClay Street in Harrisburg. In those days, they referred to the hospital as just "McClay Street".

When we left the hospital, there was no conversation. I expect my brothers were told why Mom was in the hospital. I didn't hear a conversation and they never spoke of it to me and vice versa.

When McClay Street was said, you knew people were talking about the "looney bin." This is when the treatment of the mentally ill consisted in part of being submerged in ice baths and being given electric shock treatments. The movie, "One Flew over the Cookoo's Nest" honestly portrayed the treatment people received in the state hospitals at that time.

I will never forget those visits to the state hospital to see my mother. The tall black wrought iron fences; the winding driveway among a forest of trees; The big foreboding buildings. I do not remember all the procedures for getting into the patient's area. There were many corridors to walk and heavy doors being locked behind you. Eventually we reached the visiting area. The doors which would open allowing the patients to visit with their guests had small windows.

My father and I were the only ones to visit my mother while she was in McClay Street.

Sometimes several patients would jostle to look through the window to see who was waiting. At times, there would be parts of several faces each trying to get an eye to the little window to see if they had loved ones waiting for them. Some, knowing they would not be receiving company, would just glower through the window and make horrible faces at anyone whose eye they caught. That was a little scary to me. I was in ninth grade, only around fifteen years old.

When my mother appeared, the first thing, she said to my father was, "I didn't tell." She seemed to be reassuring him that she kept some confidence.

After midterm exams that year, my homeroom teacher took me aside and asked," Is there anything you would like to talk about?

I asked her, "Why are you asking me that?

She said, "While you are not an A student, you failed all your mid-term exams."

"All of them?" I asked.

Lee's eyes swelled with tears again, his voice stopped, sniffling fills the void for a brief minute as he fights for control of his emotions. It is still very real after all these years to remember the hurt he felt when his mother threatened to shoot him as well as herself; that memory of her on the floor, the gun in her mouth.

Emily said with force, "Let it out, quit holding it in. Go ahead and cry, feel it. You really have not let yourself feel all of it. That is why the pain is so bad. You are holding back, afraid to let it burst through. Nothing else can happen, the worst is over."

Lee hates when the memory of that day overwhelms him and cripples his mind; who wants to carry a memory that jumps to the surface so painfully? Who enjoys feeling tears swell up, your throat constricts in a hot flush from your neck to your forehead? This is a memory he knows will only die when he dies.

Emily stands up, leaning over, grabs Lee's hands. She holds them clasped to her breast. "I know, if your Mother could, she would grab you and hold you close. She would tell you how sorry, very sorry she is for making you experience that moment." (His eyes flood with hot tears again) "But my child, she can't!" Emily continues, "I can. As a *mother* I know she had to be suffering that day from some demon to have given way to that awful despair."

Lee's throat is so tight with emotion he cannot talk; only small puffs slip out his shaking lips. "For her sake and yours I am pleading, begging you to try to forgive her. She truly did not know or understand what she was doing that day. She was not perfect, she had problems, too. I am so sorry she did this to you and I know she is too. Please try to let it go."

Lee's nose starts to run along with the salty tears of anguish as sweat breaks out on his forehead, throbbing from those painful memories.

Emily never knew she could feel someone else's pain as much as she felt Lee's. Yes, he certainly had been off the spiritual path, but she knew he was one of Gods children. She had to give him succor.

"Let me get a cold wash-cloth for your face and we'll make you feel better. I will be right back."

He tried to regain his control. All his life this memory haunted him constantly. Knowing his own mother said she would kill him. Knowing she did not want to take care of him. Knowing she wanted to let him confront her remains in a pool of blood that would have splattered her body through the bathroom floor down into the kitchen below.

If your mother cannot - does not - love you, how can anyone else? Why *should* anyone else? Lee learned early on not to expect love. Do not look for love.

His mother loved him so much; she had him on his knees cleaning the weeds out of the cracks in the sidewalk with a paring knife; she had him iron the families' sheets, pillowcases, and all the underclothes for the men in the family. She loved him so much that one Saturday afternoon when he had plans to go on a picnic, with his friend from Bradford's family, that she called the friends' grandmother and told her, "Send Lee home. He did not scrub the baseboards the way they should be done."

The grandmother pleaded with his mother, "Can't he please go along? We have all been looking forward to the picnic. Can't he be punished when we get back?"

Lee's mother was adamant, "No, send him home now!"

His friend's grandmother had no choice but to send him home with the promise that she would take him to another picnic as soon as possible. The grandmother said to him, "I don't know your mother very well. I know she has been sick. However, I do not think it's right that a male child *must* stay home on a Saturday afternoon to scrub floors, when he has already done them once, right or wrong.

Although Lee had two older brothers, he felt his mother always made him do more chores than the other two. One brother was two years older. She always said, "He was weak and sickly as a baby, and has never gotten over that." He never received special medical care, and he could run and play as good as anyone plays. Lee never understood why she said his brother was anything but healthy.

His oldest brother was over eighteen and working part-time jobs, giving his mother $25 a week and buying groceries occasionally, so he was spared the household chores.

One evening after Lee and his mother were done cleaning there was some conversation as he tidied up and headed for the stairs to get a bath. She was telling him how thankful he should be, and grateful for all he had, and for all that she and his father had provided.

He stopped in his tracks half-way up the stairs, keeping in mind that he had just finished helping his mother clean the whole house again. Lee asked her, "May I ask you a question without you getting mad?"

She said, "Yes."

He repeated, "But promise me you won't get angry with me."

"All right, I promise!" she responded.

He asked her, "Why do you keep casting up to me all that you say that you have done for me; and all that you say you have given me? I did not ask to be born, you two just decided to have a child, and here I am! Aren't you supposed to take care of me? You make it sound like a big deal! I do a lot of work around here! I think I deserve anything I am given."

Without answering, she glared at him, and said, "Go to bed!"

As it goes when a child is hurt, as much as they are hurt, they try all the harder to gain that person's love.

Emily returned with a basin of water and a washcloth to wipe Lee's face.

He told Emily, "After my mother was discharged from the state hospital my father took me and my mother out to the mountains. He let her know that the same bullets were in the gun from that day in the bathroom. He made her fire all six bullets. They all fired, there were no misfires.

My father told my mother, "Lene, there was nothing wrong with the gun, there was nothing wrong with the bullets; it was God telling you it is not your time to die."

Lee went on, "We all hoped she would be okay after coming out of the hospital. It was not long before she tried to hurt herself again. She lined her bed pillow with razor blades hoping to toss and turn on them during the night and cut her throat. She did not expect they would slide off her pillow and end up on my father's pillow cutting him. He was pissed.

One night we heard her ooching and ouching and found her in the cellar with cuticle scissors trying to pick her wrist veins open. Her favorite method turned out to be pills.

The doctors tried to respond to her complaints of pain and sleeplessness too kindly and she continually overdosed. There were too many times I had to hold her up while she was on the toilet and hold her up at the dinner table trying to get her to eat because she had taken too many pills.

She was not home for my oldest brother's wedding in 1962. She had another nervous breakdown and was in the state hospital again. Before she was hospitalized, she had been sticking her nose in the preparations rather than letting the bride and her family plan what they wanted. There were several arguments regarding whose church they were going to get married in. My parents pressured my brother to get married in our Episcopal church because it would make his relatives happy, resulting in nicer wedding gifts.

Unhappy, but giving in to the groom's family, the bride got married in a church she did not like. In turn, her relatives except for the immediate family stayed away with their wallets folded. To ice the wedding cake, the bride and groom had a small reception at the groom's home. It was the Hatfields and McCoys all over again; until the whiskey and the beer started flowing, then the dirty stories and laughing started.

My father asked me before we went to bed the night of my brother's wedding, "Do you have any idea what it is like to go to bed with a woman you love, and every night she prays for God to take her so she does not wake up in the morning?"

Of course, I was too young - I had no idea. I turned to my father, "May I ask you something? I heard Mom tell you, 'I did not tell them' regarding whatever was discussed in therapy. What is it she didn't tell?" I was told to go bed and we never discussed it again.

CHAPTER TEN

TWO OF THE ACTIVITIES I JOINED TO KEEP busy were the drama club and concert choir. (This was a perfect fit for a future drama queen who loved to sing the blues. Move over Billie Holiday!).

I started studying voice privately to deepen my voice quality. Some of the kids at school picked on me with taunts that I sounded like a girl. I told my voice teacher Mrs. Kerns and she said it might help. I am sure the two dollars a week helped her.

In addition to singing at school I joined my church's choir. I was asked to sing "How Great Thou Art" as a solo for Rogation Sunday in my senior year at high school. I told my parents and asked them to come and hear me. They were not regular churchgoers and declined my delightful invitation. One of my cousins was in the church when I was rehearsing and called my parents exclaiming how good I was.

After that phone call my mother said, "Nellie called and said you sounded very good in rehearsal; she asked if we were going to be in church Sunday to hear you sing. I told her no. Thinking it over I guess we'll come Sunday to hear you."

I was so angry that she said no when I asked her. Now, because Nellie called and said I sounded good, she felt ashamed of telling me she had not planned to come to hear me sing. She decided she should come; if she did not, how would it look?

I told her, "If you come now just because Nellie called I won't sing." They stayed home. During high school, I was in at least one play every year and in several choir productions. I had never asked them to come and they never said they wanted to come. *They never attended one of my activities.* They were so caught up in their own lives, my mother with her illnesses, and my father with his public service life.

A true case of "I Never Sang for My Father."

During my senior year, I was in rehearsal for the class play. I was going to be late getting home so I called my mother to let her know not to hold supper. I was the only one living at home with my parents. I thought what's the big deal? I told her to clean up the kitchen, put the food away; I would make a sandwich. She raised all kind of hell. She called the school and told them I was no longer allowed to participate in any after-school activities. She told them I must be sent home after school; she did not want me on school grounds after classes.

I fooled her. I went to the public library, since she forbade me to go to the school library. Margaretta Elder was the librarian, a fellow church member. My mother stifled herself rather than let gossip get back to my relatives, exposing her selfishness. The next day I learned that my father didn't come home for dinner and hadn't called. I thought, "Was that what really upset her, hmmm?"

I knew I wanted to get away from home and was trying to think of how I could go to college. An acquaintance of mine from concert choir told me how he received a full scholarship to go to Pennsylvania Hospital School of Nursing in Philadelphia. I decided I would follow suit and investigate the possibility for myself.

My parents being the people they were; said, "We cannot help you financially!"

They had not helped either of the other two and were not helping me. It was all I could do to get them to fill out the parent's information forms for the nursing school. They did not want anyone to know the amount of my father's disability. They never told anyone about my fathers' pension for fear they would not get the monetary and in-kind gifts from the Aunts and Uncles if they really knew how much my parents had coming in.

When it came to answer this information on the school admission forms, you cannot imagine their reluctance. I explained they would not have to pay one cent for my education, room or board. The nursing school was seeking national accreditation and federal monies. To do this the school needed a quota of male students. Male applicants were not all that plentiful, (because of the stigma of a "man" being a nurse) so if you applied and were half-decent you could get a free ride.

My free ride started when I took the train to Philadelphia for the admissions tests and interview for acceptance to the school of nursing. I had never been on a train before and here I was all by myself. When I got to the Center City Station, I had to transfer to a trolley.

Having a rash of illnesses when I was a child, I was held back in school. As I walked down the street, I felt very grown-up and free. I was praying I would be accepted so I could get away from my hometown. At the school, each man was assigned to a room already occupied by a freshman student. The first morning we were oriented and we tested in the afternoon. They kept us busy with school activities and we did not get back to the room where we would sleep until late in the evening, just in time to go to bed. I was bunked with a nice guy named Larry. I enjoyed the instant camaraderie of being in an all-male atmosphere. I felt comfortable and did not mind being away from home and fell asleep quickly.

The next morning was a replay of my awakening to my naked uncle Smittie. My brain was awakened by the sound of my roommate's alarm clock. When I opened my eyes, I was looking straight across the room at Larry. He was naked as a new born, flag pole at full mast, sitting on the edge of his bed scratching his head as he yawned. I immediately shut my eyes. Reopened them to the size of mere slits and gazed across the room. He was only a year older than me, similar builds, hairless, except for the patch surrounding his appendage. He stood up stretching and started to walk across the room in my direction. I did not know what to think. *What* was going to happen next? What did I *want* to happen next?

I shut my eyes and felt him move past me down the room to a window that looked out on the grounds of the hospital. I opened my eyes again completely and looked at his bare backside. As he started to turn around, I again shut my eyes, I don't know why. He knew he would have awakened me. A clock would normally awaken anyone. You would think he might have thought the alarm or his walking could have awakened me.

Instead, as an inexperienced chicken, I did not react until he left the room. THEN my mind said, "Get up, grab your towel, go shower with him." Moving as fast as I could was not fast enough. He must have hurried more than me, as I was entering the shower room he exited with a towel wrapped around his wet glistening body.

After saying good morning, I said something about having breakfast together. He thanked me for the offer but said his schedule did not allow it. I hurried through my shower but when I got back to the room he was gone. I was getting so tired of these missed opportunities.

I got dressed, packed my bags, went for breakfast and finished the school's agenda for the day and wistfully walked to the trolley stop wondering what life held for me. I took the train back home and worked all the hours at the five and dime I could get. I took every odd job I could find to build up my bank account that summer, while waiting to hear from the nursing school. I had no other back-up plans to get away from my home town. I wasn't looking for a full-time job if I was going to school. I was afraid if I did I would never get away.

They sent my notice of acceptance as a student in a matter of days. Excitement didn't begin to describe how I felt. Freedom was coming! Neither of my two older brothers was able to go on to higher education and this wasn't going to cost my parents a penny. They should have been ecstatic for me.

I worked even harder to earn money to save for when I went to school. My aunts bought me towels and gave me money for my first uniforms and shoes. We found out I had to buy books and another relative gave me money for them.

When my oldest brother and his wife broke up, she promptly reported him to the civil service board; he was immediately drafted for two years. He came home from the service in 1965 and gave me the foot locker he no longer needed. I packed everything that the school said I should have on arrival for the first day.

My mother remembered I sold glass to go to Joey's graduation and told me to sell all my stuff so I would have money to put in my checking account. My father told her, "No! He won't do that." My parents reluctantly agreed to deposit ten dollars a week to what I had saved in my checking account. My aunts and uncles were happy for me and I expected my parents would be. I waited for them to express something to me about going to school, never a word. It seemed like they didn't want me to go away - like they were losing a worker.

My oldest brother was living at home again and giving them room and board. He did quite a lot of work around the house that should have been enough. It was not! They really wanted all their sons to live at home as grownups, paying room and board and taking care of the house for them!

I was anticipating my departure for school, planning my trip by train. My aunts and uncles thought it was terrible for me to have to take the train. They let my parents know they should show some interest in my future; by driving me to the school. The information packet I shared with my parents described a welcoming event for the students and their families. I was so happy they were going to be involved and see where I would be attending classes.

True to form my father drove to the front of the school, unloaded my belongings onto the sidewalk, gave me a quick hug and off he went to hit the turnpike before the traffic got heavy. At least I got a hug.

As much as I wanted it, my parents show of pride for me never came. I would be getting a good education, room and board with no help from them!

CHAPTER ELEVEN

I WALKED UP THE SIDEWALK TO THE EN-
trance to the students' quarters. The welcoming sign-in desk was attended by a lovely senior citizen who identified herself as the housemother. She was looking over my shoulder for my entourage when I
quickly excused myself to go back out to the curb to bring in the rest
of my belongings.

After identifying myself and being checked in she asked, "Where
are your parents?"

I told her and she was slightly taken back saying, "Why, I never
heard of such a thing. We have a wonderful welcome reception and tour
for the students and family. It's really a shame they wouldn't stay for it."

She gave me a key to my room and a map of the campus. She
pointed me to an open door leading to the gardens, continued with
the next arrival. Leaving the building, I found myself in a large garden
enclosed by buildings. The signs told me where labs, classrooms, and
the male dormitory were located. My roommate had not arrived yet so
I chose a bed by the window and started settling into my new home. I
unpacked and explored the room and the floor I would be living in. My
roommate and his family noisily arrived, like Santa Claus on the roof
with a clatter. They were happy and laughing until they found out the
room was not empty and I had taken the bed by the window.

It turned out only did his mother drive him into the school, the
family lived in West Philadelphia. His mother was very nice, and
when she found out my parents would not be there for the welcoming
ceremony she said, "You must come with us! You can't be alone for the
formal welcoming of your class."

My new roommate's mother, Nora, realized right away I felt bad about my parents not being there. I sensed her son was not happy when she invited me to be with them during the welcome ceremony. Her saying, "I will adopt you for the day!" brought a scowl to her son's face. They unpacked his belongings and we all set out for the reception.

I surprised myself by crying during the ceremony thinking how disappointed I was in my parents. I did not know why. Why should their actions have been a surprise, not wanting to stay? After all, their non-appearances at my school activities was the norm; but *this* was different, a milestone. Everyone else had parents there to meet the school staff. Even the students from Guam and Alaska had parents there to celebrate their children's new direction.

The administrator was very blunt with some of his remarks during the welcome speech by citing statistics regarding how many students drop out or fail the first year. I knew I would not be one of those statistics he talked about. The welcoming reception lasted until six o'clock.

After the reception, the students were free to socialize or do whatever they wanted with their free time. During the socializing, I found among the male students in my freshman class a preachers' son, from a wealthy family who was a decadent genius drug addict; a failed football player from Wakefield Forest college whose father strong armed him to be there; a young New Yorker who should have been a great used car salesman; a short mouthy boy with a Napoleonic complex; a very timid religious young man from rural South Carolina; a couple of older very quiet settled men, and the rest of us who did not say as much as everyone else making it hard to gauge where we fit in the mixed group of personalities. After a noisy series of visiting each other's rooms, everyone settled down for the night knowing the next morning would be our "new day's dawning."

The freshman class was divided into two groups. The two groups would alternate between periods of lecture theory and practical experience. There were eighteen men and thirty women in our class. The women were housed in the first building and the men in the second. The women's building had an automatic locked front door except between the hours of eight and five. There was always a housemother present at the desk watching the front door. On the first floor of the women's building was a large student lounge and in the basement a game room, kitchen and laundry. Men were allowed in the common areas until ten o'clock at night.

We were given a ring of four keys. Our building had a separate front door with no overseer. They felt the men did not need a house parent. One of the administrators lived on the first floor of the building and it was felt the men would behave just knowing he was there.

On our first morning, we put on our new, crisp white uniforms and white shoes and headed for the cafeteria. The building we walked thru was the first original building of this hospital. which was co-founded by Benjamin Franklin. The entire building was maintained as a museum with medical libraries. The original Amphitheatre operating room was preserved waiting for the next procedure. The complex consisted of the Sheetz's building, the Pine Street building, the Women's Lying-In building, and Wards One and Two in the old original building. It didn't take long to learn our way around the grounds.

The first year of a three-year nurse's diploma program contains all the science courses plus all the basic nursing classes. We had Anatomy and Physiology, Microbiology, Organic Chemistry and Psychology, taught by professors from Penn State. Nutrition, Fundamentals of Nursing, Public Speaking and Psychology classes were taught by nursing school staff. They were also our clinical supervisors on the floor. It sounds like a lot but in all fairness, they did allow study time in the schedule. No students worked in the hospital past four o'clock. All academic classes were over by four also. You had a certain window for lunch but you could go for your evening meal when you wanted up until eight PM.

The lady who taught Chemistry was a normal down-to-earth teacher. The lady who taught Microbiology told everyone she had not taught for years. She had quit teaching to be a mother and housewife; now that her children were grown, she was getting back into teaching. This was sort of like an advance apology for her teaching methods if we did not think they were very good. It turned out she was probably the favorite teacher because she taught with such enthusiasm and sincerely endeavored to teach her students. She approached every class with a joyous bright smile and everyone knew she would go the extra mile to explain anything that was not clear.

Teaching us Nutrition and encouraging us to eat properly was a good old home-girl type, Miss Barnes. Our Psychologist of residence and teacher of same was Mr. Richardson. It was Mr. Richardson's job to weed out those improperly suited to the profession. He would call everyone in on a routine basis and question and evaluate their fitness to heal the sick and injured. The last thing he wanted to hear was, "I have a problem with my gender identity."

When we started classes all the men stuck together and all the women kept to themselves, because of the separate housing. As the sexes intermingled in classes and during shared practical experiences pairs and small groups started to develop. Roommates asked to be reassigned and hierarchies appeared.

My roommate (who said he wanted to be called RJ) and I, although initially frosty, became good friends. He went home often and asked me to go along frequently. His mother was a joy. His father was conspicuous by his absence. I learned from innuendo and various comments that he was not completely pleased with his adopted son of unsure linage. His mother overly compensated for the lack of her husband's interest, and RJ became a "Momma's boy."

The girl I took to both my Junior and Senior Proms also went to the nursing school in Philadelphia. For something to do on a weekend my roommate suggested we go visit her. Not knowing the public transportation system, he said he would accompany me so I wouldn't get lost. I felt he was nosy and wanted to see what kind of girl I had taken to the school dances. We registered at the housemothers' desk and soon she and her roommate appeared. It was a stilted meeting. She and her friend cut their eyes at us several times, making me wonder what was going on. I soon found out.

She turned to her friend and said, "Look they are both wearing dog chains."

I asked her, "What do you mean, wearing dog chains?"

She responded, " Don't you know when guys wear ID bracelets, it is a secret signal to other like individuals they are homos?"

I turned to RJ, "Have you ever heard that?"

Wearing his expressive, *I have been offended* look, "NO! That's just stupid. The bracelets are just something to wear!" Once we got on the trolley to go back to the school he said, "Boy, I was dumbfounded to find out they know about the bracelets."

My first visit home was about four weeks after nursing school orientation. When I returned, I found my mother had someone dig up the 40+ rose bushes I took care of and my entire rock garden, and the flowers and rocks were removed and thrown away. She had a junkman go to the attic to remove all my antique treasures and get rid of all the "clutter." She saw no antique value, just junk. Without regard, she discarded an antique French Iron bed, an original Bissell sweeper, an old parlor organ from 1890 and so many boxes I had forgotten what they contained. She explained she was alone now and had no one to help take care of the house or yard. She would have neither junked up. My bedroom was filled with old things, thankfully she didn't bother that room.

Because my nurse's training included night care with back rubs, my father would have me massage his back. He always complemented me on how well I worked his muscles. He told his friends how well I massaged his back.

When I was home for Thanksgiving from nursing school one of his friends asked my father if I could massage his back. My father sent me down to his friend's house to massage the guys' back. His wife and the kids were out, with only him and me in the house. We went up to their bedroom, he took off his shirt, and he laid face down on the bed. The cream to use was laid out and I started to massage his back.

He said," Since your arms are short take off your shoes, climb up on the bed, and straddle my back.

Okay. I felt a little strange, but I did it. As I massaged his back, he moved quite a bit, and groaned, "Oh, that's good.... I'm really enjoying this."

I adjusted his pants several times during the massage pushing them lower and lower down the back of his torso. Each time I did this he would turn his head and look back at me, as though he was questioning, "Do you know what you are doing to me?"

I was getting excited and knew I wanted to do more, but this WAS my father's married friend. By the time I was done, I had massaged from his shoulders to the top of his envelope opening. I enjoyed rubbing and feeling his skin under my hands. The friction created warmth that felt good to me and I knew inside my soul I wanted more. I had played doctor with my brother and Paul, but I did not know how to play doctor with a grownup - after all, I did not want to get in over my head. I didn't have enough experience to know what else I could have done to really enjoy myself. When I decided, I had done enough, I got up off the bed and asked him, "Where can I wash my hands?"

He curtly directed me, "Down the hall on the right."

I went down the hall; before I entered the bathroom, I turned and asked, "Which towel do I use?"

I looked back as he replied, "It doesn't matter." He had turned his head as he answered and realizing I could see what he was doing slammed his bedroom door shut. He had stripped fully and was cleaning himself up. BUT I had only put lotion on his back! A job well done!? When he walked back downstairs, he escorted me to the door, as I was leaving, he slipped me five dollars. (I wondered, in the world of adult sex, if that was the going rate.)

My oldest brother to my surprise had remarried after I started school. My middle brother having failed his physical tests for West Point enlisted in the army and was sent to Vietnam.

Returning home for Thanksgiving I felt like an outsider. I had met many other people and heard tales of others' lives and realized some glaring differences. I couldn't wait to return to the school. I had come to enjoy my life in the city, the school and the academic studies. I had kept my nose clean and free of lustful sexual fantasies, up until my roommate returned from his turkey-day holiday.

I had always had a weight problem. In sixth grade, I weighed 127 lbs. In high school my Aunt Ruth took me to a country doctor she was going to for diet pills. I had lost weight but then gained it all back with the proverbial extras. Having been overweight when I started nursing school I had gone on a diet and when RJ returned to the school and saw me in my new tight Levis' he said, "You would be a hit at Rittenhouse square."

I didn't know what he meant and asked him. All he said was, "Go up to Rittenhouse Square. Walk around, have a seat, admire the park and you will find out what I mean."

It was a mild November night when I took my first walk up Spruce Street towards Rittenhouse Square. The school was located at Eighth and Spruce and the square was up at 18th and Locust. I had never been out alone in a big city at night before. I wasn't afraid because there were so many people on the sidewalks and heavy traffic on the streets.

The first few blocks I walked were lined with old brownstones. When I crossed 12th Street the area changed to apartment buildings and small businesses. Crossing Broad Street felt like I was on the "Red Carpet." Looking to the right and seeing City Hall at night for the first time was exciting. The Academy of Music was all lit up. Chauffeurs were helping extravagantly clothed couples to the steps of the Academy. There was a noisy, obviously low-class bar on the southwest corner of Broad and Spruce. I even found that exciting. Leaning on the wall of the building on Spruce Street as I crossed over were obvious hustlers, even to my naïve eye.

As I walked up Spruce Street, I passed the Allegro Bar, great music wafting out the front door as men entered and left. Crossing 15th Street was a sign with a rooster on it announcing "The Westbury." Continuing up Spruce Street the neighborhood turned back to large brownstones. I came to 18th, turned and proceeded a block into the infamous square. "Do you know it was reputed to be a gay hangout even when you were there, Emily?"

Without waiting for a response Lee continued, "And THAT is where my education in gay life began, Emily! I had arrived."

CHAPTER TWELVE

EMILY REALIZED IT HAD BEEN A LONG DAY, even though she had tried to encourage Lee to eat, she knew his body was not going to benefit much from the small amounts he could swallow and keep down.

"Lee," Mother Anderson began, "it seems to me you may be enjoying our visits."

"Odd as it may sound, you're right. It's been a long time since I could talk to someone. That is because you're a blank tablet. You do not have any information to fire back at me to tell me I made such and such mistake or was wrong to do this or that. I can tell you things without having someone say 'I told you so!' Or 'I knew you would be sorry and regret doing that.'" he said.

"You know, I think your lifestyle and promiscuity is wrong." Emily replied.

"I really don't give a flyin' fart what you or anyone else thinks of my so-called lifestyle. You really do not know my life style. All you know is what I have told you about my childhood. And excuse me! What do you mean, promiscuity? Who told you I whored around? a trembling Lee choked out.

It was very hard for Emily to contain herself. No one had talked to her in this manner since she left her prison ministry. She used to hear words of this nature quite often from the women she counseled. She had forgotten how quick some phrases pricked her sensitivity. Her gentle nature pulled her up short and kept her tongue from rattling off a lashing at this frail man. She knew God had called her to his bedside to do His work. She prayed He would continue to guide her, giving her the fortitude to withstand the ugly truths this man revealed about his life, and that she might accomplish what He wanted her to do.

"I am sorry. I suppose you do have a point; in that I do not know your lifestyle. Since you admit you are gay, and that is an abomination in Gods', no I will take that back I think it is quite unnatural for two people of the same sex to be together in that way. However, let us have a truce, and again I am sorry for sounding as if I knew you to be morally loose. I really got us off the track of what I wanted to talk to you about. I am aware you have a medical directive, but if you would consider an intravenous, not a stomach feeding tube, it would help keep you strong enough to participate with our little conversations. If you don't you will lose your strength, and lay here, no good for anything, let alone even talking. If you do not want to take medication, that is your business. You can reject the infection fighting medicine and kidney intervention. But at least you could maintain yourself enough to visit with an old lady who wants to know more about you!" Emily cajoled.

"Why would you care about my life? I am sure there are other more deserving, less offensive patients," Lee countered.

"You just answered the question for yourself. You are not undeserving of human kindness. You are one of God's children. That is why I stopped when I told you being gay is an abomination to God. That is not for me to say. He has not written it in stone for me to carry around! Nor have I heard those words from a burning bush. My beliefs may not necessarily be God's; they are only my interpretation. Who is to say I know what God means? What he wants each individual to say, do or think? I do think I have a good idea of what he wants from me! How he wants me to think. However, it is only what he wants for me and from me that I know well. I realize I am may be small minded, or close minded. Whichever you prefer, regarding your life style. Again, God will deal with you in his way and time. That is not my job. I feel my job is to help you cross over, as ready as you can be, to meet your maker. Not to judge you."

"Okay, you can arrange the IV." he said. "I did drink a little juice from the aide that was in earlier to change my water while you went down the hall. Everything tastes so bitter now."

"Well I am glad you will accept an intravenous solution. That makes me feel better. I will stop by the nurses' station on my way out." Emily chattered as she gathered all her belongings to go home. She leaned over him and ever so lightly brushed her lips on his forehead, whispering, "God bless and good night."

As Emily entered the building the next day, she heard the code announced for a runner near the elevators. The staff had already secured the exits.

"God damn it! Leave me alone. Take your hands off me. I will have you arrested! Help! Help!" assailed her ears as she went down the hall.

The Chief was at it again. As she approached the bank of elevators, she heard the chief telling the aides, "I was only going for candy! She told me to go for candy. I told her it was too early, but she said to go now."

The aides were not sympathetic. They jostled his chair around and roughly maneuvered him back into the elevator Emily had just entered.

"Let me tell you about my wife!" Emily heard the Chief say raucously to the aides.

"When I married my wife, she was hell to get housebroke. Every time we started to undress, she ran out and jumped in the back seat of the car." The aides just chuckled to themselves and Emily was relieved he was not cursing.

When they returned the Chief to his room, they found his wife, hands on hips, loudly demanding, "Where did you go? I said I was going to the vending area. What did you do?"

"You told me to go for candy!" The chief shouted.

As the aides explained what happened, Edie apologized for her husband's behavior. "He just gets things so mixed up anymore," sighed Edie. With a curt nod, to Emily, Edie drew the curtains along the Chief's side of the room.

As Emily walked along the bed, she realized Lee was still sleeping.

She turned on her heels and walked down to the nurses' station to inquire how the IV procedure was going.

"You know Mrs. Anderson I appreciate your interest in Mr. Lee but it is hopeless." Nurse Logan replied curtly. "The IV may help keep him more alert but in reality, it might be kinder to him if he wasn't quite so aware of his systems slowly turning off."

Taken aback, Emily replied, "Please do not try to make me feel bad for wanting to help him come to terms with his maker. He needs to ask for forgiveness while God can still hear him. He needs to clarify what is in his heart, in order to send his soul homeward."

As she walked down the hall Emily considered her own thoughts regarding Nurse Logan's' words. "Of all people, I know prejudice! I think I may be as guilty of it, as guilty as some I have accused."

As she approached the room, she became aware the Chief's good friend from the old days was visiting this morning. "Good morning, ma'am. I have heard some of your conversations with your friend. Sounds like he had an interesting life."

"Likewise, your friend."

"Yes, he was causing problems again." Edie declared.

"Oh, the old boy just hates being confined. Let's take him down the hall to the rec room." Cornpopper suggested. As they wheeled the old man down the hall, he was heard saying.

> *"A foolish man named Joe Bock.*
> *At the power of hormones would mock.*
> *He said they are just for hicks.*
> *But he tried some for kicks.*
> *Now he can't pull his pants past his jock!"*

Emily just shook her head to herself and gently roused Lee to prepare him for the orderlies to sit him in his chair.

"Can I get you anything?" Emily asked after the orderlies settled him in his chair.

"No, thank you, the aide gave me something to drink this morning.

I'm losing my taste - everything tastes bitter." Emily was heartened to know the staff was being a little more attentive.

Emily began again to coax Lee to talk. "Tell me about nursing school."

Lee began, "I really enjoyed the hospital atmosphere. I loved the work. I felt I could really help people. One day in conversation with the wrong people, I referred to one of my classmates as 'Baby Huey'. The next thing I knew I was being pushed up against the wall by Hubert Bechtel. In no uncertain terms, he made me understand I was not to refer to him as 'Baby Huey' anymore.

Word got around I had not stood up to the six-foot bully. The next day some of the seniors brought me their ironing to do. They thought I was such a pussy that they could make me do their bidding. They were not six feet tall and I wasn't going to be their bitch. I pushed the ironing back in their face.

I had a hard time dealing with all the new personalities and was curious about why RJ thought I should go to the "square." The next evening, I had been finding it difficult to concentrate on my studies. A walk would do me good! I reasoned. It was far easier to give into my curiosity than force myself to study Anatomy and Physiology. I decided to seek refuge in the park.

At first, I just said "Hello"! To different people who passed by with nothing happening.

One evening a nice young man passing by asked, "Do you have the time?"

"Depends on what you want to do." I chuckled.

He stopped in his tracks, came over put his hand out and said, "Hi, my name is Tony."

I introduced myself and he asked, "Would you like to go around the corner to 'The Gilded Cage' for a cup of coffee?"

"I don't drink coffee but I am sure they have tea" I said. Looking at the handsome Italian boy with the tousled hair falling on his forehead I quickly added, "Okay!"

We walked the short distance and by the time we reached the coffee house it seemed like we had known each other for a long time. He lived with his parents in Cherry Hill and I shared where I came from and what brought me to Philadelphia. He then told me what I needed to know about the park. It was a homosexual cruising ground! We never asked each other about our own sex lives. The conversation just flowed soft and easy. He explained that men come to the park to meet and pick up other men for sex.

Other than Paul and the preachers' son, I had not been intimate with another boy. I always knew I didn't completely understand what and how two men did when they got together. Sort of like how young children don't know everything about how men and women make babies. Hell, I was still a virgin as far as girls go. I didn't know what to do there either.

I guess Tony assumed I knew what two men did together. Looking at Tony I fantasized about being able to take off his clothes and explore his body. I would have loved to found out what two men do together sexually with Tony but alas, it was not to be. I could not take him back to the school and he had no place to take anyone.

Looking back, I think he probably realized I was the country bumpkin who did not know anything. He admitted he came to the park often and had been doing it for years. We parted without exchanging phone numbers. Neither of us said, "See you again." What would be the use? I went back to the school that night with an understanding of what "cruising" meant.

The following Saturday evening, having nothing to do (except study), found me answering the call of my "Lorelei": the square. I chose my perch and decided I was ready to be forward and make an effort to get someone's attention.

An older man stopped and asked, "May I sit down?" He introduced himself. "My name is Roland Manning." After a respectable period of chitchat, he explained, "I live just a few doors down that little side street," motioning with his hand. "Would you like to walk over to my apartment?"

I knew I wasn't being invited to play cards. Not knowing what to expect but wanting to find out what happens between men behind closed doors, it was now or never, I had to say yes!

We walked the short distance around the park to the small side street beside the Dorchester. Passing a cluster of high-class antique shops, he stopped in front of a small obscure door. He had chattered the whole way like a bird telling the flock a large worm had floated out of the ground after a heavy rain. I had walked in silent trepidation not knowing if I was doing the right thing or not. I knew I wanted to find out what two men do together. I would not find out if I stayed glued to a park bench. The thought never entered my mind he could have murdered me.

He opened the door and flipped a light switch setting his elegant stairway aglow in soft red light. He told me. "Go ahead up the stairs. I'll just close the door and be right up behind you."

By the time, I entered the parlor at the top of the stairs he WAS right behind me grinding himself into me even though he still had his cashmere topcoat on. He pushed me into his parlor, as if he was doing a very "bad" Latin dance. The entire time he was slathering his tongue from my ear down my neck to my chin. Stopping in front of a sofa he threw his keys on an end table, and with no small talk, just grabbed me by my shoulders, and started kissing me.

Talk about "Roseanne's car wash of love!" When he interrupted his tongue from stabbing my throat, his lips seemed to spread open wide enough, to cover my face from ear to ear. My God, he washed my ears inside and out and the back of my neck.

His hands were all over me! Sliding my jacket off and letting it fall on the floor, his hands were on my belt buckle. At the same time his experienced lips were gyrating from my mouth to one eardrum, then the next; ever returning to bruise and nip at my lips. My head was in a whirl! I was being invaded! He was a one -mouth infantry.

As my pants slid down to my ankles, his hands, (still cold from being outside), were in my underwear greedily grabbing my young manhood. He was pulling on it with all his might like it was a rubber band. When he realized, he had achieved the desired effect on my pulsating body, my underwear was pushed down as he backed me up to the sofa. As he went down on his knees my ass was pushed down onto the sofa as ecstasy welled up inside me. He had not even removed his overcoat. It was then in that moment that I found out what some men do to other men.

Maybe I was just too green behind the ears. It was scary, overpowering. Suddenly I realized what I had done! To think I followed some strange man back to his home. No one knew where I was. I let him undress me. Slobber all over me, and I mean spittle/drool! And let him land on my privates in a way that made me think he had not eaten in weeks... When the immensity of what I had done sunk in; something like "buyer's remorse"…and all I could think was, "How can I get away? I am not doing any of this to him!!"

Feeling very satisfied with himself after having his way with me, he finished, stood up and smiled down at me. "Did I just get a cherry? You certainly acted wild enough as if you didn't know what was happening. You had no control whatsoever! You naughty boy! I'll take it slower next time and make you scream even louder. Have you ever?"

Leaving that question hanging in the air, with a wicked glint in his eye, he said, "No, I'll bet you haven't! First a cherry and a newbie; don't worry I'll be gentle with you – and I'll teach you how to give me the pleasure I gave you." He tousled my hair with one hand while loosening his tie with the other. Turning he started walking down the hall undressing as he went, calling over his shoulder, "I will be right back. I think I'll turn the shower on and give my new baby a thorough cleansing."

"No, No," I silently said to myself, "I'm out of here!"

I stood up, started putting my self-back together and ran out down the stairs as he was calling out, "Wait! What about me? I didn't get off."

CHAPTER THIRTEEN

DURING MY WALK BACK TO THE DORM, I thought about what just happened. The actual physical orgasm was such a strong bodily reflex. I felt like I was being twisted in knots. I did not know if it hurt or felt good. I could not believe what I had done. I realized I enjoyed the fear of not knowing where I was going or what was going to happen. The excitement of the stranger humbling himself in gratifying enjoyment somehow inflated my ego. Moreover, I loved being able to run away without having done anything but receive pleasure.

Sometime during my return to the school, the realization crept into my consciousness that I might, indeed, want to do this to another man. I knew I had been attracted to men. The man in the changing house, the friend of my father I had given a backrub to, my high school English teacher. I realized if I had known what to do, I probably could have quickly found myself controlling these men's bodies. I would have enjoyed making them writhe in pleasure, eager to know I could control their rapture.

When I got back to the school, I told my roommate about my experiences. He listened raptly and I thought somewhat jealously. He said, "Maybe I'll go along next time you go to the park. I could use something like that."

He was wearing his bathrobe and I walked over to him asking, "Oh, do you need some fun?" He stood frozen waiting for me to make a move. I untied the knot of his bathrobe, letting it fall open. He was very swarthy and had a chest full of thickly matted hair. Not wearing any underwear his nicely shaped manhood was nestled in silky black hair. I slid his robe off and pushed him down on his bed.

"Oh, I don't think we should have this kind of activity between us." He weakly protested. His bedroom eyes probing deep into mine. I rubbed his furry body all over. Nibbling on his earlobes, as my hand fondled his groin, I enjoyed the soft almost purring sounds he made as he mouthed, "No, I don't think we should."

It was surprising how easy and fast it was to bring him to his vortex of pleasure. I left him lying exhausted on his back as I went to the bathroom to shower before going to bed. When I returned, he was laying on his stomach with one leg pulled up, along his side, exposing his hairy backside and small round dark plum ripe for plucking. Locking the door for the night I playfully slapped his ass and said, "You better cover up. You are going to catch cold."

As I drifted off to sleep that night it dawned on me to think, "How did he know about Rittenhouse Square?"

With all levels of male students sharing the housing complex I saw quite a few handsome men. I had noticed one of the older students as he and his group went from class to class. All the male students' laundry was picked up and returned to the same spot in the entrance lobby in the men's hall. I got the bright idea one day to write a note of interest to the handsome older student I had seen and leave it in his laundry bag.

One evening a fellow student called me to the hall phone interrupting my study time. When I picked up the phone and said hello, a man's voice asked, "Is this Lee Larue?"

I said, "Yes."

He said "Hello, this John McBraide. Did you leave a note in my laundry bag?"

I was not sure if I heard anger or another emotion in his voice and suddenly, I was scared when I replied, "Yes I did."

"I wanted to call you and let you I was very flattered by your interest. And to tell you that is a little indiscreet to just put a note of such kind in an area where someone else could mistakenly read it." He asked, "Are you aware that I might be involved with someone else who could have found the note and been very upset by the contents?"

Taken back and embarrassed I said, "I did not think about that. I apologize for my forwardness." The phone call ended too quickly for me, leaving me feeling empty. I continued to lust for his body when I saw him walking on the campus. He was usually with the same man and I wondered if this was his "friend."

I did not have to wait very long to find out who his lover was. My roommate and I had been going out often in the evening to a restaurant at Thirteenth and Chancellor Streets called Dewey's. That area was known for straight strip joints, thug bars and prostitutes of all kinds working the sidewalks.

On one of our outings as we walked along Thirteenth Street a long black sedan came to a screeching halt beside us. Two large bulky men rushed out and quickly grabbed my friend and me hustling us into the backseat of the car telling us, "Keep quiet, Adelle wants to see you!" They drove us back past the school to an area known as Queens Village. We were pulled out of the car, dragged to a doorway and taken to a second-floor apartment. One of the men opened the door pushed us into shabbily furnished sitting room and said, "Adelle will be with you."

We were dumbfounded. Neither of us said a word. We just sat there waiting for some personage we never heard of. We smelled her "over the top" perfume before we saw her. A large, rough woman in a cheap, slinky, brightly colored lingerie type caftan appeared.

A face needing makeup (to say the least) opened its ulcerated mouth to say, "Hello, thank you for coming (like we had a choice!). My name is Adelle. I had you brought here because I am friends with many people associated with Pennsylvania Hospital and they think you boys need some advice.

"They are afraid your behavior and activity may also call attention to them. They are homosexual men and women who are in the closet and lead very conservative lives. I am told you guys leave the school wearing makeup, swishy clothes and are not careful about who hears you talking about gay subjects. If you bring attention to yourselves, it is feared a 'witch hunt' could develop which might bring them under scrutiny too.

"From now on, wait until you get to Dewey's to put your makeup on in their bathroom. In addition, clean up your act! Do not flame and swish around at school. For your information, Larue, Mr. McBraide has a lover, Brice Jackson. Had Brice found out that you wrote a note to John, all hell would have broken loose. He has had emotional problems and John has a hard time keeping him focused so he can finish school. John does not want any outside influences hurting his friend's concentration.

By the way," she said, "Nice choice of foundation but not your shade!" Handing each of us a cake of Nivea soap and a towel she directed us to the bathroom and told us to wash our faces before leaving.

We walked quietly back to the school. I don't know what RJ was thinking, but again I was a little scared. What kind of people was I getting myself involved with?

When we got back to the safety of our own dorm room, we talked about how Adelle knew so much about our activity. We went to talk to Geoff, the student from my hometown about what happened. He said, "I have heard about Adelle. She is a nurse anesthetist at Metropolitan Hospital on Race Street. She used to work here at Pennsylvania but was dismissed under some kind of cloud. I understand several hospital students and employees use her apartment building as a meeting place for their liaisons."

After our visit with Adelle, we calmed down somewhat, for a while...The male student whose room I had stayed in during the school interview had recently rotated back to the Eighth Street campus and was housed on the third floor of our building. When he saw me, in passing one afternoon, he stopped me and said, "I see you made it. How's it going for you?"

I certainly did not want to tell him of any of my explorations so I just made small talk about some of the courses. He in turn showed the proper interest and older student encouragement. When, "Would you like to go out to dinner on Saturday night?" came out of his mouth it took me by total surprise. Never did I think he would ask me out in front of my fellow students.

I replied, "Yes, of course!"

He drove us to a restaurant in West Philly called 'Behold a Pale Horse'. My damn naiveté; his foot kicked mine under the table, so I moved my feet thinking I had spread out too much. Dinner conversation was very mundane. I was just too unsophisticated and inexperienced to know clever gay repartee.

We drove back to the school where he parked on the top floor of the parking garage. Neither one of us were in a hurry to get out of the car. Idle-idle chitchat going nowhere.

I noticed at the last minute a very large jar of Vaseline on the floor in the back seat. I questioned, "Why do you have Vaseline in your car?"

He grinned and responded, "Some of the girls I date need lubrication before I enter them." (Having seen his appendage I knew that could be true and blushed to myself.)

I was so stupid!! I didn't know then, that gay men refer to other gay men as girls at times. Nor did I know men used Vaseline or some other lubrication to ease penetration. Getting out of the car we went back to the dorm never speaking after that evening; nor did we cross paths.

Not too many years ago, I heard he had been elected a county commissioner in rural Pennsylvania. His ruthless competitors made fun of him in their ads saying his wife had to dress him.

You know Emily, I had the best of all possible worlds. I had achieved freedom from the family I did not want to belong to; I was able to do what I wanted and I was getting an education free of charge. I had it made!

As the Christmas holiday season approached, midterm exams were sweeping everything else out of the way. I knew I was having a real problem with Anatomy and Physiology. I did not apply myself enough to the study of the subject to memorize all the things about the body and its functions that I needed to. In all my other subjects, I had B's or C's; good enough for me. Good enough for the school.

Going home for the holidays only reinforced my wanting to get away from my hometown, permanently! I was treated well enough. But I was now my own person. A different person, thinking very differently than anyone else I knew in my hometown.

I returned to school earlier than I had to, enjoying the solitude of a few days rest before the return of my school mates. One of those evenings I walked out to the Square and met a lovely young man named Donald Paul. He invited me back to his apartment to watch television. I was a hayseed, I sat and watched TV. We talked a lot but he wasn't making any overtures. I was a guest behaving according to the specified invite. Finally, he put his arm over the back of the sofa as to stretch and landed his arm ever so lightly across my shoulders. The pressure increased until I was sure the "Apollo" had landed.

I reached over, laying a hand on his lap and leaned into his face asking, "Why did you wait so long?"

He said, "I was afraid you were straight. You talked so much about your father, brothers and going hunting."

Donald Paul became the first man I was to enjoy kissing

Standing up he pulled me up with him and gently led me into his bedroom. I finally had someone who wanted to take me to bed and romance me warmly kissing, hugging and holding me... as I had wanted for so very long. Again, I know it sounds corny but as inexperienced as I was, I had to be taken down the garden path. I really did not yet know how or where to begin. I did not want to be in a "car wash!" I wanted to make love. I needed to learn how to be in a romantic sexual physical confrontation with another man. I did not know French kissing. I did not know the art of caress and titillation with the fingertips on various parts of the body.

Everyone has their preferences and it turned out he had a special talent. He liked to grasp a man's penis in the nook behind his knee and very expertly, tantalizingly, slowly bring them to an orgasm.

I don't know why I said it but when I left him late that night I promised, "If I ever learn to give head, I'll come back and give you a treat."

CHAPTER FOURTEEN

THAT NIGHT WHEN I SETTLED IN TO BED alone with my thoughts I replayed in my mind how I felt when Donald Paul put his arm over my shoulder. It was like electricity hitting my body. Finally, I had been able to put my mouth on another man's mouth who I found extremely attractive. I knew I wanted to open his lips with my tongue and kiss him passionately.

The instinctive reactions that had been trying to push through my reserve, all my life, were now out in the open. What I had thought about during those years when I looked at other men's bodies now turned into reality. I realized this is what I wanted. Not a female body to touch and feel. I knew then that I was one of those "queers" my father talked about. It was the first time I fully accepted the fact that I was what my father hated.

All the years before this moment I thought I was normal. I thought I was having horny impulses that all boys had; just like men trying to sneak a look at another man's penis at a public urinal seeing out how they compare in size. I had thought it was just a phase of feelings that would disappear as I got older and married.

No, I wanted a strong male leg, firm buttocks, muscular arms and chest to hold and caress. I was frantic. What did I do now? I was a sick pervert. I cried into my pillow pondering suicide not knowing how I could go on living. I could never go back home now. I had become one of those people the whole town would talk about.

My Anatomy & Physiology grade was in trouble; if I flunked out, then what? I had to be straight. Go back home? As I fell asleep, I knew I was going to change my ways. When classes resumed, I vowed to buckle down and improve my grades in A. & P.

During one of the bullshit sessions with some of the guys in my class, we started talking about sex; that is, straight sex. Some admitted they were virgins and I somehow left the impression I had doubts about my virility. They decided to help me conquer my indecisiveness and "hook me up." It happened with a young woman who worked in the cafeteria and lived next door in the Sarah Lawrence Home for Young Women. There was a social in the school basement. The guys gave me condoms and a pep talk on what to do and how. When I felt the opportunity was available, I sashayed a girl into a remote room and had her on her back before she knew what was happening. This was possible because she was different from other girls. The Lawrence home was a sheltered environment for mentally slow young ladies. One of the chaperons who helped guard the residents' virtues found us just in the nick of time. She pulled me away and grabbed the young lady by the arm. The last I saw of her was the back of her dress caught in her panties as she was led away while receiving a proper lecture on "bad boys."

But street life called me, and my roommate wanted to tag along. We were off and running again. We had met a college professor, Ted Brown, who hung out at Dewey's and often invited us back to his apartment. He had a lover, Donnie, a church organist studying for his Doctorate in music. Flying under my radar that sneaky bitch roommate of mine started meeting Ted at his apartment when Donnie was not home for sexual hook-ups. This gave me time to go alone to Dewey's where I met many interesting people. Harlow, Sticky Buns, Gaylord and Dannie Kelly were the stars of Dewey's.

They were all drag queens except Gaylord. He was a tall, young man who dressed in black, often leather. He had platinum white hair, I believe a wig, and wore white face paint dramatized by Chinese red lipstick and coal black eye makeup. His ensemble always included a black hat, gloves and briefcase. I was mesmerized by Gaylord. Not many people talked to or acknowledged his presence. I made it a point to meet him. We would walk up and down Chestnut Street admiring the storefront windows; it turned out he was a window dresser, if my memory serves me right, for Nan Duskins'.

During one of our window tours we almost became romantically involved. He pushed me into a darkened doorway, crushing me in a warm embrace, lifting his right leg up and wrapping it back around both of mine. I enjoyed his kiss but he looked so bizarre afterwards with his smeared lipstick that I was instantly turned off.

I soon learned that stereotyping and prejudice exists even within the gay minority. All gay people do not accept all other gay people. Asian gays were called "rice queens."

White gays who were attracted to Negro queens were called Dinge Queens. Other labels you would hear fly in the air when you were out in the gay circle were femme, butch, queen, dyke, lesbian and lipstick lesbian.

You needed a dictionary and game rules to know what and who you were talking to, and what they were into. And, you don't even want to know what "water sports" and "plain vanilla" mean among gay men. As entertaining as they may be, drag queens were shunned, looked down on, and called Pancake Patties.

Among the many people, I met at the restaurant was a gay couple; Tony and Jude. Jude lived out in Bryn Mawr and Tony lived with his brother George, in a tenement apartment building called the Graystone, whose first three floors were a parking garage on Eleventh Street off Spruce. Through Tony, Jude, and George I met more people than I can remember. I spent too much time enjoying their company, visiting with them and their friends in this derelict building.

One night when my roommate RJ was not cheating with his new love interest; I corralled him into going with me to visit my new friends. He only went with me one time and decided these people were too low class for him. I am not sure if it was class or too bizarre.

Some of the guys did wear "girl's" makeup (lipstick, rouge eyeliner, mascara, full face). Some would wear "boy's" makeup, which meant just a little powder to even skin tone and contour the cheeks, nose, and temples. Some did dress in drag all the time. Some were certainly swishy all the time, but they were fun to be with and *genuine*. They could laugh at themselves as well as each other regarding their makeup and dress.

Going to the Graystone, I was only scared when the elevator stopped on a floor where, when the doors opened, there were very few lights burning in the hall, creating too many shadows to hide in. There were times no one got on and I wanted to feel safe so I quickly pushed the button, urging the door to close. It was so frightening when a hand would grab the door at the last minute, forcing it to open. Occasionally it would be a silly queen saying, "Oh honey, I'm sorry. I had to run back for something and I was afraid I'd miss the elevator."

It might have been the building that repulsed RJ. If I were ever in a tenement or derelict heaven, the Graystone was it. I could see where walking in the parking area to get in the elevator in a dark corner would make you nervous. The elevator was very small, and shaky. It held, at the most, six people standing very close together. Even when it was not full, if there was someone else on the elevator, you knew who had been drinking, or eating spicy food, or skipped bathing.

It was a very cheap place to live due to the building's condition, so it had acquired a very motley roster of inhabitants. You never knew when the elevator doors parted what kind of people you would face. Drug dealers and buyers, "Johns," "butch" girls who would make a grown man shiver, or pretty boys who could have graced the cover of Vogue.

As the winter turned to spring, I found myself spending more time in the streets and away from the school. Anatomy and Physiology and I were not good friends, not even close. I knew what it meant if I did not pass the class; that knowledge had no impact on my need to explore my gender identity with my new friends. Like a butterfly emerging from a cocoon or an animal awakening from hibernation, people gathered in the spring on Rittenhouse Square.

The park was surrounded by fancy hotels and apartment buildings. The Dorchester and the Barclay were the fancier of the four. The residents of the area loved to visit in the park and be entertained by the variety of personalities and the colorful assortment of lifestyles that were on exhibition there.

In 1965, everyone in the big cities knew people who were gay. The more important, powerful, or higher in society you were, the more you could flaunt your sexual preferences. The area residents were intrigued by the flouncing and acting out of the gay children and the bizarre apparel of the flower children. This was the time of the flower child; Haight-Ashbury was at the pinnacle of its excitement. At the same time, gay anger was starting to build in New York City, which would ultimately result in the Stonewall Rebellion.

CHAPTER FIFTEEN

Most of the kids I hung with were not drinkers, although many of them did smoke marijuana and experimented with LSD, thanks to Timothy Leary. I never became involved with any pot or drugs but I did enjoy a good drink.

One beautiful April evening when one of the Graystone queens and I were going to Dewey's, I saw a man I recognized and called out, "Hello!" He was with another man and ignored me. They went into one of the straight bars on the corner that was known for having exotic female dancers and prostitutes.

I had met him one night when I was walking Spruce Street; as inexperienced as I was, when he said "hello", I sauntered over to him and walked along with him. It didn't take long for him to ask me to accompany him back to his apartment on Locust Street. His name was Rich and he was second something or other with the orchestra at The Philadelphia Academy of Music.

While telling me how I looked like I should have been a model for Reuben and how I resembled a zaftig Baroque painting, he had gotten me naked in his bed. He was making out and flipping me over to lay on my back as he asked me, "Can I screw you?"

I know, I know Emily, your sensibilities. Just think of it as if he was asking me if I could boil water.

I wanted to know and experience these things. And then, if I let him, I could cross that off my list of things to do! Reacting as I would if a waitress asked, "Do you want a glass of water?" I said, "Sure!" Prefacing it by saying, "But I have never done this before."

"Ah, a cherry," he gloated.

Another fruit lover, I thought, just what I need! On my back, looking at my ankles I was waiting for something to happen. I knew he was moving but I did not know what he was doing. I asked him," How is it going?"

He looked at me funny and asked," Are you kidding me?"

"No."

"Well you're not a virgin then. You must have had your butt pounded a lot because I am not small. Yes, I am in; and very easily I might say. What the hell are you telling me?" he chastised me.

"I cannot tell if you are inside me. What should I feel? Let me feel it," I said as I reached down to where I expected to feel our bodies joined together. They were indeed; it was neat to feel his hard warmth pressed into my back side. So many people do it; I thought the person receiving must feel all kinds of lustful pleasure. If they do, I had not felt it yet. His being in me didn't hurt. The rhythm after a while of having your body jarred, time after time though, got boring.

You must understand, that night when he saw me as he entered the club, he ignored me; suddenly I was a girl from Buttermilk Alley. Someone who had been used and now treated like garbage to be stepped on. Not me. I dragged my friend into that straight club and searched until I found him. It did not matter to me that he was with someone else.

I tapped him on the shoulder and said," Excuse me, how are you?"

He looked through me as his friend looked at the swishy boy with makeup on standing beside me and said, "Who is that?"

Glancing around the club as if I was not right beside him, he said to his friend, "I don't know. They must be looking for someone else."

"No, you don't!" I almost yelled. "I'm talking to you!"

He turned around and arrogantly said," I am sorry I don't know you, you obviously have me mixed up with someone else."

"Sorry my ass. You knew me well enough to screw the shit out of my ass in your apartment on Locust Street under that Reuben painting rip-off. Don't tell me you don't know me **your** sorry piece of shit!" I yelled. His friend just looked bewildered as they walked away.

My friend grabbed my arm and said," Come on, we gotta get outta here. We'll get in trouble. We're not old enough to be in here,"

The Graystone guys told me how to alter my drivers' license so bartenders would let me in the clubs. I learned how to erase the correct birth date from my driver's license and type in a date that would show I was 21. All you do is smutch ashes on the changed date and seal it between two pieces of plastic. It hides the alteration and people can either accept it or say, "No, sorry - you don't look old enough."

I heard about the Penrose club on Locust Street, a private after-hours club. All a young guy had to do was go to the club and hang out around the entrance. Someone would soon approach you, usually an older less attractive type looking for...? They sponsor you and vouch for having known you forever and a day in hopes of, let's say, companionship. Usually once in the club the younger guy would leave the sponsor and go in search of something more appealing.

The gentleman who sponsored me was very nice, so I didn't have to look for anyone else. The first evening - or should I say morning - we visited the club, music washed over my ears as soft as velvet. I could see over the crowd that someone was on a stage singing. The closer I was able to push myself to the stage the better I was able to see the entertainer. The singer was dressed in a floor length, low cut, royal blue evening gown. She wore heavy makeup and was dripping, glittery rhinestone jewelry.

She was singing in a low throaty voice, *"There must have been a thousand things…. I said wrong along the way…. Would I make the same mistakes… If he walked into my life today…. That boy with the Bugle… If he walked into my life today."*

I was one of many clapping wildly when the song ended. I learned I was watching the Jewel Box Revue. They were one of the best and most popular female impersonator shows of the day. I was fascinated and knew I wanted to attempt female impersonation myself one day. I spent the rest of my time in the club that night listening and watching the performers. That may have given me more insight into why some of the kids at the Graystone dressed up.

The warmer the weather turned the more I wanted to be with my new-found friends and join in their activities. I no longer felt "queer"- I was just one of the crowd. The convivial atmosphere, good will and acceptance among everyone who gathered in the Square allowed all who were there to enjoy life. It was a well-known fact that city matrons, nannies walking baby carriages, professional men and women, flower children and gay men and women all intermingled in the park, and there was no name calling, no cut eyes and no disapproving looks. We all enjoyed the street vendors with their ice cream, pretzels, and hot dogs. Everyone strolled and admired the innovative paintings and artistic wares for sale throughout the park. Older ladies might read or crochet. Mothers and fathers, be they professional people or flower children, would play on the grass with their children. Everywhere you could see couples, all kind of couples who had been hit by cupids' arrows and experiencing the throes of love.

While walking on the hot summer sidewalks you would pass someone with a radio playing music by Glen Campbell, the Supremes, the Mamas and the Papas, and Dionne Warwick's "Do You Know the Way to San Jose?"

I realized, come what may, I had to live in this city. I had to stay with my own kind of people!

I realized with renewed vigor how much I wanted to succeed in nursing school. It was not to be. I passed all my classes with B averages except Anatomy and Physiology. This class was so difficult for me I could not even pass with cheat sheets. I failed the class with a D. There was no room in the curriculum to repeat or retake the class, so I had to leave school.

It was May and the school officials gave those who were leaving a month to make other arrangements. I had heard other gay men who talked of how they had luck finding employment at a certain institution and decided to try my fortune. Dressing in my best bib and tucker I when to 18th and Samson Streets and applied for employment with the Philadelphia, Baltimore, Washington Stock Exchange. I knew the right person to ask for; I impressed him appropriately, and was hired on the spot as an assistant to the floor manager.

I was trained to operate the opening / closing bell and taught how to pass communications on the trading floor between the stockbrokers.

Back then there were no women on the trading floor. It was a playground for the "good old boys" club. I knew I would have an ample selection of men to choose from. Because of my age and, at that time, great appearance I was being hit on from all sides, all walks of life.

I was hit on by men with money and power, and younger men who would one day have money and power; I was in seventh heaven. Now I had to find a place to live. When visiting my friends at the Graystone on Eleventh Street I had looked at empty apartments in their building. It was one thing to run in and out and party there, quite another to live there. Maybe I now understood what RJ thought about the building.

I was still keeping company with all the guys and girls I had met there and one of them told me to find Jude and talk to him. Jude had been going with Tony who lived with his brother George.

"Brother," Jude roared when I caught up with him. "They were lovers. I walked in one night and caught George screwing Tony up the ass."

Jude said, "We had just been talking about getting an apartment in the city because I have a new job at Wanamaker's Salon.

"I'm sorry to hear about Tony, but how about you and I going together and renting an apartment?" I asked him, explaining about my situation.

We had always been good friends, able to talk freely with each other, but not physically attracted to one another. I think we both admired each other. Jude had great charm.

Tony's Graystone style should have bothered Jude right away. Jude had class, style, and an entirely different persona much classier than Tony. We discovered common likes and dislikes. We both wanted the same things in an apartment and liked the same locations. Best of all there would be no competition for the same man. We liked completely different styles of men; him, young, me - older.

We settled on a third-floor walkup at 13 th and Locust, right above the infamous Dewey's'. I still had money in my checking account and with my new employment I had no trouble managing my share of expenses. I was happy as a lark. We spent two weeks painting, cleaning and buying things for our apartment.

CHAPTER SIXTEEN

I was still living at the school during the transition time. My roommate at nursing school was continuing on with his studies and I thought doing well. When I went back to the school, the last night I expected to be there, he was not in our room. A handful of students I was friendly with came over to the room and said, "We overheard the housemothers talking on the phone and think they were saying RJ tried to commit suicide!"

I called his mother, but the normally loving Nora was gone; in her place was an accusing woman who yelled at me, "You are responsible for my son's deteriorated mental state. You have led my boy astray. You have taken him into dens of iniquity and a lifestyle of depraved debauchery. You should be skinned alive, boiled in oil and crucified upside down, and I have called your parents."

I stood at the telephone, now beeping its disconnected sound, in shock. I had always known my roommate to be a delicate, softer personality than I was, but I didn't expect him to react so badly to my leaving the school. There had been times he would come to me to be hugged and stroked like a child and want to be held as he fell asleep but I never saw any deep affection attached to this.

I went to work the next day as usual. After work that evening I was going to pick up my last personal items and few clothes left in the dorm and start living my apartment. I talked to the guys on the floor and they told me, "We heard from the school grapevine that RJ is going to be terminated for being unstable. They did not feel it would be safe to have him handle medicine and work with patients. They fear suicidal tendencies might be transferred to patients, perhaps with him becoming a mercy killer."

I wondered to myself if this was just an easy out for the school. His grades were good but since he had got in the middle of Ted and Donnie's relationship, he had become flamboyant. He expected to step into Donnie's loafers, but Ted used him for what he needed and wanted at the time, and that fling was over.

"Wait until you hear what his mother did! She came to the school with a list of names; nursing students, teachers and Doctors, who she says are gay. She threatened to go to the newspaper and expose a supposed homosexual conclave that meets at a woman named Adelle's apartment house, where they have orgies and use drugs. The school agreed to keep him on if he gets counseling and keeps up his grades," the guys went on.

I thought, yeah, right Nora. She had to know her son had homosexual tendencies for years. After all he told me to go to the square where I would be a hit. That last night at the school I gathered my things and walked through the doors out onto the sidewalk.

Cold anxiety stopped me in my tracks as I heard my parents call my name. Across the street parked behind a police car with its lights flashing were my father and mother standing in front of their car. Totally taken by surprise I never expected to see them in Philadelphia, let alone at that moment. I walked across the street and gave my mother a hug, said hello to my father and asked, "What brings you here?" Although a sinking feeling in my stomach was already sending signals to my brain connecting them to the phone call and Nora.

"Lee," my mother started, "Mrs. Baronski called, and told us you are mixed up with a bad group of people and we need to take you home. She blames you for introducing her son to drugs and a group of perverted people who are corrupting you. If we don't take you home, she is going to try to have you arrested.

She has already approached the school, threatening to sue them. Why didn't you tell us you failed out of school and were on the streets?"

It was a hot summer night but I turned cold as stone. "I am not on the streets!"

The policeman said, "Son, you need to get in your parents' car and go back to your hometown. This is no place for a young man like you. You'll get in trouble and people will take advantage of you."

"I don't know what Mrs. Baronski made up and told you but I have a job at the Philadelphia, Baltimore, Washington Stock Exchange and an apartment at 13th and Locust." I tried to tell my parents.

"How could you get a job at the stock exchange? Good God!" the policeman started, "Thirteenth and Locust? That's right in the center of the drugs and prostitution action. Either a pimp or child molester got him in his grips. You get in the car young man or I will take you to police headquarters."

"Lee you are sick. We can't let this go on. Maybe we should put you in the State Hospital in Harrisburg where I was? Get in the car!" my mother screamed.

"I have some more things in my room can I go back up to get them?" I asked. As they grimaced a silent nod I turned and walked toward the dormitory door.

I walked as if I had concrete shoes on. I looked up at the dorm windows and every one of the windows was filled with gawkers. And I was the cause of it. My world was so alive with joy when I left the school and stepped onto the sidewalk. I felt it had just been crumbled like a piece of dried up toast. I don't even remember walking back up the stairs. I could not accept my life had just disintegrated.

I didn't have to get anything else. I just thought, let me walk away and maybe I can think of something to somehow stop this from happening. I returned to my old room and was met by the same students who I had just recently talked to.

"What's happening?" they asked.

I told them quickly what was going on. "You don't have to go with them." one said.

"The front door locked behind you, they can't get in. Hide - they won't search the building," another offered.

"Go out through the garden. Exit the rear garden gate and just go. We'll ignore them and not say anything," was the final word offered.

I turned around and went back out to my parents' car. At the last moment, I looked back for a final glimpse of the school. Many of the windows were filled by inquiring faces watching this farce play out. It was a different time in 1966. You had more fear for what your parents said they would do, because back then, they would do what they said. In addition, a policeman said I had to go. I was a scared country bumpkin.

I did not know that since I had employment and an apartment, I had emancipated myself and did not have to go with my parents. Did my parents know? Did the policeman know?

They boxed my ears with threats and admonitions for the entire two-hour drive home. My mother threatened, "You are going to end up in the crazy house! I doubt you will be able to take the shock treatments as well as I did. So, if you know what's good for you, you better straighten up and behave."

I never again had contact with my new roommate Jade Plum. Nor did I have any further contact with my employer, the Philadelphia, Baltimore Washington Stock Exchange. What must these people have thought happened?

CHAPTER SEVENTEEN

My life came to an abrupt stop, as time seemed to run past me. I had become frozen in a tableau that was being created around me. I was not allowed out of the house unless with one of my parents. I was not allowed phone calls, though no one called. You would have thought I was a Japanese detainee during World War II with military secrets to blab, the way my parents guarded me. I had become a house bound scullery maid/gardener in my parents' home. The house had never before been so thoroughly cleaned and the yard so free of weeds.

My middle brother was still in Vietnam and my parents were constantly worrying about his safe return. My oldest brother had remarried his wife and they were living in a rural community nine miles away.

Because of my abominably bad behavior, my parents told all my relatives and anyone who would listen what a scum of the earth I had become. Unfortunately for my parents, when I was able to visit my aunts and uncles alone, after hearing my side regarding my job and apartment and the fact that I still had money in the bank, they turned on my parents. If it had not been for them, I probably would have had a longer house arrest. My parents were surprised to find no one approved or thought they did the 'right thing' of forcing me to come home amid threats of hospitalization in the state hospital for the insane.

My aunts said, "It is no wonder he's the way he is. You never let him get dirty or let them play with other kids. You always treated him like a girl and made him do all the ironing and housework. The other boys weren't treated like that."

That was the one time they were extremely upset with my mother.

She had always been well liked except for her spendthrift ways. They saw her threats for what they were: bitter resentful mean spiritedness.

Looking back, I think I was on my way to a major mental health problem if my mother and father had not insisted, I go for psychiatric counseling to cure my perversion. Back then it was still thought to be an illness if you did not like the opposite sex.

My Aunt Dord told my parents that a cousin told her the local hospital needed orderlies. She felt with my having gone to nursing school that it would be a natural fit for me to work at the hospital. She knew of my house arrest and decided to help free me. Aunt Dord was very influential! When the hospital found out I had been in a nursing program they gladly hired me. I fit right in and enjoyed being out and away from my parents' ever watching eyes.

It was much easier work than I did as a student nurse. The orderlies moved patients back and forth for tests and therapy, occasionally helping a nurse shift a patient's position in bed. We were the people who would take the patients to the morgue when they died and change their oxygen tanks to help them live. Once in a great while we would be called on to shave a male patient for surgery.

The head nurse on Two South called me one day to shave a man who was having pilonidal cysts removed. She told me to shave him front and back from his belly button to his… I thought that was too big of an area but that was what she said. The cysts were very small and located only at the top of the butt crack. The patient was twenty-something and was just as surprised as I was to find out what I had to shave. All the flat areas were very easy. That was my first time ever shaving a man's penis and scrotum; I did a very thorough job and handled him so much he became aroused. As he was just starting to trickle a slight discharge a senior orderly came in just in time to keep me from doing more than what was required.

I was moved off that floor and rotated through various floors. I would run into young nurses' aides who would make passes and flirt. I became close to one of them, Deb Stratton. We would meet in the cafeteria and visit back and forth on each other's area when we could.

Occasionally there would be a little quick kissing and hugging. I had decided by this point I had better try to cultivate the opposite sex.

My parents had let me buy an old car to drive back and forth to work at the hospital. Since I was dating a girl, I was given more freedom. On one of our dates after we had been to the movies we went "parking." We were both in the back seat and making out hot and heavy. One thing leads to another and we were scrambling to loosen and take off our clothes. My tight straight-leg Levi's and her panty girdle were just a little too difficult to get off while we were both in the back seat. Plus, you have to remember, I was still a straight virgin. It was too close in the car so I stepped outside to move the action to the ground. I opened the trunk lid looking for something to put on the ground.

"I'm not getting screwed on the ground if that's what you are thinking, Lee," Deb called from the back seat.

I decided to move the stuff in the trunk around to arrange a make-shift perch for Deb's posterior. I brought the spare tire, which wasn't on a rim, around so it was close to the lid and piled other stuff underneath to counteract the squishiness. The height was perfect!

I had her reclining, in a manner, on the tire and was enjoying her tight little body as she hung on to my arms so she wouldn't teeter off the shaky seat. Just as I was coming to a climax, she was moaning and digging her fingers into my arms, her ass slipped and she fell down into the center of the rimless tire. I hadn't given the crow bar in the trunk a second thought when I was positioning the tire. When Deb sank thru the hole it gouged her backside. I didn't know if she had a cherry or the blood was from her bouncing on the crow bar.

Deb was raised by her grandmother and I had the pleasure of many good meals at their home. Her grandmother was a very frank woman who told me her daughter had been a hard-headed child who ran away leaving Deb behind. She said Deb had been a handful too, but she was her only heir. She let me know she owned a lot of property and would be happy to see her only grandchild married before she died and would make that future son-in-law well to do.

Knowing my parents wanted grandchildren and thinking they

would feel relieved if I was married, I considered marrying Deb. I took her into my confidence and told her some of my experience in Philadelphia and how my parents forced me home. I told her I often wondered how my old roommate RJ was doing.

One Sunday when I was going to take her to visit the battlefield at Gettysburg she said, "Why don't we drive to Philly and visit your old roommate at the school?" We drove to the dormitory on Pine Street in Philadelphia. I knew if he was still a student, where he would have been assigned a room. I quickly found the door with his nameplate on it and rang the bell.

He called out the second-floor window, "Who is it?"

I said, "It's Lee, I was out driving with my girlfriend and we thought we would stop and say hello. She would like to meet you." Yes, in retrospect I guess I should have attempted contact in another manner first; or somehow warned him.

He quickly said, "I am busy studying for an exam." After a pregnant pause he added, "I really don't want any contact with you."

I was flabbergasted and turned away, walking in silence back to where I had parked.

Deb told me after the trip to Philly she would like to go back sometime and stay overnight. She added, "1 want to go to some of those gay clubs. I have always wondered what it would be like to be with a girl. There have been times I felt like I could be a little gay."

Yes, maybe I am a hypocrite - but her saying that upset me. We never returned to Philly and my feelings for her cooled.

My father said to me a few weeks later that a driving violation summons from Philadelphia had come to the house. Since the car I was driving was in his name and mine one of my parents opened the envelope. It contained a parking ticket from when I was in Philly with Deb. He announced since I had not been there, he contacted the people who issued the ticket and told them it must be a mistake because he had not been in Philly either.

Even though the prospects for wealth were great, my attitude toward Deb changed. The grandmother was still trying to buy me for her son-in-law. Deb sensed I was dumping her and got very angry. Hell, hath no fury like a woman scorned. Without my knowing, Deb wrote a letter to my parents telling them how we sneaked off to Philly.

She told them, "He tried to get me to go to the gay clubs and get involved with women." I cannot begin to tell you how incensed my parents were. Angry does not do justice to my father's outburst when he was haranguing me that he lied to officials regarding the ticket because of my deception. They were so disgusted with the letter (like it was a piece of filth) they just threw it down on the table after they read it.

When I got the chance, I took the letter. One good turn deserves another. I took it to Deb's grandmother and told her everything. Although she wished me well, she understood there would be no more contact between her family and myself. I knew she would not like to know everything that happened but I also knew she would punish her granddaughter.

I started seeing a counselor, Mrs. Farley, the matriarch of the first black family that joined our home church. She encouraged me to go back to nursing school. She arranged through vocational rehabilitation to get me another full scholarship for three years of nursing school. I applied and was accepted at Phillipsburg General Hospital.

During the summer of 1967, while my mother was out shopping, I met the manager of the local 5&10 Cent Store where I worked during high school. We hadn't seen each other since I had left for Philadelphia. He asked what I was doing. I brought him up to speed and he asked if I would be interested in joining the 5&10's management training program. We parted with my being non-committal because I thought I really wanted to do nursing. After thinking about it I decided to go with the 5&10. I didn't want to live the life of a student again, hoping my parents would send me a couple dollars here and there.

When I received my letter, notifying me I would start at store #27 in Red Lion, Pennsylvania, my mother decided that *they* would find me a place to live. They were leery of letting me out of their sight, afraid I would fall in with "the wrong people" again. My parents placed an ad in the local Red Lion newspaper advising the need of a furnished room for a single man.

My mother and her friend Evelyn Shoemaker went with me to Red Lion to look at the rooms and interview the people I might live with. They didn't like any of the rooms or people. One lady wearing pin curls merited the pronouncement from Evelyn, "Arlene, did you see how pink and clean her scalp looked?"

We stopped for lunch in a local Pennsylvania Dutch restaurant and learned from the chatty waitress of an efficiency apartment over the drugstore down the street. We were all very happy with the little one room apartment and it was partially furnished. It was clean and bright with big windows facing Main Street and only three minutes' walk from the store. I took my mother and Evelyn home and started working in Red Lion for Mr. Kincaid, the local 5&10 manager, the next week.

Red Lion at that time was a one intersection village. The bank was at the crossroads and a jewelry store anchored the prime spot on the other side of the street. Across the street from the 5&10 was an honest to goodness, pool hall that the country people all pointed to as a source of bad influence on their young people. The town was so small the only library was maintained in a small eight-foot trailer parked along the curb in the street, with very limited hours.

This was the smallest size store the chain operated. It had every department, just not as great a selection in every department, as bigger stores would have. The store's concept was to train you in all phases of store operation by having you actually do the work plus taking correspondence courses from the home office. There were also occasional two- or three-day regional training seminars led by a district store trainer.

In Red Lion I first started in the stock room, learning receiving and shipping. This also included checking, marking and distributing the merchandise throughout the store. I was always personable and got along with everyone very well.

The store manager took me aside. "As the only other man in the store, you know you have had a remarkable effect on the employees. Since your arrival everyone's become more conscious of their appearance."

I didn't believe it until I came in one day and the office manager, a young middle-aged lady, had changed her appearance drastically. She adopted a different style of dress, dyed her hair, styled it differently and had a flower tucked behind her ear. I don't like to say unkind things about the women I worked with in Red Lion, but I was never anywhere before where there were so many women who had faces as hairy as mine. One young lady actually had a moustache and short beard and acted like she did not know it existed.

And talk about plain! These were country people; even so, I know fashion did influence some people in town. The clerk who took care of the front end showed she thought she knew the art of makeup. She should have had someone explain to her you do not chew gum like tobacco and that flip flops, with little plastic daisies on them, were not classy work shoes.

I ran around with a couple of the younger ladies after working hours seeing movies or bowling. Sometimes one particular young lady would have a group over to her house to have snacks. She stopped speaking to me after I would not let her kiss me good-night as I was leaving. Of course, her chiny-chin hairs were a problem for me. And that news spread around and gladdened the hearts of a couple others who now felt they had an opportunity.

I always had diversion in Red Lion. I soon learned there was a motel in nearby York that had a gym club and pool membership open to non-guests. For something to do (the chance of seeing naked men had nothing to do with it) and exercise I would drive over and take advantage of the motels "facilities." There were a couple of guys there who I would have liked to take advantage of, but I still did not have the confidence or experience to achieve my desires.

The store had a summer picnic and the store manager invited me back to his and his wife's apartment afterwards. They had some delicious fried chicken and my boss asked me if I wanted something to drink. I didn't drink yet and he suggested that we both have scotch on the rocks. We were sitting on a sofa watching television while his wife busied herself in another room. After so many scotches, his hand movement went from slapping my knee in exclamation over something on the television, to increasingly resting on my thigh. I made a hasty exit. I learned that night I did not like scotch, nor did it go well with cold fried chicken.

CHAPTER EIGHTEEN

My time spent in Red Lion was as tranquil and calm as if I had been spending the time with a favorite Grandparent on a bucolic farm being pampered. The trauma and turmoil of having been pulled out of Philadelphia and being under house arrest by my ever-watching parents faded away.

In my philosophy of God and Life... I think our lives are laid out for us. I think life is just like a model train on a track. It just runs its course taking us where we are to be. That is, if the engine is driven correctly, we load the train with the proper freight and let only the right passengers on our train; it then arrives smoothly at our designated station.

If we drive like crazy, load too much weight and have too many passengers the ride is not smooth, maybe resulting in an accident and not making it to the right station. We then have the chance, to redistribute the weight, remove some of the passengers, and drive safely to where we had been going. In other words, I think if we get off the path God has for us there is always another path to take us where he wants us to be if we try to find it.

My going to Red Lion was one such turn of events. I was given a chance to restart my disrupted life any way I chose.

Of a short, stocky stature and keeping his gray hair in a flat-top, Mr. Kincaid, my store manager, was a very kind, gentle man. He was unassuming, never dictatorial, laid-back, and mellow. This man was the ideal boss.

One evening, when closing, I forgot to bring in the merchandise we displayed out on the sidewalk back into the store. The next morning, he told me, "The police called me at home last evening to tell me the merchandise was still outside when they checked the front doors. I came over and brought it in. You really need to be more careful in the future."

The company, having different size stores, always started everyone out in a small store rather than throw everything at you at once. During this initial phase is when I met the company's district trainer, Mrs. Pagano. Mrs. P, as everyone called her, was pure delight to have as an instructor. She was a gregarious Italian woman of fifty years plus, with an hourglass, full-figured shape. Thick gray hair framed her face, dusted with just enough makeup to accentuate her features and bring her dancing eyes out from behind her sensible eyeglasses.

Every three months this talented lady held a training seminar for all the assistant managers in training. The seminars were conducted in a larger Pennsylvania city at a great hotel with all meals included. The trainees were allowed to order anything they wanted to eat but were reminded there was a two-drink limit at the company's expense. After dinner, she would visit in the bar or dining room with those who decided to stay and chat over a drink. Without anyone realizing, as she quietly sipped a glass of wine, she was finding out what she wanted to know about us without having to ask any prying questions.

It was a case of the old adage where she fit in like one of the boys. She told us many times that she really enjoyed training men rather women. Don't get me wrong! There was never off-color humor or politically incorrect conversations. Family, your experiences with the company, and life challenges were the topics Mrs. P. encouraged. Men being men and drinking created conversations which gave the great lady insight into those participating personalities. Although she may have observed weaknesses and less than the best human character, she never held it against you. She would always arrange a private conversation with you discreetly if she felt she should address something personally. Her job was to make sure everyone was a good fit for the company and attained maximum growth within their potential.

The company did have female assistant store managers. These women were never included in the manager-training program. Any woman promoted to assistant manager knew she would never be a store manager, nor move beyond the store in which she was hired. This glass ceiling for women was in effect in 1967. Your promotions and pay grades in the company depended on the recommendations of your store manager and Mrs. Pagano. Their good opinions of you and your performance in the correspondence classes are what moved you up the ladder in this company. You were responsible for completing the correspondence courses at your own pace. The faster you went through the courses the faster your chance for advancement.

The powers-that-be decided I should only be in Red Lion six months. I was sent on to Washington, New Jersey quickly. Washington is a town of maybe 13,000 people just across the Pennsylvania and New Jersey border from Easton, Pennsylvania.

Mr. Kincaid may have spoiled me; my new manager Mr. Clarke would make me dot every "i" and cross every "t." The first day I arrived in Washington, as I drove up to the store, a man was standing out front by the open double doors. Leaning back against the building, standing on one foot, the other foot up against the building, his hands were in his pockets and a dying cigarette tangled from his lip. He was a tall man with a big gut hanging over his belt and a shock of pure white hair. He had narrow half-open, sleepy, eyes like Robert Mitchum and very thin lips. I did not like him at first appearance. I felt he excluded an aura of predatory debauchery. He watched as I parked my car, and did not register a flicker as I sought recognition in his eyes.

He took me back to his office and asked, "Do you want a smoke?"

"No, thank you." I responded, "I don't smoke."

"Good!" Pronounced with a southern twang, "Because I just finished mine and I was not going back upstairs so you could have one." Right off, he let me know he was former military and ran a tight ship.

The office was in the charge of Miss Mann and her young assistant, Gloria. The store boasted two buyers, Jo and Marie. Rounding out the managerial staff was a quasi-assistant store manager and personnel director, Vicky.

The lower level of the store contained the housewares, domestics, pets, hardware, and furniture departments. The manager informed me the older experienced employees who operated these areas "will bite your head off and spit it back out at you if you make any mistakes. They each know enough to run a store of their own and are quick to let you know when you've made a foul."

The street level contained the soft lines, clothing, toys, music, notions, novelties, shoes and candy. "You have mix of old timers and rookies up there. The old timers will be glad to help you. The rookies will try to take advantage of you; keep your nose clean, do your job, work hard and we'll get along all right." That was his advice as he got up from his chair, slid a ring of keys across to me and said, "It's all yours - I'm going to lunch." I was dismissed with no more thought.

Picking up the keys, I walked in his wake back up the stairs to the street level. I was just in time to see a younger woman had been waiting to pick him up. She slid over as he got in behind the wheel of the late model convertible and put the pedal to the metal.

Gathering my thoughts about the quick, acerbic details, I had just heard, I entered the store and surveyed what was to be my new work home. This was definitely going to be more interesting, if for no other reason than it was a much larger store.

Walking through the store, I found my way to the stockroom and receiving area. While exploring I met Melissa Horan, who was quick to let me know I had wandered into her domain. Listening to what not to touch, so every paper would stay where it was, being there when she needed it, I kept strolling around the store. By the time, I made it back upstairs I found Vicky had returned and expected to find me on the first floor where I should be when the manager is out to lunch. I had yet to find a shrinking violet in this store.

Vicky and I tried to feel each other out and tested our toes in each other's waters while the boss was out. Without direct wording she let me know she was dismayed that she had not been accepted into the manager's training program. She was almost distraught to find I had only been with the company six months and had already been hired above her.

Upon returning he let us know, "Glad you two are getting acquainted. By the way, do you have a place to stay yet?" I let him know I had not and he directed me to Miss Mann. I should have guessed by the woman's demeanor that Miss Mann may have been from the very old school but was on top of her game. The lady was very tight laced. For real! You could tell from the severity of how her clothes fit that she wore a one-piece corset from her shoulders to her knees.

She was the first person I ever saw who really wore old lady tie up orthopedic shoes with a proper one-and-a-half-inch heel. Her skirts and dresses were always mid-calf. It took me a while to learn she had her nose and hand in everything. Nothing passed her ear but very little came out of her mouth except what she wanted.

"I thought you may need a place to stay until you get settled and took the liberty of checking to see if a friend of mine still had a small attic apartment for rent in case you needed it," the affable lady offered. Gladly accepting the information and my boss's offer of letting me go right off to inquire, my first day in Washington was going smoothly.

The address was easy to find, a quiet street lined with old swaying trees and large turn of the century Victorian homes. The owners Mr. & Mrs. Mayfield seemed to be kindly senior citizens eager to help and glad for some extra income. An old, weathered, wooden outdoor stairs reached the apartment. It boasted a large, very nicely decorated set of rooms with a kitchen and bath.

As I drove back to the store, I explored some of the side streets. In the late sixties, the town center was a beehive of commercial sales. There were no big shopping centers, let alone "superstores." Main Street USA thrived and existed to provide your every need. As I drove back to the store, I compared my stay in Washington with my previous experience in Red Lion. My doting grandfather was gone! I felt like I had been inducted into the army, after graduating from officer's training school, and was finally a grown up and expected to accept responsibilities and oversee my own platoon.

Retailing came naturally to me; I soon found that the hardest part of my job would be interacting with all the different personalities, and in addition, putting up with how the employees would interact with each other.

When I returned to the store Mr. Clarke took me around and personally introduced me as the new assistant store manager. He instructed me on my schedule, duties, opening and closing, and banking procedures. I was not given a section to run! I was told, "The entire store is your responsibility. Every section runs smoothly, almost by itself."

I would have ample opportunity to oversee that: the inventories were done on time, Jo and Marie already saw to that; make sure all the stock flowed from the stockroom to the counters, and Melissa saw to that; counters were quickly stocked, the salesclerks saw to that; and Vicky ensured the sales floor had proper people coverage.

Working with the "Boss," as I came to call him, was easy as long as he did not catch me slacking on my duties. This meant if he walked into the stockroom and saw merchandise that he felt should already be up and out, he'd say "Why isn't it?" That was my fault. If walking by a counter he found an empty spot, or a spot that had the wrong merchandise in it, that was my fault. I had to know, "Was the merchandise on order? Why was it ordered so late? Since we have none, you're causing lost sales and money! Why was the wrong merchandise in the wrong spot? How did this happen?" If going through the under stock or stockroom he found quantities of merchandise and the item was on display, this meant we were overstocked. "Why is there excess tying up budget dollars?"

When he appeared on the floor, which was usually only when he was going back and forth for his smoke, if he did not see me, he paged me. He wanted to know, "Why, where were you and what were you doing?" and "How soon will you be back on the main floor?" When I tried to explain, his begrudging response would be, "All right, I'll wait until you're back on the floor."

Invariably when going back and forth for his lunch and smoke breaks, he would see a customer waiting to make a purchase and no one manning the cashier's desk. If I was anywhere in eye contact, he would call to me, "Lee, customer waiting!" A salesclerk could be five feet the other way, with her back turned, he would call me. He would then turn to the waiting customer with the worst imitation of a Cheshire cat and apologize. "I am so sorry you have to wait; we will have someone right with you." For that matter, he could have rung her sale himself - but that was not his job.

He would later ask me, "Haven't you trained the ladies in front so that there is always someone facing forward to see if a customer approaches the cashier's desk?"

It did not matter that this store had been open for years and he knew Vicky had trained the store personnel. After working in the store a few weeks, I came to realize no one took him very seriously. Even the staid Miss Mann would poo-poo him behind his back occasionally, saying, "It is good for him to not always get his way."

Vicky the store trainer was another case. She was one of those women who would have liked to be in the training program and some-day be store manager. She admitted she did not want to move around but she felt she could be a great store manager without having to gain work experience in different stores under different type managers. In truth, she would not have made a good store manager because of her volatile personality. She was sweet, and would do anything for you, but she could get angry with someone very quickly. She never mastered the company's concept of "organize, delegate, supervise."

Vicky would assign a task and tell someone what she wanted but not give ample time for the person to get it done. She would interrupt the person a dozen times saying, "No. Not like that." Finally, she would move the person out of the way and do the job herself as the employee wandered off visiting with another co-worker. I really was not needed in that store. Vicky would have gladly run it by herself. Truth be told she and Miss Mann really ran the store.

Lee had not realized when Emily fell asleep but her snoring broke his reverie about Washington. "Emily, you need to go home! You spend too much time with me. I'm exhausting you."

Emily grinned, "It is hard work just listening and not lifting a finger."

"You got me juice earlier," joked Lee.

As Emily gathered her paraphernalia together, she grumbled, "I don't know what's wrong with me, I never fall asleep on anyone. And, I don't even remember getting juice earlier!" They said their good nights with Emily grumbling and Lee bemusedly watching her retreating to the elevator.

Echoing her footsteps was the Chief's sending someone on their way with one of his ribald presentations.

> *"There was a schoolteacher named Maida,*
> *Who had a Swiss guide serenade her.*
> *The spinster school marm*
> *Really fell for his charm,*
> *Cause my how he o-le-o-layed her."*

CHAPTER NINETEEN

The night nurses gave Lee a gentle backrub, arranged his pillows, and settled him in for the night. As slumber washed over him, the memories of how his life had changed when he moved to Washington flooded his dreamland.

The catalyst of the change was Karen. She was among a group of hood-thug types that hung out across the street from the 5&10. In truth, he had noticed the motley crew many times. They all dressed as if they were auditioning for "Grease." They drank out of brown-bagged communal beer and wine bottles. Their loud, easily overheard, conversations always consisted of course, vulgar language. Often when closing the store at in the evenings he was serenaded with catcalls coming from the West Side Story wannabees.

One evening Karen broke away from the group as he was going to his car. Running across the street, she approached him with a silly grin on her face, "My friends think you are too tight ass to talk to me."

As he stopped to listen, her friends made catcalls that were even more obvious and with louder vulgarities.

"Come on get in my car. I'm going up to Rudy's for a bite to eat, keep me company!"

She was elated. She was happy to prove her friends wrong. She had longingly been watching Lee as he came and went to work. Karen was a petite little thing, very fair skin, turned up nose, squarish jaw line, hair pulled back in a ponytail bleached blonder than blond. Not pretty, rather plain, but surprisingly projecting an innocent naiveté for someone hanging with the group she called her friends.

They had a pleasant time together and when he came back through town, he stopped to let her out. Her jester friends were still holding their silly court. Quickly, before she moved to open the car door, she screwed up her courage, leaned over and kissed him on the cheek.

Driving away he knew he had enjoyed Karen's company. He looked beyond her costume and the demeanor she exhibited when she was with her friends. He felt she was sincerely interested in him. For that reason, he was not upset when she rushed over the next night grinning, "Hi, big boy."

Events happened as they do between boys and girls and he decided to take her to his apartment. They were no sooner in the apartment's living room when Mr. Mayfield came rushing up the stairs, banging on the door yelling, "Open up. We do not run that type of establishment here. You are going to have to get out. We can't have you turning our home into a brothel."

Luckily, when he told Miss Mann about Mr. Mayfield's coronary, the ever-resourceful Miss Mann knew of another situation. "I have an old friend who used to do alterations for Baumgartner's Clothing store. She has a small efficiency apartment behind her house and I'm sure she won't mind if you bring girls home," the affable lady offered.

"Her name is Mary Diehl. She lives up off the state road behind the custard stand, 62 Lynwood Road. There is an old boarded up diner right on the other side of her road. You can't miss it, been closed for years all run down. Someone should light a match to it."

Sure enough, Mary did not care what Lee did if he paid his rent. And years later he would tell his friends he did not know how he ever lived in such a rundown shabby place. The neighborhood was distinctly low class. There were no sidewalks, only worn dirt paths. Mary's house and two others were off to a corner by themselves. It was a very run-down area, crowded with broken, discarded automobiles, some with weeds growing where there used to be an engine.

The apartment, reached by a rear side door, had originally been Mary's dining room. It was a 12 foot by 12-foot room. Immediately inside the door the only sink in the apartment hung from the wall; a small 12-inch lavatory sink. Immediately next to that was a metal shower stall. The shower opening faced the toilet on the sidewall. This was the bathroom and kitchen. There was a chifforobe on the same wall as the toilet; a heavy cot type bed, not as big as a single bed, filled up the rest of the wall. There was a comfortable worn-out chair; a television sat on a stand next to the chair and a dresser filled the space. The heating source for the room, a space heater, warmed the people at a table for two. A large coffee table sat in the center of the room helping disguise the bed as a sofa.

Mary was a good landlady, minded her own business, and paid no attention to who was coming or going. People in glass houses do not throw stones. Her glass house was her son. Lee had heard his father use the term "rummy," describing a male drunkard. When he first saw Mary's son, he thought, this is a rummy. He was filthy dirty and unkempt; so, drunk he could not be understood when he talked. He could not walk unless he held on to something, still almost falling on his face with every step. Her son remained in this drunken condition constantly, which made Lee curious. How did he get that amount of liquor to drink in the first place?

The neighbors and Mary did not mind Lee's comings and goings. They did not care who was traveling with him, or whether they stayed overnight or just an hour. Realization came upon him that the neighbors probably enjoyed his living nearby. He provided them with activity they could watch and talk about amongst themselves. This area was home to poor people who could not afford to have televisions. They depended on the life passing by their doors and windows to provide their daily banter. They were ignorant of the fact that if they worked hard and made more of themselves, they could be part of the divine comedy, not just watch it pass by.

Lee enjoyed the neighbors' interest. He could always count on them to greet him when he came home with someone, man or woman. Likewise, they would call behind him, "Have fun," when he left to go trolling. Mary would often call out to him as he passed by her porch, going or coming from work, "Wait a minute - I have something for you." She would have hot soup or a piece of delicious chocolate coconut iced cake for him.

Karen was trying to become a fixture in his life, taking every opportunity to try to get closer to him. Karen had told her best friend Sheila,
during their "girl talk," that she and Lee had not been intimate yet. Sheila
suggested that Karen and Lee go along with her and her boyfriend, Hulk
for an overnight stay at a hotel in the Poconos. Karen confided in him that
her friends thought he was a fairy. The incident at the Mayfield's spooked
him and he hadn't tried to go all the way with Karen again. Apparently,
this had been discussed among the friends. This planned weekend was
supposed to tell Karen's friends if he was queer or not.

Sheila's boyfriend picked Lee up from work one evening saying,
"We have to get the girls some sexy lingerie for Saturday night." Hulk
took him to the local adult store that sold gay and straight magazines
and paraphernalia; each bought a baby doll set for their respective partners. While in the store Hulk called Lee's attention to the magazines
with the naked women's boobs and asses showing. He did not get the
response out of Lee that he wanted. He picked up a magazine with a
naked man showing an erection on the cover saying, "Maybe this is
more your type!"

When the "sexy" evening came, the foursome spent the beginning
of the night together drinking champagne. After relaxing and mentally
preparing, they parted company and locked the doors between the adjoining rooms. Although there was ample foreplay and making out, Lee
was unable to perform. Blaming it on the champagne, Karen consoled
Lee. "Don't worry - I'll tell them you were great."

After that evening, Sheila still was not satisfied about his sexuality
and decided she and Karen would have a girls' night out. Her boyfriend
Hulk would spend the night with Lee watching television in his apartment. When the designated evening came, Hulk appeared in unlined
white shorts, athletic shirt and moccasins, bringing with him a case of
beer. Lee never drank beer. He endured one of the longest nights in his
life. Hulk was a good-looking handsome man who looked like he could
have been a prize fighter. He had a couple scars on his face but they only
gave him masculine character. His crew cut went well with his toned
body. Lee suspected he was a natural blonde from the muscular hairy

legs that crossed and uncrossed so often. He thought he spotted some soft blonde fur on Hulk's chest, but trying for a closer, more definite validation could have got him in trouble.

As the case of beer emptied, Hulk kept manipulating his engorging crotch. He used the john in the tiny apartment, to recycle the beer, letting his shorts drop to the floor revealing he wore no underwear. Yes, he was a true blonde, with a tight chiseled belly. This man was very appealing and probably would have engaged in anything that might have happened. He could later blame it all on that queer, saying, "I only went along with it to prove Karen's boyfriend was queer."

He knew this was not the place nor the time to throw caution to the wind. He thought the Hulk left a little begrudgingly. He was complaining he had drunk all that beer and didn't know if he could drive home. No, he was not going to let Hulk sleep over. He had stopped him once from stripping off his clothes. Laying on the narrow bed, as Hulk said," Boy! Are we going to be close in this bed?"

Lee mused to himself that maybe Hulk was upset because he would have a bad hangover and nothing to show for it; and nothing untoward to tell anyone. From then on Lee made it clear to Karen he would not entertain spending any time with her friends again. The next evening, he took Karen to bed on his small cot. Any doubts Karen had about his manhood were resolved in that bed that night.

Lee found real attraction in a woman for the first time. She smelled exotic. He enjoyed the softness of this woman's mouth on his, plunging their tongues together in a dance of passion. Her soft body twitched under his lips as he licked her armpits down to her elbows to nibble on her fingertips. Her small round breasts were supple fruits to squeeze and titillate with wet sucking kisses. He traced his tongue down her side finding her hip. Lightly nibbling, he left a wet trail to her velvet honey pot. This was the first time he performed cunnilingus on a female. It did not smell like fish and did not taste like chicken. He found great pleasure in her twitching and squirming. His tongue probed deeper and deeper, licking and pulling at the same time on a certain area to give Karen convulsing pleasure. His manhood could wait no longer! It ached from being so hard. He gently let himself slide inside her open hips, floating on a mixture of her fluids and his saliva.

Yes, he knew Karen was happy with their sexual encounter. She purred and stroked his hair saying, "Oh, yes, harder, more; Oh no, oh God!" Amid cries of pleasure, gyrating hips and gasps of sucking for air were shouts of, unrecognizable sounds and "I'm coming!" As they lay spent, bodies glistening from nature's best form of exercise, Karen mewed, "Baby that was great!" He had found happiness, again.

Work was demanding at times but he came to enjoy the people he worked with. One of the older women in the basement, Gina, would occasionally bring him homemade food: lasagna, meatballs, and manicotti. Everyone knew about Karen. It was a typical small town. Those who didn't see Karen rush to meet Lee as he left work, heard all about it. Those who didn't see them together in a restaurant, heard about it. "Go find a nice girl!" she would say.

On one of his exploring forays into area towns, he visited Allentown, Pennsylvania. When he was leaving the Hess's department store, (famous for their Patio restaurant and meandering live models), he saw a little bar called "Rube's" across the street. From a poster outside he learned it was a small intimate piano bar with a duo "Candy and Noel" entertaining on Friday and Saturday nights. He started going there on the weekends by himself. It wasn't exactly that he was ashamed of Karen. She lacked a certain level of manners; or maybe it was her bad teeth. He liked her enough to screw her as much as he could. But not enough to buy her the kind of clothes, stockings, and shoes she would have to wear to appear in a place like this, with him.

Rube's attracted, what was then called a "mixed" crowd. At that time, for that place, it meant there would be straight and gay, men and women bar customers. He really enjoyed listening to the music the couple performed. Once or twice, he met someone to go home with. It was there that someone told him about the bus station in Easton, Pennsylvania being "cruisy." Easton was right on the Pennsylvania/ New Jersey border and he drove right past the bus station on his way to Allentown.

There were many guys who would drive around the bus station block looking for men to pick up. Sometimes there would be guys sitting in the park across from the bus station cruising other guys who frequented the park. He met one guy on an isolated park bench, shadowed by trees, who told him about his childhood. The man joked, "We were so poor when I was a child, my mother cut the pockets out of my pants so I would have something to play with."

He must have still been poor. That night in the park he stood up hidden from view by a nearby tree and whispered, "Come here I want to show you something." His pants were loose and he must have been well endowed because he was able to bring his flaccid penis out through his side pocket. He and the man never got together except for the man to show off his air-conditioned trousers.

The man was nice enough to point out a young attractive Cuban who drove around the block looking for action. Lee had seen him before but he never got a head turn from the handsome Latino. One night he parked his car and propped himself against a light pole waiting for the hot Cuban to go past. He almost had to throw himself in front of the man's car to get him to stop. He got the impression he was not exactly the Cuban's type but since the Cuban stopped, he would accept whatever was offered.

The young man knew the area well and drove his new convertible, his daddy back in Cuba bought him, out to an isolated farmers pasture. After they parked, they jumped into the back seat to explore each other's bodies. Possessing that hot Latin blood, and feeling a naked body rub against his own, their mutually stimulating passion caused the Cuban to explode into a sex machine. There wasn't an area left un-tongued on his body as he turned Lee around to lubricate his Cuban cigar. Lee was pushed head first out over the back seat, to rest on the closed car trunk. His back side was plowed as deep and hard as the local farmer plowed his fields. Lee wondered if the farmer's tractor has as fast a ride as he was getting. He had never gone stargazing quite like that before.

The Cuban certainly knew how to ride a tractor and milk a cow at the same time. After he exploded with gusto, he laid back and said, "I never do repeats, so don't be surprised when I don't pick you up again. But you can tell your friends about me if you like." When their paths next crossed, he didn't pick him up again or even acknowledge seeing him.

Another night at the bus station he met Earl. He really liked Earl. He was about the same height, stocky and very hairy. Best of all he was passive in bed. He enjoyed Earl's company quite often on his small bed until Earl screwed up. One night, as they lay spoon fashion, with Earl's backside getting a workout Lee suddenly smelled something. "Earl did you fart?"

"I don't think so. My bowels were loose earlier today, I'm afraid to fart for fear I'll shit myself!" Earl whimpered. Reality halted all action; as he realized he had been **shit** on. Whether accident or not. there is a limit to how much shit you can put up with for a good piece of ass.

Having just turned 21, Lee had the stamina to keep up with all the action regardless of which direction it came from. He and Karen were seeing quite a lot of each other. After having Karen out too late, too often, requiring her to actually crawl in through a window, the parents rebelled. Her father told Lee, "You cannot date my daughter anymore."

After hearing, Karen cry for most of a week, her mother laid in wait for Lee at his apartment. Angry and almost spitting, she asked, "If you get my daughter pregnant will you marry her?"

Quickly responding "Yes" (He really liked Karen and his parents did want grandchildren.)

Her mother was happy enough to permit her daughters' sexual escapades with an (up and coming??) store manager. From then on, Karen had a door key for when she got home late but the mother said, "Why don't you just drop her off in the morning? Then she won't wake the whole house when she comes in late." He remembered all the times Karen's period was late and knew this was what prompted her Ma to want to know if she was going to have to have a shotgun or an amicable wedding.

Everyone knew everything about everybody in Washington. When he came back from lunch one afternoon, he saw Mary scurrying out of the store like a mouse looking for a mouse hole. Uncombed hair, bedroom-slippered feet and her best housedress, Lee tried to think 'which juicy piece of gossip did Mary take to Miss Mann. He wasn't too concerned; he had only taken one man back to the apartment. It wasn't unusual for buddies to stay over when they had been out late.

As he told Miss Mann he was back from lunch, he felt he detected some uneasiness from her. He felt that Mary was probably sharing some tales of his shenanigans. Vicky later told him that Mary had told Miss Mann about Karen's mother paying her respects. Apparently, while she waited for him to come home, Mary saw her waiting and started up a conversation with her looking for information. Mother was hot under the collar and announced there may be a wedding in the future.

When he and Melissa went down to the annex the next day to get ready for another furniture shipment, he sensed something was coming. Melissa moved close to him and softly murmured, "I do not know why you are going with that girl Karen. She has a bad reputation. She isn't educated and comes from a bad family. She's not the kind of woman you should be dating."

Moving close enough that he could smell her muskiness, she gently took his hand and placed it under her sweater onto her full breasts. Dropping the papers, he had in his other hand he pushed her sweater and bra up so he could gab both her breasts. Unlike Karen's sweet youthful freshness, Melissa having had a child had full firm melon-type breasts.

"I don't know why you are dirtying yourself with that piece of trash. You know she has been with Puerto Ricans and Blacks. I'm available. I am more your age and better suited for your future than she is. Have you heard that Mr. Clarke met his wife when he was an assistant manager and she worked in the stockroom as I do? She was good for him like I would be good for you. I do have a child, but I have a lot more to offer in more ways than that little whore!"

She pushed her breasts together up into his face urging him to enjoy her. He massaged her breasts and sucked her nipples until they were hard. As he buried himself in her breasts, she slid her skirt and panties down. Letting his pants fall down to his ankles his manhood was at attention, Melissa pulled him back on top of her, falling on to the loveseat they were going to move. She eagerly brought him inside her volcanic furnace. Being a divorced mother who had not had sex for years, she was like a vacuum sucking him into her not wanting to let go. She grabbed his hands bringing them to her tits. She wanted to be handled rough almost as if you were squeezing oranges on a grater to get all the juice out. She was certainly practiced on how to thrust and get the most out of each contraction.

Enjoying an active sex life enhanced his longevity. He knew how to perform. A slow circular dance, around each wall of the vagina; first this way, then that way, thrusting hard in to the center with each thrust; whirling constantly around and sideways leaving no area unstimulated, repeating the steps over and over again. Grabbing, squeezing those tits and sucking that mouth, nibbling her lips, brushing soft kisses on her closed eyes. She moaned and grabbed him as if she was falling off the face of the earth. All hell broke loose. And it did. Thank goodness, the furniture was covered in plastic. This girl had wetness, as he had never felt before. They walked around the rest of the day, with no underwear. She had to use her slip and panties to wipe herself off. Lee had to use his undershirt and shorts to try to clean her off him. They knew they were covered with that smell, left from hot wet sex, but he had to return to the main building.

Returning to the store, Vicky questioned them as to what took so long. She listened to their rambling response and walked off muttering. A few steps away she stopped, turned around, smelled the air in their direction then started off again, muttering louder. It was something about behavior in the workplace.

The next day Melissa caught him in one of the stockroom aisles. Leaning in, grabbing him around the neck, smothering him in kisses she implored him to understand. "I want you know I'm not a whore. I just really like you. I hope you still respect me." He was not ready to settle down with anyone and Melissa wanted something permanent.

Karen's parents accepted his relationship with their daughter to the point that he was a guest in their home for dinner often. Karen's father liked him enough to put his name up for membership in the local Moose; where the four of them spent many happy Saturday nights dancing. While there one night an older couple came over and said hello to Karen and her family. They quickly introduced their daughter's boyfriend to the older couple. When they walked away Karen whispered in his ear, "That's Barry the fairy, my old boyfriend. The old lady is Ella. He takes her around so people don't suspect he's queer."

But he'd become so happy with his life that he lost the urge to visit the bus station and desire to visit Rube's. The only thing uncomfortable was always worrying when Karen's period was late.

CHAPTER TWENTY

Never accused of being a shy person, he was surprised when he was reluctant to confront one of the store employees. Vicky came to him and said, "Lola and Barb in the dress department are complaining that one of the store's employees has a bad case of body odor. It is one thing to have to work with a smelly co-worker. It is quite another when she wants to try on the clothes we sell. It is not just underarm odor; it is also coming from below the waist. We think it would be better if a man told her about the complaints. She won't take it as personal."

Taken back by not knowing quite how to tell Angelique about the complaints he went to see if the problem was evident to him. He would be more comfortable and feel justified if he was aware of it. He went back to Vicky, "I can't smell anything. Why don't you talk to her?"

"No, you are the assistant manager."

He countered, "But you are the personnel director!"

"Your job!" Turning on her heel, Vicky left him to deal with the problem.

Going back to the children's department, the unsuspecting Angelique greeted him," Hi! How are you today?"

"I'm fine, but I have an unpleasant job to do today," he lamented. "I have to tell one of the ladies that other salesclerks have complained that she has a problem."

Sweet Angelique asked, "What is the complaint?"

"They say she has body odor. And if that is not bad enough, they say she emits olfactory offenses from below the waist," Lee weakly offered.

"Those stupid girls... Why don't they just take her aside and tell her? Do you want me to do it for you? I wouldn't mind. Women can talk about this to other women - who is it they say suffers from this problem?"

"*You*," he stammered.

In an instant she quickly sank to her feet and lifted her skirts to smell herself. Lee didn't smell anything the entire time they were talking. Rising to her feet Angelique raised her chin in the air and said, "Please excuse me unless you have more to say I have some business to take care of." Turning on her heel she went straight back to the ladies in the dress department.

"You shrews… Of all the mean, unkind things to do, to involve Mr. Lee in this argument I had with you. You are the ugliest women I have ever known. I don't mean beauty wise - I mean inside, spiritually."

"Go back to where you came from! I am sure your opinions would be extremely welcome in your own country. But not here!" Lola screeched. "We don't need you here, thinking you're better than we are. Our families have been here for years, since the 1880's. You come here; you and your ignorant husband, who can't even speak English without sounding funny." Barb threw in.

"Since the 1880's! You think your family owns the country and has a right to say who can come here and live? Maybe your people were some of the white people who drove the native Indians along the Trail of Tears?!" Angelique hurled back. Lola and Barb looked at each other. "Trail of tears…? What are you talking about?"

"And you think my husband's ignorant?"

"All you foreigners come here and take jobs from our people. You get business loans, home loans at little or no interest. You get all the opportunities that we have worked all our life for. You get tax forgiveness, free education, counseling, mentoring, and church sponsorship by the bleeding hearts," Lola complained.

"Yeah you come and take everything we had to work for. You have people coming over here, getting a free education, a degree, officially licensed. Then what? They leave the country and go back where they came from. They use their education and all the benefits they reaped from their experience in our country and help their own people in the country they came from. All we get is the bill to pay for all they took from us. Our foolish politicians have created all these programs that give everything to your kind. While our own go homeless. Children grow up without an education. The elderly can't afford their medical treatment, let alone their winter utility bills!" Barb spit out.

"You forget! It was my country that gave America the Lady Liberty. She welcomes all who want to have a better life and don't mind working for it. All this because I said something, about how you dress, then hear this.

"You dress in worn, faded flowered skirts. I have discarded ta-blecloths that looked better. You wear cheap sleeveless stained white blouses. My cleaning lady uses better clothes for cleaning. You wear dingy white bobby sox rolled down and penny loafers. You look like cleaning ladies. My cleaning lady dresses better than you. Her clothes are clean, pressed and spotless. You are an embarrassment to the Ladies' apparel department and the clothes you sell.

"If your husband, or that family that goes back to 1880, was half as successful as my husband you too could have a better life. We were not always comfortable. We worked very hard, my husband and I both worked while he went to school. After he got a job I went to night school to better my English. We both continued to work while he got his degree. He got a better job; he doesn't want me to work. Since I don't have children to care of it is my choice. My clothes are old. But I take care of them. Those of us who have had to work so hard are not as wasteful as many of you, who take much for granted; so, matter-of-factly. And many people think my husband's accent is delightful; cretins!"

The petite French woman turned on her heel, these truly ignorant imbeciles were not worthy of her conversation. Lee could see why they would be jealous of the pretty French girl. Her clothes were not the height of fashion but they were stylish and clean and she wore them well. Barb and Lola came running to Lee to complain about the woman they made their nemesis. "You have to fire her - we can't work with her kind."

Vicky who had been cowering close by and heard the exchange walked up to the confrontational Barb and Lola. "It seems you made some spurious accusations about a co-worker that were unfounded. You know she has a point. You don't dress very well to be working in the Ladies department. Maybe you could take some pointers from Angelique."

"You are going to side with that foreigner against us?" Realizing Vicky was serious Barb stormed past her leaving her resignation in the air.

"I quit! "The toady Lola followed suit.

"Well, that settles that. I have been trying for the longest time to find a way to get rid of them, so I could ask Angelique to take over the Ladies' department. She will feel so guilty about their quitting I will have no trouble getting her to make the change."

Vicky walked away leaving him dumb founded. He had only been a pawn. Vicky had used him to get what she wanted without soiling her hands. As he walked away, still deep in thought, he almost collided with Rose, a high school part-timer filling up the candy counter. "Hi Rose, how are you?"

"Mr. Lee, I have ants in the nuts again."

Until he came to this store, he didn't know the procedure for this problem. When ants appear in the nuts display, you take everything out of the case. Wash it thoroughly with soap and water and then lavishly sprinkle borax under the trays. When the ants walk thru the borax, they will lick it off and die. You may find ants, but they will be dead.

He previously enjoyed buying from the display until he found out how often there were live ants in the nuts. The warm, shiny, silver rotating display featured warmed: cashews, red-skinned peanuts, plain peanuts and pistachios. Looks were deceiving, the display could get you salivating until you knew what was underneath the trays.

Rose was a dark-skinned Italian girl, tall and husky, 5 '10", 172 lbs. She had light brown hair cut in a boy's style with a shingled (tapered) back and sides. She was always laughing and smiling so much you didn't notice her glasses. A little loud, slightly shy of boisterous. Wide hips, big bust, the kind his friend Gina downstairs would say, "She'll make good babies."

He remembered Gina words ringing in his ears when he almost fell over Rose that day "Find yourself a nice Italian girl!" He was just 21 and Rose wasn't 18 yet. He didn't think this was what Gina had in mind. The next time he saw Gina she called him over. In a conspiratorial tone she whispered, "Say, I heard you almost fell over yourself with our Rose. You know my husband teaches music at the high school. He speaks very highly of Rose. Good Catholic girl. You could do a lot worse than our Rose! Good strong body, wide hips, make a good mother." As he walked away her lips were laughing as much as her eyes.

Being close in age to many of the employees he sometimes forgot his position and talked inappropriately to them; one evening he was talking to one of the young ladies and mistakenly called her a broad. The next Friday evening they were open his boss had him downstairs in the back of the store doing busy work. His back was turned and he was bent over and had not noticed the well-dressed lady who approached him.

"Excuse me, are you Mr. Lee?"

"Yes, I am; how can I help you?"

"I am Mrs. Martin Fillmore and my daughter told me you called her a *BROAD*. I will have you know my daughter has not been exposed to such street vulgarity at home and I will not have her talked to like that by anyone. I know what people mean when they call someone a broad and I will have you know sir; my daughter is no broad. I want you to apologize to her and treat her with proper respect and decorum. Do I make myself clear?"

"Yes ma'am, I am sorry. You are right. I should not have used that terminology in regards to your daughter. I will apologize. I am sorry I caused you the inconvenience of having to come down here."

"Then I won't expect to have to talk to you again. Good night."

Lee watched her ascend the stairs, like a queen going to her awaiting carriage, waiting a few minutes he trailed behind her. The dear old boss was standing at his favorite place right outside the door having his smoke. "Did you know Mrs. Fillmore was coming to talk to me?" he asked.

"Yes! That's why I thought it best if you take care of that task, I assigned you. There wouldn't be anyone in ear range and save you embarrassment. God, she almost ripped my head off when she called me. When I thought about it, I decided it would make a bigger impression on you if she confronted you. And she was eager to confront you! Quite the tiger protecting her baby! Now go back downstairs. Throw that display you are working on back together. The girls can finish it tomorrow and you can get back upstairs where you belong so I can go back to my office."

CHAPTER TWENTY-ONE

HIS FIRST CHRISTMAS WORKING IN Washington was a joy. Lee loved the town; it was the quintessential small town with the huge, brightly lit Christmas tree in the center of the town square. The people were like characters out of "It's a Wonderful Life." Everyone was friendly and bustling up and down the snow-covered streets with all their purchases from where he worked.

The boss was the perfect Scrooge. He knew Lee had to drive almost three hours to get home but the store was open until nine o'clock. That is when he was able to start driving to his parents' home. As he drove the snow cleared interstate to his hometown. He was serenaded by the chords of, *"I'll be home for Christmas…. You can count on me…… Please have snow… and mistletoe…. and presents around the tree. Christmas Eve will find me..."* on the car radio. The Philly fiasco that broke his heart and soul had healed, so he could actually enjoy going home for the holiday. His brothers secured leave from their respective military duties and were waiting for him to get home so they could relive old times and cook a hot dog in front of the fireplace's dying embers.

Before going to bed the family gathered around the kitchen table to watch Mom and Dad stuff the 20-some pound turkey. When they were done father would announce, "Well Mother, we stuffed the bird and now it's time to stuff you. Let's go to bed!"

It would cook overnight, awakening the house to the aroma of the promised Christmas feast to come. As was their habit, aunts and uncles would arrive around one o'clock on Christmas day. They would sit around the table holding hands while Aunt Dord would say grace. She would always remind everyone to give thanks for all their blessings and each other's company.

Mother was a plain cook, nothing fancy. The meal would consist of the turkey, potato filling, gravy, mashed potatoes, corn, and homemade pumpkin pie. If she wanted to dress up the dinner, she would buy those cylindrical cans of biscuits; The kind from the dairy case that you had to unwrap, and whack on the side of the table to get them ready to "pop" open. Just like grandma made, hot from the oven!

The gifts received were never an important part of the holiday. The brothers enjoyed buying their mother gifts and watching her face light up. Father always got the traditional manly gifts of socks, underwear and plaid or corduroy shirts. Mother loved him to wear a blue shirt to match his blue eyes, so every year there would be a new blue shirt. As sure as they knew they would receive money envelopes from their aunts; they knew the uncles would share after-dinner beers and whiskeys with their father; and the aunts would have to drive home.

Around seven o'clock in the evening the turkey and fixings would be brought back out for the gratuitous cold turkey sandwich for supper. Watching the Christmas shows on television, basking in the warmth of the fireplace, the glow of the Christmas tree lights bouncing off the walls would always be his happiest memories of Christmas.

The nature of the business of working in a 5 and 10 cent store embellished his enjoyment of the holidays. Articles in the newspaper would tell about large department stores depending on a successful Christmas to put them "in the black" (meaning a financial success) for the year. In the five and ten, which was being promoted as a "junior department store," you didn't rely on any one particular season to make the year. A successful Christmas was just icing on the cake.

Transitioning through the calendar's holidays, (Valentine's Day, Lincoln's Birthday, Easter, Memorial Day, Independence Day, Labor Day, Halloween, Thanksgiving and Christmas,) each manifested its own banners and window signs declaring the celebration's arrival. In those years, people shared the holiday spirit within their neighborhoods. This was the era when everyone's family had reunion picnics during the summer and neighbors were really neighbors. Back then if a neighbor told your parents you did something you shouldn't have; they believed the neighbor! They were glad to hear what happened, so they could correct you, to make you a better person. Whoever said it takes a village to raise a child must have known how parents were back then, (glad to know neighbors were looking out for their child's well- being). They were not thought to be meddling, as parents think today when neighbors complain about a child's behavior.

Lee developed a serene life in Washington, Karen had become a good habit for him and he seldom strayed from her gentle love. Gina, from the store's basement departments, started him on a bad habit when she sent him to Zackies' for a drink and to find a "nice" girl. Besides having a collection of plastic sword fish swizzle sticks he developed a fondness for whiskey. Whether it was because he enjoyed Karen or knew drinking and driving didn't mix, he stopped traveling the forty-five-minute drive to Allentown.

However, the guys he met at the Easton bus station cruising area told him about a bar in Phillipsburg, Pennsylvania. The two towns were connected by an old metal five lane bridge. One minute you were in Pennsylvania, you drive a couple feet and you are in New Jersey. He easily found the little rundown bar owned by an older lady named Elsie. There was never a huge crushing crowd, but he always found a welcome and someone to talk to. He never pulled anything out of the bar to take home, but did indulge his taste for liquor. He rationalized it was only a 15-minute drive home.

There were evenings he stayed out so late between the bar and the bus station that he was afraid to go to bed for fear he would not wake up in time to go to work. Sometimes he would go home, shower, dress for work and go to the store, maybe just two hours before opening. He knew when the person opening up for the day arrived, he would wake up him from where he would sleep in the furniture department. He would drag through the day but by store closing time would be rejuvenated and capable of repeating the events of the last evening.

After the Christmas store party, he became friends with the part-time candy girl, Rose. He hadn't taken Karen to the get-together and somehow during the festivities he and Rose were partnered for a couple of the games. Sometimes he offered Rose a ride home and accepted an invitation to come in for a homemade dessert. Lee still hooked up with Melissa once in a while, never as often as she would have liked. He was just having fun with everyone.

The straw that broke the camel's back for Melissa was when she heard that Lee had added Rose to his time share list. She didn't believe he and Rose were just friends. She told him she would no longer see him, or (you-know-what with him), thinking she could coerce him into being with her more. Having never enjoyed her as much as Karen, it was no problem for him to drop Melissa.

He didn't know Melissa well enough. She spat fury, she ran to the manager complaining how he had led her on and it was now impossible for her to work in the same store with him. She in turn didn't know the store manager well either. He sadly accepted her resignation and within a heart-beat his wife who had been looking for a job was back doing the job she did when she met her husband and loving it. Additionally, Rose was moved from the candy department and worked part-time with the boss's wife in shipping and receiving.

Things in Lee's life were going smoothly until his mother's health took a turn for the worse. The problems she had put up with after her stomach operations were getting increasingly harder for her to deal with. She had been suffering from a dumping syndrome problem, accompanied by cold sweats, stomach pain and shaky weakness. Because of the stomach surgery her intestinal track and stomach were reduced from normal size. In a normal size stomach food may take 30-45 minutes to travel from the stomach to the intestines. Because of her surgery that could now happen as fast as ten minutes; hence the dumping problem. Because of the shortened time span the food was not diluted with water and liquefied as in a normal stomach. The body would pull water out of the circulation creating a loss of blood leading to stomach distention and fainting, causing a shock to the body. The whole process makes the intestines work harder affecting her blood sugar levels. The stomach problems irritated her hernia, and her adhesions from all the scar tissue were a surgical obstacle when the hometown doctors considered how to help her.

They told her to go back to Philadelphia but she felt she couldn't always run to Philly for help. Somehow, she ended up going to the Geisinger medical center in Danville, Pennsylvania. It was there that doctors first told her there was something terribly wrong with her blood. They were not able to tell her what was going on in her blood stream; they only knew there was something wrong.

She had been anemic all those years and often had to go for transfusions, maybe twice a year. All they could do for her stomach problems was to suggest she change her diet, drink less fluid with meals, lay down after eating, and eat less or smaller amounts more often. She went home and tried to help herself by changing her eating habits.

The spring of 1969 brought change once again to Lee's life. The store manager took him aside and told him he had to break it off entirely with Karen if he wanted to have a future with the company. He told him the company would not stand for having a store manager who associated himself with such a low-class woman. Lee wanted a career with the company so he told Karen the truth as hard as it was and walked away never looking back.

Melissa being out of the picture, Rose became his sole female friend. They became very close, often having meals with her family. Rose's mother was a terrific cook and taught sewing and cooking classes at the county extension offices. Rose's father was a hundred percent true Italian. The man's worst habit was hitting his wife. She often told Lee, "He doesn't hit me as much as he used to and not as hard."

Rose's mother fascinated Lee with her sewing skills and ability to make beautiful creations out of scraps. There were two sisters (one younger and one older) and a brother that still lived at home and an older sister in college. The family included Lee in many of their activities, singing around the piano being one of his favorites. Everyone seemed to like him, although the younger sister would often tease about him being a "fairy." She made up a poem, "Rose and Lee will get married, but their name will be Criberri, because he is such a fairy!" It struck a chord with him but apparently no one else. The first of May the town celebrated its two-hundred-year birthday with a big fancy dress ball. Rose made herself the most beautiful antebellum ball gown to wear for the festivities.

A few days after the ball, Lee's store manager told him to come to his office after the store closed because he needed to talk to him. The boss said it so sternly he walked with a heavy heart when he went to the office. When he knocked on the door, he thought he was going to be fired. The boss called, "Come in." He and his wife were sitting in the room waiting for him. Lee was really skeptical when he saw the wife there too; he couldn't figure what she had to say.

He tried to replay his memory tapes, thinking, "What could I have done wrong or said that they are going to reprimand me for?"

"Congratulations Lee!" The boss stood up and offered his hand to Lee.

The Mrs. Broke into a big smile and laughingly said, "If you could have seen your face."

He still didn't know what they were talking about. "You are being promoted and transferred to Philadelphia. It is a big move for someone who has been with the company the short time you have. They must think you are doing a good job to move you up to the district's highest volume store! You are to report to the Woodland Avenue location in two weeks."

"I am so happy for you Lee. Congratulations. You know, I wonder if we are going to lose anyone else to Philadelphia?" the misses mused with a twinkle in her eye.

He had never seen either so friendly or smile so much. A lot more was said and exchanged between them, but he lost track of the conversation. He was immediately concerned with his parents' reaction. He knew they would recall his previous stay in Philadelphia and they would worry for fear he'd fall into the same behavior and crowd again. He thanked his boss and his wife for the felicitations and left the store with a heavy heart. He wanted promotions; he just never thought he would end up being sent to Philly. He didn't know what to do. Instead of being happy he was faced with a problem. He just could not fathom telling his parents he was returning to the city of sin.

He thought they would not take it so hard, and maybe not think at all of his past life in Philly - if he went as a married man. His parents always wanted grandchildren so he decided to do his duty and get married. His older brother botched it and the middle brother had no interest in girls, so he might as well try his luck.

He remembered telling Mrs. Smith when he was a teenager, "I will only marry a woman who can sew her own clothes and knows how to cook extremely well!" Rose was due to graduate high school in the beginning of June and would turn 18 on June 16th. He had turned 21 that January, their ages were close enough. He took Rose out to grab a bite to eat after work a couple nights later. While she was mid bite and chewing on a hamburger, he casually said, "Rose I am being transferred to Philadelphia - would you like to come along as my wife?"

Amid food projectiles she dropped her sandwich and throwing her arms around his shoulders, food crumbs flying, and gleefully cried, "Yes! Oh, yes!"

After she regained her composure, they decided they should return to her home and ask her parents if they would sign off for her to get married. When they approached the house Mother Criberri was working in the kitchen. Through silent hand motions they beckoned her to come outside with them. They knew her husband was in the next room and would hear the conversation they were about to have with Rose's mother. They wanted to tackle one parent at a time and felt the mother was an easier "Yes".

They first explained about his going to Philadelphia and Ma's jaw dropped. Dismay, then extreme happiness lit up her face when she heard, "And, I have asked your daughter to go along as my wife," he added.

She shared in her daughter's happiness and said, "If she had said no, I would have gone with you! Well, walking back to the house, "Let's go ask your father." Trailing in behind Mrs. Criberri they waited outside the father's room as Rose's mother called out to her husband, "Tony, the children want to get married."

After a pregnant pause a gruff voice responded, "About time."

CHAPTER TWENTY-TWO

ROSE WAS LIKE A KID IN A CANDY STORE. She was thrilled to be able to tell her classmates she was engaged to be married and moving to the big city of Philadelphia. The ladies at the store were excited for her almost as much she was and started immediately to plan a bridal shower. The Italian mama, Gina, took him aside and congratulated him on his good choice of a nice Italian girl.

The boss could have cared less. His only concern was filling the part-time position Rose held working in the stockroom with his wife. Despite the age gap the two women had gotten along well and the boss's wife was sorry and happy at the same time, to see her young helper leave. Vicky was happy! She saw it as another opportunity to try for the assistant-manager position.

While he was tying up loose ends in the store, and trying to gather information about his new job, Rose was left to sort out the wedding plans. She and her family went to the local Catholic church she attended to make plans to get married there. The priest would not marry a Catholic to a non-Catholic and told them they should get counseling and not rush into a marriage.

Rose went to Lee's religion, Episcopalian. The Rector at the local Episcopal Church would marry them if they agreed to counseling before the marriage. Rose made the arrangements and he agreed to travel back and forth from Philly every Sunday until the wedding to meet with the Rector.

Whether frugality or desire (it was a coin toss), Rose and her mother decided to make the wedding gown. They also decided to save money and have a garden reception after the service in their backyard.

Mrs. Criberri would make the wedding cake and together she, Rose and the sisters would make the food.

The two weeks' notice before going to Philly went very fast and a sunny Monday morning found him traveling toward Philly. Even though he encountered a broken fuel pump on the way he still arrived at the appointed time at his new assignment. It was a very large store on the corner of 62nd and Woodland Avenue on which trolley cars still ran. His old roommate from nursing school lived on 57th Street just off Woodland on Kingsessing. His previous Philadelphia lifestyle started to climb to the surface.

Walking into the store, he found the manager's office in a secluded corner of the lower floor. His new boss was leaning so far back in his reclining wooden office chair he might have fallen ass over teacups if Lee's arrival had captured his attention. As he walked toward the open office door the old gray-haired man peered over the rim of his glasses sizing up his newest recruit. He was about to ask the office ladies for the manager when he said, "Come in. Come in. You are my new assistant?"

"Yes sir," and Lee introduced himself.

Standing up and extending his hand, "I am Ralph Morse. Welcome to store 237. Let me put my coat on and I will take you around to meet your co-workers." Putting his coat on, the older gentlemen escorted him out of the office and to the stockroom. Lee was introduced to Burt, a fifty-something black lady who was the head of his stockroom, wearing a high bun on top of her head filled with different colored pencils, and her crew Lena and Joe.

While walking through the basement, the older man introduced Lee to Janet the head office cashier. Going up the front stairs, he took Lee to the front section of the store: candy, notions, books, and electronics. After meeting Mr. Hendricks, the front 1st floor assistant, they meandered to the soda fountain where he found the right-hand man Mr. Marshall. He was Morse's number one assistant. He oversaw the basement and the entire store. Just as they were saying their hellos, Margie Draper, in charge of the ladies' and girls' department, came by and met him.

Mr. Morse stood back and with a motion of his arm said, "This is your section." The side corner consisted of men and boys, seasonal, and toys.

"Here I am, Mr. Morse." A pinch-faced, very thin, very tan bottle-blonde women came around the corner.

"Pat, I want you to meet your new boss Mr. Lee."

"Pleased to meet you. I'm glad you're here. We haven't had a manager of our own for a while. I need some relief, having run this section by myself. Well, I have to get back to a project I am working on. Mr. Morse, I have those counts you wanted. I'll lay them on your desk."

With that he asked the restaurant manager, "Gert, page Hendricks and tell him I want to see him at the fountain." As the younger blond-haired man walked up Mr. Morse asked "Where did you stay when you came to town?"

Hendricks responded, "With a Mrs. Evans on Elmwood Avenue."

Ralph said, "Well, take Lee down there and see if you can get him a room."

He followed the blue-eyed blonde man, who always wore suede hush puppies, to his car. He was professional, not friendly - a very matter-of-fact person. Mrs. Evans only lived four blocks away. On the way he told Lee that she ran a clean house and minded her own business. He stopped at a duplex located on another trolley line in a pleasant neighborhood. The lady herself greeted them. She remembered Mr. Hendricks and affirmed she had an available occupancy.

She let them know she never used a sign. The people who found her through word of mouth kept her busy. She showed him an inside room on the second floor by the bathroom and said she only had one other boarder at that time. He gladly took the room and they headed back to the store.

He checked back in with his new boss who gave him the rest of the day off to go back to Mrs. Evans and get settled in. Walking away he heard, "Since I am giving you this day off you will be working both Friday and Saturday 9-9."

Lee drove to Mrs. Evans' place and unpacked his stuff and settled into the room. For those who don't like hotels, a boarding house is even worse. No television. Mrs. Evans was very nice. Her house was clean and she wasn't a chatty old woman. She gave you a key showed you the bath, where the linens were and you are on your own.

Well, here he was, in Philly around 6:30 p.m. - what to do? Of course, he headed into the city where he knew he could get a drink and feel comfortable. It was just a short trip out Passyunk Avenue, up the expressway; get off at South Street, down to 15th and up to Spruce Street. Although he had been away from the city a long time it didn't take long to find out from friendly guys in the bar what was happening in the gay scene. He didn't stay too long but headed back to South West Philly and his bed away from home.

The next day he found out that before the store opens all the employees use the rear door in his section by the Seasonal Goods to enter the store. He went down to his mailbox to find out what awaited him. He discovered it was his new boss's habit to greet you every morning with a list of comments, suggestions, guidance and sometimes an ass-chewing. It was also possible to receive one from the store's first asst. Mr. Marshall. Using the trickle-down effect, the section managers wrote one for each counter girl to help keep her on her toes.

Heaven help the section manager who when reading a morning missive from either boss was asked a question regarding, "Why are we out of? Get back to me." You better be able to show when it was ordered, and that we had a reasonable quantity on hand at that time.

Mr. Morse was very involved in keeping merchandise on the shelves. The first person to complain about a morning review was Adele. She let him know that the boss already knew exactly what sizes of men's and boy's underwear we were out of, and complained it was his fault because he wouldn't okay the order. The store received merchandise two ways; WD and direct. WD meant it came from the store-owned McKeesport warehouse and each store could order the quantity they wanted. Direct means you had to order from the manufacturer and the boss had to initial those orders because the money for these came from another part of the budget. The company preferred you spend your dollars on WD merchandise rather than buy outside-direct. Since the boss was only allowed a certain number of dollars for direct; he spent them where he wanted.

As long as the departments beat yesterday's dollar goals, the home office didn't care if you needed fill-ins on direct merchandise. This particular man had a great feel for inventory control and ran a tight lucrative ship by keeping his finger on the pulse of sales.

Mary was Lee's seasonal department girl, and Pat took care of toys with the assistance of a part-timer since she had added responsibilities as head salesgirl. There were two cash register stations in his section so he had one other extra floater. When anyone needed change, they would call their station number. It didn't matter what section called - whoever heard, responded.

When he talked to Rose on the phone that evening, he found out the minister set the date for the wedding, for June 21st. He would see them for counseling every Sunday afternoon until then. Many of the store's employees were curious, interested in the fact they had a new manager who would eventually be bringing a new wife to the store. Maybe because he was a recent arrival or going to be a newlywed, his co-workers were taking it easy on him, trying to make the transition to the big store easy. He enjoyed the departments he had to work with and his employees were very experienced.

The previous store didn't have windows that needed dressed so he never had that experience. Window dressing was covered in his training course so when he found out he had to do the window dressing he was glad for the challenge. The window well was 3-4 feet wide and maybe 8 feet long. The trick was to build the height from front to back, showing as many varied products on sale in the store as possible.

He enjoyed the work and the various department people would bring him the merchandise to put in and take back merchandise that had been removed. It might have bothered him somewhat, being in the window on the street, where all the passersby would often stop and watch. At times he would have to contort his body, almost standing on his head and stretching to place some things or remove something that sold out and should no longer be displayed.

This store in particular had a large number of poles in the store that required a banner on each side. Thank goodness, they used a stock boy for that. Once in a while one of the assistants would be pulled to help in receiving if they got swamped. The head stock lady Burt would call up to the floor and tell you when certain merchandise would come in, "How much of this do you want?" If she was not happy with the quantity you told her she would go to Ralph and complain. She would then call you back and say "Papa (her pet name for Mr. Morse) said.... send it all. So, prepare a place for it."

During his first week he found time to look for an apartment. From a local shopper type paper, he found an older couple who had turned their second floor into a separate furnished apartment. Like many people he encountered they also thought it so romantic, newlyweds. They were impressed that Lee was working in the city and going back and forth to see his bride and going through pre-wedding counseling. They were very happy to be involved with helping him make a love nest ready for his new bride and her honeymoon.

Lee hadn't minded staying with Mrs. Evans, until he realized what he had missed. She was as good a land lady as you would want. He rarely saw the man who used the back bedroom. Coming back to his room early one evening he saw light flowing out of the open back bedroom door. As he undressed for bed, he decided he felt "frisky." He excited himself to a state of arousal and went back to the man's open door to say hello.

Nothing ventured, nothing gained, what did he know? The door was open wide. Lee's bare feet slid silently across the hardwood floor as he approached the doorway. The man was lying in bed with the covers casually covering his groin. His feet stuck out from under the covers exposing very hairy toes. Lee's eyes followed the contours of his body up to a hairy chest with a matched set of well-muscled arms. What if it was 10:30 at night? Lee was only in his underwear with a hard-on. The man in the back room hardly looked up as he approached the open doorway. He was not interested in saying hello or talking about the weather. Lee's dick had subsided to just a nice bulging prominence by the time he lowered his book realizing he wasn't alone.

"What the f.... Whether it was surprise, anger or just the uninvited intrusion; the man was not happy. Getting nowhere fast he went back to his room and jerked off. He thought, "I should have tried... How about getting something to eat? But, no! I had to show my nakedness, probably scared the guy." He moved from Mrs. Evans with her blessing into the apartment he would eventually share with his bride. He could stop eating out now and stay home and watch TV the nights he wasn't working, something he couldn't do at Mrs. Evans'. He also rediscovered the freedom of coming and going more freely from his own home. Enjoying being footloose and fancy free, he started running down town to his favorite old haunts, the Westbury and the Allegro.

The first Saturday night he stayed in his new apartment he made a run downtown to the Westbury. That was the night he met John Davis Tuttle Glendenning the 3rd. He was older than Lee, 42, and way more experienced. Very conservative appearing, someone you truly would not have picked out as being gay. But gay he was. He had an apartment on the Parkway facing the Philadelphia Art Museum, and was attached to the diplomatic service.

John convinced him to go home with him the first night they met. He was a few inches taller than Lee with a tennis player's body. His wavy dark hair, complementing his darker skin tones, was combed straight back accentuating a masculine bone structure and full lips. His European background was evident in his manner of dress and masterful stride. A constant expression of confidence made other men move aside to let him pass.

Anyone challenging him soon changed their mind when they saw the take-no-prisoners threat in his eyes. The same characteristics that made him someone other men wanted to respect were the same attractions that could draw a man to John's dominance, where he became the most passionate loving man Lee ever knew. Bathing his eyes with kisses trailing to the small hollows behind his ears. John whispered with choked emotion, "You're a beautiful man. I have imagined you for years. Your straight dark hair, I curse my unruly mop, and deep green eyes set me afire. You are the perfect size for me to hold and love. I never wanted someone too big, but I didn't want someone I could lose under the sheets either. Where have you been? I have been in the city for three years. I was giving up hope of finding you!"

Before he could think what was happening, they were in his bedroom and undressed quicker than you can peel a banana. Holding Lee's face between his hands, gently prying his lips apart with his probing tongue, he rubbed his furry body against Lee's, creating growing excitement between them. John sucked and squeezed Lee's chest as if he was a woman with breasts. Gently laying Lee back on his bed John gently rolled him over massaging his shoulders and back as his swollen manhood swayed back and forth against Lee's upper thighs. Playfully he dragged his hardness up and down the valley between his buttocks tickling Lee's twitching rosette; begging it to loosen and invite him in. As John massaged his buttocks, he felt a wet finger slide into his butt. As John reached up and sucked his ear lobe and gently bit his shoulder, one finger was replaced by two, by three. John found his walnut sized prostate and aroused him.

"Quit teasing me," Lee moaned.

Invitation issued, R.S.V.P. not required. John reached under Lee and gathered some of Lee's honey. Milking his own manhood, he lubricated himself. He gently placed the head of his proud pole against an inviting orifice. Reluctantly Lee's inner passage loosened and gave way to John's invading spear. Fighting to withstand the desire to plunge forward and deep he slowly explored the soft walls of his Lee's insides with his probe. Sometimes not being able to withhold the desire his strokes were vigorous, other times a gentle, massaging lunge.

Lifting one leg at a time, keeping himself engorged in Lee, he turned him over onto his back. Pushing his legs back over his head he folded him like a bent playing card. Bending forward he explored Lee's mouth again and again with his searing tongue; all the while passionately thrusting himself in and out of the tunnel of love. John did not hurry; Lee didn't want him to. He could feel every swollen, bulging blood vessel on John's throbbing projectile. Neither wanted it to end. The hot skin to skin contact that produced a warm mist on both of them was pure ecstasy.

They were kissing when John could no longer hold himself back and let his hot liquid spew outward as his body trembled with grateful release. The hot volcanic eruption inside him hit the target prostate and let loose his own eruption, his muscles spasmodically pulling John into further depths of pleasure. Slowly lowering his legs John again grabbed his face in his two hands kissing him and telling him how wonderful it was. He slid down his chest licking the sweat off his body as his mouth found a still swollen oozing appendage. He slowly pushed his nose until he bounced against pubic hairs. With a few practiced strokes he drained all the energy left in Lee's body. It was as if all was right with the world and Lee had no cares or worries. John pulled himself back up to lay beside him, gently kissing his cheek and forehead. He cuddled up to Lee casually throwing one of his legs over his and pulled him close and started to murmur something quietly loving in his ear as their relaxation turned into sleep.

CHAPTER TWENTY-THREE

Awakened hours later by roaming fingers playing in his chest hair trying to rouse his body, Lee realized he had to hurry and get on the road to Washington. The false sense of well-being he had felt just before dozing off was now gone. The little boy late for school stood in his place. Last evening when they met, he shared his life plans with John. Now as he got dressed and made it known his departure was imminent John became agitated.

"Yes, I know what you told me last night, but I can't believe it. I thought you were just trying to represent yourself as forbidden fruit to make me more interested. I never for a moment believed you. How could you let me do that?"

"Me? Let you do what?"

"Make a fool of myself. Get in over my head with someone who now tells me they are not available."

"Listen I had a great time. You were great. But that doesn't change the fact I am getting married and have an appointment I must get to."

"How can you say that after what happened between us last night? We may have just met but I know there was a magic; Serendipity. It was so special, so right."

"I explained to you I have to get married or my parents will go out of their minds with worry that I will turn out queer."

"Sorry it's too late! The man who was in bed with me last night is as queer as I am."

"Maybe I am bisexual?"

"Guess again!! I've been around. You responded to every sensuous touch, every intimacy with total abandonment. You were not just half here, visiting for a while. You were totally into me, into us and what we shared, I could tell. This, whatever it is between us, has the makings of a great love affair if not a lifetime love."

"They want grandchildren. I am their last hope!"

"No, you are *your* last hope!"

"John. I can't begin to tell you how very much I enjoyed what we did last night. How much I enjoyed you, your touch, in every way. The closeness; the intimacy; the electricity between us when our bodies touched.

"But that is all it can be! I have to get married and I have to go now."

Frantically John pleaded, "Please don't do this to us! Don't throw away what we could have! Please! Stop and think what you are saying."

"John, I have to go."

"No! I won't accept this. There was too much emotion in play from both of us. You are too good to let go to a woman, especially one you don't even say you love. It isn't fair to her; you're not meant to be with a woman! You're meant to be with a man. ME!" John's voice was trailing off behind as he closed his car door.

During the drive up to Rose's parents' house to keep the counseling appointment, as a matter of fact for the rest of the day, all he thought about was last night. He remembered he hadn't showered and wondered if anyone would be able to smell last evening's love remnants on his body.

He was so satiated that he felt he could not hide the inner gleeful contentment left from the previous evening's romance. Giddy, like a kid with a secret he should not tell. Yet he wanted to tell the world. He wanted everyone to know how great he felt; but he couldn't tell anyone.

All these happy feelings disappeared when he arrived at the Criberri home. Almost sick to his stomach from the realization of what he did, what he felt hit him like a cannonball in his midsection. Breaking out in a cold sweat he couldn't move, because he knew to marry Rose would be the wrong thing to do.

"Lee!" Running out of the house Rose was all aglow. Running on automatic, he got out of the car and gathered Rose in his arms as John had held him a few hours earlier. Rose found his lips and welcomed him kissing him warmly, tenderly. Hers was not the kind of kiss that flamed his groin to arousal. Not the rough masterful lips that pushed his mouth open only to make him captive with a deep kiss. A kiss that now burned into his soul with guilt.

"You are almost late. We have to hurry - we have so much to do." As they sat with the local Rector and listened to his platitudes regarding the sanctity of marriage, he felt his ass squirm as if he was on fire. There was no fire, no squirming, just a vivid knowledge of shame. As hard as he tried to focus on what they were discussing he was somewhere else in memory.

Enough! He screamed inside his head. I will not do it again. I have to stay true and marry Rose. I have to be normal for my parents and my future children. Finally, relaxing, he was able to participate more enthusiastically in the counseling. Driving Rose back to her parents' home he once again felt loving toward his future wife.

When they got back to the Criberri kitchen the women cornered him and made him come up with a guest list for his side of the family. He still didn't have a best man. He hadn't been able to decide which brother to ask to stand for him. They talked about the arrangements made for the different foods, table settings, flowers and discussed the drawings and material for the wedding dress. Rose already purchased a small tiara with a train. He really did not care how Rose might wear her hair or what kind of shoes she may buy.

Mother Criberri made a delicious Italian dinner of lasagna and his favorite chocolate cake. After dinner the betrothed couple took a walk and coo-coo eyed each other and talked of the future.

Having to get back for an early store opening the next morning he took leave of his wife to be home around nine o'clock. Driving home, he considered all the arrangements that were being made for the wedding and knew how upset everyone would be if it fell through - everyone but him, that is. The closer he got to Philadelphia the more pressing the memories of the previous night became again. He told himself he would not see John again and vowed to work hard keeping himself busy at the store.

When he got home the phone rang and rang but he turned the ringer off and begged Morpheus to let him fall asleep. Guilt, greed, and shame were his companions in bed that night. None of them helped him sleep or made him feel comfortable. Nothing he did the next day had his full attention. He struggled just trying to keep focused on what was in front of him at the moment. If anyone noticed anything strange in his behavior, they probably thought it was due to the pending nuptials. For most people, the struggle to concentrate and focus on daily tasks would be from obsessing on something terrible that had happened to them or something terrible that they had experienced.

But for Lee it wasn't something bad he obsessed about. It was something wonderfully sensuous his memory banks kept rekindling. The hard-strong warmth of a body pressed against his, John's Anteaus cologne that just slightly wafted against his nose when John held him close; The crispness and smell of the bed sheets, the passion of love that he never before experienced. The joy of falling asleep held by someone who made you feel complete, loved, wanted. How good he **resist** this magnet of desire?

He delved into cleaning out the under stocks of his department to immerse himself and keep busy. He was on his hands and knees reaching deep into the underneath section of the toy department when he realized there were two feet stopped in front him. His first thought was, *"It must be the boss or first assistant! What did I do?"* Glancing best as he good from under the counter, (he was in almost up to his waist,) he thought the figure in dress trousers must be one of the managers. Stopping his cleaning for a minute expecting one of their voices to say something he was curious when nothing was said. The two feet just stood there.

"Can I help you?" he was asking the body as he pulled himself out from underneath the counter. Looking up at the figure beside him he met the darkly strained eyes of the previous Saturday nights encounter. A strong male hand reached out and raised him to his feet.

Pulling him close, John said, "I have to talk to you."

"Stop! Back up! People will see!" Lee stammered.

John continued, "We have to talk. I am sorry I came to your job, but you didn't answer your phone last night. We must talk."

Mixed emotional reactions made him cold and sick to his stomach at the same time. He didn't know what to do! He did know what he wanted to do! He was so twisted mentally. "Can we go over to the counter for a cup of coffee?" John begged.

Finding his voice, "NO, we can't go over to the counter for a cup of coffee! You shouldn't be here!"

"If you don't tell me you will meet me after work; I am going to act like the biggest love-sick teenager you have ever seen and call all kind of attention to us."

"Okay, Okay, now let me get back to work; I have to start the closing duties."

"Thank you - I'll follow your car out of the parking lot, then pull over and we'll go from there." Even in a loose suit that man had a body that shouted when he turned and walked away.

"Oh, my God what have I got myself into?" he asked himself. Then the chords from a West Side Story song rang in his ears, *"Tonight, tonight, I'll see my love tonight..."* Lee knew by all that was right that what he was contemplating was wrong. But, like Scarlett, he would think about that tomorrow!

As he pulled over a block from the store, John's car was screeching to a stop. He hurriedly exited his car and came around to Lee's passenger side, opened the door and slid across the seat. Grabbing him close and kissing him boldly, Lee was putty in John's arms. They drove back to the apartment he was readying for his bride holding hands. As they walked in silence to the front door his breath came faster and faster with anticipation of what would come.

John closed the door behind him, turning the deadbolt and grabbed Lee's out stretched hand and followed him upstairs. "I have never felt so strong an attraction to anyone so quickly before, Lee. I have been beside myself."

"You're beside me NOW; let's make the best of it." Hand in hand they walked into the bedroom meant for a wedding night three-weeks hence. Slowly kissing each other, their hands as in chorus undressed the other. Lee felt as if he was touching a live wire as he lowered John's underwear to be greeted by a bouncing pole.

He in turn felt as if his skin was crawling alive as John took his underwear down. Bending over, he lifted one foot at a time; his thick hair brushing against Lee's privates; so, Lee could step out of his shorts. Instead of straightening back up, he sank to his knees, slowly pushing him back onto the bed; Lee's resolve not to be with John again disintegrated.

They made love again and talked long into the morning about what was in the future for them. Having moved into the living room with a cup of tea and coffee they curled up together on the sofa to try and sort out more rationally their 'at odds' differences. John knew what he wanted and was ready to persevere and pursue Lee whatever it took. Lee knew he had to marry Rose.

He left it to fate to help him keep his resolve. As often as they could, they spent the nights together in each other's arms pleasing each other and exploring each other's physical reactions to the joy of love. Much to John's dismay Lee kept traveling back and forth to visit his bride and continue the counseling sessions. Sunday nights when returning to the city he also returned to John's arms and bed. John knew Lee would eventually give up this foolish idea to wed and have children. He continued believing this up until the night before the wedding.

Lying in bed that night John decided he needed to *prove* to Lee, once and for all, that he was meant for a man and *not a woman*. He rolled him over and roughly pounded his backside so hard Lee thought his head would go through the bed board. When he released his load into him he turned him over and almost *viciously* attacked his swollen prowess. *Not gently* and loving, but *demanding*, pulling, stretching; he serviced Lee greedily. As soon as he knew he had him in a place of *drained complacency* he pounced on his chest and ***plunged*** himself into Lee's mouth. Almost suffocating, choking him, he **ramrodded** himself *in and out* of his throat until he poured himself down his throat like cough syrup.

Although Lee was not *entirely* displeased with being handled roughly, it was quite unlike John to have behaved that way and he wondered, why? "You want to marry a woman! Will a woman have what I have? Can a woman deck you *and* dick you whether you are willing or not? *Can a woman service* you with that much passion and strength? Hold you down when you would push her away? All the time wanting to be *controlled*, over powered; *desiring* a man's *hardness* in your body. What will she shove down your throat that makes your body throb and ooze begging for release?"

Lee was scared and taken back by this sadistic side of a man he had come to feel so strongly about. He had been ready to tell John he had second thoughts about the marriage and would not go through with it. That was before John ill-used him and he heard the venomous tone of the stinging tirade John threw at him.

Yes, he could enjoy being submissive for someone he loved. But he was not there with John yet. Seeing this mean streak told him...STOP! Step back! Think! This man just told you he could control you, would control you if he wanted. He doesn't have the only hard dick in the world; it could just as well be attached to another face and body.

John pulled him close and kissed him, saying, "I am sorry if I sounded mean but I had to show you what you'll be missing, and losing."

He let John hold him close knowing he had to do something. Nothing had to be done right then and there, tomorrow would be soon enough. He wanted this small amount of time left before the wedding to savor and remember for the future. John knew in the morning he would understand and see the folly of getting married.

"Good morning, love of my life," greeted him as he opened his eyes. John was on top of him distractingly kissing his neck expecting it to lead to a passionate breakfast treat.

"John, I have to go. I have to rush home, shower and gather my clothes for the wedding. Thank God the wedding isn't until one o'clock after the Church's scheduled morning services."

"YOU mean!! You are still going to marry that child?"

"Yes John. You fully explained last night what you can give me; All about physical sex. You just don't understand you can't give birth. I had decided to tell you I wasn't going to get married, until you explicitly defined all you were capable of doing to me. Had you stayed true to the person who made me fall in love with him these last week's I wouldn't be getting married today. Instead of being loving and gentle you were mean, vindictive and bordered on being physically abusive."

"I just wanted to make sure you know what you are losing. What you will miss. She will not satisfy you like I have. I love you. I'm sorry I was rough with you but you have to understand I don't want to lose you and that means not marrying her. Please don't throw our future away!"

There was just no way he could continue this endless discussion. He grabbed his lover of the last few weeks, gave him a hug and a good-bye kiss and left to get himself together for his wedding.

John was upset that this whippet of a young man had scorned his love and offer of a lifetime of passion and adventure. He immediately decided there was only one thing to do. He too got himself showered, went thru his closet and pulled out a Versace suit. "We'll see if he has the strength of his conviction!" John muttered to himself.

Lee ran back to his apartment, showered and looking into the mirror, realizing his cheeks were irritated from John's hairy thighs rubbing him the night before. He rubbed his wrists where they were slightly sore from being held down. His groin started to stir again. "No, stop, get out of my mind; don't think about him!"

He told himself, *"A new day has dawned."*

CHAPTER TWENTY-FOUR

DRIVING TO WASHINGTON TO GET MARried he kept telling himself he was doing the right thing. As much as he had enjoyed the physical pleasure with John, he knew he was out of his league. John came from money and he felt eventually with their different resources there would be too much conflict. John had talked of their going to Europe for long vacations and Lee didn't have the time available, or the money. Considering hotels, food, and recreational costs (drinking, theatre, excursions) and the unexpected, he knew he could not afford the expense.

John said, "I can afford it, I'll pay our way! All you will need is spending money." Having seen the look on Lee's face, he sputtered, "I have enough money for both of us. I just need you."

Even spending money for a European vacation could be a lot of greenbacks. Add on a suitable wardrobe, and yes, he was out of his element. And if the questions regarding the difference in social status weren't enough, he could not forget the controlling roughness John displayed when trying to prove he had so much more to offer than he would ever find with Rose.

"You'll never know until you try," he told himself. Pulling up to the corner, the Criberri family lived on; Rose was outside in shorts and a skimpy top washing the wedding car. Yelling, "You shouldn't be here yet!" the unsuspecting bride disappeared into the house.

Her sisters came out and chided him, "You saw the bride before the wedding, that's bad luck. You're not to be here, you are supposed to meet your family at the church."

He returned to his car and drove to the church. His parents and brothers were waiting in the vestibule to greet him. "Are you sure this is what you want?" "Are you sure this is the right girl for you?" "You haven't known her that long!"

"Oh. Mother, leave him alone; he just wants some of that wild Dago pussy!"

"She's a nice girl, not wild, and can make her own clothes and she is a good cook. I'm sure you'll like her. Remember, you wanted grand-children!" He responded, fielding questions from his parents.

Slowly other members of the family arrived: his fathers' sisters and brothers-in-law from Roxborough, Pennsylvania and his hometown, and a handful of cousins from around the state. The bride's side of the church was occupied more than the groom's side when all was said and done.

Time passed quickly and he heard the wedding march begin as he took his place at the altar rail. Unknown to him, before the bride's music was cued; a late arriving guest hurried in the rear side door and quickly sat down in a back pew. Now as he turned to watch his bride proceed down the aisle with her father, he saw a familiar male figure stand out in the crowd. He would have stood out anywhere in this town, (because of his impeccable grooming and expensive suit), and his ruggedly handsome European countenance.

Nervous beads of perspiration danced on Lee's forehead. Panic momentarily shook him as he wondered if John was going to make a scene. When the bride's father placed her hand in his he forgot about everyone else in the church and without a flicker of conscience thought only of the vision in white. Later he would not be able to even talk about anything else that happened in the church except he and the lady he met at the altar rail that day had become husband and wife.

As the recessional started the happy couple kissed and walked down the aisle. With relief he saw that John was not in the pew he had occupied. Walking outside the bridal couple stood in the shade of the church doors and received the families' felicitations. As he was receiving congratulatory hugs from his wife's aunts and uncles, he saw Karen standing partially hidden by a tree. The wide tree, nor the large jacket she wore, could hide the fact that she was pregnant. Just as he made eye contact with Karen her mother appeared and pulled her away.

Amid the traditional rice throwing the bridal couple proceeded to the wedding parties' cars. As he helped Rose into the car his gaze swept across the car's roof to the other side of the street where he saw John standing beside his car. Tears, gleaming like diamonds, were flowing out from underneath the sunglasses he wore to cover his weeping eyes.

The gratuitous ride through town serenaded by the honking of car horns and bouncing cans trailing the car did not give him time to think about the phantoms he left behind him in the shadows.

When they arrived back at the Criberri family home, they were led to the bridal table. The yard was decked out with all kind of festive decorations and a phonograph played loud happy music in the background. On-lookers would have thought they were watching a party-scene that took place along the river in the movie "Roman Holiday." The home-made food was wonderful and the father's private stock of Italian wine flowed freely. Fathers, mothers, aunts, uncles, cousins, all were happy as they could be for the newly married couple and wished them every wish for happiness and prosperity.

With the regaling of good wishes pealing in their ears the happy couple departed on their way to the bridal bed awaiting them in Philadelphia on Doral Street. Arriving in southwest Philly they stopped at the Horn and Hardart restaurant on Passyunk Avenue for a bite to eat. Neither had eaten much in the excitement of the wedding. As the waitress walked up to the table, she asked, "You're newly-weds, aren't you? Just married?"

"How can you tell?" they both wondered, looking at each other.

"Well the bride is wearing her wedding corsage, and what I would take as a traveling suit. And you both are so radiantly happy!"

The waitress called the manager over and told him about their just being married. He shared in their joy, ''Your first meal as husband and wife is on us."

Arriving home, he realized his heart wasn't singing, *"Tonight, tonight, won't be just any night. Tonight, there will be no morning sun!* "As he took his new bride upstairs, the excitement he anticipated was not there. He rationalized the difference in moods by telling himself this wasn't forbidden fruit. It would be normal not to be overly excited. This was meant to be slow and easy; passionately warm, not on fire with a fever.

After he took her on a short tour of the living room, bathroom, and bedroom. This is where the glasses, knives and forks are in the kitchen. He settled down in front of the TV to let Rose unpack and get a feel of the place.

When the eleven o'clock news went off, he went in the bedroom where Rose was just finishing her unpacking. Turning off the lights he took his new bride to bed. He soon discovered he was not lying beside a Melissa or a Karen; let alone a John. Her kisses did not have the "warm welcome, there's more waiting for you" that was seared into his memory by John. As his fingers slipped Rose's top off her shoulders, he found Rose had large crevices on her shoulders. He turned the lights on and looking at the indentations asked Rose, "What happened to your shoulders?"

"They're from my bra."

"Your bra... (They were so deep he could lay a finger in them and there was still space up to the skin level.)"

"I'm a 36 double D and I have to keep them cinched in or they bounce too much and hurt."

Well that was a new one for him! Turning the lights back off he started to kiss his wife and fondle her breasts. He stopped in his tracks when his fingers, while squeezing her nipples, came in contact with rough skin. Turning the lights back on he examined what his fingers had felt and found small round scar tissue spots all over her chest.

"What's that?"

"I find little pimples, bust them and they leave marks." Out went the lights again and frying to avoid tongue contact with those pimple bumps he proceeded to mount and enter Rose.

Her body was large! It was lacking the alluring velvety softness of Karen and Melissa. She didn't have that enticing female scent that pulled him to them and made him want more. He had seen pictures of He-She's and thought this must be what their body would be like; but with a penis.

He didn't enjoy Rose's garden patch. He didn't enjoy Rose; Period. As he tried to finish himself Rose asked, "ARE YOU DONE YET? ARE YOU DONE YET? You're so heavy!"

With hurt feelings he thought how Rose wore a size 14/16 and was two inches taller he was; and he was only a 36 waist.

Rolling off his new bride's body, his mind was reeling with the realization that *he had made a terrible mistake!!*

CHAPTER TWENTY-FIVE

As Emily unlocked her front door that evening, she was still surprised that she had fallen asleep at the bedside of one of her patients. While settling into her cozy little apartment she remembered sleeping very well the night before and wondered at herself, mystified, her dozing off like that.

Recalling the day's events, she had been listening so closely to Lee that she really couldn't remember the aide that came by and offered them the juice. She thought it odd that he thought she had brought it with her.

Making herself half of a celery stalk and cold roast chicken sandwich (with a dab of mayonnaise), she took her cup of chamomile tea with her to her favorite arm chair in front of the television. As she enjoyed her repast, she decided she needed to call her eldest daughter to say 'hello'.

Her visits with Lee especially brought to mind her need to stay in touch with her own children and tell them how much they were loved. Being a southern Baptist minister's daughter, it was natural for her to be stern with her two girls and easy on her son.

Her oldest daughter was so agreeable she made her mother proud with everything she did. As a child she was always trying to please and was a joy to behold. The youngest daughter had always been a challenging child, forcing Emily to the edge of her reason at times. Sneaking behind her parents back she would attempt new fads, be it clothes or hair styles. She always attracted the wrong friends as far as her mother was concerned. Both daughters graduated college with the eldest having a career working with under-privileged children in the same city in which her mother had attended nursing school.

The younger chose a path in the financial world reaching a moderate success, but never quite succeeding as much as her mother would have liked. She was luckier in romance though; if you can count yourself fortunate to have a successive line of live-in boyfriends. They were sometimes so fast and furious she ended up with a child she could not match to the father.

The eldest remained single and happy until she moved back home in later life. She helped take care of her father so her mother didn't have to give up her nursing position. She fell under the spell of a fop, a man twenty years her senior. They met when she was asked to accompany him on the piano for a vocal solo at her church. Every church has one; an older man with a fantastic baritone or high tenor voice, impeccable grooming and clothes, manicured nails with a clear coat of polish. He is adored by the women in the church.

He always knew the right thing to say, "Oh, I love your perfume Mrs. Smith! My you certainly make that dress look good! Love the shoes and hat! Your makeup is flawless!" He knows everything there is to know about how women should look and how they can achieve their best look. At a church gathering you will sometimes hear his falsetto laugh or the feminine side of his voice; when he forgets himself and gets too animated with those flying gesturing hands adorned with expensive rings.

Emily always gave her daughter credit for marrying smart; *someone older with his own money.* In this case the hubby was a real-estate entrepreneur, with a coin operated Laundromat here and there and a chain of drive -in movie theaters. He sold the land to a development company and made a good deal. Yes, she married well and he didn't bother her for that silly sex stuff.

Only as she had gotten older and wiser did Emily come to the realization that her eldest did not marry well. There is comfort to be found with a man who loves you and enjoys your body even though he may not have such a large bank account. She could see the emptiness in her eldest daughter's eyes caused by not having the loving man /woman relationship God intended. She was a good daughter to a fault, but there was a joy of life missing in her personality. Her mother thought it was because she lacked that nurturing fulfillment that comes upon a woman who is loved and treasured. A wife needs to have a husband who loves her with all his heart as Emily's husband loved her.

She never worried about her son. He didn't get anyone pregnant as so many young men ruin their lives. He was too busy with his friends.

After calling her daughters she was getting ready for bed when she spied the piece of paper on her dresser. She had forgotten she had tried to call Lee's friends for that record and any information she could glean about him. Remembering she had not yet received a response, she called again, leaving a message. Answering machines; everyone has answering machines! At least she hadn't been subjected to a multiple tree of push one for so and so. Push two for so and so. Just straight forward, "Can't answer the phone, leave your name and number, we will get back to you."

Although the more she heard from him about his life the more she was drawn in, she still did not know all she would like to know about his family. "Surely, he must have someone who would want to see him before he dies. All God's children must have someone, somewhere, who cares enough to be sad that their family member is dying. Someone who regrets they did not make enough of the time they had together."

The next morning as she was going down the hall, she saw someone come out of Lee's room. She found him with a glass of juice in his hand he had just received from an aide. "She encouraged me to drink some while she was here. It is very sweet. And cold! I always liked very cold drinks. You can have some if you like - she left a small pitcher."

"Maybe later" Emily replied. "You were talking about New Jersey yesterday. Had you told me that you were married and that was where you met your wife?"

He thought there's that razor-sharp mind again. He remembered only hinting once that he had had a wife with a connection to New Jersey. Emily was very good with remembering detail.

"No, I'm Edie. I am your second wife not your first. "

Emily thought she heard what might have been a slap to the face as the voices behind the curtain raised in decibels. Both Lee and Emily were disturbed by the loud voices coming from the chief's bed. He realized the old man didn't have a razor-sharp mind.

"Morning, Chief!" called Cornpopper.

The Chief, happy to see his old friend, began, "You know what they call a cotton picker? A little girl who lost the string on her tampon."

> *There once was a laddy named Herkin.*
> *Who always was jerkin' his gherkin.*
> *His mama said, "Herkin!*
> *Quit jerkin your gherkin!*
> *Your gherkin's for ferkin, Herkin!"*

The Chief was off again. Couldn't remember his wife's name but he could play a comedy club with his raunchy humor. As Cornpopper wheeled the old boy off to the day room he passed by the open bed curtain and glanced in to where Lee lay on his bed.

Emily thought she saw a look of something cross the man's face. Could have been disgust for what he might have heard about Lee. But it could have been Emily's vivid imagination.

Lee's memory tapes having played back so much of his earlier life in dreamland he didn't know where to start when Emily brought up his wife. *"And they lived happy ever after!"* were not the words reverberating in his thoughts the morning after his wedding night.

His father had always told him you don't screw the girl you intend to marry before the wedding. Why he chose that pearl of wisdom to accept as gospel from his father escaped him. After the fact, he knew he should have had sex with her when they were dating. He would have known this was not somebody he would be attracted to physically; or she him.

The next morning, he didn't even quite like her. Rejected by her saying, "Are you done yet? You're too heavy!" Of all the people, he had been with, and God knows there were many, no one had ever told him, "You're too heavy" or wanted to end their intimate time together quickly. That little Keopeke ruined him for women!

On the plus side, was the fact there seemed to be an easy relationship between, them regardless of their physical dysfunction; Neither minded being naked before the other or sharing the bathroom. Rose enjoyed cooking her husband his first married life breakfast. Afterwards he took his bride to see where he worked and introduced her to the store employees.

Although the apartment was small Rose liked the neighborhood and was happy the store was so close that she could walk to where her husband worked. Being Italian, she was elated to have so many Italian families in the area. Any kind of store she would be interested in shopping in was located around the Five and Dime or on the way to their apartment. It all combined to make it a clean safe area to start married life!

They had a week for their honeymoon and his parents asked that the newlyweds come home to visit, so relatives who hadn't attended the wedding could meet Rose. While home, they invited Rose to extend her visit so they could get to know her better. Lee drove back and Rose took the train to Philadelphia the next weekend.

When his mother was able to get him on the phone out of Rose's ear-shot, she had much to say about her daughter-in-law. "You know she sits around here watching television all the time hardly wanting to go anyplace. If she is not watching TV, she's reading a paperback novel. Early in the evening, she spends a lot of time in the bathroom. She comes downstairs in her baby doll pajamas to watch TV, in front of your father, with her legs crossed exposing herself. She has a nasty habit of picking at bumps on her legs!

"I asked her, "What causes those bumps?'

"She said, 'It is from shaving my legs!'

"Imagine a woman so hairy, she has to shave! She squeezes her bumps until they bleed. On my good furniture!"

No, he didn't know where to start telling Emily about Rose. Remembering all the sordid details, he remembered he had already told Emily he'd decided to try to spare her some of the more colorful highlights, or at least try to tone them down.

CHAPTER TWENTY-SIX

"Yes, I met my wife while I was working in New Jersey for the five and dime. It was right before the company transferred me to Philadelphia." Shaking his head, Lee thought how much the poor old woman did not know, nor would want to know, about his life in New Jersey.

"Was it love at first sight?" Emily questioned.

From an amused face, yet almost sardonic contempt, Emily heard, "Hardly. We settled into a routine of sorts with my playing the dutiful husband. The store was open six days a week, 9-9; my schedule was Sundays off, Wednesday afternoons off, two weekdays 12-9, two days 9-9 and every other Saturday 9-9. Rose became the 'stay-at-home' housewife. At first, she kept herself busy with sewing projects although few were ever finished. Her attraction to paperback books (that I didn't know she enjoyed before we were married) became time consuming, preventing her from doing normal day to day housekeeping chores. She loved to cook and always had a great meal ready. Unfortunately, she decided she did not like to wash dishes. The dishes from the previous evening were often in the sink unwashed when we sat down the next evening.

"On weekends I took her to the grocery store and had to motivate her to house clean, meaning I had to help. It was a very small second floor apartment, living room, bedroom, tiny bathroom and even smaller kitchen. Everyone ironed their clothes back then, but ironing was not one of her favorite tasks. One end of the sofa back had a stack of clothing waiting to be ironed. The other end had a growing pile of paperback books she had finished but was not ready to discard. One wall in the living room had two closets with an alcove for a desk in the center. The desk quickly disappeared under the ever-increasing moun-tain of her unfinished sewing projects.

"One day Mrs. Evans, a woman I rented a room from when I first went to Philly, came up to me while I was working and said, "Hello! How is married life treating you?"

"Me being me, I told her how unhappy I was becoming with my wife.

"'Oh honey, she's just out of high school. She just does not know everything she should. I will stop by, introduce myself, and try to guide her a little.' When I got home that night, Rose let me know Mrs. Evans had stopped to see her and that she didn't want any more visits from her. Our sex life was almost non- existent, so I'll spare you the details, Emily."

"Well, that is a first! Maybe I will have a swallow of the juice. I forgot to take a pill this morning."

"We consummated the marriage, but only, what, maybe a handful of times in the first year, if that."

"My, that juice doesn't taste very good."

"Rose didn't want children so she bought a spermicidal female spray. When we were getting ready for bed at night, I would pass the bathroom door. She would be standing with one leg propped up on the closed toilet seat and her hand aiming an aerosol can of up inside in her, as she asked, 'Do I need this tonight?'

"My memories: a tall, naked woman with drooping double Ds, legs and tits covered with red swollen little shaving bump pimples, aiming a loaded can up her vagina was not a pretty sight. It made me quickly answer, 'No!' I could never enjoy my wife intimately. She could be a good friend but as a wife, she failed. As I said at cooking and baking, she excelled. Anything else about housekeeping not interested.

"I am going to tell you something I am very ashamed of, Emily."

"What! You? After everything else, you are going to tell me some-thing you are ashamed of? If that doesn't take the cake; go ahead."

"When my wife persisted in not doing the dishes, I got to the point I would literally drag her out to the kitchen and demand she do the dishes. She would turn to walk away and I would grab her and demand again that she washes the dishes. She would turn to walk away again and I pulled her back into the kitchen and slapped her. My memory is forgiving but I am afraid someone else might say I beat her.

"We went home to visit my parents after one of those scenes and she had taped her glasses together over the nosepiece because I broke them when I hit her. My mother asked her, 'How did you break your glasses Rose?'

"'Ask your son.' she smartly answered.

"'They were broken when we had a fight,'" I countered.

"'It was no fight. He beat me!

"'LEE! You didn't hit your wife?'

"'Yes, I did. I am not proud of it but, she wouldn't do the dishes and I was tired of them gathering in the sink.'

"'You don't hit your wife, especially for something like that.'

"'Mother, stay out of it. It is none of your business.' my father warned her.

"My mother glared at me but never spoke of it again.

"So that was Rose's last trip to my parents' home. Hearing the shock in my mother's voice shamed me so bad I knew I would never hit her again. I started ignoring her and going out by myself. She cried after me as I went out the door, 'You don't love me anymore! You don't even hit me anymore.'"

"I talked to Tim, a stockman who worked at the store and told him how unhappy she was. He thought she would be different if she had her own home to take care of rather than living in a furnished apartment. He invited us over for dinner and in the course of conversation asked, 'Hey! Ma, could you help them out with finding a house?'"

"I did not know there was a special way of selling and buying real estate in this part of Philly; or that it was secretly 'white only.' Real Estate agents would not open their portfolio of available houses to anyone unless you came with an accepted member of the community. If you were black and went into a real-estate office you were told, 'Sorry, we just don't have anything available right now.' If you were white and not introduced by somebody trustworthy, you were told the same thing. They did not want white people helping the undesired to 'break open the block.'

"That is why my friend's mother, Celeste Simonetta, took us to meet Joe Hiller. He in turn showed us the 'houses for sale' listings he had hiding under his desk blotter. That was the beginning of closeness between Tim and his mother and Rose and me.

"We bought a two-bedroom row house in southwest Philly, only a couple of blocks from the store where I worked. My parents gave us an old living room suite and found used appliances for the kitchen. The house needed some improvements and Rose's parents talked their oldest daughter's husband into redoing the electrical work. They came to live with us, Debbie, Harold and their children, while my brother-in-law rewired the house.

"Before coming to stay with us, Harold being unemployed, they lived with Rose's parents. Harold was caught between low self-esteem and the bottle. A major dose of guilt from Debbie kept him on that path. She blamed him for getting pregnant twice and not finishing college. I thought they were coming to help, as in volunteer. It was soon apparent, when they started asking for money every week, they expected to be paid the same sum we would have paid an electrician we hired off the street. The difference being we would not have housed, diapered or fed his family, and we would have had our privacy.

"I started going out to a neighborhood bar just for a little peace and quiet. I was on my way out the door one evening when Debbie shouted, 'Wait! Take Harold along. He could stand to get out too!'

"Harold was always a little loose, as if he had a slight buzz. He came up to me as we went out the door and put his arm around my shoulder saying, 'Thanks buddy I could use a couple drinks.' When we got to my corner source of libation, we sat down and visited with a woman I knew from the store. One of my female clerks came in and we moved to a back booth.

"Harold was a cheap date - he only drank 15-cent beers. As I was walking back to the table, from getting a round of drinks, I heard someone make a remark about our being faggots. I was in shock. I sat the glasses on the table and told everyone what I heard. No one acted surprised or cared. I cared. I had not done anything to deserve a slur like that to be said about me.

"My co-worker, seeing I was upset, said, "Don't worry!" followed by loudly calling out, 'Two beers for two queers and two more for two whores!' You will be surprised Emily, but I was shocked!

"When we left, my brother-in-law said, 'Let's go for a ride down around the airport - I always wanted to see the planes come in up close.' We did live close to the airport and I enjoyed watching the planes come and go too, so I thought, 'What the hell, why not.' I drove the short 15-minute drive down to Island Road circle and found a road that ran along the airstrip. We decided on a good spot to eyeball the planes and parked. We watched the planes and in between oohing and ahhing would talk of our wives. After 30 minutes, he put his hand on my knee, swung him-self over on my lap, and threw a lip lock on my face. I was suffering from a case of morals (for once), I did not return his affection and he flipped himself back over to his side of the seat.

"We continued watching the planes when I heard, 'Man, am I messed up, I gotta go home.' Neither of us ever mentioned it. He never looked at my face again when talking. He finished the wiring quickly and the last I heard was they moved in with my wife's cousin in south Philly.

"After the house was fixed up, my wife decided to throw me a surprise birthday party. It was a surprise she invited all the young people her age from the store, including the older women who worked for me. At that time, I had a toy department clerk named Betty Doitch. The party ran late and she needed a ride home to Upper Darby. I volunteered to take her home while Rose cleaned up after the guests left.

"I was always a crybaby, complaining to everyone and anyone who would listen about my problems with Rose. Betty was one of those sympathetic shoulders so our time during the drive to Upper Darby was filled with my laments about Rose. She understood and said, 'You need an older woman, someone like me.

"I half thought she was right since I had already learned how soft and warm her body could be. A few stolen kisses here, a grope, a pat, heavy petting whenever we caught a few minutes in the stockroom together. More than once, one of us was pinned against the shelves by the other's body weight always with one piece of wood between us. By this time, after massaging her leg on the trip, I pulled up to her door wanting more. I reached across the seat and brought her to me. Our lips met and our tongues reached for each other's tonsils.

"My goodness!" Emily said, "How you describe situations! I have heard of people like you who work on the telephone. They talk to strangers with this kind of intimate smutty vulgarity. I think you missed your calling."

"I'm just telling you how it was... When my hands went under her blouse to caress her, she pleaded with me to stop. Reminding me her son was probably watching from the front window, she tumbled backwards out of the passenger door, blowing me a kiss as she disappeared into her apartment. Soon after that evening, she was transferred out of my department. She always thought my wife figured something out, complained to my big boss and therefore responsible for her being moved.

"Emily, I had a red Testament. Look through it please for a beige envelope."

"Is this what you are looking for?"

"Yes, open it and read them."

"My, they are old and fragile. I am afraid they may disintegrate while I hold them."

"They are over 30 years old." He sighed "This one is titled

Mr. Wonderful
My boss in more ways than one.
He's not an easy one to know,
But yet I go on trying.
To read the thoughts his mind doth sow,
Through eyes of mystery and hiding
Eyes that say much more than words,

But not enough of them are heard.
He's a wonderment to me,
which I shall never understand.
Nor shall I know, why my feelings are such-
when' ere I feel his hand.
And why do I allow his eyes to reach out and touch my
heart?
Making it impossible, for me to depart"

"That was the first note she hid in my section book for me to find. Emily continued. "This one is titled

A Very Special Guy
There was a night not long ago-
A special guy got me all aglow.
It came as no surprise to me,
For I have loved this special He!
For quite a spell not knowing why.
My heart has chosen this special guy.
He touches me and I am through,
with even caring what's wrong or true!
I told him this and he seemed to
Not minding my answer which said, No! no!
to the one only 'special guy'.
Not knowing- if or when-
he'd hold me in his arms again
Does he know my happiness shall never be
Until he's made his love to me.

"And yet another, Lee…Whatever did you do to deserve such attention? She writes,

Driven Away
And First a demotion away from your presence.

Seeing you only for a fleeting second.
Now to talk has become forbidden.
I meant no harm. I really didn't!
So not wanting to harm you, I will stay away.
Not seeing; Not talking; will hurt all day.
But in time, the hurt will heal and go away.
I will remember you in my mind, Lovingly still.
And dare a reader of minds, at his very own will.
To bare my thoughts that linger there still.

"Lee! Whatever possessed you to get involved with another woman?"

"I don't know. Was it forbidden fruit? Was it just an early sign of my masochistic tendencies? I did feel a great fondness for her. I can't say love. But she made me feel special; I felt she loved me. When I was with her, I was a man.

"My boss threatened to fire me if I had anything else to do with her. So, I dropped her, too. But that didn't stop my trouble with women. The woman who was working in the boys and men's department when I started had personality differences with my floor girl. Since I couldn't wave a magic wand and make everybody happy, she quit. Her replacement was lovely transplanted southern girl, Billie Totton. We became friendly and occasionally would meet for drinks behind everyone's back. This was the first person I worked with who I told I was 'gay'. It didn't matter one whit to her. 'That's your business, and what you tell your wife is your business,' she'd say.

"We had a nice friendship. Everything settled down again after Betty quit. Did I forget to mention that? Anyway, Billie and I went out on a Saturday night staying out somewhat late. My wife had learned not to say anything to me so I was cool.

"The next morning Billie's husband called complaining I was seducing his wife. I quickly told Rose of the previous evening escapades. The next thing I knew there was a hammering on the door. Looking through the curtains, I gasped, It's Billie and her husband.

"Rose said, 'Let me handle this.'

"Billie had not told her husband she was with me. I was visiting Billie one day when he came home from work. Billie told me he assumed from then on that we were having an affair. I had shared that with Rose and told her that Billie thought he was the one having an affair with a co-worker. Rose opened the door, 'Good morning.'

"'I came to see your husband; he was with my wife last night.'

"'Well, I don't know where your wife was last night, but my husband was with me all last night. Take your problems home and look to yourself.' And then she slammed the door in his face.

"I could not believe she stood up for me like that. However, that did not stop Mr. Totton from going into the store and telling the big boss during his coffee break, 'I am taking my wife away from this store and that whoremonger she works for.' Within days, he packed up his family, backed up a truck to the front door, emptied the house and moved to Northern Pennsylvania. After the boss cleaned up the coffee, he spilt because of the husband barging into his office, he told the office manager to summon me to his office.

"'What is your problem?' he asked. 'Hot nuts? Trying to ruin my store? I guess we should be glad you are picking on the older women and not getting the young girls. You had better clean up your act. One more situation like this and it is out the door for you. No questions asked. Do you understand me?'

"Just think if it happened now, I could say I was inspired by some politician's behavior. You know, Emily, there really is some humor in that somewhere. I never thought I would have someone tell me to quit chasing girls!"

CHAPTER TWENTY-SEVEN

THAT BROUGHT FRATERNIZING WITH MY female staff to a screeching halt.

Tim from the stockroom and I started spending more time together, each needing a co-worker to complain to. He was unhappy with his future with the company and, well, you know why I was unhappy. He would come over for meals and television, and in turn, he would have his mother invite us for dinner. He would goad me to tell his mother her lasagna was stringy. I never understood why that was supposed to border on a complaint/insult regarding an Italian woman's lasagna.

He decided to quit the store and started working for a private investigator. I thought that was quite a leap to go from stockroom clerk to private "I" but that is what he did. He would ask me to go along with him on my nights off. He was encouraging me to quit the five and dime and join his company. Observing him, I found he would go visit people who were involved with an accident and try to get them to tell him what happened. Depending which side, he was working for, their insurer or the other person's insurer, his job was to get them to commit to a statement he would help them say; write it down and have them sign the document.

I felt he was being deceitful; he would fast talk people in to saying what his employer wanted, inflammatory descriptions or damning actions against themselves. He would write their statements up slanted for his employer's best interest. Convince them to sign an affidavit that could be used against them in court. I was there to witness their signature. I didn't agree with him tricking people to hurt their own case; I didn't want to be involved.

In our travels, we would pass the old haunts I used to frequent. Instead of spending my nights off with him I started going back to those haunts for a more comfortable shoulder to ... hmm... on.

He started to invite me over by myself and when I got there, he would have another "buddy" visiting. He would bring out pot and booze and encourage smoking and drinking. I never smoked anything so the pot was wasted on me. He was cheap, he only served beer! Beer would never pass my lips. I had always been very particular what touched my lips.

I felt uncomfortable not knowing his friends and questioned his motivation to introduce us. He invited me over several times after that night but I stopped going. I had no interest in pot and felt there was an underlying reason for his invitations. He kept dropping in at our house even though I was not visiting him. One night he asked Rose, "Do you know where your husband goes when he goes out at night by himself?"

"That is my husband's business," Rose curtly told him.

I retorted, "Why would you care where I go? You jealous I didn't want to hang out with you and your pot smoking friend?"

Even though we did not get along as well after that, he still hung around long enough to meet my oldest sister-in-law, and damn if they didn't get married. After the wedding, I met his mother in the grocery store. From the little she said I knew she was not happy with her son's choice of a bride. She wanted a pure Italian bride with a better pedigree for her precious boy.

"Emily, listen - the Chief is reciting again."

"The old man was saying to his doctor, you know, Doc, *when I was young it was hard as a rock! As I got older, I could bend it a little, now I can bend it a lot. Does that mean I'm getting stronger?*" The Chief was entertaining his company as they wheeled him down to the day room.

"I am so glad the Chief is getting more company lately. He truly enjoys himself." Emily told called out to the chief's wife as they passed. Rewarded with only a sour look Emily turned to Lee.

"Tell me - didn't things between you and your wife look like they would improve?"

"In what way?"

"As husband and wife?"

"Not intimately. We became good friends. She really did not seem to mind the lack of, you know... I convinced her to get a job. The five and dime had a store in South Philly and she worked there. She moved up the ladder from sales girl, floor girl, office girl, office manager to where they asked her to be a traveling training director."

"If you were good friends, what happened? Where is she now?"

"The last I heard she was living in Norristown and had a boyfriend named Fred Brown. As to what happened ... She went back home to visit her family one weekend and I decided to go out in drag. I do not know exactly why... I just wanted to see what I would look like dressed as a woman. Other guys did it and I wanted to feel what it was like to experience cross-dressing in public.

"A friend told me Timmy Schaeffer and his drag show were playing at a bar that weekend. Gay guys in drag are always welcome to come and sit in the audience. I went through her closet and found a long gown she had worn as a matron of honor for a girlfriend's wedding. It had a dark burgundy, long sleeve, plain scoop neckline top and a straight pink crepe skirt. I could even wear her shoes she had to go with the dress. I wore my hair long and straight in those days so I just washed it, shook it and put some of her makeup on. I thought I would be the belle of the ball.

"I walked to my car proud as a peacock and drove up to the northeast. I did not even stop to think the neighbors might see me and say something to her. It was a small bar up off the Sears circle on Adams Street. My peacock feathers began to shed as soon as I got out of my car and started walking. As I walked, I thought I must have lost my mind. But! I knew, once I got inside the bar, everything would be all right. I opened the door to a void of darkness and smoke. Stepping inside the doorway, to let my eyes become accustomed to the low light, the voices I had heard as I opened the door had slowed to a stop. My only thought was to become less conspicuous by finding a seat and blending in. I waltzed myself to a bar stool and slid up on to the seat. I had to grip the bar tightly because my heels were slippery on what seemed a very wet floor (it smelled of urine). The dress was so silky I almost slid off the other side of the stool.

"Gathering my composure, and glad I did not land on the floor, I realized everyone was looking at me. Elbows were poised on the edge of the bar holding wafting cigarettes as people looked through the smoky haze at me. Hands that had been lifting a beer bottle stopped mid-movement as if frozen in time. Lips that have been poised to wrap around a bottle now echoed, 'What the hell?'

"A bartender who had been lying across the bar chatting up a female patron broke his pose to saunter over to me. Looking me up and down he announced, 'We don't what your kind in here. Get the hell out.'

"Well, I can tell you Cinderella had gone to the wrong ball that night. My carriage had gone to the wrong castle. I was fortunate enough to slink out of the bar with only a deluge of slurs and catcalls thrown at my back. I promised myself I would never to do that again!

"Not five minutes after my wife returned from her weekend away, she hollered down the stairs at me, 'You were wearing my clothes? What were you doing?' I denied it, but she of course knew I was lying. However, nothing else was ever said.

"On one of my forays I met a young man named Eddie Peeples. He lived in Upper Darby and worked at the local Food Fair. By now, I was doing the grocery shopping by myself. As I was going through his checkout, he would flirt with me and me with him. I did not realize one of my former associates worked there in the front office. We had arranged a date while we talked and I drove out that night to pick him up. When I arrived at his apartment, he did not answer the door so I went in town to the bar where we met. When I got there, he was already sitting at the bar nursing a drink. He acted rather coy and distant when I sat down beside him and said, 'Hi. I thought I was to pick you up at your apartment.'

"I squeezed his leg and he made a big deal of standing up and moving his stool away from me. He turned to me and said, "You know when I closed out my drawer and took it to the office; Millie said she saw us talking and asked, 'How do you know him?'

"'I told her you were just a friend I met out in the bars. And I added... he is such a nice man! You know what she said? His wife is nice, too! I told her, 'You must be mistaken - he lives with his sister.'

"She said, 'No! I know him and the woman he lives with is his wife!'"

"Emily, I felt awful! I could tell he was really hurt. I liked him a lot. We had one short brief meeting and I was looking forward to being with him more. I tried to explain; I did not want to tell people I met in the bar I was married, because no one wants to get involved with someone who already is in a relationship, let alone married to a woman! You were considered a pariah. Well, that nipped that affair in the bud."

"Different times when we were talking Rose would ask me about the bars. 'What are the guys like? What are the bars like? What goes on in those kinds of bars? Can I go along sometime?' She told me she wanted to go out to the bars I went to. By now, we were sleeping in separate bedrooms and she told me I could bring my boyfriends, home if I wanted. She offered to make breakfast for everyone in the morning! Therefore, I started taking her out to the bars with me.

"She was a hit! We were of the same size. I say that only because she was not a small girl who looked like she needed protected. She looked like she could take care of herself. She did not need a knight in shining armor to guard her. She wore tailored clothes, penny loafers. She just fit right in. I outright introduced her as my wife. Everyone loved her. She was attractive, not pretty in a girly overly feminine way and not demure in her mannerisms or speech. She had a beautiful smile; she was always making everyone feel at ease, and had a laugh on her lips. She would even drag a cute guy across the bar to introduce them to someone they were too shy to walk up to and say, 'Hello!' She was not gay. She seemed to truly enjoy being out with me and loved everyone she met.

"Our going out together ended one night when I left her in the front bar of a club and she was necking with another guy in the back bar. She sent a 'friend' back to look for me, he opened the door and shouted my name out followed by, "Your wife wants you out front. She needs some more money for drinks!" My lovely Rose had turned into an albatross around my neck.

When I was ready to go out again, I left Rose at home and went to a new club, Maxine's. It had a reputation for being a "wrinkle" bar (gathering place for older men). Besides attracting older men, it was also a piano bar. Upon opening the door on my first visit a loud baritone voice kissed my ear;

> *"Just a gigolo, everywhere I go, people know the game*
> *I'm playing.*
> *Paid for every dance, selling each romance,*
> *every night some heart betraying.*
> *There will come a day, youth will fade away.*
> *Then what will they say about me?*
> *When the end comes I know, they'll say just*
> *a 'Gigolo' and life goes on without me!"*

I made it my business to meet the owner of that wonderful voice. His name was Henie Sachs. Within five minutes of shaking his hand he told me, "I am drunk, I am usually drunk. I am a drunk! I look masculine, you may think I am masculine in bed, I am not. I only roll over. When I am not on my stomach, the only other thing I do is ... fellatio. I perform fellatio. I do not receive. I am so inebriated my 'bad boy' does not work. I get myself off in the mornings before I go to work. If that interests you, we should be leaving. Are you interested? Even drunk I can roll over and entertain you. And I do my best organ playing drunk!"

I did drive him home and liked everything I found out that night. I became a regular visitor to Mr. Sachs apartment and Maxine's. The lifestyle I was pursuing back in the late sixties, early seventies -before the advent of AIDS - was exciting. Yes, there were sexually transmitted diseases! Between penicillin and drugstore remedies for crabs and lice, you were home free. People looked out for you back then. Bartenders would tell you if someone who was hitting on you was bad news.

At Maxine's there was a hat-check lady known to all as "Mary the Hat." When I first started going there if I was not with Henie, I would look to Mary for advice. She could be depended upon for a recommendation. If she personally did not know the individual in question, she would ask around until she found someone who did. If she did not know the person and could not find anything out about the person, you did not go home with them.

One person I asked her about was a doctor. "Oh, honey. Yes, he is more than all right. Lovely person, rich doctor, lives on Washington Square. You would do well catching that fish!"

Right after I met him, he invited me to a party at his house. When I turned the corner onto his block, the street was full of parked cars. Literally, sidewalk to sidewalk, cars parked and blocking the street! Right in front of the doctor's door was the biggest Rolls Royce I had ever seen. There were flags on each bumper of the car and a liveried chauffeur standing at attention beside the driver's side of the car. Another man in a similar uniform stood beside the Doctor's front door as if he was a guard at Buckingham Palace. The owner of the fabulous car, and retainer of the liveried men, was a real-life English "Baroness" attending the party.

Doctor Ben tried his best to sophisticate me. He introduced me to Philadelphia's gay society. Every weekend we met one couple or another to attend the theater, such as the Forrest, the Locust, or the Academy of Music. I was young and a toy for him. He showed me off in lovely restaurants like Le Bec Fin, Bookbinders, the Three Threes, and The Pub Tiki. The relationship started to wilt when he ordered me an antipasto. I looked at it; had no idea when it was, I wanted meat and potatoes. I think he really wanted someone older with the same kind of wealth he enjoyed. I did meet many other great people through him and had a chance to attend Henry David's fabled out-of-this-world Halloween balls. We remained friends but drifted apart - maybe I was not comfortable with his hoity-toity crowd. I do not know. I knew I wanted to swim in those waters and Rose was an unwanted sinker on my line.

Desire for the chance to have a relationship with another man demanded I get Rose out of my life. Making the decision to change one aspect of life led me to decide to change jobs also. I wanted a brand-new start. I had met many guys who worked and lived in center city Philly and decided I wanted to be part of that scene. I interviewed with the Gimbel's Department store at Eighth and Market streets. In 1970, Strawbridge and Clothier and Lits Brothers were on the opposite two corners. Wannamaker's was on Market Street at 13th. The guys always joked, if you took all the queens who worked in those stores away the stores would have to be self-service.

I was lucky enough to be hired on my first interview, although not for the center city location. They gave me a job as assistant manager of the men's department in King of Prussia, the pearl in the Gimbel necklace chain of stores. I went home, called Mrs. Paggano my home office trainer, and told her I was quitting. She knew from her last visit at the store I was not happy with my store manager, she asked me not to make any decisions until she could come to Philly and talk with me. She suggested I consider transferring to Pittsburgh, she promised me a nice store location there. I told her my mind was made up, and I accepted employment with Gimbel's.

No sooner did I start working at Gimbel's than Rose complained she wanted to change jobs. Without discussion, she had interviewed with the alterations department at Gimbel's where I was just hired. She was hired as a seamstress and for a while we drove back and forth together. This was getting me nowhere fast on being able to develop a new relationship. I was ready to tell her either I was moving out or she would have to move out but fate intervened again.

She had been spending more time on the phone with her parents and before I knew how it happened, her youngest sister Vivian and husband Gary moved in with us "for a while to get re-established." I never understood why or how this was best achieved by their living with us. They both found jobs at fast food restaurants although

Vivian worked longer hours than Gary did. I did not mind having them around as I did her other sister and family. Not having children might have helped.

I was going out at the time and had started to exercise to improve my body. I would lie on the floor in the hall at the top of the stairs doing: stretching exercises, sit-ups. And that exercise where you lay on the floor, push back on your shoulders, hold your back end off the floor, lifting your feet in the air peddling like riding a bicycle. I exercised in my shorts. You only saw me if you walked up the stairs while I was exercising and looked. I did not think I was inappropriate or flaunting but I got catcalls from all of them.

I was going out one night when Gary asked, "Can I ride down town with you?" Rose told him where I liked to go and he said, "Looking in the phone book I found a pool hall close by where I would like to shoot some pool." I dropped him off a block from where I was going and purposely parked my car farther away than usual not wanting to lead him to where I was. Unbeknownst to me my helpful wife told him the name of where I liked to go. No sooner did I have a drink in my hand when he came in and plopped down beside me.

"Did you really think I wanted to shoot billiards? I want to play pool with your cue stick. I guess I will have to settle for pocket pool until I get you alone and get that pool stick of yours out in the open. Do you know how I am going to 'chalk' the tip?"

"Where is this coming from?" I questioned.

"Who are you kidding? Exercising in your skimpy briefs; you had to know how you were affecting me. I almost jumped you in front of the girls." Sitting sideways on his chair he had one leg propped on the back of my chair and his other long leg stretched out in front me. He was leaning close, breathing on my neck, flicking his wet tongue lightly inside my ear, one hand across the back of my chair and the other working its way into my pants pocket.

"And you were going to spare me the details," Emily exclaimed. "Hard to believe both of your wife's sisters ended up with likeminded husbands."

"I'm not talking dirty; I am just explaining how people reacted to me. Gary of course blamed me for leading him on. I hardly found myself that erotic! Enough was enough. Even though he was attractive, not my wife's brother-in-law. I took him home and told Rose and Vivian what happened.

They left within days, and I was right back to square one, move Rose out. Rose didn't want to split up. "I married you for better or worse. I meant to keep my vows when I married you!" Not proud of it, I had dishonored my vows and felt the right thing to do for both of us was to live apart.

It was all about what I wanted.

Since she did not have a car, it made more sense for her to move closer to her job. We found her a nice little apartment in Norristown where she could get a bus to work. We divided the furniture and bought her some things she needed to get started being on her own. I paid five months' rent for her, hugged and kissed her good-bye and never looked back.

She called a couple of times after we first split up, wanting to get together to do dinner or the movies. To be honest I did tell her during the separation process we would get together, go out, do the dinner and movie thing, but it never happened. I was all for me! Saying whatever I had to say to get what I wanted.

Working together at the same store, we would run into each other and people talked. The situation became too emotional for her and she quit and became the office manager for J.C. Penney's auto center. That is where I took my car to be worked on and even though I treated her shabbily, she always made sure I got my car worked on quickly and economically. If I did not have the money for the needed repairs, she would arrange that I could pay later. She was a good person. To this day, I still say I did her a favor because she was too good to have to be shackled to the likes of me, a gay man who did not appreciate her as a beautiful straight woman. She deserved to have the chance to find someone who would want, appreciate and adore her for exactly how good a woman she was.

I did the right thing. I was happy, calmer. On my own I began developing friendships with new people who were not just "hook-ups." I was promoted to an "area manager" in Gimbel's and became close friends with the other managers on the floor.

Shirl Conway came into the framing department with a picture she painted to be framed. She was a big star on a show called "The Nurses." We were all star struck. Of course, we were also star struck when singer Leslie Uggams and soap star Eileen Fulton visited the store.

I saw this man come off the escalator one day and his manner of dress was so different I knew he had to be somebody! He disappeared back toward the general offices and never reappeared so I went looking to see where he was. I found he had gone into the beauty salon. I should have guessed by his appearance; he was a hairdresser. Some stereotypes run true. His appearance and mannerisms announced everything, leaving nothing to the imagination. Some people flaunt things, shove it in your face. In the beginning, he was like that. Over the top, the hell with convention; arm the torpedoes.

Because my department was right in front of the escalators, I often saw him coming and going. I would watch fascinated by his outrageous attire and affectations. He wore bleached blonde hair, a wild handle bar mustache and carried a "man's" purse. One day while I was dressing a mannequin, I was particularly taken by his colorful ways. That was until I realized he was walking towards me. I was half-afraid people would associate me with his kind and was embarrassed knowing people would see me talk to him. I already knew who he was when he stopped in front of me, holding out his limp hand. He introduced himself, in a silky voice that would do his alter ego "Ida Lupino" justice.

"I'm Ronald Derby, the salon manager. Eva in credit told me you live in the city. I told her I have been having trouble getting the bus back and forth. She suggested I ask you, if I could ride with you."

Silently I thought, "I'll get you Eva!" Being a nice person, I said yes and told him my schedule and where we would meet, outside after work. Looking back on the first night I took him home I acted like he had a disease I might catch. He was the first older person I met who was so out and proud. He presented himself like everyone else was abnormal! This wasn't Rittenhouse square, teenagers and young adults. This was the family oriented conservative, straight mainline. He was pushing the envelope, breaking barriers. There were other gay hairdressers in the salon but you would never know it by their appearance or presentation of themselves.

After about a week I loosened up and he invited me in for dinner and to meet his other half. They lived in a beautiful basement apartment in a three-story brownstone off the Art Museum circle on Green Street. The doorway was very unique; the door was hidden in the woodwork of the staircase. It was their little world. It was decorated beautifully, slightly exotic but homey at the same time. It was the first time I saw cloth billowing in soft folds float from the sidewalls up to the center of the ceiling, creating a tent effect.

His other half, Tom, was an interior design student who experimented at home. He wanted to have one wall mirrored but could not afford it. He pasted Reynolds wrap on the wall and painted a faux frame around it. They had a very small but highly functional kitchen where Ron prepared meals. There were times he would say, "I'd invite you to stay for dinner, we are having company, but I know you wouldn't like the food I'm serving." They were having steak tartar, raw ground beef. "No, thanks - another time."

Gradually we became very good friends. He relaxed his dress style at work and we often visited back and forth. People who would not normally talk to his kind would talk to him when they met him in my department. The old adage proved true; you cannot judge a book by its cover. I do not know if anyone assumed, we were more than friends; some would ask, "Does he ever ...get ... You know... friendly with you?" I could honestly tell them no.

In the summertime, if the expressway was backed up, we would use the river drives to return to the city in the evening. People, especially young men, would jog along these drives. He was ten years older than I, and he'd previously lived in Manhattan and Washington, D.C.; he had obtained an advanced degree in "gay society." One night we were returning on the East River Drive when he asked, "Do you know how you can meet these handsome men with the bouncing balls?"

"What?" an incredulous Emily queried.

I know. That was my reaction also. I shook my head and told him, "You are too much!"

"Nonsense! All you do is look in all your mirrors, side and back, know how the traffic is! When there are no cars around, turn off the engine." Which at that point that is exactly what he did; He reached over and turned off my ignition, saying, "Mother's going to show you how it's done. Don't worry - I've already checked the mirrors. There are no cars coming. Now let your car drift slowly to a stop."

As the car slowed, he said, "Now use the brakes and stop the car!" I did what he said. He continued, "Get out; open your engine hood." I was sitting looking at him. It was a slow traffic time. The crowd, of mostly young, men in the park were looking at us sit in the car. "People will assume you are having car trouble. Get out... open the hood.... Jiggle the wires. Find an attractive naked body and ask for help. They never know how. After you find out their name and get a phone number, you act as if you are jiggling a wire. Get back in, start it up, tell him you'll call him and wave good-by."

I was dumbfounded. I could not believe he would do something like that. "Not on your life," I laughed. "Be outrageous on your time not mine." I turned the tables on him, becoming the outrageous one, when I left him in front of his house saying," I'm going to see a guy about being in a drag show."

I read in the Philadelphia Gay News that a man was trying to get a group together to start a female impersonation show. It interested me so I called and made plans to meet him at his apartment that night. He lived in a bad part of North Philly and I was not even sure I wanted to leave my car alone on the street for the time I would be in his apartment.

The building was dreadful, his apartment terrible and he had no plans. He just had the desire and was hoping to find people who'd done it before and would have the necessary sound, recording equipment, wigs and costumes. The next day I talked to Ron about it and he told me how he had done drag in Washington at the Club 55 and participated in the Gay Academy Awards. The man I met really had nothing going for him and Ron said, "Let me talk to Tom before you decide to hitch yourself to this guy." I had made plans to meet with him and the other guys a week later. "Miss Lupino" asked me to take her along. She did herself proud and took command of the room when she entered it. By the next day, he and Tom had a plan of action on starting a group, even succeeded stealing two of the guys from the other group he met the previous evening.

On our first get together in their apartment, they announced the group would be called "Charades." A friend of Tom's was introduced as our choreographer. "You must have an opening number with dancing!" Within minutes chairs were pulled out and the former Miss Lupino (now "Miss Star") and the two new guys were being walked through the "Charades" version of 'Big Spender' from Cabaret. "Oh, Lee! We have to have someone for a second number after we open; that's why you aren't in the opening."

Uh, huh......I don't want to seem like sour grapes but the other two guys had no experience either. They were not attractive drags. Mike was built like a linebacker and did Diana Ross with white face. His dress was gorgeous and the red hair was styled like Miss Ross, but that was it! No! He did snap his fingers and sway like she did

The other guy, Teddy, was a sweet boy but a diminutive munchkin. He was knock-kneed, pigeon toed and his claim to fame was his Barbara Streisand impression. He could cross his eyes! Can we talk? Between these two, of course, Miss Thing was the best looking! I think there is a picture of us in the testament.

"This picture of people around a table?" she asked.

No, not that one. Let me see them a minute. Here we are: this is Tom, Ron and myself; this one of us on stage has everyone. The group around the table has my wife in it; the woman in back with long brown hair.

"You certainly put a lot of effort into changing your appearance.

How did she come to be at the cabaret with you after you moved her out? I thought you wanted her out of your life?"

"I told you we remained friends, mostly due to her good graces."

Tom and Ron had us going out to watch the current drag show in town and we were at the Forest Theatrical Cocktail Lounge on a particular Saturday night. They were nosing around the back talking to the Fabulous Fakes who were appearing there at the time. When they came back around the bar Ron whispered, "They're getting ready to leave town. They are putting costumes and wigs away in suitcases as they are done with it, rather than leave it out to use next Wednesday. You kids go on to the 'Roulette.' We're staying here to see what happens."

He was right. The next morning at 7:30 AM, my phone rang. "Wake up, crazy person. The Fakes left after last night's show. They did not tell Joe until they were paid and had their stuff out that they would not be performing there next week. They were off to Atlantic City! I stayed late and as soon as they left, I called Joe over and told him we had a show and we could be ready by Wednesday night."

I told Ron **he** was the crazy person. We did not have all the acts together, let alone costumes. "Well honey, we have to get ready. Tom and I are calling off sick until Thursday and devoting our time to this." It did not take much to convince me to do the same. We were planning on what to sew first, second, etc., when Ron said, "If we had another sewing machine Tom and I could both sew."

I had a stroke of genius and said, "Maybe we could borrow Rose's!" I called Rose and rather than lend us her sewing machine she came with the sewing machine. They talked to Joe and it was agreed we could open a day later on Thursday. Like us, she sewed until Thursday before the show getting everything ready. She helped backstage doing whatever she could do to help. That is why she is in that group picture taken at the bar.

We did a show Thursday and Friday night and two shows Saturday night. I had the only car so Ron would drive my car home early and Tom would come back to get me after I was done working and take me right to the club. Two weeks later as we were going up the expressway to work Tom's sultry, silky Ida Lupino voice (with his southern accent more pronounced than usual) surprised me by announcing, "Honey, we won't have to borrow your car tonight. We bought ourselves a little car over the weekend."

For some reason my porcupine quills went up suspecting there was more to the story that I hadn't heard yet. That afternoon Ron came back to my department and asked, "When are you going to lunch? I thought we could have a little chat."

Never did he do lunch with anyone! When he was in the store, he never left the beauty salon saying, "You have to watch them like a hawk they are always giving services away to their friends!" I was taking a late lunch that day, usually his busy time, but we walked out into the mall and found a place to sit down and "chat."

"I find it hard to tell you this," he lamented, "Joe told me I have to put you out of the show. He thinks you are too masculine to make a good drag.

"Oh," I said, "A white Diana Ross built like a linebacker and a cross eyed midget Barbara Streisand is okay! However, me with my great costumes and wigs, I have to go? What are you going to do? I ask you?"

In the next breath he says, "I collected your things from the club and Tom's bringing them with him when he picks me up tonight. We can put them in your car for you and save coming to the club."

I was out of sorts for a while but really did not mind very much. It was a lot of work and made for a very tight schedule. The little bit of money we were paid was always spent on more stuff for the show. It was not as if I was getting rich doing drag. We got past it. It was not too many months before they announced they were going to Atlantic City to perform. By this time, they had replaced the other two with prettier drags who were very good and added a couple more.

When I drove to Atlantic City to see their show, I was quite surprised. The bar was rundown and hard to find on a back street. Not big time like New York Avenue was back then for gay bars. They were not playing to a gay crowd. It was at best mixed and lowbrow. Not sophisticated enough to accept a drag show.

It was in the hottest part of summer and their dressing room was in the attic, no air conditioning; anywhere. A drag with all that heavy makeup needs air. They had to walk up and down an outside wooden stair to get back and forth from their dressing room to a tiny make-shift stage. It was a hastily built platform suspended in front of what had been a window now turned into a rear stage door. They lasted two weeks and that was the end of the Charades. The guys in the show scattered. Casey Cook, one of the new kids, did continue in the business establishing a drag show still playing in Las Vegas. He hit the big time even appearing on a major afternoon talk show. That gave him exposure and he landed a small, but pivotal role, in a major motion picture. To this day, the old boy is still dressing as a female and drawing crowds.

Ronald continued to enjoy his renewed interest in cross dressing. He decided to start hormones and began to entertain men behind his lover's back. He found several advertisements in the Philadelphia gay newspaper, more often than not married men who wanted to meet and have relations with transsexual men. Many times, when his lover had the car, I would transport him here or there. At first, he would go to their place and have them send him home by cab. The longer he did it the bolder he got and began to receive them at his apartment.

I was very intrigued by it all. He had some dates that would go all out and take him to lunch in swanky restaurants. Many did not even want sexual favors just his company. Some would want to watch from behind a partially closed door as he changed clothes. Others would want to undress him down to his essentials and just apply lotion to his body. He received cash and jewelry from his admirers; always reminding them he had a lover who would beat the hell out of anyone he found fooling around with him.

CHAPTER TWENTY-EIGHT

My memory is filled with glorious moments of sweet dates, the joy of dressing for fine dining, sing along, around the piano at Maxine's, closing the bars at 2 AM, closing the afterhours clubs and partying until 4am, driving to Atlantic City to party until dawn - I was living the life! Or so I thought.

"Now, now don't get upset," Emily cooed.

"I was so stupid!" Fighting a constricting throat, trying not to not to get choked up Lee continues, "I had the best of everything. I was welcomed in every bar and club. My youth and looks opened the doors of all the private clubs in Philly. They told me I was fun, a good conversationalist and listener; and for whatever other reason people found *me* attractive."

I met a scion of one of the best Philadelphia families, with ties to "tinsel" and "tiaras," in one of those clubs. After dinner and bar hopping in Philly, he whisked us to the seashore for more partying. We partied up and down New York Avenue: Ceils' Palace, the Saratoga, anyplace still open and serving. He wanted to be the first to show me a sunrise emerging off the ocean crest as it rose up in to the sky. I was like a kid wanting to take some of the beauty and joy of the moment home to my mother. I stood, leaning on the boardwalk railing, staring hard and long at the sun creeping up in the horizon.

I wanted to remember every color changing nuance to be able to share with her. She had been sick for such a long time. I had to absorb the sunrise like a sponge absorbs water. I wanted to run home and wring this beautiful sunrise out for her to enjoy. I felt she had been cheated out of the joy and fun of life. Even then, before my greatest adventures, I felt undeserving. Who was I to have so much fun, freedom, gaiety?

She had always wanted to travel. The only places she saw were all the different hospitals she was a patient in. She never got any enjoyment out of her life. She never got to see the sights or experience the wonders and enjoyments a large city has to offer. I planned in advance, asking Rose if she would spend the weekend and join us. I thought it would make my mother happy to see Rose and me together and I bought tickets to see Howard Keel in "Man of La Mancha."

My father did allow my mother to come to Philly for a long weekend. He didn't like big cities or city people. He felt "city" women painted their faces and dressed like whores. He didn't feel "city" men were "real" men. Real men were like him; they went hunting, dressed in work clothes, they didn't wear fancy expensive suits as if they were women. Men wore tie shoes not fancy slip-ons. A nice white T-shirt and clean jeans could take him anywhere.

Although my mother was a "country" woman I was so proud of how nice she looked that evening. She brought along a lilac colored, linen shirt dress with dainty white cuffs and collar. The dress was fitted through the bodice and flared out at the waist. She only wore a size 4B shoe and had shoes and an evening bag dyed to match the dress. She wore a dainty amethyst earrings and bracelet set. Rose did her hair into a French twist and applied just a smudge of lilac eye shadow and rouge. My mother looked lovely. Rose treated her like a queen. I'll always remember how radiant she looked, walking into the theatre that night.

She was so happy. After the show we had a late supper at Palumbo's nightclub. She reminded me of a naughty child saying, "Your father wouldn't be happy knowing I was out this late, in a bar; even though it is a restaurant!" I don't know if I ever saw her that happy, before or after that night. No, I know I did not.

My father had brought her down and dropped her off and I was to drive her home. Ron and I had just become friends, and somehow it worked out that he and his lover would ride along when I took my mother home. Out of the blue as we were getting in the car to go pick up my friends, my mother asked, "Is that why you and Rose didn't work out?"

"I beg your pardon?"

"You and Rose not getting along... was it because you like men?"

"Yes, but somehow I thought you caught on to that ages ago."

"I didn't want to accept it. You and Rose seem to get along so well. She treats you just like she should, as your wife. She treated you so nice! If I didn't know you were separated, I would think you are happily married. It's a shame it couldn't have worked out for both your sakes."

My mother seemed fine but when we got back to Lewistown, she found a moment to take me aside.

"Lee, I like your friends. They are very nice to me, but I don't want them here when your father gets home. You get along well, they like you, you like them. But your father would be very upset just seeing their manner of dress and affectations, let alone the earrings and handbags, the hand movements and if they opened their mouths... I don't know. I am just afraid your father may say something terrible and I don't want you upset or your friends' feelings hurt. Here is some money - take them back home and stop somewhere and buy them a nice meal and explain how your father is."

Knowing she was right; I told the guys we were leaving and we went home. I remember my father saying in later life, "Your mother told me she told you to leave before I got home, when you brought her back from Philly. She didn't want me to see your friends. She said she was afraid I would have been rude. I was talking to Bob at the firehouse and told him how she chased you and your friends away for fear of my actions. Bob told me, in the city it doesn't matter whether you are gay or straight. It is equivalent to whether you are a Democrat or Republican. It is no big deal."

"Emily, you are looking tired and I feel worn out and can hardly keep my eyes open."

"Well then I'll let you rest and take my leave until the morning."

Although he was sleepy, he was restless. It was hard for him to find the right position to sleep in, when he did, he fell asleep quickly. His illness did not make him suffer. Nor did it rob him of his extensive memory tapes of life gone by which seemed to play back like a movie as he slept.

He had enjoyed all the social life the big city had to offer. The Christmas after he moved his wife to Norristown, he ended an evening on the town, with a visit to his favorite after-hours club, the Penrose. As usual, on a Saturday night, the bars had been full. Remaining fairly sober, not having his usual foggy headed buzz, he enjoyed the club's loud music and festive Christmas decorations.

He watched the gyrating dancers and observed the eye games play out around the bar. As people tried to make last minute hook-ups, he thought a guy across the bar was watching him. Glancing again in that direction, the man raised his beer bottle in a salute. Lee in turn raised his glass and sent a salute back. Immediately the man was up on his feet and came around the bar asking, "Hey buddy, is anyone sitting here?"

Quick to take someone's measure he saw the exaggerated swagger and almost laughed at the man's attempt to lower his voice to a very masculine range. Using his deepest basso forte, he replied, "Not until you put your ass down, sailor."

Quizzing Lee's face for a spark of interest, the guy sat down and started small talk, introducing himself as "Tim." Using his normal speaking voice Lee asked, "Is your voice really that low? Or are you doing an impression, looking for an ovation?"

The guy's head snapped around and in a more normal voice questioned, "What do you mean?"

Laughing Lee introduced himself explaining how he heard the inflection and tone the guy used when he came over. "You seem more relaxed and your voice sounds normal rather than affected." They spent the rest of the evening together talking and exchanging stories with each other like friends of long acquaintance. The young man was home visiting relatives in northeast Philly.

"Boy, my Aunt is going to be screaming at me for being out so late with her car." His parents died early in life and he was raised by his mother's sister Margaret and her brother Ben. Right after high school, he left Philly and joined the army. When he was discharged from the service, he settled in Florida, met a young service woman, becoming engaged. He was returning to Florida on Christmas Eve to get married on New Year's Day. Tonight, he was out "sowing his last wild oats." As the low bar lights turned bright, signifying closing time was approaching, Tim emptied his beer bottle and turned to Lee... "You know dude, you're a nice guy, but we're too much alike; I only top. We want the same thing out of a partner in bed so I'm going to hit the road. It was nice talking to you!"

Lee was furious for being cast off so out of hand. "I don't know you! But I know me! You have no right to assume I am as self-absorbed as apparently you are. I have never met anyone, man or woman that I couldn't take to bed and find something to do that was mutually satisfying! If that is your attitude, then yes, you better leave. I'm going to tell you, if you are that rigid and narrow minded, then you are in for a rude awakening and a lot of missed opportunities. I am going to the men's' room and when I come back, I will expect you to be gone!"

When he returned Tim was still there, "Man, I am sorry, I didn't mean to insult you. I just know how I am. I just like to screw! Guys, girls it doesn't matter. Where do we go from here?"

Having spent time working this number Lee wanted some reward so he said, "Let's go! Where are you parked?"

"In the parking lot across the street."

"That's where I'm parked. I'll drive slow – just follow me." They drove tandem style back to South West Philly. While he was driving home, Lee talked to himself questioning his motivation. Why would he knowingly take someone home who was so one-sided? He normally would not get involved with someone who more or less announced he was only trade, that is, someone who doesn't do anything, who will only let you get him off, usually orally. Not do anything for you leaving you hot and horny. He always felt sorry for guys who were so uptight that they couldn't let themselves experience full pleasure with another man. Now he has this guy on his ass, so to speak, who only likes to screw... anything... whatever!

A man gladly accepts head from a woman. If the lights are off could he tell the lips on his penis were from a man or woman? Lee always said he could tell; because the man would do a better job. By virtue of being a man, with an intimate knowledge of how it works and what makes it feel good, men best how to give another man optimum pleasure.

There are women who enjoy performing oral sex; so why is it so hard to think a man couldn't enjoy doing it to another man? Many men, if not most, giving head get aroused when performing this act for his lover; the same with anal sex. A man can ask his wife to roll over so he can screw her in the ass and she'll do it. He'll not think it strange but something that his wife should do to please him! Some women find pleasure in it, some don't.

A man having a prostate gland behind his anal entrance can derive a great deal of pleasure from anal sex. It's no different from a man using lubrication and entering slowly with a woman. Some men will automatically climax when they are being screwed by another man. The active man massages the other's prostate bringing it to an unforgettable climax. Some men even buy a strap-on for their wives so the woman can screw their behind. Yes, he knew any man could find pleasure in bed with another man, if he allowed it to happen.

Driving home, he was looking forward to exploring Tim's body with his hands and mouth, feeling the hairy skin, muscular arms. Finding that manly part and feeling it pulse and expand under his touch. That's why he was taking him home! He was horny!

Arriving at Lee's, Tim went upstairs to freshen up. After Lee locked up and turned off the downstairs lights, he found an anxious naked Tim in his bed eagerly awaiting him. Quickly doing a pits, tits and ass review in the bathroom he went to his bed wondering what was going to happen. Surprisingly, he was pulled into the warm embrace of a man who didn't seem quite so one-sided.

Tim was an excellent lover as far as he went. Translated that meant he would kiss, touch any part of a man's body but he would not envelope a man's organ with his mouth. He would permit the man to screw him between his legs under his balls, but no anal penetration. He in turn wanted everything out of his partner. Given these parameters there was a lot of area for him to explore and many ways to enjoy Tim's body. Tim was a great make out, terrific French kisser, with roaming fingers in just the right places at just the right times. He enjoyed the bodily contact and closeness after the physical release, kissing, hugging and holding for long periods of time. Definitely not the typical wham, bam, thank you Ma'am kind of guy. He didn't jump out of bed saying, "Got to go. That was great - we'll have to do it again sometime." He enjoyed what happened between them and was just as eager as Lee to savor the moment.

Having gotten to bed around four in the morning neither was rushing to get out of bed. Around one in the afternoon Tim called his Aunt to let her know he was all right since he hadn't made it home. Not knowing his sexuality, she teased him about hooking up with some girl he had met. Promising to be home soon he hung up and they repeated in quicker fashion some of the things they found out they mutually enjoyed during the wee hours of the morning.

Finally leaving around four thirty he promised he would call. Not expecting to hear from Tim again Lee was taken by surprise when Tim called soon after he returned to his Aunt's. He implored Lee to let him come back that night. Lee told him he had plans to meet friends for drinks, but Tim would be welcome to join them when he was available. Tim joined them around nine thirty and within an hour they were once again in bed giving each other goosebumps.

Aware tomorrow was Christmas Eve Lee had had no compunction having a flirtation with Tim because he knew it had no future and accepted that from the start. He hadn't expected it to expand beyond one night. He was unprepared for how hard he fell for Tim. Tim felt the same feelings and didn't want to return to Florida but felt he had to.

That last night together neither slept; the hours were filled with tender kisses and passionate intimate love making. First, fast and furious then slow and measured, making each tingle explode into a hundred fire cracker explosive moment of unbridled pleasure. Tim learned how he enjoyed having his shoulders lightly nibbled and his neck kissed and playfully bitten. He was very careful not to leave a blush of a bruise on

Lee's pale skin. He kissed his back, up one side and down the other, lightly chewing on Lee's love handles. He even nibbled on his inner thighs so close to Lee's manhood that his nose nuzzled against his scrotum at times. When he felt his whole body glowing with small embers of fire Tim slowly entered him from behind. Reaching underneath Lee, he stroked him in unison bringing them both to a mutual toe-curling climax.

Emotions were running high for each of them as Tim dressed to leave. Lee was to be at work by 10 and it was already half past ten. As he got himself ready for work all he could think of was how much he had enjoyed being with Tim. John had been an excellent lover, but he had not felt this emotional connection.

Now that Tom had gone, it was unattainable. By the time he arrived at work, Lee was crying for the love he would never have.

CHAPTER TWENTY-NINE

Using a rear security entrance, Lee was able to enter the back of his section without anyone seeing his tear-stained face. Going to his desk he gathered his name tag and record book to compare how business was doing against last year's figures. Walking out through the boy's department, he greeted the ladies he knew he could depend on to open up for him when he was late. Cleo and Marie were taking care of the customers in the infants and scout department. Harriet was waiting on a mother trying coats on her son.

As he passed thru the department Harriet called over her shoulder, "Tom Cezel is looking for you. I told him I didn't know where you were, that maybe you went to check on a shipment in receiving."

Grateful for the heads-up he continued across the floor looking for Bella, the supervisor of the section next to his. As he spotted her talking with a couple of her salesgirls, she called out to him. "Boy, you are in trouble! Tom Cezel is on the war path." Leaving the sales ladies to start the after-Christmas markdowns, Bella walked towards one of the few men she ever considered a good friend.

Approaching him she saw the emotion building up in his face. She grabbed his arm, "Come back in my stockroom - you look terrible!" As the door closed behind him, he fell into her arms and cried out the story of his broken heart. "Boy, you have it bad! Better compose yourself! I hear Cezel coming. For God's sake, don't tell him the real reason you're late."

Clipping her words off as the stockroom door opened, Tom Cezel stood us if at attention and loudly exclaimed, "How could you be late on Christmas Eve! You know that's one of our biggest days!"

Losing his control, Lee started sobbing. Bella burst out, "His dog died! He fell getting out of bed this morning and landed on the dog. Before he could get the dog to the vet, the dog died. He's blaming himself; he is full of guilt and remorse for killing his dog!"

Dropping his jaw and shaking his head, he listened to Bella and looked at Lee's lack of composure with disbelief. The personnel manager turned on his heel slamming the stockroom door behind him, muttering, "For Christ's sake!"

Last minute exchanges, refunds without sales slips, gift givers looking for particular sizes and colors helped keep him distracted from the heavy dismay in his heart. When he did take a lunch break it was with a supportive, but otherwise chastising Belle!

"What were you thinking? Married? Well he is getting married! Do you have a hole in your head?"

He tried to explain he "never expected" anything but an overnight tryst. He'd had many one-night stands, retaining friendships with quite a few of the guys. He told Bella that the male gender is far more lenient with their conscience than women when it comes to casual sex. Men often want only the physical interaction, and maybe some gratuitous emotional groaning and ahhhing at the time of release. For the most part they not are looking for "strings-attached" sex. They prefer it to be anonymous.

For many men sex is nothing more than turning on a faucet. The water is hot until you have sex with the person, then the water turns cold. When the water turns cold, you turn off the faucet and walk away and don't have sex with him again. Having done it, and having had it done to him, Lee knew many men don't think twice about getting out of bed abruptly. It can happen in minutes, hours or the next morning. All that is left is an echoing trail of the smallest good-bye, "Boy that was great," and maybe not even that much. "Gotta go, gotta get to work early in the morning!"

There were times when he just got up and left without saying anything. He had gone home with a very nice guy, Jim Cline, who lived on Spruce Street in Philly. They had fun; kissing, hugging, teasing each other. During their making out he discovered the guy had lubricated himself. Not one to turn down an invitation he topped him. Waking up hours later, he got dressed and went to the front door to find it locked. He went back into the bedroom and picked up the man's keys off his dresser. Going back to the locked front door, he unlocked the door, left the apartment. Locking the door from the outside he pushed the keys back through the letter slot. He never thought about seeing the guy again. It turned him off that the guy lubricated himself so he would be ready to get laid. Lee thought that he was slutty! Not looking for anything permanent, just freeing himself from Rose a short time ago, the last thing he thought he wanted would be to get tied down.

As Belle sat with him during break trying to raise his morale, he was almost despondent. He knew many think of homosexuals as deviates, perverts, and people unworthy of being part of our society. Just as many have said that all black people should be sent back to Africa, many thought homosexuals should be put in hospitals because they are mentally ill. It is still a debate among thinkers whether people are born homosexual or decide to be homosexual. Either way he prayed to the God he knew for answers. Of course, he prayed for there to be a way for him to be with the object of his broken heart; Tim.

Like the mother who prayed her daughter would find a doctor, lawyer or professor to marry, since the mother knew her daughter was sure to have a have a good husband marrying one of those, he prayed for his chance with Tim, because he knew they would be happy.

People forget God answers prayers in a Godly fashion not in a mortal fashion. The mother found it hard to accept that her daughter could find total happiness with a regular guy, one who works hard and makes a success of himself creating a wonderful future for his family, without him being a lawyer, doctor or professor. Lee never considered it was God's will that he and Tim should not be together. But again, maybe that God knew it wasn't best for Tim to be in his life. He never remembered how he made it through that day until the store closed at six o'clock. Heading upstate to be with his family gave him some comfort. He wanted to feel good. He wanted to feel whole again. He had a sense that all would be well, being home with his family for the holiday.

Unfortunately, he found that once he got there, it was if he was playing a part in a rehearsed play. Sometimes he muffled his lines. Other times his actions were uncoordinated. It was like he really wasn't there in mind, just body. The holiday visit became one big excruciating wave of anxiety after another. He wanted the event to be over so he could leave and be alone with his thoughts. Driving home, after the big meal, gift exchange, good-bye hugs and kisses, he was once more alone with his depression, the kind which is only experienced when your heart is breaking. You see no chance of a future between you and the one you desire. You can't see yourself being happy again! You think dark thoughts, bordering on dreadful consequences. Driving straight home, he wasn't even up to going to the bars to find someone else to sleep with to help him forget Tim. He couldn't let go. He didn't even want to.

His house seemed especially cold and lonely that night. He went from room to room turning on the lights and the television to make noise. He made himself a drink and sat down in front of his Christmas tree to look at the colorful lights. Chance would have it that the movie "White Christmas" was playing on the television. Bing Crosby started to sing *White Christmas* and all the emotion in him welled up. When Bing sang.....*may your days be merry and bright...* he jumped up!

Crying angry, hot tears he attacked his Christmas tree. Like a wrecking machine he tore it to shreds. Pulling off lights, entangled in branches, sending glass ornaments to the floor; Grabbing at the icicles and taking decorations to the floor with them. Just reaching out willy-nilly and destroying something that stood for happiness and good cheer. When he realized what a mess he had made, he fell to his knees landing on the broken glass ornaments. Now feeling pain, and even madder and sadder, he fell backward on to the floor in a sobbing heap.

The telephone rang. Knowing he was too upset to hide the emotion in his voice he didn't answer the phone. He unplugged the tree lights and went to bed. By the time he laid down he was cursing ever having met the bastard. How could he be such a fool, to get so wrapped up in somcone that he let it destroy his Christmas! How did he lose all control and make that mess downstairs with his tree? His soul was rebounding;

His self-survival defense coming back. As he was about to turn off his bedside light his phone rang again, and this time he answered it.

"Hey dude! What's happening?"

Anger! Gladness? He wasn't sure which he felt. "Tim?... I didn't expect to hear from you ever again."

"Man, I can't stop thinking about being with you! I felt awful leaving you. I didn't want to. But I had to come back to Florida."

"Did you call a little while ago?"

"Yeah - I guess you weren't home yet?

"I went home to my parents. I had a terrible time. My mind was distracted over this guy I recently met."

"Oh yeah, tell me about it. My day was the same dude. I got it bad!"

"Where are you Tim?"

"I'm at my apartment, I just left my fiancé. I don't know what to do! I love her, but I don't want to marry her. What can I do?"

"You tell her you are gay! I think that will do it!"

"I am *not* gay; I like men *and* women! I always have!"

"Well there's your answer, go ahead and marry her but I won't be with you again! There are lots of other guys out there, you will find someone."

"You have to understand" Tim begged. "How could I tell her now? That I don't want to marry her? What could I say to my family? How do I explain to them that I'm not getting married?"

"You have to stand on your own two feet and stop this merry go round you are on," Lee explained.

"I would love to say 'good-bye' to this mess and come live with you, but I can't. They expect me to be with girls."

"Hey, that's your problem, if you want to live a lie."

"I don't want them to them think I'm queer."

"If you want to bounce back and forth make sure you tell everyone you sleep with what you're doing."

"Oh sure! I'll just say, by the way I am with you tonight, but I may be with someone of the opposite sex tomorrow. Tonight, is just fun and games."

"Isn't that what you have been doing, just enjoying the fun and games?"

"Until now - I am not enjoying how I am feeling now."

"And what is the difference between before and now?"

"You! You're the difference! Before I met you, all the guys I was with were straight. I got them drunk and before they knew it, they were naked and I was screwing them. None of them were gay! They were just like me, out drinking, got horny, grabbed an ass, and grabbed a crotch. Usually it would start in the bathroom with someone shaking their dick too much. Someone would get a hard on. Someone would remark on the size. Another would say mockingly, 'Oh, I am scared! It is so big! Don't stick that in me!' Just horsing around - but eventually one of the guys would come over and start a conversation. The next thing out of his mouth would be 'I have wondered what it would be like being with another guy.' That was all the opening I needed. Before he knew it, I would have him in bed on his stomach fuckin' the shit out of him. The next morning, they forgot it ever happened. None of them ever took it seriously. No one thought anyone was gay!

"I never was with an actual gay man before. I didn't know it could seem so normal. You are so straight. You aren't a pansy like so many queers. I mean, you know how they are! Limp-wristed, dress girly, talk and act sissified. You are normal-acting; no one would ever pick you out as being queer. Your house is normal, not like some girl's house, frilly and flounced. My relatives would never think you were queer."

"But you have forgotten one thing, Tim! I am queer! We prefer Gay though, thank you! We do not put ourselves down by referring to ourselves using a term straight society uses to dehumanize us. Listen, I have to go. You have too many hang-ups and the word queer rolls off your tongue far too easy. Especially for a man whose nose was brushing my balls just the other night. Good night and good luck!" Ignoring the phone when it quickly rang again, Lee was quick to unplug it from the jack.

The next day, the day after Christmas, was an easier day for him to get through because he could see that Tim was too screwed up. He had lunch with Bella, who was very glad to see her friend back to his usual spirits. The store was busy with the after-Christmas exchanges and post-holiday sales demanding him to focus on his work.

That evening he and Rose met for dinner. Supposedly it was so he could deliver the Christmas gift his mother had sent back for Rose. Exchanging stories of each other's Christmas visit with their respective families, the evening became a story of explanation and a cleansing apology.

He tried to explain to Rose why he felt it was in her best interest when he moved her out to give her a chance at a normal life. He had never told her about going to nursing school and his experiences in Philadelphia. She had not known how his parents reacted to the gay inferences in his youthful past. He confessed he never should have married a woman and explained the pressure he was under when he was transferred to Philadelphia. He apologized for marrying her and asked her to forgive him for involving himself in her life.

Having never heard anything about this part of his life Rose was now able to piece together and accept with more understanding why he behaved toward her as he had when they lived together. Moving from her parents' home straight to marriage handicapped Rose with an immature view of life. That short time on her own enabled her to develop an adult personality and perspective. Having put her toes in the dating pool since they separated also showed her more of what was and wasn't available out in the real world. This maturity allowed her to understand and forgive him for many of his past actions.

He told her about Tim and his plans to marry his fiancé in Florida. They both agreed it was a terrible mistake he should not make, but it wasn't their mistake to correct and they would be unable to stop him. As they left the restaurant that evening, they embraced each other with more warmth then they had felt for each other in several years. He was happy Rose was evolving in a good way and Rose left hoping he might find peace of mind in self-awareness.

Trying to push aside his emotions over Tim, he decided to get back on the merry-go-round that threw him. Driving downtown he went in search of a new thrill ride. Arriving in Center City he headed for his favorite haunt, the Westbury. Roberta Flack's recording of "Killing Me Softly" was playing as he walked through the doors. As he went around the bar to a sit down the words wafting through the air haunted him. They rekindled the memories of passion he had recently shared with Tim. Although there were many attractive invitations being sent him by way of the coy smiles and heavy eye contact, a cold chill weighted his heart down and sent him home alone. It was too soon for him to think about finding another body to place salve on his injured heart.

As he unlocked his door the phone was ringing like a firehouse siren. The fire was his instant headache and emotional turmoil of both wanting and not wanting it to be Tim, knowing he would be better off if it wasn't Tim. Extinguishing the flames of his tormented mind were the words, "Hey Dude, what's happening?"

Lee's emotional train ran from seventh heaven to ground zero, "I didn't expect to hear from you."

"Hey man, I am really sorry I talked like I did last night, I didn't mean to offend you. I thought about all you said and I guess...I'm bisexual!"

Lee's blood pressure hit the boiling point. "You know, I think bisexuality is a lot of bullshit. You are either gay- queer as you say- or you're not. When you stick your dick up another man's ass, let him blow you, and enjoy jerking him off, and all of the other intimate stuff like kissing, hugging, touching, you get my drift? You are not straight. Or bisexual! You are gay!"

Lee didn't stop to catch a breath he was so furious. "Yeah, I have been told some men say they go both ways. To me that only means they perform with women as a means of hiding their true homosexual nature. They are not strong enough emotionally to accept their gayness. They are afraid and unwilling to risk the reactions of the world if it was known they were gay. Queer as you say!"

"Stop that, man," Tim interrupted. "I got your message - you don't like that word. You won't hear it from me again!"

"That's right, I won't - because I'm ending this conversation!"

"STOP, please, I need to talk to you. I don't know what to do! I feel I love you! But I think I love my fiancé too!"

"Tim, I don't know what to tell you. I never had mixed feelings about sexuality as you do. I always knew from the earliest memory of my father rocking me to sleep. The intimacy of laying on his hairy chest and playing with his nipples; I was told my mother breast fed me as a baby but the defining moments were with my father. I certainly did not have all the knowledge to understand everything. Just the same I knew from early on I had a desire to be with, to feel, and to touch men in an intimate sexual way. Of course, my mother handing me off to him while he was in the bathtub, so he could bathe me at the same time, may have had something do with it. All those games of hide the soap, ending in a tug of war, with me pulling on I don't know what, and how he would stick his finger up my ass to wash it.

"I don't know, it was never girls for me! I knew I had to date them. Flirt with them in junior and senior high school to be like the rest of the boys.

But anywhere, anytime, it was the men and boys that had my attention. In the bathroom, locker rooms, on the sports field. I would be trying to see what their tight shorts revealed or hid. I would watch grown men walk, looking at their crotch to see if there were any protruding bulges suggesting what lay beneath the layers of clothing. I was a pervert, a young child with lascivious thoughts and adult desires. I don't know if it was good or bad that I didn't have the knowledge to know how to act on those thoughts.

"It was a long, diverse path that led me to where my sexuality is today. Along the way I used and hurt people, and for that I am truly sorry. You haven't ever spoken about your sexuality exploration. You are at the cross-roads where you can choose to do someone a great injustice or accept the cost of the life you want. Don't make someone else an unwitting financier of your sexual fantasies. In the end you won't like yourself.

"I married Rose because I felt bad about my parents not having grandchildren. I was afraid to tell my parents I was going back to Philadelphia. Why are you still thinking of getting married, Tim?

"I never had sexual exploration. It was a one-time thing. A guy was watching me pee in the W. T. Grant's department store public bathroom. As I shook it, he asked if he could touch it. Next thing I knew he was kneeling in front of me taking my pants down. My legs began to shake, I exploded, led out a primal sound, almost fell over but grabbed the urinal top. He quickly stood up, wiped his mouth with his handkerchief and was gone before I could take the whole thing in. I have never understood why a guy would want to suck another man's dick. I have had many girls do it, that's natural. I like to screw guys because their ass is tighter and grips the whole penis better than a girl's loose pussy. Some girls aren't too bad. With many, put them on their back, that thing just opens wide, swallows you alive! You could drive a Mack truck in there.

"In high school, everyone had a buddy they would screw in the ass. Girls were too young; you couldn't get at them unless they were your sister. They weren't interested in sex like guys. We had a dick that got hard. We knew what it could do and how to do it. Girls don't know that stuff as early as guys do. We needed something, so we would corn hole each other just to get off - nothing else, man. Men outgrow it and turn naturally to women."

'No, Tim I never had the desire for girls and should have stayed away from them. The women in my life chased me. I was flattered. Yes, it is common knowledge all younger men are oversexed so it was no hardship to perform or enjoy female sex. Fair to women, no! But they got what they wanted. They always say leave them wanting more! My goal was to please. But listen, "dude," I gave you all the information you need and as much advice as I can emotionally afford - you have to do the rest. I can't talk to you anymore, Good-bye"

The next day (the 27th) Rose surprised him at work and suggested they go to lunch together. He told her about his phone call with Tim and as far as he knew Tim was going forward with getting married. They both lamented that decision but what could they do? Rose thanked him for all he said to her at dinner and told him she was still interested in sharing a home together if he was. She reminded him when they got married the vows said "for better, for worse." She said she would respect his lifestyle if that's what it took to get them back together. He thought to himself, "She just doesn't get it." He walked Rose to her car and returned to work. When the opportunity presented itself, he went in search of Bella. Bringing her up to speed regarding Tim's "train-wreck-to-be," he told Bella how Rose wanted to get back together.

"As if Tim isn't playing with your head enough, now Rose wants to get back together. Believe me- she may say it would be just platonic, but she would be chasing your ass all over that house looking for some. She's been out on her own, had a boyfriend, probably learned how to do it and wants to try to win you back with some new tricks she's learned. I don't know which of them would be the worse choice. Maybe I should throw my hat in the ring?"

"No, no Bella, wrong number, wrong plumbing!" With those words he parted company remembering the saying, "Many a truth was said in jest!"

Thank God, he had enough work to occupy his mind with getting ready for inventory to keep him occupied for the remainder of the day. Wednesday was always one of his long days that he never minded. It was in the middle of the week; no one was in the bars so he had nowhere to rush to. He decided while he was driving, as soon as he got home, he was unplugging his phones. He had had enough of the Florida basket case. He really loved his time with the guy and sexually…wow! Tim seemed so intelligent. How could he be so stupid when it came to his sexuality and thinking he had to get married to please society?

How many people can ignore answering a ringing telephone? We all know there have been times when we ate too much and didn't need anymore, but we ate more anyway. We or someone we know didn't need another alcoholic beverage sometime in life. Like a moth to a flame, he could not resist that blasted ringing phone calling to him as he walked into his living room.

Instinctively knowing who it was, without the usual politeness, he picked the phone off the receiver saying, "Yes!"

"Hey dude!"

"Do you know that I hate the word dude?"

"Well who pissed in your skirt?"

"You did! You have been doing it regularly ever since you went back to Florida!"

"Man, I am so sorry! I am just got caught up in a catch 22. I have been talking to some of my buddies down here. I told them I met this swell girl up home that I think I love. I really like Yvonne.

"Oh! Is that the lucky girls' name? You know, you never said her name before!"

"I didn't?"

"No, I wondered why now it is Yvonne."

"Probably because I'm starting to think of her as just another person, not my wife-to-be."

"I think you need to change your thinking about a wedding also."

"As much as I would love to, I don't have the balls to do it. It's like being in front of a speeding train. I am too scared to move. I mean we had the rehearsal dinner, the caterer, the flowers, suits rented. When can I possibly say? Or do?"

"You know I have an idea. Give me the phone number where you are at. Let me get settled in and I will call you back."

"No, you won't. You just want to get me off the phone. I know there at times this week when I called and you didn't answer the phone. You were ignoring me; probably fed up with me. I don't blame you."

"No, you have it wrong I am going to call you back; I promise! Give me the number!" Having changed his clothes while trying to find the right words to say.... he sat down in front of the phone. It was late in the evening; he must try this last-ditch effort. Gathering his courage, dialing the number, he prayed she would answer the phone.

CHAPTER THIRTY

REACHING OUT THE HAND STILL WEARING his diamond, set ablaze by the moonlight, a very sleepy voice answered the phone. "Hello?"

"Hi, Rose! I am so sorry to call you this late but it's important! I need a favor."

"You sorry ass! You know when the phone rings this late at night people always assume the worst. You think there's an emergency in the family. Someone's hurt, injured, dying or already dead. What could be so important for you to call me at this time of night?"

"I apologize for worrying you, I am sorry. It's Tim, in Florida. He insists he is going to get married without revealing his sexual background. I thought, maybe if you talked to him and told him what it was like for you to get married, only to find out later you married a gay man... I don't know. It's not right that he gets married without her knowing he is at best bisexual."

"That is not your business, and certainly not mine. What could I tell him? Maybe the girlfriend already has a suspicion and doesn't care? Hell, I didn't even see it in you. Although my own sister knew you were gay. Remember how she used to say our children's name would be Criberri, because you were such a fairy? Maybe I did see things and denied them. You know, when you hung around my mother showing such a passionate interest in her sewing and cooking. Asking, how do you make this? And why do you turn the material this way or that? What is Frenching a seam?

"All those see-through shirts you made yourself and wore when you went out alone at night probably should have been a clue. The light bulb flashed on briefly when I came home and found you had worn my bridesmaid dress. I really didn't know what to think then... I had heard of men wearing women's clothes, so I didn't automatically assume you were gay. Whoa, boy was I wrong!"

"I am truly sorry, Rose. If I could go back and change things, I would."

"No, Lee I would not want you to go back and change anything. We did have fun. Going to the theater, the night clubs, the academy of music, the Latin casino, Palumbo's. We had some wonderful times. I love your Mother; she is a dear. Your father...is your father! If you hadn't asked me to get married, I probably would be a carbon copy of my mother. Married to a boy from high school, with no ambition, pregnant with children and stuck in New Jersey. Since we separated, I made new friends and returned to some of the places you took me to. Yes, I had sad moments.

"Now I can look back and say I have found contentment. I am on my own, away from my parents and Washington. It was not a trip without emotional difficulties. I worked through it, and I'm all the better for it. My car is paid for. Through my jobs, I improved my sewing and business skills. I am making good money and am saving for a down payment on my own home. I could be a lot worse off. Maybe, just maybe I did lack some skills as a wife.

"Maybe I married you for the wrong reasons. So, as for this favor - how am I supposed to talk to Tim?"

"I told him I would call him back. I will call the operator and ask her to arrange a conference call between the three of us. I hope that you will be inspired to say something to bring him to his senses; or do you really not care that he screws up that girl's life?"

Rose wondered to herself, "Are you doing this because you want him or do you really care about another woman getting screwed over? I have no idea, but at least I don't have to get out of bed or get dressed.

"Okay, go ahead; I'll do what I can."

"Thanks Rose! I'll hang up and the operator will call you back in a few minutes."

Gathering his thoughts, he called the operator and told her what he wanted to do. Within moments, the operator had connected Rose to Tim and Lee, and he was saying, "Tim, I have my wife on the phone. I had the operator connect us altogether so she can talk to you. I want her to tell you as a woman who married a closeted gay man what it was like. I want her to explain what you will be doing to Yvonne, which is exactly what I did to her. I hope you are not upset; you need to hear a women's perspective on what it is like to marry a man only to find out he also likes men. Rose -Tim. Tim- Rose. Go ahead, Rose."

As Tim said…"Yo, Ro!" Lee dropped out of the conversation put the phone down and let them talk alone. He could slightly hear their voices knowing they were talking but not able to distinguish what they said. He didn't want to listen to Rose even kindly describe how disappointed she was in her marriage. He could imagine there would be things Rose would need to say that could hurt his feelings. After a half hour of back-and-forth conversation, he heard no one speaking.

Picking the phone back up Lee questioned him, "Well now, was that so bad? How did it go?"

"I told him every argument I could think of; as to why he shouldn't get married, the ball is in his court!"

"Hey, Ro I appreciate the information, but everyone is different."

"Okay guys I am going back to bed. Good night."

"Thanks Rose! Moreover, Tim you need to shake some cobwebs loose; good night to you, too."

"Wait!" Hanging up the phone, Lee had had enough of this melodrama for the night. Mentally exhausted he went to bed content to let fate play out.

Friday the 28th came and found him busy at work getting ready for the end-of- year inventory. It was calming to only be asked…."Are we to physically separate the spring stock from the winter stock?" "Where do you want the spring coats to be displayed?" "We have, don't have all the inventory mark down prices yet." "Should these be counted at full price or marked down?"

Lunchtime brought he and Bella together and he told her about the late-night conference call. "Boy, I don't want your phone bill. Why are you wasting time and money on this person? He is in Florida for God's sake. It's not like anything is going to happen between the two of you."

At this point Bella saw his lower lip quiver and realized his heart was still with Tim. "Oh, Lee, I'm sorry. I didn't realize you were still so involved. I thought you had lost interest in him when you were fed up with his antics about hiding his lifestyle from his fiancé."

Trying to hold on to his composure he mumbled, "I know I probably should have never left this whole thing get this far. I guess I can't let go of the dream."

Our intimate moments were so loving…I could still feel his body touching mine, the memory of his biting my love handles, his furry chest rubbing on my body, his hands playing up and down my arms, grabbing my fingers and kissing them when he was on my back. He made me feel like I was the only person he ever touched that way. I felt so special when we made love. He made me feel that he loved me. I know love is not just sex! And when we sat and held hands and talked of childhood exchanging family anecdotes over lunch.

It was as if we had known each other for years, it was so easy and comfortable being with him. Every time I heard his voice, even though I soon felt rankled because of his lying to his fiancé, I got chills. When he talked to me, it is as if he was still beside me, not in a different physical state. Although we are only connected by a phone line, I can still feel his breath feathering against my skin as he speaks; his body heat, warm against me."

Bella was aghast at the emotion she felt inside her. She wanted to rage out at him and tell him what an idiot he was. She was angry that he was such a fool and so out of touch with reality. She stood up to leave; afraid she couldn't contain her emotions. Fearful she would say something to her friend she would regret, when she realized what she was really feeling. She caught herself thinking she was … jealous? Had she ever felt like this about someone? Had anyone ever felt this way about her? She was never with anyone who made her feel as desired as Lee expressed Tim made him feel. Was she angry because she thought he could not see he was being made a fool of?

She had been made a fool of in her lifetime. It was never done as sweetly to her as it was being done to Lee, indeed, if it was. Was she feeling sad? Was it because she knew she could never be as vulnerable as he has been; so brave to open your heart to such pain from this degree of loving someone? She thought she should be happy for her friend. You know, "Better to have loved and lost, than never to have loved at all." She was not able to figure out why she just couldn't say, "I am happy for you, it must be wonderful to have found someone to make you feel that special."

That was it! He hadn't found someone to make him feel that special - he found someone else's fiancé! He might as well have gone to the local lost and found box looking for a pair of gloves. He found one glove that someone else lost that fit his hand. One glove, not a pair! What good is one glove without its mate? Her lunch was ruined but she didn't want to reveal her inner musings to her dearest friend. "Well, you know he's not married yet!" Her heart was not in the words. She didn't know how it sounded, but it was the best she could muster at the time.

Time passed quickly but Lee was not eager to go home. He found the prospect of facing another phone call from Tim daunting. To avoid getting out of bed to answer the phone he watched TV until early in the morning. The evening went and morning came without his phone ringing. Was he glad, or sad?

When Bella saw her friend the next day, Saturday the 29th, she couldn't tell from across the floor what expression was on his face. He seemed to be into his work and focused, very busy, but not talking to his sales help very much. She thought she saw Hazel try to talk to him but walk away shrugging her shoulders when she didn't get a response.

When she got the chance, she walked across into Lee's area. "Hazel, how goes it today?"

"I don't know what happened to him this last week, but something did! He's like a roller coaster; One minute happy, the next morose and quiet. I don't know if someone died or if he came down with a terrible illness! He just isn't himself. You two seem close, maybe you can find out what's eating him," she murmured as she continued straightening up the clothing.

Finding him in the back room, "What's up my friend?"

"Not a thing."

"What's new?"

"You mean!? Did I hear from Tim? And what did he say? Well, you will be very happy to know he didn't call! As we stand here, he's probably putting the final changes to his wedding plans. Is that what you wanted to hear? Does that make you happy?"

Bella was experienced enough to know when she heard misplaced anger. She apparently was expected to absorb the price of Tim's not calling. Well, she was not in the mood to be the bull's-eye for her friend's arrows. "I'll see you for lunch. Maybe by then that boiling pot of yours will have lost some of its steam. If not, we will lay you down and take everything out of the steam table and put everything on you. Maybe that will absorb your head of steam and cool you down!"

He skipped lunch, working the rest of the day cleaning out under stocks and back rooms and doing all the necessary markdowns so he would be prepared for inventory. He thought about going to the bars after work but was too angry with himself. Yes, he knew it was his own fault. Yet, it is human nature to feel self-pity and want to hide and lick our wounds.

The phone rang soon after he got home. Tim never called that early so he expected it to be one of his friends.

"Hey, dude. I did it! I told my fiancé I couldn't marry her. You and Rose were right. She suspected I was a swinger. I quit my job and I have been getting rid some of the things not worth bringing back to Pennsylvania. I called my family and told them the wedding was off, I didn't go into detail. Told them I quit my job and was moving back to PA. My aunt said I could have my old room back. I told her I think I have other plans.

"She asked, 'Are you going to shack up with that floozy you laid with Christmas weekend?'

"I told her, 'Yes, if she will have me.' Will you have me?"

Ecstatic beyond words, Lee responded, "Yes, of course. When are you leaving? When will you get here?"

"I have to drive my car back to Pennsylvania. I was hoping you would fly down and help me drive home. I'd like to leave tomorrow. My rent is due on the 1st, my landlord said if am gone by the 31st he will let me out of the lease."

"Yes, I'll call right away to find what flights are available. Are you still at the number you gave me the other night?"

"Yes. I hope you know what you have gotten yourself into, dude. You are responsible for changing my whole life. Facing issues, I never knew I had! I am looking forward to our making a life together. I have never lived with anyone in this kind of relationship. They will be adjustments for both of us. Are you up to it?"

CHAPTER THIRTY-ONE

BORROWING MONEY FOR THE PLANE TICKET
from Ron and Tom, Lee arranged to fly to Miami Beach. The next evening, Sunday the 30th, they hugged their friend good bye and watched the attendant take his ticket. As Lee disappeared into the plane, they called out "Good luck!" hoping everything would work out for him.

Walking back to their car Ron said to Tom. "Dear me - I think our boy has got himself into trouble."

"I should say so. He doesn't even have the money for a plane ticket because he's out in the clubs all the time. I know he's your friend but I think he's asking for trouble! I am not saying you should not have lent him the money for the ticket. But he doesn't even know this guy! Couldn't you have talked to him?"

Giving him a sideways glance from the corner of his eye, Ron recalled how it was when they first met. Lovingly, he murmured to Tom, "No, dear. I remember how the memory of seeing you the first time tortured my soul. I was already emotionally involved with you long before I caught your heart."

Hearing the loving sentiment softened his heart for a moment, "But how is this guy going to live up here? Is he expecting to be supported? Moving right in when he has family! What is Lee thinking? The guy could murder him in his sleep. I'm telling you; this will end badly. Nothing good will come of this," Tom growled.

"I wish I thought you were wrong, Tom." He said quickly hugging his lover close. "Regretfully, I think you are going to be proven right. Let's hope for the best!"

Lee couldn't appreciate a moment of the flight, because of worry. His thoughts were centered on a tall young man with russet hair waiting for him in Florida. What if he has changed his mind? What if he isn't at the airport when the plane arrives? He had purchased a one-way ticket and didn't have the money for a return ticket. What would he do if there was no one to meet him? Working himself into a frenzy of emotion, the flight attendant passing by asked him if he was all right. Gently sobbing, he told her he was rushing to see a sick friend, and the flight attendant went about her business. The gravity of what he had done, on words from a perfect stranger, grabbed at him in his throat. Too late now! Too late for recriminations! He had better be there! Or you will be the laughing stock of all your friends. These were his thoughts as he beat himself up emotionally. The miles between the cities disappeared quickly as he played out both sides of the drama in his mind.

As the plane taxied to the gate he thought, showtime! As he walked off the plane into the gate area, expecting to see Tim or at least hear his name called out, there was silence. He looked and looked for that lanky red-haired man. But there was no one in the waiting area.

Lost, he felt the heat of despair washing over him. Out of a dream-like quietness, he heard running feet hitting the floor and a loud frantic voice calling, "Lee! Lee!" Looking up he saw Tim running down the corridor. "Thank God you're here!" The words rushed out of Tim's mouth.

"Just as your plane landed, they announced that the arrival gate changed, at the very last minute! They moved the plane to a whole other terminal. I had to take a shuttle bus to get here. I was so worried about you arriving and not seeing me. I was afraid you would walk off and I wouldn't know where to look to find you. And you would think I changed my mind and didn't meet the plane. I am so glad I got here and you're still here. Were you worried? How long have you been here? Come with me - I have to do something."

Uncharacteristically Tim grabbed him by the hand and dragged him to the nearest men's room. Once inside, checking for feet under the stall doors, he threw Lee against the back of the door, passionately hugging and kissing him until he could hardly breathe.

"I am so very glad I met you! I am so very happy you are here! Thank you for coming. Come on dude, we have some driving to do." It was eleven o'clock at night as Tim drove him past the swanky Fontainebleau Hotel showing him some of the sights as they drove out of Miami heading north to Pennsylvania.

It was a long hard drive, non-stop Miami to Philadelphia. Yes, there were stops for gas and quick fast food meals. Of course, they stopped frequently for needed love breaks along the road, hoping the police didn't go past. With all the distractions, they made it home, inside their front door, before the clock struck midnight the next evening. They ended their first New Year's Eve together by going straight to bed, sleeping until around eleven the next morning.

After celebrating the next morning, as any young couple who just moved in together would, they forced themselves out of bed when Tim said, "Well I might as well face the music and introduce my family to the bimbo I am living with... Get dressed!"

Avoiding the traffic downtown, caused by the New Year's Day Mummers Parade, Tim drove up Roosevelt Boulevard. Driving around the Sears Circle brought back memories of the night he drove up the boulevard, getting off at Adams Street to go to that bar. Laughing aloud, he remembered the evening he wore his wife's bridesmaids dress. Oh, how he was going to be the belle of the ball that evening! He decided to share the story with Tim.

"You did what?! What's the matter with you? You will never do that with me. Don't tell any stories like that to my family. Unless you 'act queer' they won't suspect anything!"

Pulling up to the curb in front of a block of attached houses Tim got out and ran towards the steps in front of 6708. Remembering he wasn't alone he turned around, "Come on, just keep your mouth shut?"

This was not sitting well with Lee. Knowing he was stuck up in the great northeast with no alternatives, and not in his own car, he had to fight to move one foot then the other to follow Tim up the steps. As he stopped behind Tim, the door opened.

"You spoilsport! Why didn't you tell me you were coming? I heard the car pull up, saw it was you and ran to take my apron off. I wouldn't want your girlfriend to meet me for the first time in a soiled apron. Where is the siren that can stop a wedding? Where is she?"

Leaning around Tim, looking past Lee, she continued to look up and down the street. She knew she must have missed the third person. She knew there had to be a third person, a girl. Her heavily made-up eyes focused on Lee. It was his first impression of Tim's Aunt Margaret. What he saw was a seventy-something, wrinkled Marilyn Monroe- type well past her prime. He knew, at first glance, that the local drugstore's best customer of Tangee firehouse-red lipstick and Clairol's platinum blonde bleach was standing in front of him.

"Maggie, get out of the doorway! Let Timmy in. I want to meet the new girlfriend, too." Uncle Ben scolded.

"Well good luck!!! A disgusted Margaret barked. "Someone's pulling our leg, unless it's a helluva Halloween disguise."

"No! I left my dresses at home, but I can wear one another time if you like!" He spit back. Glaring at Lee over his shoulder, Tim was pulled into the house by his Uncle. Ben was left looking confusedly at Lee. He too looked around him as his sister had, then focused on Lee, although not as severely as his sister.

Quickly regaining his civility; "Come on in, don't be a stranger. We don't bite. You must be a friend of Timmy's?

"Come on down Irma, dinners almost ready. Timmy and his friend are here. You'll want to say hello," Maggie cattily called upstairs.

The siblings' older cousin from Ireland had been making her home with the brother and sister ever since her husband died. It was an easy financial arrangement for all concerned. She learned early on not to confide in Maggie, keep anything personal in her locked chest and keep to herself. She always liked Timothy and thought she knew him better than he realized.

Quickly grasping the situation as she came down the stairs, she said a silent prayer. "Dear Lord please watch over us." She thought Timmy was about to see a side of his Aunt he did not know well. Her eyes landed on Lee and she was immediately sorry for him. She regretted a visitor would be subjected to what she felt was a certainty to happen. In a thick Irish brogue, she greeted her cousin. "Tim, so good to see you; glad to have you home. Who is your friend?"

"Irma, Aunt Margaret, Uncle Ben, this is my friend Lee. We met through mutual acquaintances and he was looking for a boarder. I thought it's time I try to get out on my own so I'm going to rent a room in his house until I find my own place. I won't be disturbing you guys and intruding my late hours on you. You know how I like to stay out and party!"

"Party? Good idea, let's have a drink! Tim, do the honors, while we get to know your friend," Maggie announced, devilment dancing in her eyes.

"Do you think you need to check the stove Maggie?" Irma asked. "We don't want the food to burn while we have a nip." The dinner drawing Maggie's attention to the kitchen, Irma went to Lee's side and whispered, "She's been drinking already, she's a hellun' when she's drinking - be careful what you say." She brought her fingers up to her lips, as a librarian would do to silence noisy kids in a library.

Amazed to hear this camaraderie type statement from someone he just met, she set him on edge. He didn't know what to think. The Uncle seemed, nice and "normal," but Irma and Tim's Aunt were questionable.

Tim and his Aunt came back into the living room with a tray of glasses. Maggie suggested they all have a toast to new friends. No sooner had the glass left her lips and Maggie was all over Lee. Not wanting to see bloodshed Irma slipped into the kitchen.

"How did you two meet? Where did you meet? Who are Tim's friends that you know? Who are your parents? What do you do for a living? Are you married, been married, or divorced? What parish are you in?" Being a good Catholic, she wanted to make sure she was entertaining a fellow Catholic.

Lee was waiting to be asked, "Are you circumcised?"

Before she got all her answers, she turned to Tim. "Well what happened to the marriage? What made you leave Florida? I thought for sure you were going to shack up with that tramp you met Christmas weekend. Who was she? Where did you meet her? Do you know her Lee? Come on so many questions... No answers? What's up guys?" Turning back to Lee, "So, you have a boarding house?"

Irma returned from her supervisory tour of the kitchen and called, "Come on now everyone! Dinner's ready!"

Lee tried to decline, "Really we should go, you were not expecting us for dinner."

After a couple of shots of his Uncle's best Irish whiskey, Tim was ready to take on the family. Turning to Lee, Tim announced, "Nah, we'll stay - they always cook like they are expecting an army!"

The food was wonderful; Lee had never tasted roast lamb before. The previous tension had seemed to pass and he was enjoying the closeness the family enjoyed. The meal was passing without incident, until Maggie started lamenting how much she missed her dearly departed sister Sarah Ann.

Tim only took so much of her cry for sympathy until the whiskey he drank spoke out, "You didn't appreciate her while she was alive."

"What do you mean?' Turning a stricken look on her nephew, "I loved my sister, it broke my heart when she died."

"The only thing that broke was your pocket book. I heard you yell at her, 'Die and get it over with!' All you wanted was her retirement checks to pay the household bills and to steal money to buy your booze."

"Now Tim," Irma pleaded, trying to stop the confrontation.

"Now Tim my ass! My sweet, generous Aunt lies in Holy Sepulcher while she sits here pissing about how much she loved her. Bullshit! You all know I'm telling the truth. We all heard how she would yell at Aunt Sally. Sick as she was. She'd yell at her and tell her,' Stop shitin' the bed! Get yourself to the bathroom!' She would sit down here and listen to Aunt Sally crying for help, waiting until she had messed in the bed. Then she would go and scream at her, berating her for making the mess. I know how it was. I didn't forget."

"As God is my witness that is not how it was; I only tried to encourage her to help herself more, instead of turning into an invalid. I was grief stricken when she died - she was my best friend, not just my sister!"

"I remember how she died too. Aunt Sally made it out of the bathroom by herself and called you for help. She pleaded for you to help. Then she lost her balance and fell down the stairs. You taunted her and called her a cripple and wouldn't even call an ambulance. It was only when Uncle Ben came home and found her lying at the bottom of the stairs that you stopped rummaging through her bedroom looking for her money. Uncle Ben had to call the ambulance."

"Timmy! That is enough!" Ben's booming voice rang out over Maggie's wailing as he slammed the palms of his hands on the dining room table. Lee watched the action play out as Irma sat further back in her chair. Her thin lips pulled closely together in a tsk, tsk manner.

Throwing his chair back that it fell on the floor, "I don't know why you want to protect her Ben. How often has she threatened to grind up glass and put it in *your food?*"

Standing up and leaning into Tim's face, his Aunt said, "You are a hateful nephew. All we did for you. Sarah Ann, Ben and me - we took you in and gave you a home. We did everything we could for you when your parents died! Raised you a good Catholic and look how you turned out. You were going to get married, and now you're not! You show up here. We don't know what kind of person you turned out to be. What kind of people you got yourself mixed up with!" Her eyes landed on Lee "Letting them influence you".... her voice trailing off.

Again, Ben tried to defuse the situation, "Sit down everyone, we still have dessert! Irma isn't there a cream cake out there? Let's bring it in. Maybe that will sweeten some dispositions."

Rallying, before Irma could get out of her chair, Tim gave tit for tat, "I am a much better person than you are. My parents taught me what I needed to know before they died. You just gave me a roof over my head; you were no example of what kind of person to be. My not getting married was the right thing to do."

"I used to think you turned out all right," Maggie attacked. "You were such a sweet child....I found those Playboy magazines you hid under your bed! What do you do with them? Jerk off!"

"Margaret Mary Lewars!" Irma cried out. Even Maggie turned red, knowing she had gone too far.

"Your poor saintly Mother, God rest her soul, is turning in her grave. To think you would talk like that, anytime, let alone at the dinner table," Irma spit out.

Silence finally returned to the dining room. Ben sat there in disbelief, cradling his shaking head in his hands. A stunned Maggie recoiling as if she had been shot with a gun stuttered, "What! What did I say that would make my poor saintly mother, roll over in her grave?"

Tim picked up the gauntlet, "Why would you allude to such a personal bodily function anywhere, never mind in mixed company, not forgetting you are at the dinner table?"

With a completely innocent face she looked around the table, at everyone in turn questioningly then turned to Tim, "What are you talking about?"

"You asked me if I jerked off with the magazines. A lady would never say such a thing!"

"What's the big deal? The kids over at Grant's Store say it all the time to each other."

"You hear them asking each other if they jerk off all the time?"

"Yeah; they always call each other jerk offs. They say it all the time! Jerk off, it means 'drop dead.'"

"So, what you meant was…Did I look at the magazines, then drop dead? Margaret stared blankly at his face. Tim pushing his chair back again albeit more controlled said, "Come on let's get out of here!" Lee was thinking that he at least enjoyed the food, but he wondered what it must have been like to be raised in such an atmosphere.

As they drove home, he asked the pensive Tim, "What are you thinking about?"

"My sister Margaret, we always called her Peggy, to not confuse her with Aunt Margaret."

"I didn't know you had a sister?"

"We haven't spoken since she graduated high school and went to college. She never came back after she left my Aunt and Uncle's house. We were both home the day Aunt Sarah died. It was the only time Aunt Margaret went upstairs to help her sister back to bed. We heard them arguing... Maggie had been drinking and called her an invalid, scolding her for not trying to do more for herself. We heard a scuffle.

"Sarah told Margaret, 'Maggie you are hurting my arm, stop pushing me.' It sounded as if she was holding her arm too tight and pushing her too fast for her feet to keep up.

"Maggie said afterwards, 'She got huffy and pulled away from me and fell down the steps.' My sister had gotten up from the dining room table, where we were putting a puzzle together, and went to see if she could help Aunt Sara as she laid at the bottom of the stairs Aunt Margaret said, "She's alright, let her catch her breath. Let her rest a minute then we'll get her back upstairs." That's when she went into Sarah's bedroom, where she was when Ben came home.

"Ben threw a helluva fit and called the ambulance right away. Peggy told Ben, 'I saw Aunt Margaret sort of push Aunt Sarah towards the stairs. Aunt Sarah's hands were flailing out trying to catch hold of the wall, but her fingers just slid down the wallpaper as she tumbled down the stairs. She wouldn't talk to me; her eyes were open but she wouldn't talk to me!'

"Before the ambulance got there, Ben told my sister and I to stay in the dining room and say nothing. By that time Margaret was sitting on the sofa, crying alligator tears. The entire world would have believed, at that point, she truly loved her sister and was mourning her death. The minute they took the body, and the door was closed, she was back upstairs. All we heard were dresser drawers opening and closing as she went through her sister's belongings. She came to the stairs and called to us to look at the black dress she had taken from her sister's closet saying, 'Won't this look nice on me for the funeral. There's another subdued floral I can wear for the wake!'

"Both of them had worked at the Philadelphia Naval Depot all their lives, getting very good pensions when they retired. Maggie spent her money foolishly and Sarah invested hers. When she died, we found out Sarah left everything she had to Margaret. With her own money and Aunt Sarah's savings she could have had life easy. Instead she drank it all and now has to work at the W. T. Grant store across the boulevard. If we're lucky she'll be drunk one day and run across the heavy traffic at the wrong time and get hit by a car.

"My sister never forgave me for not saying something, rather than keeping quiet, about Aunt Margaret being responsible for her sister falling down the stairs. I didn't see anything. She says she saw what she saw. What could I do? I didn't see anything."

CHAPTER THIRTY-TWO

THE NEXT WEEKEND TIM TOOK HIM TO meet his girlfriend Patty. When they were settled into the cozy Fishtown living room, Tim told Patty how he told Lee what a slut she was and never paid cash for anything.

"That's right honey! My doctor, my hairdresser, any work I got done around the house. I'll either fuck or suck 'em. Usually they end up owing me, even if I did get something out of it. A girl has to know how to stretch her husband's meager little pay! There's a little grocer around the corner. All the neighbors say how expensive he is and they wonder how I can afford to pay his prices. All I know is I phone and tell him what I want and within hours I have my order and he's gone. How he explains it to his wife isn't my concern. My husband is as stupid as the grocer's wife. He should see I couldn't afford all I do around here on his pay."

Before they left Stan, Patty's brain-dead husband came in and Patty rushed over hugging and smothering him in kisses. Stan and Tim seemed to be on good terms. Stan reminding Tim, "Hey man we have to go out drinking again - had a great time, haven't done it in a while."

As they left Lee wondered why Tim would have friends like this; something felt off. Having endured meeting Tim's family and friends Stan and Patty; Lee decided to have a small dinner party. He wanted to introduce his new lover to his friends and establish his style of a dinner party: white linen table service, matching china and stemware, and polite company. Ron and Tom, Lib and Liza, and Eddie and Lorenzo attended the small soirée. Without anyone saying it out loud, they all knew they wouldn't miss the party. They wanted to see who had captured their friend's affection.

The evening had all the required elements for success. Good food, pleasant conversation, well-mannered guests. Everyone displayed their best company manners. When everyone left, Tim let out a sigh and said, "I am glad that's over!"

Mystified he asked, "Why did you say that?"

"They are not my kind of people, that's' all." he replied. "Ron and Tom are sissified. Ron acts like the only southern debutante who forgot the cotillion is over and does not know he is the pariah of the season. Who does he think he is, batting those fluttering, massacred eyelashes at everyone? You would think the way he acts so grand that he was Liz Taylor. He has a Cheshire cat grin, but never smiles. It's almost a grimace; he never opens his mouth to show he has any teeth. Does he? When he was talking to me, I felt as if he thought he was looking at a fly. It was as if he was trying to inch closer to the fly without the fly seeing the flyswatter behind his back. He acts as if he wants to distract you and then smack you down.

"And his friend Tom, a drop-out from thug school because his friends found out he took ballet lessons. No one would ever think he was from Fishtown and Kensington. The guys from there are rough. His mother probably had to walk him by the hand to school every day and pick up at the end of school to protect his little pink ass from getting beat - or worse. The boys from Kensington know the meaning of butch. Not that one, such a mincing walk. His wrists are so limp it is a wonder his watch doesn't slide right off. Who does he think he is impressing with that put-on oh-so-proper accent? Elizabeth - oh!! excuse me - Liz! Such a butch!! And Liza, talk about a May-December romance. How much older is Liz than Liza, forty, fifty years? It certainly isn't looks or manners. And what do they see in each other? Liz must have big tongue and know how to make Liza squeal like a pig.

"And Lorenzo? I never did like Spics. Eddie? Eddie is the only normal friend you have; and since you won't be needing those drag outfits you have upstairs you can give them to 'darling' Ron."

Slightly surprised by Tim's impression of his friends, Lee wondered why he'd blasted them in that manner. "You're just giving me a dose of pay-back. Because I told you I didn't think much of Patty. Bragging how much money she was able hide from her husband to stash away for a rainy day for herself. How she never used cash to pay for anything. Groceries, furniture, car maintenance, doctor's visits, dentist, hairdresser and some clothing by trading sex for them. Sometimes saying she made extra money in the bargain! She admitted she thought of trying to approach her manicurist for free nails but the girl was too ugly! Although she did say, if the woman would have been satisfied just eating her out, she probably would have let her. She smokes pot and abuses pharmaceuticals." Lee knew he lived in a glass house, but he really did not like Patty's "ways."

"And she's a hypocrite! She told me how good a Catholic she was, and what a great Mom she is! Bullshit!"

Tim defended her by saying, "Ahh, her old man is probably doing something behind her back. He has to know she could not afford everything she puts in that house on the little money he gives her. I have always thought he might be screwing around with his buddy Wes. They spent a lot of time out in Stan's workshop. By the way I was putting some of my things in the back-bedroom closet. Those women's' clothes make me uncomfortable, give them to Ron and Tom. I think they may have a use for them."

Lee could hear Tim was feeling quite comfortable in his new surroundings. If only he could find a job! Having acquired some measure of balance in his life, Lee settled back down to his own job and everyone was happy. Bella had her old friend back and Hazel was not feeling so put-upon and ignored.

One morning right before the alarm clock went off for Lee to get up for work, the telephone rang. It was on Tim's' side of the bed so he answered it. Lee heard Tim's side of the conversation.

"Yes - hi! Uh huh, uh huh. Okay!"

Lee had gotten up and was getting ready to go to the bathroom to shower when Tim hung up the phone. He jumped out of bed and started to get dressed.

"Who was that?" he asked.

"A friend I met when Eddie and I were out the other day. He is up at the drugstore and wanted to know if he could come over here and crash. He's been out all night and didn't want to go home."

Lee didn't know which question to ask first. Since when are you running around with Eddie Peeples and how did that start? How often and where do you two go? Why can't he go home? Why did you give someone you met out with Eddie just the other day our phone number? He's now your friend, comfortable enough to ask to "crash" here? You didn't tell him the address so he already has that, too. And why does he? Why have you not told me all this before some stranger phones? From the end of the conversation I heard, he tells you he is coming over here, to my house, when I'm not home?

Nothing about this seemed right to Lee. He went to the bathroom and got himself ready for work as all manner of questions and accusations went through his head. As he was going out the back door, Tim was letting his new friend in the front.

When he got to work, he felt very unsettled and talked to Bella about it. Bella felt sorry for her friend but also thought to herself, I told you so. Lee called the house several times during the day to inquire what was going on but no one answered the telephone. He worked until six o'clock that day and hurried home full of questions waiting to be answered,

He opened the door to find an aroma of something cooking in the air. He couldn't tell what Tim was preparing from the smell and didn't get the chance to lift a pot lid to see for himself. He was greeted in a bear hug and thrown onto the dining room floor. Thank God for that faux fur rug! Tim proceeded to undress him sliding his pants off his ankles. You would have thought he was the main course for dinner that evening and his body was Tim's smorgasbord. He took a lick of that, a smell of this and a big helping of everything else. Quite out of character and as equally unexpected... Tim engulfed his manhood in his mouth. Stopping, starting, tickling with his tongue, swirling, going underneath, attacking every angle, he worked him into an explosive frenzy.

After his dessert, he announced, "That is the way I want to satisfy you from now on!" Slapping his thigh, grabbing himself and shaking it in his face he said, "Now roll over I have some business to finish."

After dinner that evening Lee finally came back down to earth and remembered he had some questions he wanted answered. For some reason they didn't seem so important, now. Having been laid bare on his fur rug seemed to make all his thoughts about the morning phone call unimportant. He was spoon fed some story that amounted to Tim's' going out with Eddie only a couple times when Eddie was off, and only because Tim was so bored.

We believe what we want to believe, and that was enough for him. It was enough for Lee until he went to bed and found a strange man's tie on his bedside dresser. He did hear the warning bell but he was too much in love with Tim to believe something terrible was developing.

Tim landed a job as a debit insurance agent; the old-fashioned kind that came to your mother's door. He would collect that quarter or dollar that was squirreled away each week in the stiff, thin cardboard sleeve that advertised the company logo. Collecting the money, he would mark the amount on the appropriate week's dates, initial the book; replace it in the envelope. The sleeve was always kept in the same safe place for quick retrieval when the agent retuned the following week.

Although it was steady work, Tim was not happy driving door-door and sought an office job. He secured employment with the city's teachers' credit union, finding his niche working with mostly women. He started out as a clerk and worked his way up to loan officer. It was a good, steady job, well-paying. The only objection Lee had was the office would frequently go out for drinks after work. Everyone was expected to go along, according to Tim.

Irma encouraged them to start a novena at The Shrine of Blessed John Neuman; asking for holy intercessions for whatever they felt they had a need for. Many women pray a novena asking God to help their husband find the church again. Lee prayed God would help Tim find happiness in their relationship, since Tim had reverted to his one-sided sexual self and the frequency had dwindled. They had tried several times but were never able to complete the nine-week novena.

On their trip home, after an evening of prayer, their car was rear-ended in an accident. After talking to a lawyer, they were immediately admitted to Metropolitan Hospital with severe trauma to the back and neck. They both had to have daily intravenous injections of muscle relaxers, lumber traction and cervical collars.

During the hospitalization Lee discovered Tim liked different sex outside the home. He would have Lee crawl on top of him in his bed, after the last bed check and sit on his face. During the day when the afternoon nurses came on duty, and were busy catching up on nurses' notes, Tim would lock them in the bathroom. He'd bend over and tell Lee to take him from behind. He always cautioned Lee, "Don't touch me!" Of course, he wondered why. When he did touch him, he found out he was rock hard. The slightest touch made him shoot the load he had other plans for.

One of the afternoon shift nurses came to their room to chart temperature, pulse and blood pressure and found they were in the bathroom together. She knocked on the door and called to them, "Come out I need to chart you, then you can resume whatever you are doing."

When they appeared red-faced, she looked at them quizzically. Lee said, "We were meditating and wanted privacy."

She commented, "I use Mah Wong Balls to help me meditate!"

When she left the room, he told Tim, "I don't know what the hell Mah Wong balls are."

Tim explained, "They are balls on a cord, maybe eight or six; the size of small tennis balls. A woman lubricates herself, lubricates the balls and pushes them up inside her vagina. She masturbates, massages her clitoris. As she starts to climax, she pulls them out, it helps heightens her orgasm."

And Lee thought he had heard it all. "Men have been known to do the same thing!" Tim added. Asking Tim if he knew that from personal experience, he curtly responded, "No."

Lee did make mental note of that info though. It was on the same card he noted Tim's proclivity for different sex outside their home, along with how Tim reacted when Lee "entered the back door." He was perplexed because Tim was so one sided at home.

During their confinement a priest came by to visit. Tim of course acknowledged he was Catholic and Lee appreciated the priest's visits. Often, he would leave the room to let them fellowship together. On a particular visit after he prayed with Tim, he asked to speak with Lee privately. The priest explained to him that he was leading Tim into eternal damnation. He told Lee that if he loved Tim, he would break off this sexual relationship and just be Christian friends. The conversation took him back a step or two and he confronted Tim with what the priest said. Still, Tim admitted that if he wasn't in a relationship with him, he would still be with a man.

After their two weeks in the hospital they had to stay home from work for two more weeks wearing cervical collars. Even though it was a slam dunk, because the other driver ran a red light, it was going to take time to settle the car accident. The events surrounding the car accident slowed Tim somewhat in his extracurricular activities.

Once back to work it didn't take long for Tim to start running again. Working downtown did have its advantages! To try to prevent Lee from curtailing his outings Tim invited Lee to go along. Lee found he enjoyed a couple of the co-workers. Some of the partiers let the cat out of the bag that it was usually Tim who instigated the Friday night drinking parties.

It was at one of the office-get-together parties that he first heard African-American people make unkind remarks about other African-Americans. Several women of color were in the group this particular night and fussing with each other. One chose to say something about another of the lady's shade of complexion. Quickly remarks were flying about whose ancestors worked in the masters' fields and whose ancestors were the house n____ s. They easily used the word that white people weren't supposed to use. It was a word that made his skin crawl; he always felt it was an ugly vulgar word. Yes, we know there is another meaning in the dictionary for this word. This time it was said in the context of being a form of Negro.

When this word is used by anyone, of any color, regarding a person of color, it is always wrong. There is no sugar coating thick enough to make this palatable to anyone. It would be a step towards a better world if everyone of all colors could refrain from calling someone else this slur again.

As the frequency of after office hours drinking increased, Lee was invited less and less often. He usually found out about it when Tim called from the bar to say he would be a little late. Lateness came to be until two or three in the morning. Tim would explain the "girls wanted to go for breakfast."

The first Christmas they were together, the credit union hired a portrait photographer to take pictures of the members with their families as a holiday gift. The morning of the day the photographer was to be at the office, Tim suggested they meet in town for dinner. When Lee left work at six o'clock, he went to the office to meet Tim. Taking the elevator to his floor, he found the door to the office locked, but could hear loud music playing and the lights were on. He went back to the lobby and used the pay phone to call upstairs to the office. The phone rang, and rang, with no one answering. He went over to the guard and asked him if Mr. Lewars had signed out for the day.

"No, Mr. Lewars and the photographer are still upstairs, everyone else has gone home."

He went back upstairs and banged and banged on the office door. He even yelled out Tim's name, to no avail, no one opened the door. Once again Tim came home late it was becoming common for him to crawl in anytime between one, two, three in the morning. (His excuse was he didn't know anyone locked the door and the music must have drowned out the phone.) "Since you didn't want to go out for dinner the photographer and I went to McGinty's for a brew."

Moreover, the sex life they once enjoyed had dwindled to the point that sex may happen every four or even six weeks. Lee had a religious grounding of some sort, somewhere inside himself, so he decided to try another avenue for help. During Mass, at the Cathedral of Saints Peter and Paul on the Parkway, it was announced that St. Raphael's Men's

Shelter was in need of volunteers. He talked Tim into volunteering to help there on Sundays, thinking it would curtail Saturday night drinking parties. He called and talked to the head of the shelter, Brother John about he and Tim helping out. Glad for the offer of more helping hands, they were told to be at the shelter at 4 AM on Sunday morning.

The first Sunday he was there Lee learned out to make oatmeal in a 40-gallon batch, starting with how to light an old-fashioned gas flame under a 4 foot by 2-foot kettle, swinging the faucet over and opening the spigot, letting water flow in until the water was ten inches from the top, dropping in ten pounds of surplus butter, so many five-pound bags of dry oatmeal, and a few 5-pound bags of sugar. Stir constantly, with the aluminum boat oar given specifically for that job, until it was done so it didn't stick. Because they knew Tim worked in an office, he was assigned work in the shelter's registration office.

The second Sunday they were there Lee learned how to make French toast. The toast came pre-coated and frozen. The brother instructed him to lay the toast on the griddle in rows of 8 deep and 12 across. By the time you get the last piece on the griddle, you go back and start flipping the toast, in the same order you put them on the griddle, as they would be cooked on the first side. When you have flipped all the pieces you then go back to the beginning and start taking them off as they would be done. Do this fast as you can as there are maybe two hundred men to serve. He wasn't quite as fast as the brothers would have liked. He ended up with a brother on each side flipping and turning and laying down what he wasn't fast enough to do. God doesn't like it when you burn the food and waste it! Meanwhile, Tim was assigned office work.

The third Sunday he was there he learned what you do after you serve the starving throngs of lost souls. You clean up the kitchen and dining room. You make precisely three hundred bag lunches. On long rows of tables, you lay out foot square sheets of wax paper. You go back and open up and place above each wax paper sheet a paper bag. You then open as many loaves of bread that you need and place a slice of bread in the center of each wax paper sheet. Next you go around and lay on each slice of bread a piece of cheese. After the cheese you repeat the process with a slice of ham. You then finish off the sandwich with another slice of bread. Going back to the beginning you wrap each sandwich and place it in the bag. Finding whatever fruit, you have for the day you place an apple, banana or pear in each bag. Finishing off the contents for the bag will be the muffin, cupcake, or cookie du jour. All that is left is to close the bags, fold down the ends and place the completed bags in boxes, moving them to the side table by the front door. At exactly 11 0'clock, you ring the bell, open the front door and hand them out to the people who appear for the next half hour or until they are gone, only one to a customer. Meanwhile, Tim sharpened pencils in the office.

On the 4th Sunday he was at St. John's: he helped prepare breakfast, helped prepare sandwiches, gave out sandwiches and at exactly eleven thirty-five policed the area. Policing meant you went around with garbage bags, picking up everything the homeless men you just fed had taken out of their bags and thrown away. Homeless, supposedly hungry men, if it wasn't their favorite type of cheese, lunchmeat, fruit, or sweet, they would throw it away immediately on the street. Or you would see them walking away going through the bag pulling out whatever they didn't want and throw it onto the ground. Half-eaten, just bitten into, sometimes right in front of you; and then they'd growl "Is that all you have?" Meanwhile, Tim alphabetized papers in the office.

On the 5th Sunday Lee learned the last of his volunteer responsibilities. After you pick up everything that's had been haphazardly discarded on the front sidewalk, you go to the basement. You bring all the clothes that have been donated throughout the previous week upstairs to the side yard. You hang them on the chain link fence surrounding the shelters driveway. At 2 o' clock you open the gates and let the men run wild carrying off everything they want. However, many will sell what they take for booze, or as with the bag lunches, discard items along the street. When all is done, you police the area. Tim looked pretty when he answered the telephone in the office.

If you were still breathing after all the morning/afternoon activity you were invited to stay and socialize with the brothers. It was during this time Lee found out about Brother Sebastian, who shed his brother's robe for his casual play clothes and sandals. His boyfriend didn't like to take him out for the day in those gloomy robes. The other "girls," otherwise known as the brothers, would treat themselves to pornographic movies and beers. Occasionally nuns from St. Beatrice would visit their brothers in charity. To say their behavior was questionable would be most kind.

Observing the interaction of the brothers and nuns, seeing Tim sit on his ass all day smoking and drinking donated soda, pissed Lee off!

Thank God for the sanity of his drab job at Gimbel's. Life seemed so normal at work! None of Tim's bullshit. Sign in, do your work, sign out. That was until Tim started wrecking his nerves at work, too.

Tim got so bold that he called Lee at work one day to tell him he had a venereal disease and said, "Maybe you should call a doctor for a checkup - I caught it from sitting on a toilet seat that one of the women used who had an STD."

Their relationship came to the breaking point months later. They were out for a Friday night drink at the Westbury one evening. The bartender came over to ask them what they were having, asking, "Hey, Tim, how are you doing?" After the drinks were served Tim got up and went to the bathroom.

Curiosity got the best of Lee, "Excuse me, bartender." When the bartender turned around Lee asked, "How do you know Tim? We just met and I don't know if he is safe to go home with?"

"Oh yeah, nice guy, great screw. We were together last weekend."

"Does he have a nice place?"

"I don't know - we went to my place."

"Oh! Thanks a lot!" When Tim returned Lee casually asked him, "How does the bartender know your name?"

"One time, when I was out shopping with Eddie we came in here for a quick lunch and he introduced me."

"You goddamn liar!" He raged, as he knocked him off his barstool onto the floor. "The bartender remembers you screwing him in his apartment last Friday! When you had to stay late and help 'paint the office.'"

Lee picked up the cringing figure on the floor only to throw him into the wall by the door. He caught him sliding down the wall and threw him head long through the double entrance doors into the street. He continued to pick him back up when he fell and bounced him, as you would bounce a rubber ball, across the street to their car.

When Lee stopped and took the car keys out of his pocket to unlock the car, Tim jumped on his back and dug his finger nails into the soft skin on each side of his nose. He didn't stop digging into his face until he got to his ears. He yelled in pain and threw Tim off his back and moved away from him. Blood was streaming down onto his clothes from the deep wounds on his face. Tim had grabbed the keys and backed the car out around him and sped off. Grabbing the handkerchief from his pocket he moved out to the curb and hailed a taxicab.

"God, you look awful, are you going to the hospital?" was the cabdriver's response when he saw his bloody face.

"No, home, 6459 Randolph Street. Down the expressway to Passyunk, out to 62nd Street, between Elmwood and Buist."

"Were you mugged?" the cab driver asked, as he drove to southwest Philly.

"No, my lover fights like a girl."

"A man did that to you?" the cabbie queried. "Well, I hope he looks worse than you."

"Unfortunately, he doesn't."

"If I see your ass in town again, I'm going to stop and you better tell me, you beat the shit out of this guy or I'll kick your ass. No way should you let a punk do that kind of shit to your face!"

Even though he babied his face with Clinique skin products the evidence of what happened was apparent to everyone the next day. He tried his best to hide the scratches with makeup and powder but he was met with comments like, "Somebody throw a cat on your face?" "Did you get drunk and fall in a rose bush?" When he transferred to the downtown store, he was co-manager of the men's departments which comprised two areas of the first and second floor. In a back corner of the first floor was a hip new department called "The In Place." Lee hid his scarred face in that department when he went to work on Monday.

"Oh honey, someone really did a number on you." Steve, the young clerk who worked in this department, lamented. Lee had never been too friendly with the clerk before, thinking him snobbish. Talking to him that day he found out just the opposite. He was quiet and minded his own business, trying to encourage all to "live and let live." Steve was in his middle twenties, living at home. He had a lover named Greg ten years his senior, who also lived with his mother. Greg had stolen Steve from the cradle when he was only 16. Recently Greg had been campaigning like a politician, for Steve to agree to move in together.

Steve, although totally gay, was very conservative in his appearance. He dressed his soft athletic six-foot two frame in ensembles of tan slacks and navy blazers, coordinated with light blue shirts and politically correct blue striped ties. He exuded an aura of calm nonchalant superiority from a very plain "GQ"-style face. Greg was the older, ruggedly handsome, greaser type no one would suspect is gay. That was until you met his best friend, Lenny, who was such a femme.

Steve's mother was a live-in housekeeper on the "main line" and didn't come home except on the weekend - and those were few and far between. When she did come home, he would retreat to his basement apartment. They both had privacy and only had contact when they wanted to see each other. He was used to having the run of the house. He enjoyed living alone and coming and going when he wanted.

Greg would have loved to be with Steve all the time but was kept at an arm's length by Steve's demand for space. They would go shopping on the weekends and Greg would get enthused about furnishings he saw. "I am going to buy that so when we move in together, we will have it."

His mother required little of Steven in exchange for a roof over his head. Cutting the grass and planting impatiens along the sidewalk seemed to be a small price to pay for free rent and total freedom. The only thing that ticked him off about living at home was that his sister and brother, who lived out of state, would call him with last minute shopping errands. Using him as a personal shopper for their mother, he was to buy a gift for whatever occasion and sign their name to the card. They never reimbursed him for any of the gifts thinking his reward and payment was that he lived at home rent free. They had no concern for how much effort was needed to find just the perfect Aigner bag or Gucci shoes.

Every weekend they were together Greg continued to stockpile furnishings and accessories, storing them in his mother's garage for the day they would move in together. That day came, and the first night they stayed together, Steve complained it was if they moved into a hotel room. He would have rather started out with second hand furniture replacing items with new ones as they were needed.

Steve said to Lee, "I feel like I am living in somebody else's house! All the furnishings are brand new, but they aren't mine. They are things Greg bought himself. Not us!" Steve would have rather waited until they found an apartment. Then they could go shopping, knowing the space they had and what would fit well. Everything went together very nicely, but Steve felt he had no input into the selection of what was bought. Greg paid for it; this is what we are buying.

He and Tim had been frequent guests at Greg and Steve's, feted and treated like royalty. Steve would sometimes berate Greg in front of them and sometimes Lee would join in and pick on Greg also. Greg never got mad at Steve or ever said anything unkind to Lee when they were both out of order. Steve would throw loud hissy fits and Greg would just walk away, trying to find a remedy to make Steve happy. Always the perfect gentleman, Steve minded his own business and never criticized Lee for putting up with Tim - even when he told him how Tim was staying out late and he suspected he was cheating. When Steve saw how Tim had scratched Lee's face and heard what happened, he blew a gasket!

"Honey, I have been trying to mind my own business, but I have to tell you! You got to get rid of him - he's no good! I know you want to believe he isn't doing the things you think he is and that he isn't cheating, but take it from me, he is!"

Tim called during the day and told Lee he had been to the house and picked up his clothes, and was going to stay at his Aunt and Uncle's for a while. He took it hard but knew it was for the best. Lee didn't remember who initiated their phone contact but there were soon phone calls back and forth and it seemed reconciliation was in the offering.

When he called and couldn't find Tim at home, when he had said he would be, he started tracking him down. He would go downtown and cruise the streets looking for his car. One time he spotted Tim leaving the gay merry-go-round: an area of streets, 17th to 21st, Spruce, Pine, and Lombard Streets, with Delaney being a favorite. Gay men would drive through the area circling the streets looking for a pick-up. In turn gay men would walk through the area circling and circling, hoping to catch someone's attention. He chased Tim's car wanting to confront him and call him a liar to his face. They raced up the Schuylkill expressway at speeds of a hundred miles an hour. At one point he thought about just giving up, turning the wheel of his car so he would crash into the guardrails and kill himself. Realizing he was irrational and acting unstable, he slowed his vehicle and returned home.

Missing Tim so very much, he called him and begged him to come home. Tim made him promise he would not be so possessive and not complain when he went out drinking with his buddies. Tim returned and all was fine for a while. He would occasionally meet Tim and a few of his friends and go bar hopping. In 1973, South Street and Society Hill's rejuvenation was in full swing and Harlow had opened her night club, Harlow's. Lee had met Rachel at Dewey's while in nursing school; she was not pretentious, but sweet and kind to everyone.

They tried to go out more often, just the two of them. To this end Tim mended hurt feelings with Maggie. Occasionally Patty and Stan invited them to their house for dinner. On one of those Saturday nights after dinner Tim and Stan got into a pissing contest about who could drink the most shots. The trio ended up in a roughneck Kensington area bar.

Lee felt uncomfortable because he didn't feel as masculine as everyone else in the bar. Leather biker boots, worn or torn jeans, muscle shirts, and rough language personified the crowd. During the shot contest, Stan's buddy Wes joined the throng of shot drinkers. Of course, no one knew he and Stan were gay or slept together. This small part of the world thought they were "buddies."

They had started drinking around ten and sometime after midnight Lee's bladder needed relieved. He was always a person who had trouble using bathrooms in public places to urinate. He had no trouble cruising in a bathroom known to be gay, a whole other issue. But he truly did not feel comfortable in this bar. He was out of his element. To have to go to the bathroom, especially in a rough and tumble straight bar, was nerve wracking for him. He managed to go in to the bathroom when it was empty and was close to zipping up when Wes came in. The only interaction he and Wes had up to that time was their introduction.

When Wes came in the bathroom he was as chatty as if he had known Lee personally. He stood at the urinal beside him. Not standing very close to the urinal Lee could see without turning his head as Wes unzipped. The room was getting too small and perspiration started rolling down the small of his back. Lee went to the sink on the side wall to wash his hands. As Wes said something to him, he turned his head in his direction. He saw Wes had turned sideways exposing himself playfully. Grinning and smiling as he talked, he bathed the urinal, side to side, with his amber stream. Only half listening because he was dumb struck by Wes's actions, he was further taken back with what Wes said next. "You know it's getting late and you guys have been drinking a lot. You really shouldn't drive all the way to Southwest Philly. Why don't you stay at my house tonight? I know Tim can stay at Stan and Pat's; he's done it many times before." He moved over to the sink and rested his hand on the wall and leaned close to Lee.

"Wouldn't that seem a little strange, my going home with you - a perfect stranger?" He asked.

"Nah, a lot of guys sleep over at their buddy's houses when they have been out drinking and had a little too much to drink!"

"But we aren't buddies. We just met; I don't know you! The only conversation we had at the bar was 'Hello.'"

"I have a big bed! We can talk all the way home, and as late into the night as you want. That's the thing about guys. We don't need any overnight kits with shit in it. Peel off your clothes, get in bed, shower in the morning, use your finger to brush your teeth and away we go." He leaned in close to Lee's face as to kiss him saying, "How about it, you and me?"

Flabbergasted Lee turned away from the beer stanched breath of Wes and exited the bathroom leaving Wes groping a bulge in his pants. Finding Tim, he announced, "Time to leave, we got to go!"

Without looking at Lee, continuing to watch the sports on the television, evil turning the corners of his mouth up; "Hey dude, I'm having fun. I'm not leaving yet!"

"Stan's buddy Wes just made a pass at me. He wants me to go home with him!"

"Ahh, guys stay over at guys houses all the time up here; Too much to drink. Nobody thinks anything of it."

"He was shaking his dick at me."

With interest gleaming in his eyes, he turned and asked, "Was it hard? How big was it?"

"I didn't even look at it; I was too surprised! Come on - I want to leave."

"Then leave. Don't make a scene like a girl."

"Then give me the car keys," he said pleadingly.

Wes crept up behind him, reaching around him to pick up his beer bottle. Leaning in close to him as if he was only reaching for the bar pretzels, he whispered in his ear, "Don't do this. I really like you. Please don't make a scene in here! You're different from most of the other guys. Just calm down and play along, he won't care if you come home with me. I already asked!"

Infuriated, a stricken look on his face he turned to Tim, "Did you give me to him for the night? And what is your goal? Shack up with straight buddy Stan? Done that before, have you?"

He could see the glazed look in Tim's eye and knew it would do no good no argue in this bar. If he had been in his own kind of bar, anywhere, Tim would have heard what he had to say and there would be a different ending. In this bar he would only come across as a "girly man" who didn't fit in. "I'm out of here." He turned and went for the door.

Wes followed determined to try one more time. Catching him outside on the corner, "Come on . . . have a change of heart. It wouldn't be that bad. I'm a sweet, gentle guy. You saw I have a lot to offer. I'm really much better than Tim. Ask Stan."

Shaking his head in disbelief he headed up the street hoping he was headed toward a subway stop. Before he found a subway, Tim squealed to a stop threw the door open yelling, "Get in!"

They drove home, neither finding words they wanted to say to the other. Lee felt alone and worthless; given away to another person, like a prostitute only worth what her pimp gets. My God - this is what my life has come to? All of the emotional trauma he endured with this man, and he wants me to sleep with someone else. Wes as much said he, himself, had Pat's husband Stan; and apparently Stan had Tim and Wes, since he offered up Stan as a reference. This is one shitty mess. It appeared to Lee that he shared quite a few of his Aunt's bad habits.

History repeats itself, the same patterns appeared again. Tim was out late and he decided to play detective. Lee drove down to the merry-go-round and sure enough spotted Tim standing on a corner talking to someone. Lee parked as soon as he could find a parking place and walked back to where the two were standing. Tim, absorbed in trying to get together with the guy he was talking to, was oblivious to his approach. He was clearly trying to pick up the guy.

Lee walked up behind Tim and said, "I hope you've told him you have a lover." Looking into both their faces he stuck out his hand to the stranger and said, "Hi, I'm Lee! The lover he cheats on but isn't man enough to leave! Oh, don't let him fool you. He does like to suck dick. Only, if you jam it down his throat as you sit on his chest!! And don't touch his dick if you fuck him, because he comes right away. No self-control!" Leaving them speechless on the corner, Lee left and went home, Tim pulled in minutes later.

"What the hell was that about!? He is one of my co-workers I was just walking him home. Nothing was going to happen."

"Well, "Lee said, "If it walks like a duck and quacks like a duck...."

He continued being a doormat without knowing why he put up with Tim's bad behavior. One Sunday afternoon when Tim had come home around ten o'clock in the morning, he called Steve. It was the usual type of phone call even good friends get tired of listening to. The hurt lover who keeps taking the bullshit hoping the other party will change and see how good they have it. The good friend has heard the same story over and over, just different incidentals. The teller being so lost in denial and needy, they can't change because they haven't hit rock bottom yet.

A couple hours later Steve called back. When Tim answered the phone Steve asked, "Where is Lee?"

"I don't know, man – I'm reading the Sunday paper. He got pissed because I was out all night and he went up to the bedroom and locked the door. He's probably pouting!"

"No! I think something's wrong. I can't say why but something made me think he was going to, you'll think I'm dramatic, but I think he was going to kill himself!" With Steve in mid-sentence Tim hung up the phone and ran upstairs.

He remembered he had a shit load of Thorazine, Stellazine and Phenobarbital pills in his closet. Banging on the door, calling, he did not get a response. He threw himself against the door, jarring it open. Seeing Lee asleep, he ran to the closet and found the pill bottles. All had been opened and some removed from each. Lee was breathing, slowly, and Tim wasn't able to wake him up. He dragged the limp figure off the bed and pulled him down the hall to the bathroom. He laid him over him the tub and turned the cold water on, letting it pound on his body until he showed signs of alertness.

When he could utter some words, Tim moved him up in the tub

and stuck his fingers down his throat, making him retch and vomit until he thought he got all the medicine Lee had swallowed out of his stomach. Cleaning him up and putting him back to bed, Tim apologized for driving him to such desperation and promised to change his ways. But Tim couldn't change his ways any more than a leopard can change its spots.

Lee's childhood friend from Bradford Pennsylvania called his parents and asked for his address and phone number in Philadelphia. He had relatives in New Jersey and the next time he went to see them called Lee and received an invitation to come visit for a couple days. It had been a few years since they had seen each other and both had matured. Lee developed his dark handsome Italian looks favoring tight jeans and open shirts that exposed his manly hairy chest. Joey outgrew his lanky gainliness and was now a blonde crew cut Adonis, a la Tab Hunter, although a geek.

Joey arrived on his day off while Tim was working which allowed the two friends time alone to catch up. Tim came home on time for once and everyone enjoyed the pot roast dinner. They sat around the table afterwards drinking and chatting about their childhoods. Joey still remembered when Lee visited with him at his parents' home for his high school graduation and the present, he gave him for graduation was a hand job.

Tim found it hard to believe they had no other sexual adventures beyond that experience. "No," Joey said, "although we often talked about some of my friends and whether or not they were gay or acting on impulse."

Plying everyone with drinks, Tim suggested, they all to go to bed together. Tim made it clear he wanted to screw Joey in the ass. He had never been screwed and Tim wanted to be the first to do it.

"No, I will only trust Lee. Maybe, if like it I can let you, but only him first!"

They went upstairs and undressed each other, Tim going right for the fresh meat. Turning off the lights they got in bed and Lee and Joey were making out. Tim positioned Lee on his back and maneuvered Joey onto his stomach ass up. As the two old friends made Tim put a bottle of poppers under Joey's nose.

"Oh God! What is that?" Joey cried out.

"Just poppers, man, it will help you relax." Tim cajoled.

"What are you doing back there?"

"Just putting some lubricant in your ass, so you can relax." That done Tim opened Joey's buttocks and aiming his prowess at that virgin hole, mounting Joey in one impaling action.

"YEOW!! STOP!! STOP!!!" Joey screamed, jumping out of the bed.

The pain expressed by his childhood friend sobered him up immediately. Lost and out of control he started yelling at Tim, blaming him for wanting to have a threesome with his old friend. He knew he had lost the friendship of his old friend; Joey was dressed and gone before he stopped to draw a breath from haranguing Tim.

Tim wasn't going to listen to any of that shit. All he wanted was to get laid by something new and strange. After dressing, he too headed downstairs to leave. Lee pulled him back and started hitting him but he escaped his clutches. As Tim ran out the door, a distraught Lee threw his head through the glass pane in the door and shoved his neck down on the glass shard sticking up from the broken glass pane.

The old couple who lived next door was awakened by the noise generated by the bedroom fiasco and came over to complain. Finding a bleeding Lee on the floor, the wife called for an ambulance while the husband pressed a heavy kitchen towel against his neck. Arriving at Mercy Douglas hospital with the deep neck wound and reports from the neighbors of a terrible fight it was assumed someone had pushed him into the glass door window. The police were called but he refused to co-operate. He knew if he told the truth they would probably hold him for observation and admit him to a psych ward.

After he was stitched up, his neighbors took him home and told him how fortunate he was to be alive. Giving him advice on getting rid of his roommate they told Lee they would look in on him and said, "Call if we can do anything."

Lee knew he was in trouble and needed mental health counseling.

The next day he called the area mental health center. He told a half-true and vastly altered story of the night before. He was extremely honest when he stressed, he felt he was out of control of his emotions. They had him come right in and talk to a counselor. He was asked, "Do you ever have suicidal thoughts? Have you ever tried suicide? Do you consider yourself depressed? Do you get despondent?" He had to lie to his intake counselor or they would lock him up.

He realized he had to get Tim out of his life. He called Tim's Aunt, without inquiring about him. He told her if she was going to be home, he wanted to bring some of Tim's things to her house. When he arrived at her house Tim met him at the curb. As he unloaded the things he packed and put on the curb, Tim was going through the boxes asking, "Where is such and such?"

As Lee got back in his car, he told Tim, "Who the f.... knows and who the f.... cares?"

"I want, where's my.... I want.... " was all he heard as he drove away.

CHAPTER THIRTY-THREE

HE WENT FOR COUNSELING BI-WEEKLY, then weekly, meeting with a grandmotherly type named Mrs. Lloyd. During the one-on-one therapy sessions, she talked to him about abandonment, esteem, self-worth, and self-hate issues she felt had developed after his mother's suicide attempts. Somewhere, somehow in his mind when she locked herself in the bathroom with the gun and tried to kill herself and threatened to kill him, his mental health was damaged. From religious and familial teachings, you are told your Mother loves you unconditionally.

He didn't think his mother loved him. How could she not love him enough to want to raise him? He didn't feel she loved her family or she would not have wanted to leave them by killing herself. If she did not deem him worthy of love, or wouldn't or couldn't love him, why would anyone else in the world.

His father did not see or in many ways know he had been psychologically damaged to the extent he was. Should he have known? Seen? Yes, of course, in a perfect world.

He had been carrying the burden of being responsible for his mother's poor health because "your birth was difficult" since he was old enough to understand what he was told, that "Your mother has been sick since you were born!"

During an emotionally draining session Lee sobbed out loud, "If your own mother doesn't love you, who will?"

He hadn't felt it before. Do parents understand that an incident like this can make a child feel unwanted and worthless, erasing any chance for feeling self-esteem among the peer group.

He was right to tell his mother that day when they were cleaning (when he was 12-13 years old) and she cast up to him all she and his father had done for him, "I didn't ask to be born, you brought me into this world, you owe me clothing food and shelter." His mother felt he should earn it each and every day by doing gardening, house cleaning, ironing, and washing.

There were weeks of discussing what he knew of his mother's relationship with her parents. She was an unwanted late life baby, rejected by her mother. She was parented by a doting father, abandoned by older, jealous siblings. Because she didn't want to eat her mother's hurried "throw it on the table dinner," her father gave her nickels and dimes to go to the corner store. There she would buy candy, potato chips, or dried beef.

In the old days, the large cast iron kitchen stove heated the house in the winter. Her mother would turn off the lights and bank back the kitchen and parlor stoves. Being younger than her un-interested husband, her mother would go out and tell her children to go to bed to keep warm.

Mrs. Lloyd was able make him understand that parents are not born. People who have babies do not come self-equipped with what they need to know to raise a child. Only through parenting do you become a parent. Not everyone becomes a good parent. Everyone could, depending on their experience as a child with their parents. How and what they were taught, if was there love in the family, and how was it expressed and valued. The most necessary requirement to be a good parent is to want to be a good parent.

Lee benefited greatly from his time with Mrs. Lloyd. Accepting his mother had her own baggage which she exposed to her children like a virus helped him understand she could only react to whatever she experienced with the limited love and education her parents gave her. She probably did do the best she could.

Living with the thoughts that no one is going to love you because your own mother didn't is not corrected easily. Like dieting, one day at time you have to retrain and force yourself in to different life scenarios. You can't reject someone simply because you want to reject them before they get a chance to reject you. You need to want to treat yourself better, with more dignity, more self-love. You deserve a clean home with furnishings you can afford. You deserve to keep yourself neat and clean, wearing as nice clothes as you can afford.

You need to cultivate wholesome television viewing, read good books and keep current on affairs. Be part of the whole, not a tumbleweed blowing in the wind annoying the world. If you continue to be a doormat, people will use you for a doormat. If you let multiple, anonymous strangers use your body as a sex object and not treat you as a worthy, deserving person, you will come to see yourself as a loathsome, undesirable creature not worthy of respect. You will become round shouldered from looking down, never looking people in the eye. You have to open yourself up to be vulnerable, and maybe get hurt, before you can change the past and create a new healthier future for yourself.

With several months of successful individual counseling, Mrs. Lloyd suggested he join group counseling to wean himself from the dependence on counseling. Reluctant at first, afraid of people perceiving him as a fool, he found he enjoyed the camaraderie. It was a small group of twelve people with a myriad of problems; nobody had just one. Many times, he was accused of being a ringer. The others in the group challenged the psychologist leading the group saying he didn't need to be there. To the others in the group he seemed to have all the answers. It is always easier to see the faults in someone else, rather than yourself, and tell them how to correct their lives.

His involvement with the group counseling came to a screeching halt when he confronted another member. He and others would meet for ice cream or snacks outside the group. It's in human nature to talk about people who aren't present. They had been discussing a young man named Jordan, who was seeking help with a self-hate problem. He was born of a biracial couple, and much darker in complexion than anyone else in his family. He had been discriminated against by his own family and wished he had been of a lighter complexion like his siblings. Lee found himself in the men's room with him during a break in the session one evening. He controlled himself and did not act out on his fantasy of getting ahold of this guy wherever he could.

Jordan was complaining how he did not get anything from the counseling and didn't feel like he fit in. He didn't feel anyone wanted to talk to him or cared about why he was there. He didn't feel included in discussions. They were both finished doing what they came into the restroom to do and moved over to the sinks to wash their hands. Lee asked the man if he could speak freely.

Jordan said, "Yeah, man! I feel like such an outcast!"

"Some of us have got together after group and discussed it and we think there is another issue - your sexuality. You said you don't like girls, yet you've also said some people have made comments about your genital size. We don't know if you meant girls have made comments, be it big or small, which would explain why you don't like girls. Or by people, did you mean when you were in school and showered in front of the other boys - did they make fun of your size, big or small?"

"Hey man, I am not small!"

"I don't know! I was a gentleman and didn't try to check you out at the urinal. Well, that is a lie! I did! You stood too close."

"That's why I never got along with the girls. They said it was too big, complained it tore them up. This is hard to talk about, man! In high school I played baseball, and one evening after practice the coach asked me to re-line the field. You know, that white powder had washed off from the rain, and more needed to be spread. When I got back to the locker room everyone had left. Alone, I undressed; I enjoyed being naked with only the exhaust fan on. You know a man's shower room has that certain stale smell. I don't know if it's the sweaty clothes and sweaty jocks on the floor, or all the 'cum' squirted on the walls, when the guys see who can jerk off the fastest and furthest.

"The wet slab floor was cold and damp under my feet. I enjoyed the feel of the surface under my feet; that physical skin on floor contact took over my senses. I enjoyed a heightened sense, so much so when I reached the showers I sat down on the floor. God, I can't explain it - I felt so sexy! I spread my legs and rubbed the head of my prick on the cold damp floor. My boy responded, and with a little stretching, it was growing bigger. It was feeling good. I realized I had to get up off the floor. By the time I got under a shower it was at full mast waving in the breeze, proud as you please. After I soaped up and rinsed off, my hands just went there again. I was really going at it. It felt good, there was some feeling I can't explain. It was all about being alone where all the naked bodies cavort and shower, I knew this was out in left field. I moved over to the lockers to get dressed and take this party home.

"Standing, there, in a public place, knowing I could just play with it…all I wanted, as long as I wanted, man, it was showing off, it seemed to get bigger than usual, really swollen. At one point it felt so good. I was sort of bending over and I saw a tear in its 'eye.' Something inside my head told me to see if I could touch it with my tongue. Next thing I know I'm grabbing it at the base and pulling it up and stretching it. I didn't have to stretch it too far or bend over very far. I stuck my tongue out and flicked the end of it with my own tongue. Man, I was going crazy inside. I thought, wow! What if I could do myself? I always thought how lucky dogs are, that they can lick themselves.

"Say man, don't look at me funny! Any man who exercises and does stretch has had that thought. I straightened up and let it relax a minute. That quick, I decided I had to see if I could. I stroked it, took a good hold and bend over forward. First, I flicked it again. Then I swirled my tongue around it and went for the gold. Man, I could get two inches in my mouth with good suction. I stopped; thinking Jesus Christ! What am I doing? I've had B. J's before. It must be okay; people do it! Why? I knew it had felt good! But I felt scared, because I had enjoyed it! I can't tell you how it felt to know I could control the feeling in my own penis. You know like masturbation; everyone has a different way. Some like it wet, some want spit, others want oil, others want it dry. You know some want the hand upside down, pull it to the side, squeeze the head, others want more tightness on the shaft. You know if you do it with the opposite hand you usually use, it's altogether different. It's like some stranger's doing it to you and feels great to have a more exciting feeling for a change. Every man, somewhere in his life, has had another male jerk him off.

"Standing there, allowing myself to abandon all principle, I got caught up in the moment, real into it. I bent over and captured myself again. It didn't take but a few motions. The feeling swelled up, my legs became weak, and like it was my first climax and I came in my own mouth. I didn't swallow it! I was scared stupid. I straightened up and it rolled out of my mouth over my lips dripping to the floor. As I raised my arm to wipe my mouth, I realized someone was standing in the doorway of the showers. I was so scared I didn't look at the face. I was too worried about what I had just done. Was I queer? Did I want to do that to another man? What did it mean?

"I came back to my senses and wondered how long someone was watching me without my realizing it. By the end of the next school day everyone knew what I had done. Some of the guys were bold enough to ask me to do it again and let them watch! Others taunted me and called me faggot, grabbing themselves and saying, hey - take this!"

Lee found himself aroused by the narrative and nearly lost his train of thought. He was almost motivated to pursue his first desire, but sincerely wanted to help Jordan accept himself. "That was in high school, Jordan - you are 28 years old. It was an embarrassing moment – but why does it define you now? You said so often you never had a girlfriend and don't like girls, they get on your nerves. Not all girls would kick a man with a big dick out of bed!"

"No, girls just want your money!"

"You don't like faggots! You say it's a crime against God! You are quick to add, 'I do have faggot friends, but that isn't for me!' What are you saying? What is for you? No girls? What is the alternative?"

"Man! What are you saying man?"

"I am saying you say you even hate being black. How could you deal with yourself if you had to face the truth, and accept you are a n____r cocksucker?"

That black man jumped on Lee like the proverbial white-on-rice! He had him down on the floor, straddling his chest, hitting him, punch after punch in the face screaming, "Don't you call me a faggot! I ain't no cocksucker, I don't want screwed in the ass." As the other group members standing around in the hall heard the loud yelling, they called the group's leader. They rushed in and pulled Jordan off the bleeding Lee.

As they pulled him up to his feet, Lee yelled, "How did you feel on my chest; with your crotch so close to my face? Did it make you want to unzip your pants and stuff something down my throat? Who were you hating as you hit me, me or you?"

Again, he showed up at work leaving co-workers and customers alike wondering what happened to his face. Counseling ended for him, and he lost himself in his work. The store was a great place to meet people, sex partners in particular. Steve said to him one day when they were straightening clothes, "There goes a shopping bag queen."

"A what?" he asked.

"Whenever you see a queen carrying shopping bags under her arms you know she's heading for the restrooms.

"What are you talking about?"

"Cruising queens go to the bathrooms or maybe even meet somewhere else, but neither have the time, or maybe a place, to go. One will get two shopping bags and they'll go into a public restroom. When they are alone, they go into a booth together and they open the bags. Someone steps in to the bags and stands there either getting done or doing the other. If someone comes in, they just get quiet and no one thinks anything other than someone has two shopping bags full of goodies... if they only knew what kind of goodies!"

On the days Steve worked at "The In Place" alone, Lee would cover for him when he went to lunch and had to use the bathroom. On one of those days, as he straightened stock and tidied up the area, a nice-looking guy came in. He seemed to spend more time than necessary looking at the clothes. Lee felt he was being cruised because he noticed the man kept looking up at him and making small talk. As Steve walked back in to the area, the customer asked to try on a pair of pants and went into the dressing room. He told Steve he thought the man was interested.

The man called out, "These are a little too big. Could I try on the next smaller size, please?"

Steve said, "Here, honey - give him these to put on." Handing him a pair of pants exactly like the customer was trying, but, two sizes smaller.

"When he says they are too small, ask him if you can check the fit and go from there." He handed the man the pants through the slit in the curtains and the man said, "Excuse me, these aren't the right size."

"Try them on please, they all run different."

The response from behind the curtain was very authoritative, "Sir, these pants don't fit!"

"May I step in and check them? I will be better able to understand what size you need." Winking at each other he left Steve to stand guard while he went behind the curtain. Entering the small fitting room, and making sure the curtains overlapped, Lee asked the man to turn around and face the mirror. Raising his eyebrows questioningly he started to rebuff him but decided to play along, and turned around crossing his arms in front of his chest. Standing behind the man, Lee put his hands on the man's athletic bubble shaped butt. "Yes, they do feel like they are very tight."

Surprised to be accosted but enjoying the attention, the man didn't move as Lee ran his hands around his waist. "They feel all right here, but my oh, my, they don't even meet here in the front," as he swung the two sides of the fly as if to fan a fire.

At this point the customer grinningly sneered, "They are way too tight in the crotch!"

He confirmed this when he gently snuggled his hands down each side of the man's smooth belly. "Oh, I do apologize, sir! It seems I put my hands *in* your underwear instead of on top of them to check the feel and fit!'

"Well, while you there, why do you think they are too tight?"

Moving his right hand to encircle the man's swelling organ and lifting the hairy orbs with his other hand, he said, "I think you have too much in your pants to start with."

"Well, I can't make them smaller." the man huskily said.

Nibbling on his ear Lee whispered, "I can help reduce the size."

The man uncrossed his arms and put his hands behind his back to explore Lee's bulging pants. Turning around he gently offered, "Not here, I have a room over at the Ben Franklin. Can you sneak out for a little while?" Softly kissing Lee, he convinced him to take a short break.

Lee came out and told Steve what he was going to do. Steve said, "If anyone comes looking for you, I'll say you went up to alterations about a customer's order."

The man came out and threw the pants over the rack, grabbing Lee close to him and hugging the breath out of him. Grinning ear to ear he said, "No sale here. Come on!" It was a delightful one-time fling; the man was an Air Force pilot in town for a recruiting seminar. They enjoyed a wonderful matinee in the Old Hotel at Ninth and Chestnut, never seeing each other again.

Another time Lee was folding shirts when a guy walked through the department and took the escalator upstairs. He had been talking to Gill Wheaton as they straightened the stock and Gill said, "That guy was cruising you; he's probably going to the men's restroom. Go get him!" (It was a standing joke in Philadelphia that if you took all the gay men out of the department stores the stores would be self-service and devoid of customers.)

Sure enough, when he got there the guy was standing at a urinal. Not wanting to be obvious Lee went to a stall and opened the door getting some toilet paper to blow his nose. The guy looked around twice to see what he was doing and looked down at his hands both times as he did. Another customer came in and Lee ducked into the stall. The second man used the urinal without the first man leaving; when the second man left, Lee came out of the booth. The first guy turned around, zipped up and said, "Can't stand here anymore I might get reported. Are you interested?"

Lee said, "Yes, but... let's get out of here." Introducing themselves to each other Tony said, "I would like something more than a one-night stand."

He invited Tony out to dinner. They exchanged phone numbers and promised to get in touch. He called Tony later that night and after a long dinner date followed by cocktails at home the romance was on. In this small world they found out they had something unlikely in common: cheating lovers. Discussing their respective former lovers, they discovered Tim had been cheating on Lee with Tony's lover Eric. Ironically, as soon as both were available, neither wanted the other. Each now were making overtures to get back with their former partners.

Tony came from a large family with several brothers and very loving, supportive parents. They were seeing each other at Easter time and he invited Lee to dinner on Easter Sunday. The mother loved pound cake so he made a huge pound cake in the shape of a cross, since this family was Catholic.

They enjoyed each other's company and decided to become roommates. It was Tony's first move away from his parents' home. There was no controversy, no confusion. It was dull. It was going great, but blah. No excitement. He knew the end was coming when Tony woke him up in the morning with a blowjob. He had nuzzled up to him talking sexily into his ear. He started to go down and jumped back, right away, covering his mouth with his hand.

Lee asked, "What's the matter?"

Through the hand covering his lips, he said, "My teeth!" Embarrassed, Tony looked around and then leaned over the bed and picked his teeth up off the floor. Excusing himself he went to the bathroom to wash off his teeth. As Lee watched his bony, skinny ass rush away he knew this wasn't for him. His way out was Tony going to the hospital. He was a cancer survivor since he was ten. As a young child his body grew proportionally for his age and height. He attained normal height, and it didn't stunt his genital growth, but he was extremely thin. Occasionally a flare-up caused him to go back into the hospital for a short stay.

It was during one of Tony's hospital visits that Lee became familiar with Peter. Peter was a youngster who worked behind the camera department at Gimbel's. When opening his department one morning, Lee happened upon a letter addressed to him. It was from a secret admirer who wanted to meet him but didn't want to step in to the middle of an existing relationship. If he was available and interested, he was to place the envelope is his blazer jacket so it would be visible. The sender would than interpret the placement as a sign of availability and interest and he would identify himself. Later when he passed by the camera department, young Peter spoke up inquiring if Lee was having a nice day.

Pausing a minute, looking quizzically at Peter, he thought - Peter? Lee asked him, "Did you leave me this note?" tapping his breast pocket.

"Yes, I hope you don't mind, but you never stop and speak. You are always busy or on your way to do something else."

"Well, well young Peter! What am I going to do with you?"

"You don't have to think about that. I know what I want to do with you."

"Why you rascally Peter Rabbit; how old are you?"

"Old enough - 19! Does that matter?"

"Yes. Your parents would have me arrested for robbing the chicken coop."

"Well, you can eat chicken. I'll pull a long hard carrot out of my garden for you to chew on. Besides, my mother knows and my father is never home."

"The offer is very interesting! Such tender, young meat! We'll have to talk later about our likes and dislikes."

As Lee walked away, young Peter exclaimed, "I like what I see from this side!"

Stopping in his tracks, he turned around and saw the young man in a new light. He decided he would knock on that door and see who answers. During the day he thought about cute, attractive, nubile Peter and wondering what he should do about Peter's overture, because of his age. Lee was in his middle thirties. He was soon relieved of wondering about young Peter - it was taken out of his hands.

Lee was taking the subway service cars back and forth to work and so was Peter. Lee took the Elmwood Avenue car and Peter rode the Woodland Avenue car that went into Darby. That evening going home as he usually did, he saw Peter coming down into the waiting area for the West Philly cars. Peter came over, stopping at his side, stood very close and in a low voice said, "I am going home with you; and I'll show you **why** you should let me move in with you."

Shooting Peter, a surprised look, he thought, Tony's in the hospital, his parents will be seeing him, I have a free evening... It is just a trolley ride home right now, let's see what happens. They got on the trolley, Lee first, walking down the aisle to a seat in the back. Peter followed along and swung into the seat beside him. He sat down in such a manner as to squeeze Lee between him and the wall of the trolley car. Peter took off his jacket and laid it across his lap, making sure it overlapped onto Lee's legs. Catching on to the fact he was being pursued was exciting. It was getting more exciting every minute by the forwardness of the youthful hunter.

As the trolley pulled out of the station, the lights flickered as usual while going under the Thirtieth Street station. He felt a hand creep under the coat exploring his private area as Peter quietly sang Judy Garlands' "Trolley Song" in his ear. His head immediately pivoting, searching the surrounding faces to see if there was an awareness of what was happening. A smile and chuckle escaped his lips. Thinking he may enjoy this young man after all. He relaxed and let whatever Peter wanted to happen, happen. The trolley had emptied out and they were alone in the back of the trolley as it pulled away from Bertram's Gardens. He had to remind Peter to stay seated and stop trying to squeeze down on the floor in front of him. Experiencing the most pleasantly distracting ride home he ever had, the two exited the trolley at 65th Street and Lee led his new love-struck pup home.

Undressing the youth was like taking a diaper off a baby boy. The youthful manhood, no longer withheld by the clothing, bounced rigidly into sight pointing straight up and out, its unforgiving demand for release refused to let it bend for any amount of time. Ahh, youth, Lee thought. After 45 minutes the steeple still stood strong. The steeple swayed in the storm of convulsing gales, twice. It still stood after withstanding pounding forces. What would it take to bring this structure down? Two hours into what had become a marathon, bringing the jack hammer home to Lee, guilt again came over him as he said, "You know this is great. You could make an old man out of me - but I still have a problem with your age."

Jumping out of bed Peter picked up the clothes he had peeled off as he got in bed. Throwing them at Lee he said, "Get dressed, we're going to see my mother!" Getting dressed and following Peter back to the trolley stop, two transfers later he was walking behind Peter into the boy's parents' home. Opening the door Peter called out, "Its only me, Mom, I'll be up in a minute." Peter went in to the kitchen and checked on the food in the oven.

Turning to Lee he explained, "My mother is very sick. She has cancer, that's the main reason she would like to see me settled before she dies. My father couldn't take it when he found out my mother had cancer. He thought life had thrown him, and his biggest disappointment was when he found out I was gay. When they told him, she was terminal and only had so long to live, he couldn't take it. He doesn't come home often anymore. My aunts take turns nursing my mother. She is lucky she comes from a large Italian family that takes care of its own."

Hearing this brave young man sound so stalwart of his parent's plight was very hard for him. It was as if he was hearing the news about his own mother, it affected him so greatly. Peter led him upstairs into the softly lit mauve colored bedroom. Against the cushions lay the remnants of a once beautiful bride, the beauty only remaining in the pictures on the walls. Introducing him to the sweet woman, she raised her eyelids to better see the man her son has presented to her.

"My son tells me you are co-workers."

"Yes Ma'am."

Unable to hold back Peter rushes forward, "Mother, Lee has concerns that you or Dad would cause problems for him if we have a sexual relationship." He thought he saw a perceivable wince but her speech never revealed a hint of disgust or animosity.

"Be it you or someone else my son has made it clear what his preference is for a life partner. Am I happy he wants to be with men?"

Wearily she continued, "Heavens no! I would much prefer he dated girls. Married a girl, had children, raised a family; but even if he did all those things, I wouldn't be here to see it. I am on borrowed time. My main concern is that my only child is as happy as he can be when I am gone. His father has made it clear he cannot stand to be around either of us anymore. He is a very weak man. I am not making excuses, I understand. Where Peter is concerned, he favors me so much he says, it is too hard to look at Peter when he can only be reminded of me. It is not that he doesn't love Peter, he does! Peter's strong. He just needs someone to love him, look out for him, and help him care for his soul."

"Oh, Mother I'll be fine." Peter leaned over and lifted his sweet mother off her pillow in a painful hug. With a weak smile for Lee, she closed her eyes. His aunt left the corner she was hovering in, gathered them as she would a newspaper with potatoes peelings on it, she was discarding, and gently dismissed them.

"Okay you two, let her rest. I will wait a while and then try to get her to eat a little something. Go have your supper. Dimitria has left a lovely stew on the stove." Lee left Peter to finish his stew and fondly looked forward to enjoying his company again.

The next day Lee went to visit Tony in the hospital to explain he should move back in with his parents. He did not mention Peter; he only talked about the relationship between them. Tony had come to know several people who worked in the store with Lee and continued to pop-in to say hello. It was on one of those pop-in visits from one of those people that Tony found out about Peter. Men can be bigger gossips than women. Tony was told everything that the rumor mill knew about how and what transpired between Peter and Lee.

Having his feelings hurt and feeling betrayed, Tony searched out Lee to accuse him of leaving him for another man. "Why didn't you tell me you met someone else? Jeez, a guy can't even go to the hospital and feel sure that his man is at home waiting for him." He saw a movement in Lee's eye and turned around to see Peter walking away from them.

"Just a minute, you tramp!" Because of his cancer Tony's voice hadn't reached its more masculine note. When he was excited, he sounded more like a girl. "You knew we were an item. What the hell's up with you? You know you shouldn't shit where you eat. How long do you think this will last? You are too young. You are just a ribbon clerk; how long do you think you will hold his interest? I am a lawyer and I couldn't keep it. Well you just better stay healthy and not go to the hospital. There's always going to be someone else waiting just like you did."

Unfortunately, Tony was right. He and Peter didn't last very long. Peter could last, that wasn't the problem, but that is all he had. Lee wanted something more than cuteness and sex. After they broke up Peter could not cope with seeing him, but not having him, and he transferred upstairs to the shoe department. Lee was co-manager of that area also, but his assistant handled that department more frequently.

Just as customers often return items they have bought and worn it also happens that store employees do the same thing. Lee knew of many games' employees played. If customers didn't take their receipts some unscrupulous employees would keep them. After altering it to show their name, they would take something from stock. Attaching the orphan sales slip to their package, stolen merchandise walked out the front door under store security's noses.

A young geeky man went so far as to buy a very expensive designer suit. He took the suit to a private tailor who took it apart, made a pattern and put the suit back together. The employee returned it for full refund. He and the South Philly tailor made a bundle selling ripped off designer suits. The young sales clerks had a reputation to maintain in the bars and dressing well was a prerequisite. Everyone had game for a five-finger discount! Lee had a pair of shoes he purchased outside the store that he had worn and decided they were not the right size. Knowing many other store employees routinely exchange items and sales clerks look the other way, he took advantage of his position and did the same. The difference was that he went in early when no one was in the department. He took a new pair of shoes out of the box and put them on. He put the shoes he wore to work in the new box. He put the box with his old shoes in it on the return to vendor table.

When Peter was getting the shoes ready to send back, he called Lee over and said, "I asked Mark where these shoes came from. He doesn't know. Do you know where they came from?"

Asking himself why Peter would care, they never worried that much before if a receipt wasn't in the box. You didn't need a receipt to send the shoe back to the vendor. He told him what he had done. Peter said, "Oh, well, that's all right then, I just wondered."

Two or three months later, long after he forgot about the shoes a security guard came to the floor and asked him to accompany him to the office. He was offered a seat and the guard went around the desk sat down. Leaning over to get something from a drawer he said, "You know I am sorry this took so long but I had to wait until you wore those shoes into the store again." He sat the old pair of shoes Lee exchanged on top of his desk. "Do you know anything about these shoes?"

The light not flickering on yet, he asked, "What do you want to know?"

"Well, slick! I have information that says you stole the shoes that you are wearing and put these old worn ones in stock."

Along with the pain in pit of his stomach, it felt like his chair was falling into space. "I didn't steal them. My wife bought me the shoes for Christmas and I did exchange them here because of size. We often take back merchandise that we can't prove was bought here because we sell the same brands other stores do. As long as it is an exchange, nothing is said and we build good will."

Remaining silent the guard got up and left him alone in the office. He returned with a voluntary resignation form and threatened to have him arrested if he didn't sign the form and leave the store. Feeling very ashamed, and just glad not to be prosecuted, Lee signed and was escorted out the service door onto Eighth Street. Alone and jobless, in despair and wondering what he would do, he walked down the street.

"Lee, Lee!" Tim came rushing from his idling car at the curb. "Steve called me, saying while he was at lunch you were taken away by security. He was worried, and not knowing who to call to help you, he called me. He said the only time security takes anyone away is because they're caught stealing. Word spread through your department that you had been removed by the store detective.

"Peter in the shoe department bragged, 'I reported him for stealing. I told them he stole a pair of shoes.'" Vengeance doesn't belong only to women scorned, Lee thought. He also thought he was very glad Tim had come; he didn't feel quite so lost. He had been trying to ingratiate himself back into his life and he felt he saw the perfect chance when Steve called.

"You know I still love you - why don't I move back in until you get another job? Things would be back to normal. You know I can help you with the bills."

Feeling instant relief for Tim's offer, he thanked him and told him, "I can't think straight right now - let my nerves settle before we talk about that again." Arriving home earlier than usual since he was terminated, he was feeling desperate and was considering Tim's offer. He was surprised by a knock on the door. He immediately thought Tim had come back and would press him to get back together. He found Mr. Melnyck his insurance man at the door.

"Come on in, I'll get my envelope." Not knowing where or when his next paycheck would come from, he told the kindly old gent, "I may be late next month – I'm not working right now." Mr. Melnyck fixed that problem within minutes. He explained they were shorthanded and he was again carrying the book for this area of Philadelphia. The district manager has to collect the premiums when he is short an agent. This was the same way Tim got his job with the insurance company. Mike had come there collecting when he was short staffed and got Tim his first job in Philadelphia.

Fate again presented him with an irony. A job offer appeared just when he needed help to get back on his feet. He knew he was going to be offered the same job Tim had. They really didn't care who they hired; any warm body will do; just so the district managers didn't have to be responsible for collections.

Lee was hired the next day when he went to the insurance office in the Northeast to fill out an application. Until he passed the state licensing exam, he could not sell insurance. He could only carry "the book" and collect premiums. The book was the size of a shoebox, which Lee thought was apropos. Mr. Melnyck gave him a large leather wallet and told him to keep his collections separate from his own personal money and to never borrow from the account collections.

Because Mike, as he came to call Mr. Melnyck, had 7 other agents he didn't spend much time with him. It was his job to push his agents to sell and had to go on an expected number of sales appointments with each agent every week. He was left on his own to study for the state licensing exams. Remembering the route fairly well from driving Tim around the streets of his neighborhood, he found it easy to find the customers' addresses. As the weeks went by and he adjusted to his new job he was pleasantly surprised to find Kathy Derickman was one of his customers. She had been a fun customer from the 5 and 10. The last time he saw her was when he was out with his brother-in-law. Happy to see each other after so long they agreed to meet for a drink at the local bar, Angelo's, to play catch up on what they had been doing. Being weak minded when it came to Tim, he was glad to have an excuse to give Tim as to why they couldn't get together that weekend.

Saturday night he and Kathy amused each other with stories about her away-from-home truck- driving husband and his head-over-heels love for a looser lothario. They talked of her suspicions regarding her husband's sexual adventures while he was away and Lee's fatal attraction. She insisted on buying the drinks and impressed him with all the money she was throwing around buying everybody drink after drink. During the evening she introduced him to women around the bar adding, "I help them out once in a while, because they're not married and sometimes need a little extra cash."

She explained, "It would be better if they were with a man. They wouldn't appear so obvious. I have a lot of male friends who want companionship and I make introductions." And she lifted her glass and swung it around the bar at all the women she had introduced him to.

"Sometimes, depending where they are to meet, it would be better if they arrived at the place where they were going with a man." She offered Lee a chance to make some extra money by helping the girls get to where they were going. He was trying to decide if he had had too many drinks or did, he actually *understand* what she said, that she's a Madam running girls. He realized then that she had been telling the truth that time when she shouted, "Two more for two whores!"

Out of the corner of his eye he saw her slip a twenty-dollar bill off the bar that the bartender gave her when she broke a fifty. As she put the twenty in her purse, she deftly replaced it with another. Whispering to Lee, "If he says anything about this being phony, back me up that this is the twenty he gave me when he broke my fifty.

"And I have had gentlemen who request a gentleman for a date. You could make some money!" My God, I had just been approached to be a male whore, Lee thought. Remembering his embarrassment when she made her proclamation in the bar with his former employee and brother-in-law, he wasn't going to stay. Making a hasty exit he thought how lucky he was not to have gotten involved with her passing counterfeit money. Fired for stealing! Then out with a woman passing fake money. And a Madam at that! And he could have been a prostitute's escort, and more!

Well I guess you should expect one crazy person now and then, although this may not have been the first crazy lady.

He collected insurance premiums from a Mrs. Rosemont in Darby; among her insurance policies, she was paying for a policy that belonged to her son Rusty. She told Lee one particular Friday, "I am going to send you to Rusty's to collect his premium. It's about time he takes care of his own business. I'll give you the directions; he doesn't live far from here, down by the mall in the Fernwood Apartments." He could understand the woman wanting not to continue paying for her son's insurance policies. After all, out on your own, you pay your own bills.

She gave him the address and told him, "Rusty's apartment is on the third floor - he doesn't like to come all the way down to the first floor to open the door. They don't have those electronic locks. Just go around to the back of the building and there is a fire escape that goes right to Rusty's apartment."

No problem, Lee thought. After he found the address and was going up the stairs; he found the higher he went, the wobblier the old iron fire escape became. As he reached the apartment door, he realized the fire escape was not attached to the building. The bolts had rusted away. As he leaned to knock on the door his shifting weight caused the fire escape to swing away from the building. As the structure started to sway, he grabbed a hold of the door knob. Just then the door was pulled open from the inside. The retreating figure, swathed in only a bath towel around the waist announced, "My mother called! Come on in, I'll find my book."

He reached out for dear life at the door frame trying to catch a hold of something for safety. The noise of his jumping into the doorway caused the young man with a long red pony tail to turn around. "Oh, I'm sorry I thought you were the insurance man?"

A visibly shaken Lee said, "I am! Your mother told me what time would be best to catch you home and to come up the back stairs."

"I don't know why she told you that. She knows this is the time I just get home from work and I would be in the shower." Grinning he offered the consolation, "My mother! She does have her ways."

The young man loosened his towel and re-wrapped it around his waist. The suddenly bashful Lee lowered his eyes as the young man offered him a handshake saying, as Lee introduced himself, "I guess you already know my name - I'm Rusty. Come on in and sit down. I'll get my book and money."

As he walked away, Lee could still see beads of water from his shower lying in the red hairs of the triangle that went from his waist down his back under the towel. Sitting down on the loveseat, he tried to calm himself as the red-haired boy walked back toward him. He was struck by the boy's beautiful hairy chest and impressed by what he thought was evidence that Rusty could be a great model for men's underwear.

Sitting down obviously aware his leg was pressing against Lee's leg, Rusty gave him the book. "You'll have to show me what you want. I mean, tell me how much to give you. I mean, I have never had a man sit me down and talk to me about this. You know someone to sit down and tell me the 'ins and outs.' I mean, tell me what you need, I'll give it to you." Thinking he was being handed double entendres, he quickly told Rusty how much he needed to pay, marked the book and took his leave. Although he was still clad in only his bath towel, Rusty followed him out into the hall and stairway, making conversation the entire time Lee was going down the stairs.

At one point, Lee stopped to turn around and look back up as he was talking to Rusty. The staircase was wrought iron and Rusty had lifted one foot up off the floor and propped it on the bottom rail of the banister. The moved foot caused his towel to drape open and reveal his entire sexual prowess Lee turned and headed for the front door, thinking "That's too much for me to handle!" Rusty called out, "See you next month!"

Fate can lead you down different paths, sometimes leading you back to a path you encountered before. Lee was caught short and had to go to the bathroom urgently while collecting on his debit one Saturday morning. He was passing a Clover store in Media and recalled the bathroom was pretty clean and made a beeline for the public toilet. Running into the toilets, he could see there were only two, both already occupied. Through the cracks in the door he could see something going on, that looked like someone was putting paper on the wall of the toilet partition. He called out, "Please someone give up your spot I have to shit really bad!"

Soon an old gent came out of one of the booths saying, "He doesn't want to play." Not understanding or caring what the man was talking about he rushed in and got his pants down just in time for a loud explosion. The person on the other side called out, "Thar' she blows, don't blow a hole into the floor!"

Ignoring the person on the other side of the wall Lee finished what he came to do and left the stall as fast as he entered it. Washing his hands and leaving the washroom he could tell the person in the other stall was leaving also. Being a fast walker, he was focused on what he was doing and today was no different. As he went into the parking lot, he heard someone rushing up behind him, "Whoa, thar' she blows..."

He turned around ready to face some unknown heckler only to come face to face with a laughing Rusty.

"Boy, you walk fast - what's your hurry?"

"Do you always accost men in the Clover store parking lot?" Lee countered.

"Only those who slipped through my fingers the first time"

"I didn't slip through your fingers; your legs were wide open and you scared me off when I looked up the stairs to talk to you. You knew you were exposing yourself."

"That's my best view. I like cute guys looking up at me through my legs, all the better if they're naked and we're making love. How about coming back to my place?"

"Another time - I have to collect from some customers out here in an hour, and if we went back to your place, I'd never make the appointments."

"Well then, how about going for a short ride with me? I know a spot close by that has an excellent view of the countryside."

He thought about the handsome young man and acquiesced, saying, "I can't spend a lot of time with you right now - I have work to do."

Lee left his car in the store parking lot, and Rusty drove them up into the hills surrounding Media to an overlook with a spectacular view. They got out of the car and walked over to the low wooden barrier. The natural beauty of the area took his breath away. Rusty walked up behind him and hugged him around the waist. "Beautiful view isn't it?" Dropping his hands lower he groped Lee's crotch to arousal while grinding himself into his back side.

"Boy, I'd like to plug this ass." Rusty growled.

"I think it would be more like drilling, and I don't usually carry Vaseline with me! Do you?"

"No, usually I take who I am interested in home to my bed or we go to theirs - but you don't have time!"

Lee was thinking, he brought me to this spot; he's probably done this before. With the thrill in the idea of outdoor sex, he turned around to face Rusty, hugging him close and laying light kisses on his cheek, jawbone etc. "Well, if you really want my ass now. Get down on your knees and polish the knob. Use what you get in return for lubrication."

With surprise showing on his face and a wide grin, Rusty said, "I always said I liked the view up here; I'll grant you your wish." Eager to plunge himself inside Lee, he sank to his knees. Lee was soon to bend over holding, onto that that low barrier for support. He felt like an oil rig was banging his back side.

As they drove back to the Clover store, Lee asked Rusty if he ever went downtown. "No, I don't have many friends who want to be seen in gay bars so we just hang out here picking up the occasional trick in the parks or bathrooms. Sadly, mostly married men or old fat men, like that old geezer who was in the john when you came into the bathroom."

"You're wasting your talents on the guys you find out here. You would be a hit downtown, with something that size all you would have to do is hang on the corner of Broad and Spruce Streets. Cars would be screeching to a stop to pick you up and take you home. They would be parking their cars and running over to find out who the new meat on the rack was."

"What about you? Aren't you interested?"

"You're too easy. There's no challenge with you. You service and screw. Anyone apparently, if you'll excuse me for saying."

"What the hell do you mean?"

"I need someone who makes me work a little for want I want. I'd always be thinking when I turned my back you were out shopping the tearooms. There's an old saying, 'Where you meet them is where you'll lose them.' You're young; you're a whore by your own admission. Look what you did the first time I came to collect your insurance! I don't think I'm unique."

"You're right! One time I answered my door to find a delivery man. Asked me to hold a package for the lady next door. 'It's fragile' he says. I told him, "You had better bring it in, and set it down. Since it's so fragile, I'll have the owner come over and pick it up herself.

"Yeah he didn't get out before he dropped his drawers and I 'dicked' him; walked a little funny when he left. You didn't seem to mind taking it all though; too small for you?"

"No," Lee thought, "Too whorish."

He went back into the store using the same bathroom stall, to clean himself up, when an old timer came in. He saw the older man looking at him through the hole in the partition and the old guy stuck a finger through, motioning for him to put himself through the hole so he could service him. Lee thought, the old goat, if he wants it that bad, I'll give him Rusty's leftovers. "Twenty dollars, man!"

The old gent pushed a twenty-dollar bill through the hole and Lee thought, "Why not?" After pushing his underwear down again he pushed himself through the wall. "Hey," the old guy complained, "Someone has already been here! Give me my money back." Since the old boy rejected what he offered, he started to put himself back together as the disgruntled would-be buyer started banging on his stall door. The man's voice rose louder and he was worried at first.

"Hey you little fuck! Give me my money back! You're not clean; you still have someone else's slobber on you. Give me my money back."

The more he thought about it the braver he became. By the time he opened the door to his stall, a couple of other men had come in and looked quizzically at him. Raising his own voice, Lee said, "And why would I owe you money?" Knowing the two men saw him come out of the booth and knowing they would have heard him shouting and banging on his door, he thought, let him tell these two guys why he gave me twenty dollars.

As he drove away, he thought, "Who did I call a whore?" He also knew he enjoyed the challenge of making eye contact with a stranger. The cat and mouse game of seeing if he could capture the person's interest, get them in bed and then flip them over, no - Rusty would never have been enough.

It was during this time of easy money, borrowing from the insurance wallet, that he started going to Atlantic City more. New York Avenue was at its height of gay hedonism. You might find a few lesbians or fag hags (straight women who liked hanging around gay men), in the bars and clubs but this was a man's domain.

The gay clubs and bars were centered on New York Avenue and Snake Alley. There were two popular hotels on New York Avenue, the Bellevue and the Chesterfield, with a shared parking lot between them. The guys would walk around their rooms naked with their windows open. They would open the windows and doors in the communal showers flaunting and advertising themselves. Men would yell across the open area making contact, ending with many men running back and forth between the two hotels. It was commonplace to look out your window and see a naked guy in his bedroom, across the way, combing his hair. He would go to his window, lean out and call to someone. In the next minute you would see him open the door to his room and invite a new friend in. Only after some grand Hollywood style kissing and hugging, to make sure they had tantalized the peeping tom queens, would they then pull the window blind to shut out the world they had invited

Mr. Melnkyn had stepped down as staff manager and taken a debit, or insurance route. His asthma and years of heavy smoking caught up with him and his health was declining. The new man on campus was young and full of vibrato. He was all get up and go-go-go! Chuck Conrad was one of the cutest, dark haired, button-nosed Italian men he had ever seen. He had a pretty, young, blond wife and new baby. He had everything going for him but he chased anything in a skirt. He bragged to Lee, "The other guys sell enough insurance on their own, so we spend the days at the malls looking for pussy. Some of these men have female policy holders who pay their insurance premiums the old-fashioned way, on their backs."

When he worked with Lee, he told him how he had worked with another gay guy in Reading. If the guy had a really good week, he would let the guy suck him off. He promised Lee if he had a good week, he could have the same treat. Not being impressed, Lee felt there were already too many spoons in that bowl. Lee tried at times to get his head together, staying home hoping to find some remnants of peace.

Late at night Tim would ring his phone, as the jukebox in some bar was playing Gilbert O'Sullivan's "Daniel's leaving today, something about an airplane, and Daniel my brother, you are older than me, do you still feel the pain..." He would listen and when the song was finished the phone would go dead. Other times Tim would call from his bedroom in his aunt's house.

He would tell Lee, "I really miss you! I miss our being together. I miss caressing your body, grabbing you and making you hard; bringing you close and then rolling you over and entering you and stroking you as I pumped your backside. Do you remember how that felt for you? I'm working on myself now as I think how warm you felt underneath me, your shoulders wide and strong, the hair on your legs rubbing against me as I cling to you. Your fingers turned upwards grabbing at my thighs. How your climax would clench your ass muscles against me and pull the load right out of me." That was Lee's introduction to phone sex. Tim even tried enlisting mutual friends to help get him back.

Ralph Jones called Lee inviting him to dinner. After dinner and movies Ralph suggested they visit the Penrose, the gang's old stomping ground. As they sat at the bar enjoying a drink, they saw Tim circulating among the crowd. Up until then Lee had been enjoying Ralph's company. He was considering going home with Ralph if the conversation headed in that direction. He was so emotionally wound up in Tim that his head told him he needed to break loose from Tim, he was no good for him. Yet his heart wanted to prove to himself that Tim could still love him and be the man he wanted him to be.

Ralph put his hand on his knee, and in his sweet southern voice echoed, "Honey, I can see you are still in love with that man! Go get him!"

"I was hoping to come home with you tonight."

"When did you decide that?" Ralph questioned.

"All evening I have thought how kind and gentle you have been, understanding."

"Yes, maybe I have been kind and gentle, understanding both your views. But what I see is, you still love him, and you are too stupid to see him for what he is. He will never change. I am speaking out of turn here, but I really do like you and if he wasn't in the picture... yes, I would take you home and prove to you. You know, once you have Black you don't go back! But, honey you are too sweet to take advantage of. Yes, I would like to puncture that nice round bubble of yours and show you what these lips can do, but only for the right reasons. Not to compete with Mr. Slut over there. Oh, child! I have had too much to drink. I gotta hit the head."

When Tim saw that Ralph had left him alone at the bar he slinked over and sat on Ralph's stool. "Hiya, kid! What's up?"

God! Lee thought. He is polluted!

"Ready to go home with me again?"

His head nearly fell off his shoulders, it spun around so fast. "No! I'd rather go home with Ralph. But he won't have me out of respect for you and what we used to have."

"You'd rather go home with him? Are you saying you want to become a dinge queen?" (A slur for a white man who sleeps with a black man.)

"He has just been himself, the same man who you introduced me to months ago - someone who doesn't whore around."

"How's it hanging, man?" Ralph asked as he walked up to Tim.

"What the fuck you been doing? You were supposed to soften him up and make him see we should get back together."

"I am sorry Tim, but you don't deserve him and I can't sell something I don't believe in."

Turning to Lee, Tim bellowed, "Well, you faggot, you can have your n____r!" as he stormed off.

Lee turned to Ralph to hug him, "I am so sorry for what he said! Let's go home."

"No! If that happened, it would be for all the wrong reasons. You would be using me to try to get back at, replace, and punish Tim. And for my part, I don't know if I would be trying to punish you for being so stupidly in love with a goddamned fool or pushing my own agenda, feeling I had to prove to you that as a black man, I could be a better lover than Tim. Now I am confusing myself as much as you two fucked up. No, thanks. Good night!"

Reeling from his ongoing Tim problem, Lee left the club intent on finding a new interest to decrease the chance of romantic entanglements.

He always enjoyed the bar scene, and his friend Matt Barlow told him of "Miss P's." It was a new bar that opened at Eighteenth and Lombard Streets around the corner from the Graduate Hospital. The well-known drag queen Patty Paige and her lover Frank had opened a welcoming small bar for "gay family only" that required you to know the combination on the door's lock to get in. Frank would guard the door in case a "non-family member" tried to get in. Lee ingratiated himself with the drag queens there and was soon performing in their shows. It was strictly volunteer, no pay - strictly camp for camp's sake!

Lucille Ball had just banished Angela Lansbury's version of Mame by doing the movie version. Movie goers reeled as much to Ball's performance as the Miss P's regulars reeled when Lee portrayed Streisand. "That's the fattest Streisand I ever saw!" was heard in the audience.

Having given away all his drag clothes, he occasionally borrowed from his insurance collections to pay for material for a new frock; after all, a decent drag queen can't be seen in the same outfit more than once! Well, maybe you could repeat the outfit every month and a half or so. Then there's shoes, makeup, drop-dead gotta-have-rhinestone shoulder-duster earrings. And panty hose! Can we talk panty hose? Layers of pantyhose! And don't forget those fishnet stockings to make a man's leg shapelier.

One of the drags worked on the Hospital's switchboard and talked the security guards into letting him park his car there. The guards would stand and watch as he walked across the street with his wig boxes and gowns over his arm. To save space in the small dressing room, carved out of space under the stairs to the second-floor apartment, he would dress at home. This meant he would do his face, put on his under garments, slide his tits in, put his high heels on, and just throw a large sleeveless chambray work shirt on over top. The shirt was long enough to cover his crotch and almost cover his ass. The front was left unbuttoned enough to show the top of his black one-piece merry widow corset.

When he walked in front of the headlights of the cars at the intersection he always got whistled at. The people would think they were looking at a real woman involved in theatrics, or a prostitute. He didn't care what they thought, as long as he got catcalls and attention. As he was going back to the dressing room one night, he saw Big Al and asked him, "Who do you have visiting you? Bring a trick home from your latest trip?" (Big Al was one of the first male airline Stewards.)

"What the hell are you talking about?"

"I just saw someone going up the stairs to your apartment."

"There's no one up there - quit trying to rattle me!"

"Oh yeah? Listen! Turn off the radio Jackie. "As it became quiet everyone could hear footsteps on the stairs and in the apartment above them.

"Shit, call the police! I'm being robbed!"

The police came as Big Al caught one of the robbers by the legs when he tried to get out through a window. Al did get an honorable mention for bravery during the show as Patti tap-danced up and down a stack of suitcases on the stage. "Watch my feet; this is about as fast as Big Al's feet moved when he flew up the stairs to catch those boys robbing his apartment. Now watch this," as she tapped faster, "This is how fast he chases the boys down the street!"

Doing the show, he made a friend of one Barton Mathews. He was tall and homely and just knew he owned Rita Hayworth's "Put the Blame on Mame, Boys" better than Rita did it herself. They became fast friends with Bart, moving into his back bedroom, once again resplendent in drag clothes.

They had fun together. Bart made him laugh and almost made him forget Tim. He and Bart weren't sexual friends, just hanging out and running around friends. On Saturday nights after the show they would go down to Thirteenth and Locust Streets and give the prostitutes competition. They weren't selling, but baby, they had takers. It was nothing to walk up to a car where a prostitute could be leaning into a John's car talking price and break her balls.

"He is not a she! He has a dick just like I do. And he may rob you or give you syphilis! I don't charge! I don't have a disease! The only thing I want to know... do you like hips, lips or finger tips. Or a small side order of each?" They were both of a size as to dissuade any one of the "girls" from becoming physical.

At rehearsal Miss P. was saddened to announce, "It came to my attention that two of my 'girls' were supposedly seen at 13th and Locust Streets. I assured the person who told me that none of my 'girls' would be seen there. They tried to describe them, one as very tall, and well, they weren't too kind about the facial features - Bart. And, the other was stockier, and wore her hair back like this." Miss P made a grand sweeping gesture a la Veronica Lake, the way Lee wore his in drag. "I know I won't hear anything like that again."

He found a few men who actually liked going out with drag queens. The only drawback was they wanted you to stay in drag the entire time they were with you. He met some gentlemen who only wanted to visit at home during the day. He never questioned their scheduling. To accommodate those men, he shopped the local bargain store. He bought himself a sexy nylon caftan that zipped up and down the front. Because it was tiger print, he called it his "Tiger Lilly" outfit. It was easy to get in and out of or just lift up depending on the activity they would engage in. He also had to purchase ladies crotchless underwear. Married men who came to visit him wanted total domination. They wanted sex with a man, who dressed up as a woman, but would use them as the woman.

Bart dated married, single, straight, gay - it didn't matter. Lee didn't know until Bart disappeared suddenly that they had a lot more in common. He heard from a mutual acquaintance who worked with Bart at the same restaurant that when he left, they found a shortage of cash in the amount of three thousand dollars. And he left owing Lee rent...the bitch!

Word of the fun shows at Miss P's got around. Lee saw Tony and his new boyfriend in the audience one evening when he was doing

Edie Gourmet's rendition of "I Don't Care." His second number was a take-off on Della Reese.

Tony went backstage to congratulate him. "You look great! You have the presentation of someone who would have a big voice, big enough to sing 'Della Reese's "If You Don't Know." He never knew for sure if that was a back-handed compliment.

Tony didn't want to leave his new friend alone for too long in a bar full of adventurous faggots but he visited with Lee long enough to tell him he found his new love cruising the Frankford elevated train stop.

"It's just the hottest cruise spot! Here's my number - give me a call sometime and we'll catch each other up on tricks."

Well, if Tony can find a number at the elevated, so can I! First chance Lee got he went up to Frankford and Olney, parked his car and cruised for men. He met an older man named Jasper there and made a date for a weekend rendezvous at "J's' Mountain Get-Away" near Reading. It was out in the middle of nowhere. But no was the operative word here, as in Jasper had no hair, and they had no chemistry.

His next visit to Frankford proved better in the person of Oscar Pettijohn. They liked each other right away and agreed to put off sex until they knew each other better. After several weeks of movies and dinners they decided that the next time they got together they would consummate their relationship. Oscar greeted him at the door with a glass of wine. Escorting him to the sofa they talked, embraced and introduced each other to the other's body. Going into the bedroom, Oscar proved himself an excellent lover, attentive, slow, gentle, affectionate, and teasing. After his amore had exploded, he focused even more at giving satisfaction.

When Lee signaled him to slow down and cuddle, Oscar inquired, "Did I go to fast? Should we have waited longer? What can I do to give you pleasure?"

"It's not your fault! I was afraid I would really enjoy sex with you and fall in love with you. I jerked off several times before I came here tonight, thinking if you didn't get me off, I'd be able to keep my distance from you and not fall in love with you. I've had trouble getting past my ex and I'm afraid you could make me forget him. As much as you enjoyed yourself and I enjoyed you, I can't bear to think what it would have been like for me. If you got me off with the same explosiveness you experienced.... I'd be head over heels in love with you."

Oscar got up. "Get dressed and get out. I don't have room in my life for the likes of you!"

Feeling rejected out of hand and misunderstood, Lee dressed. As he walked to his car, he remembered he had Tony's phone number with him. He called him from a pay phone asked if he could stop in since he was nearby. Tony met him at the front door and took him back to his apartment. Lee told him about meeting Oscar.

"Ozzie? You mean the tall blond, wears it back in a ponytail? Drives a red import convertible?"

"Yes." he said and told Tony every stupid thing he'd done and said. Tony jumped up and grabbed him by the shoulders.

"You idiot! All the queens want him. He very seldom picks any one up and never takes anyone home, and you did that to him? You threw him away?"

Lee started to cry and headed for the front door. By the time they reached the front steps leading out of the building, Tony calmed down and tried to console him. "Sit down, calm down; let's talk."

As they talked, he leaned back on his hands looking up at the stars, trying to forget his stupidity. All of a sudden, he felt like his hands were covered in pins and needles. He shook them to increase the circulation and saw there were little black spots all over his hands. Upon further inspection he found the little black spots were moving up his arms. He jumped up and found he had sat on an ant's nest being built between the cracks in the cement. Tony pulled him into the foyer.

"Take off your shirt. My God, they're everywhere! Take off your pants. My God, you're covered! Take off your shoes. We are going back to my apartment, and before you enter my door you take off all your clothes. Run like hell for the shower and wash these ants off. I'm going to take your clothes behind the building and put them in the dumpster. Now go."

He was able to wash the ants off and feel clean again. Tony being much thinner than Lee, it was difficult to find something for him to wear home as he drove the expressway back to Southwest Philly. Tony finally produced an old pair of farmer's jeans. They had to split open the side seams and wrap a table cloth around him to prevent him from being accused of indecent exposure.

CHAPTER THIRTY-FOUR

IT WAS INEVITABLE THAT LEE WOULD BE faced with an alarming shortage in his insurance funds. He learned to keep his job by selling policies to people who didn't want them. He would make up fake applications and submit the money for them. When they were issued, he would return them to the office for a return of premium saying the customer changed their minds. Once in a while he would be able to talk the customer into keeping the policy, especially if it was for a child where the premiums are low. He had a customer, Fanny Adamato, who had come to like him and he confessed to her what he had been doing. He explained he was going to ask his aunt for money to cover up the funds he had taken from the insurance company. He begged her not to hold it against him.

"Why would I hold it against you? I have a similar situation in my own home!"

"What do you mean?"

"You know my husband drives for SEPTA? Well, he used to come home with pockets full of change. At first, I didn't think anything about it.... but it got to be more and more change. Here he told me he and some of the other guys were jumping on other buses sitting in the garage during their lunch hours, after work, whenever and stealing the money out of the fare boxes. Not their buses, other buses, so it wouldn't look like they were involved. That's how they were caught. Theirs were the only buses whose boxes weren't robbed. I have a thief in my own home. How could I judge you?"

She didn't judge Lee; she introduced him to her brother-in-law, Bruce. He was not quite as good-looking as her husband (who Lee was hot for). When Bruce found out Lee used to do drag, he told Lee that he had done drag, "big time," under the drag name "Flossie," because he was known to always floss his teeth after seeing his tricks. He was a hairdresser working in a rented shop in Penbrook. During Lee's slow periods during the day, he would stop in to visit and meet some of the customers.

Margo was a bleached blonde, fiftyish woman, plump, well-dressed, and attractive with a great personality. After she left Bruce revealed she was in the numbers, a bookie and a loan shark. He said, "You know those guys you saw leaving, they were her collectors. As in break your hands, bust your kneecap."

Another time Bruce took Lee to a wedding reception for his friend Harriette's daughter. As they left the restaurant Bruce said, "Take a last look. Tomorrow this place will be ashes. The owner owes Harriette money and gave her daughter the reception hoping he could work off the rest of the money he owes. But it wasn't enough, so she's burning the restaurant tonight because she knows he has insurance. Her enforcers will make sure she gets her money." Bruce said she was a female mob boss, and had inherited her father's...men.

Bruce told Lee he was taking him out for his birthday. "Make sure you get very dressed up - we are going to the Drury Lane Supper Club. Julie Wilson is appearing there." When Lee picked him up, he was in full drag. "Flossie" didn't look bad. He looked like his grandmother, only a more youthful version and more stylish.

Hearing about how these friends of his dealt with money, he decided he needed to get out of the insurance business before he couldn't pay back what he owed. Whoa. ... Too late for that! When he figured how much he had "borrowed" from his turn-ins, the amount was a couple thousand dollars. Not having that kind of money, he called his Aunt Peggy and asked her to loan him the amount. She called his father who in turn called him.

"Lee, your Aunt Marg called and told me you got in trouble. She is going to send the money. You need to quit that job. Her first husband had the same problem: sticky fingers. You're lucky to have her to help you, I couldn't. Now goddamn it, straighten up!"

His aunt sent him a little extra cash and Lee was like a drunken sailor, running to all the bars and buying new clothes to gild the lily. Before he knew it, he had borrowed another small sum from the insurance company. Not being able to go to the one well he knew about, he drove home to see his mother when he knew his father would be at work. His mother broke down crying when she was told he had dipped into funds that did not belong to him again. "Oh, Lee! It breaks my heart to think of you going to jail, but we don't have that kind of money!"

He realized she thought he said twenty-five thousand.

He quickly corrected her and said, "Twenty-five hundred." Drying her face, she got up and went to the phone calling the local bank where she and her husband had done banking all their married life.

Her high school friend's son Leonard worked at the bank now. He listened to his mother's conversation.

"Len, I need to get a personal loan for my son for $2500, he got himself in trouble. I will co-sign for it; you know we're good for it. I don't want my husband involved. He would skin him alive! I want you to make the check payable to he owes the money to." Upon hanging up the phone she turned to him and told him in no uncertain terms, "When you get back to Philadelphia, you take this check to the insurance company and tell them what you have done. They will probably fire you! Good, because you evidently can't handle large sums of money. Get yourself another job and keep your nose clean. Give me a hug and get going. Mind you I will expect a phone call to let me know what you have done."

When he walked into the insurance office and asked to see the manager, Mr. Ebaugh, the man seemed to know what was coming. Lee laid the check on his desk, "I have to quit. This belongs in my account."

"I see," he mused, lighting a cigarette. "We have scheduled an audit of your book for this week suspecting something was going on. We won't prosecute, but of course you are no longer associated with us. We'll contact you if we find any monies other than this missing.

We have your bond you have been contributing to, so maybe that will cover the rest, if this amount doesn't. Do yourself a favor and never take another debit insurance job. I appreciate you trying to handle this like a man."

Lee had made an acquaintance with a woman on his debit whose husband worked at the state liquor control board. He had told her he was quitting and needed a job. She talked to her husband and he was fortunate to quickly get a part time job with them. To make ends meet, he went back to the Five & Dime store where he used to work hoping to get another part-time job there. The man who had been first assistant manager when he worked there was now the store manager. Knowing him to be a good worker and having a soft spot for him, he gave Lee a part-time position. It wasn't the kind of life he had been living, but at least he had an income, could keep up with his expenses and still enjoy frequent visits to the bars.

Tim's phone calls were easier to avoid now that he was busy on the weekends. After a particularly hectic weekend Lee was looking forward to being home alone on Monday night. He sat down to watch television only to have someone knock on his front door. Opening the door, he saw a married man, who lived with his family three doors up the street, slowly backing down his front steps.

The Gorman family had lived on the block when he and Rose moved to the street. The man came home in the summer, usually shirtless, exposing a nice chest and a heavy tan. The hotter the weather became he shed his long pants in favor of denim cut-offs, but kept on those heavy, muddy boots. He could have posed for a magazine, with his rugged good looks. Lee always thought he must work in the construction business from his appearance. Their only awareness of each other had been a nodding of the head to acknowledge the other in passing.

The only time Lee spoke to the man was when he had to tell him he was responsible for an injury to his son. His son and some of his friends were running up and down his front steps and chasing each other over the neighbor's porch railings. He had gone out to tell the boys not to play on his porch. He was leaning on the old rusty cast iron railing talking to the boys when it broke loose. It swung down to the cement pavement. Lee landed on the railing and the Gorman boy was pinned underneath it. He picked himself up and took the wailing, bleeding boy by the hand to his mother.

She answered the door, listened, slapped her son and told him, "Stop crying." She dismissed Lee with, "It's his own fault - he shouldn't have been on your porch. He's fine, don't worry."

Indeed, he did worry! The boy had a deep nasty gash on his head. "I really would feel better if you took him to the hospital. My home-owner's insurance or I will pay for it. It would make me feel better. I think he heeds stitches!" He called to the closing door. He waited and watched for the father to come home so he could run out and tell him what happened. He was afraid an excited mother would incite fatherly anger, leading to his receiving an ass beating. Instead all he did was grunt a "Thank you for telling me."

That being their history he wondered what brought this now well-dressed man to his front door. He obviously had been at the front door but was now standing on the bottom step awkwardly looking back. He looked like an embarrassed cowboy caught serenading under the wrong window. "Hello, I'm Jack Gorman."

"Yes, I remember when your son was hurt - how is he? I felt really bad about what happened."

"Oh, that was his fault. He's fine - as he grows you won't notice that little scar very much. Can I come in?"

Well, he wasn't belligerent, or unpleasant, why not let him come in? "You caught me by surprise but you're welcome to come in." Lee wondered what had brought Jack to his door.

As Jack stepped up into his living room, Lee shut the screen door behind him realizing how snug the man's pants fit. When Jack sat down, his sport coat slid open and away from in front of his lap, and Lee could swear the man had no underwear on. It would appear Jack could more than satisfy his wife. Lee's eyes danced from the man's lap to the healthy exposed tanned chest. Nervously the Jack saw Lee check out his body and he quickly crossed his legs at the knee, pulling his jacket together. This maneuver only exposed his bare ankles, revealing how the sun had bleached the brown hair on his tanned legs to a light sun- kissed blonde.

Seeing Lee shamelessly derive pleasure from looking at his body, Jack felt very awkward. Suddenly aware he was the sex object of another man; he conspicuously placed his hand over his lap. He felt very uncomfortable, not knowing if he was excited or repulsed by the open admiration. Thinking he appeared foolish he stood up saying, "Excuse me! I ... this is a mistake - I have to go."

"Sit back down! I will only make eye contact. That's what's bothering you, isn't it? My checking you out, like you and your buddies have probably looked at women all your lives. Gay guys do the same thing to men. To every man we see. In the quickest, fleeting glance, we gauge right away whether or not we would have sex with him if possible. Straight men look at a woman and automatically, depending on her body type and appearance, fantasize what they would do with her if they could have their way with her. Do you want to deny you ever looked at a woman in that manner?"

Met with silence he continued, "You look very nice tonight, all dressed up - were you and the family out?"

Slowly Jack sat back down, relaxing, stretching his legs out in front of him, making it hard for Lee to keep his eyes on just his face, but he did. "There were two important functions in my family this weekend; my sister-in-law's wedding and my nephew's confirmation. Both were equally important to each of us. She decided to go to her sister's wedding out of town and took the kids with her."

"Confirmations are usually on a Sunday. Yet here you are dressed to the nines on a Monday night. Were you out to dinner with friends?"

Jack looking at the floor saying nothing only urged Lee to continue. "So, you are home, alone, nothing to do. Why not call a buddy?"

"Hey, I can go - I have other friends to hang out with, I can sit home with a beer and watch the TV." He spits back.

"But you didn't! You stayed home, got all dressed-up and knocked on my door. Why didn't you wear your street clothes? You would have if you were sharing a beer with your buddies."

Mike didn't have a quick response for him because he knew he wanted to impress Lee. He wanted to look nice. "AND you came here because you wanted to. I just want to make sure I know why you came to visit me. You seem awkward and embarrassed; you know you are very attractive. If you think I was checking out your crotch. I was and am. You must know I am gay. I am sure the neighbors watch me and my guests' comings and goings. I like guys. I like to have sex with guys. One would assume you know how we do that. I am thinking you came here tonight to find out what I'd do with you!"

Mike stood back up, "I gotta go, man I shouldn't be here."

"Oh, I'm sorry. Am I too bold for you?" Lee stood up ready to see if he could get away with undressing this handsome neighbor. Putting his hands out to bring Mike closer, he said, "You have to realize, you are the fly in a spider's web. What did you come here for? What do you want me to do? What did you expect I might do?" Lee teased, running one hand over Jacks rising chest, and the other ready to explore the shape of Jacks butt.

Interrupting the tension of the moment was another knock on the door. "Hey Lee!" and another loud rap was enough distraction to make Jack open the door and run out. "I'll leave you to your company!" and Jack was gone.

Quacking like a chicken, he called out after Jack, "Chicken!! I'll see you later!" Waiting on the porch, watching the retreating Jack disappear up the street was his former boss from the insurance company. "Well," he said. "It doesn't rain that it pours married men coming to my door. And to what do I owe this pleasure?"

"Hey, hope I didn't break something up... I was out with Roberts on his debit and well.... you know I need to shower before I go home. Can I use your bathroom?" Already walking up the stairs, loosening his shirt and tie, he said, "He introduced me to these two sisters. Man, you should have seen them! Big tits, great asses.... Man, they give great head. They straddle your lap and take it all the way up the poop shoot.

Becky would certainly smell something on me." As he dropped his trousers on the floor and hooked his thumbs in his shorts he asked, "Is it all right to shower?"

"Sure, if I can watch."

"Shit, man I don't care who sees me naked! I was never embarrassed in the YMCA showers."

"And what were you doing at the YMCA, that you say that so blithely?"

"Racquetball, man!! What do you think?"

Lee went to his bedroom and took a few items of clothes off in case he got carried away. Walking over to the bathroom for a look-see, he found a sudsy Chuck in his shower working up a lather stroking his dick. He exclaimed, "That is the Dick of Death? That makes girls swoon? We gay guys would toss a catch that size back in the water. *Pulllezzzze*, the way you talked I expected something much bigger."

"Hey man, more than a mouthful is wasted. You want to find out? Go ahead try it for size. What are you going to do with those big ones? Grease 'em up and use 'em like a sliding board?"

"Well, you'll never know! With that five inches of nothing! You ought to be ashamed how you always talk in the office telling the guys how the girls complain of your size, making out like its *soooo* big! Your dick is so small it probably irritates them, because it's too small to really lunge in and out. You probably pull it out too far and jam it back in quick; hitting the sidewalls, hurting them. You need to rest that thing, fertilize it and hope it grows. Or find a small, tight Asian girl. They're used to small dicks!

Having never been put down because of the size of his penis, Chuck quickly dressed. "Thanks for the shower!" he called over his shoulder as he was opening the front door to leave.

"Oops, sorry! I didn't know there was anyone out here." He heard Chuck saying to someone. When he went to see who Chuck was talking to, he saw Gary, Rose's sister Vivian's husband, broadly smiling at him.

What the hell, Lee thought.

CHAPTER THIRTY-FIVE

"HEY LEE! I TOOK THE LEAD FROM YOU, and left Vivian! We were not good for each other anymore. She wanted to be a porn star. Tried to get me involved but that's not for me. Can I come in?"

He had been attracted to Gary, but did he have to show up just now? He was stunned. He thought he might as well put in a revolving door. "Gary what are you doing here?"

"I'm sorry about your company leaving - new boyfriend?"

"No, former boss; as a matter of fact, you're the third man to show up totally unexpected in the last hour."

"I was hoping, now that you and Rose aren't together, and I split from Vi, that there would be a chance for you and me."

Lee sent Gary upstairs with his backpack, commenting, "Use Rose's old room and clean up if you want to." He needed a few minutes to collect his wits. This parade of manhood was making his head spin. Digesting the maelstrom of visitations, he fondly remembered Gary's husky smell in the bar that night when he had locked his long legs around his bar stool trying to seduce him. The indignation he had felt back then, because they were both married to sisters, was gone.

Anticipation was now making the little hairs on the back of his neck tingle with excitement. He changed clothes again and freshened up. Opening a bottle of wine, they regaled one another with stories of what they had done since they'd become single. Sitting close to each other on the sofa caused a tension of sexual excitement building in each other's minds of the possibilities to come. It reminded Lee of the old times with Tim as they enjoyed a flirtatious conversation over steak, green beans and baked potatoes. Tim and Gary were both tall and fair-haired. Tim, redder; Gary blonder. Gary knew how to sweet-talk a person; he had a very calming, lower register voice that would have made him an instant star on the radio. When Lee listened to Gary it was as if he were being bathed by a heat lamp. Gary's eyes and voice were hypnotic, increasing his desire for physical contact.

Just talking with Gary made him tense; Lee was afraid he might miss his chance for the unspoken promise of physical intimacy to come. It was as if Gary was a magnet, sending out wave after wave of seductive fingers pulling him closer and closer. At the same time Lee's ambiguous emotions tried to repulse him backward out of reach at the last minute. Succumbing to physical need, Lee said, "It's time to go to bed."

Gary hesitated, "If you don't want me in your bed I'll understand."

"No, I want you in my bed, And I want you in me...."

Gary stood up and moved over to him. Lifting him up out of his chair, embracing him warmly, he whispered, "We don't have to do anything you don't want to do."

Lee's eyes spoke for him. He smiled as he laid his head on Gary's chest. He luxuriated in Gary's soft gliding touch. He was a complete lover; he was expert in French and Greek culture. He was a joy. Gently caressing, a strong caress where appropriate, the perfect, softly spoken verbal instructions and freely given complementary gratification responses. Only at the end as they fell asleep did Lee realize, without knowing, sometime during their love making, he had replaced the live Gary with the ghost of Tim.

Before he left for the state liquor store the next morning, Lee talked with Gary. "If we had met years ago, before Tim, this would have a completely different ending, I am so sorry, but I still love Tim. As long as I feel like I do we won't have a chance. You need to move on and let me find my way, on my own. I'm sorry. You don't want unrequited leftovers."

"Is there anything I can do or say to make you change your mind? I'll get a job! Work shoulder to shoulder with you; we can build our own life. You told me you enjoyed our lovemaking. Give us a chance. Don't we deserve a chance?"

"You deserve someone who can commit a hundred percent. Not just let their body have its way with automatic reactions to great stimulus. You don't want someone who can't be there mentally, someone who would always fanaticize he is with someone else.... You are physically very attractive and you know how to play me like a cheap violin. But when we are together and I'm caressing you and feeling your body move with mine I am thinking about Tim."

"I can make you forget him. Let me try. You have been honest! You told me more than I wanted to hear, but I appreciate it. Now let me take your scared soul and heal it with my love. Let me rewrite fanaticizes you had with Tim. Let Gary make you his love offering. You gave Tim enough tries and he screwed up every one. Let me show you the difference! Let me make new memories for you to enjoy, and permit me to make you happy. Why won't you let us try to have a life together?"

"I do have feelings for you, Gary. Just not enough of the kind you deserve! With you it would just be pure raw sex. I have to make this right for me, with Tim, before I can try to repeat what I had with him. I don't want a repeat of what I had with him. That's just it! I don't know how to have what I want. I don't want what I had with him in so many ways! Yet I do want that feeling I have when I am with him and everything is right between us. I am too screwed up with him to have anything but sex with someone else."

Gary listened to this final pronouncement. He knew he would never get from Lee what he wanted. He heard he was screwed up in his head. He couldn't understand how a man could get so screwed up over someone who had screwed him over so often. If he wanted to waste his time he could, but Gary wasn't wasting any more of his.

"You know Lee, I think I understand and appreciate your tenacity in trying to make Tim treat you how you want to be treated. I don't agree with your thoughts. I think you are damn stupid and I resent your throwing our future away. Think about it and call me around one o'clock today if you still feel this way. If you do, I'll leave and you'll never see me again. Then you better call Tim, and get back together! Nothing is going to work out for you until you and he are right."

Lee spent the morning selling Thunderbird to the winos and expensive bourbon to the ladies who secretly drink too much while their families are away. He made change, bagged the purchases, for those who didn't slip their bottle under their coats; all the while thinking of Gary. He called Tim, telling him about Gary's visit.

Later he talked to Gary, "I called Tim and he has agreed to come over to the house this evening and talk about getting back together. He promises to be faithful, and work hard to make a future together for us. I hope you understand."

Tim met Lee at the house and he was no sooner in the door before Tim swept him up in a bear hug, promising him the sun, moon and stars between kisses. They went upstairs to the bedroom. Lee immediately saw his room was in disarray. Feeling a fist pull his stomach muscles into a ball of knots he looked around the room. The drawers in his dressers were open and clothes from his closet thrown around on the bed. It looked as if someone had done a hasty search.

Tim went to the closet where he had left a small locked box when he had left. He had forgotten about it because he'd pushed it way back in a comer and left old shoes on top of it. Lee never looked in the closet and didn't know the box existed. When Tim pulled it out, he stated, "The lock's been broken open. My mother's wedding ring and several family heirloom diamond rings were in here, along with some rolled coins and old money. My leather coat is gone too, along with a flexible duffle bag."

"Yes, my good watch and onyx pinky ring with a diamond center are gone too."

He went next door and asked the couple who took him to the hospital if they saw Gary leave. "I'm sorry to bother you but I was wondering if you saw anyone come and go from my house today."

"Why, yes - a tall fellow; a cab pulled up and honked. He came out carrying a duffle bag of sorts and got in. Is everything all right?"

Thanking them and apologizing for the intrusion he went back to find Tim sitting in the living room. "Well, it's my own fault. If I hadn't behaved badly, I wouldn't have ever left and Gary would not have had the chance to take advantage of the situation. I'm awfully sorry about the stuff he took."

"It's only material things that I should have given to my sister anyway." Moving over to enfold Lee in his arms and holding him tight, "The important thing is we're back together and nothing is going to come between us again!"

Lee was happy. He knew this time everything would work out for him and Tim. For the first time in a long time he felt at peace.

CHAPTER THIRTY-SIX

LEE LAY IN HIS BED WHILE HIS SUBCON-
scious replayed his life on an endless loop. Standing by his bedside,
Emily could not help wondering what had happened. He was very tired
two days ago, when he last talked to her but yesterday, he did not wake
up all day. And he was enjoying their conversations! She felt she was
helping him come to an understanding of how God might view his life.

Hoping to help him see the error of his ways in time to ask for her
God's forgiveness, she listened to abominable tales and stories. When
she first met him, she felt he seemed stronger than his health warranted.
Yet, recently, he did seem to be tiring quickly. She considered it might
be due to his medical condition.

When she talked to the nurses at the central station, no one appeared interested in whether he was talking or not. They left her with
the impression that she should be aware of how the human body shuts
down. That she should be used to seeing life turning downward towards
the end.

Intuition told she was not watching the "normal" chain of events
that happen when someone is dying. She felt he wanted to stir but was
not strong enough to break through Morpheus's veil. She called out,
"Lee! Lee! Please try to stir yourself."

The Chief did not stir yesterday either, yet today he was moving
around so she suspected he was going to be awake. He seemed to be
acting like he was trying to shake off a night of heavy drinking. (She
remembered how her husband acted the morning after he drank too
much of her homemade Elderberry wine the night before.) She was not
aware of the Chief's treatment plan, but she had knowledge of Lee's
directive requesting only to be kept from excruciating pain. He had

not ever complained of pain! He never complained, just accepted the closing of his book of life.

Today she had news for him. Trying to get through the cloud of sleep he was in, she raised her voice, "I had a response from your friends Burdee and Tuck. They both said they would try to get here today. You want to visit with your friends, don't you?" She waited, hoping; but no response was forthcoming. She left the room in search of the head nurse to inquire if something had changed that she did not know about.

If only she knew which nurse had been taking care of the room; the kind person who always brought him fresh juice, maybe she would offer some insight as to why he was in a deep slumber. Walking up to the socializing attendants at the nurses' station, she queried, "Excuse me I hate to be a bother," a pronouncement that made some roll their eyes. "I was wondering if I could find out which nurse has been caring for room 204. She is short, stout and has dark hair sticking out from under her cap. Large oversize glasses! She's been in and out of the room since the second day Lee got here."

Mrs. Gaston, the charge nurse for the day, exasperatedly responded, "Mrs. Anderson, none of us wear caps anymore! I have no idea who you are thinking of."

"Oh my! That's right!" Emily said. "How odd!"

Mrs. Gaston continued, "With the wellness program our employer demands we all participate in, we have to exercise and maintain an average weight for our sizes. We do not have one short, stout person, or anyone wearing a cap on staff. Furthermore, no one who wears large glasses. With contacts and Lasik surgery, our people are too vain for glasses."

"Oh my! Well, I tell you something's wrong! If he was dying, his kidney function would be shutting down and he would be losing strength. Not just sleeping; he is in too deep a sleep for the last stage of death. You know yourself when people are dying, they drift in and out of sleep. Restless most of the time; fighting, wanting to go, wanting to stay. They do not just lie in a state of calmness and sleep deeply as if they have had a sleeping sedation! Something is wrong I tell you!"

Mrs. Gaston suddenly raised her head, awareness in her eyes realizing Emily was suggesting something most upsetting. "Are you accusing someone on the staff of doing something criminal? Do you think his condition is related to an 'angel of death'? We have never had anyone make such an inflammatory accusation before."

"Good morning, everyone," called Edie, the Chief's wife, as she passed them on her way to the elevator.

"Well, something has to be done, I tell you. I think it is very abnormal for him to be sleeping so deeply," Emily went on. "The patient is near death; non-responsive! There is no family! No next of kin, and the patient cannot advocate for himself. Without a formal complaint of inquiry, registered with the Facility's Administrator, nothing can be done!"

"If that happened, the administrator could instigate an investigation," said Mrs. Gaston. "Nevertheless, I am telling you the hospital must be very careful because of the new HIPPA laws, with patient confidentiality and all. And in the end, what purpose would it serve?"

"Patient confidentiality - what purpose?" Emily almost choked on the words. "Are you crazy? I tell **you**; something is not natural!"

"That is a very serious thing to say, and not to be taken lightly. After all he came here to die, there is no family. To suggest we have someone on staff acting in such a manner is ludicrous!"

Emily spit out, "He has friends coming today, people who love him. What do you think they will say?" Visibly shaking with anger, Emily turned away from the nurses' station and headed to the first floor. She was not sure they loved him, but she still wanted the staff to do something. Show some concern. Not say, "Well, he came here to die – what's the problem?"

She left the administrator's office knowing she had done the right thing by lodging a complaint of inquiry, even though it was again explained to her that the only thing they could do was a simple blood test. There was no proof - just an old woman's suspicions. Without the next of kin's consent, and with the living directive in place, their hands were tied. Still, Emily knew she had done the right thing.

Because her prime concern with Lee was not communicative, Emily decided to stop and visit with some other patients. The last person she stopped to see was a courageous, sweet young woman, resigned to a slow death. It was with some guilty pleasure of relief that she enjoyed talking to people who shared her understanding of life. Diane Bigelow was a young mother diagnosed with Lou Gehrig's disease.

"Good morning, Diane! My goodness, don't you look charming!"

"Mrs. Anderson, so good of you to stop. How are you? I hear you are working with a very sick young man on two."

"Yes dear, a sad case - no loving family like you have," Emily shared. "Look at you. What a pretty necklace!"

A beaming Diane explained, "My daughter made this for me out of her pop-it-bead kit. She is so happy when she comes to visit and sees I am wearing it."

With motherly pride, Emily assured her she knew she treasured it. Leaving Diane to visit with her husband and daughter she thought how brave they were as they shared Diane's remaining days together.

As she took the elevator back up to Lee's room, her hand sought out the necklace he had given her. She had worn it under her blouse every day since he gave it to her. Often wondering where it had come from. Was it a special gift? For a special occasion? Stopping a moment in the hall, she slipped the locket out of the top of her blouse and looked at it again. It was a beautiful piece of jewelry that she felt must have meant quite a lot to someone.

It was so quiet in the hall, her footsteps echoed in her ears. As she approached Lee's room, she could see two people, one on either side of the bed. Each was holding one of his hands. She was surprised the Chief was still quiet. Without his normally noisy television on she heard them talking as she approached.

"He sure doesn't look like himself!" The taller, fatter one said. "I wouldn't have never recognized him if they hadn't told me this was him."

"Sickness certainly doesn't become him!" the other stranger added.

She was not comfortable with people talking ill of the dead before they were dead. It was especially disturbing to her to hear them discussing his looks! Before they had a chance to turn around Emily blurted out in an agitated state, "You must be Burdee and Tuck!"

Hearing her footsteps, they turned around as Emily finished her pronouncement. Temporarily forgetting her manners, Emily audibly gasped as she came face to face with her first real drag queen.

Recognizing the reaction, he created in some people, Tuck said, "Oh, honey don't have a conniption fit, this is my street drag. Out of respect for Lee."

"Who is Lee?" asked Burdee.

"I felt I should doll myself up a little," continued Tuck. "You know, we used to perform together at the Boulanger Theatrical Cocktail Lounge in Philly. He would have expected me to come with a little glamour banging, you know?"

Feeling like a duck out of water, watching emotion rush across Emily's face, he excitedly continued. "Well anyways, my name is Tuck. That's my stage name, Tuck! My real name is Howard, Howie for short. They called me Tuck because I have so much to tuck!"

Quickly interrupting him, the taller one stuck out his hand, abruptly, saying, "Hi, I'm Burdee - you must be Mrs. Andersen? Thank you so much for calling me."

"Yes, where are my manners? Thank you for calling me, I am Lee's oldest, *bestest* friend," Tuck interjected.

"You are not!" Burdee claimed. "Although I'll admit, we drifted apart when he hooked up with his lover Fred."

"Well, I don't know nothing about no Fred," Tuck admitted. "Lee always called on my birthday and holidays. Every time I called him, I got the phone company messages that said, 'Number disconnected, no further information available.' I stopped asking him for phone numbers. I just waited for him to call me."

Almost whispering conspiratorially, Tuck continued, "I think he wanted to forget about his life in Philadelphia. You know?"

"You're probably right, because he never wanted to talk about his life in Philly." Burdee said. "He told me, 'I couldn't handle my emotions and I lost control of my life' He would just say, 'It was a bad experience.'"

Burdee continued, "And I don't know why you both think his name is Lee. His name is Douglas Powell. We grew up together in Lewistown."

"I know him as Lee Larue..." Emily began, "I have been curious as to his real name. He explained this name was a stage name."

"When I met him in Philly, it was at a drag show." Tuck responded. "When we met, he introduced himself as Lee Larue. Some others thought he was lying, that he was really someone else. But the circumstances were such that it really didn't matter to anyone if he wanted to be incognito. He never spoke much about his family when we met. As we became close, he told me he and his brothers were raised very strictly and kept at home as much as possible. They were not allowed to visit other kids' homes and were not allowed to have their friends visit them in their house. It was as if the parents felt someone might find out about something they were hiding. He'd mention seeing them, visiting them now and then but never in great detail. Almost as if he was ashamed of them, or maybe they didn't want him to tell anyone he was their child. I don't know," Tuck shrugged.

Having listened incredulously, Emily found her voice again, interjecting "My grandparents were from Mount Union, they often visited relatives in central Pennsylvania.

"Really?" Burdee responded, "Small world!"

Burdee was not surprised her family had moved away; he grew up knowing his hometown did not like black people, period.

"Yes, I would love to know more about his family. He told me about his mother's illnesses and poor health. But there is so much more I am curious about."

"Yes, his mother had a long history of illness." Burdee offered. "One Sunday morning he invited a bunch of us over for a breakfast 'soiree'. While he was preparing the food, his father called to tell him his mother had fallen and needed to go to Philadelphia. He wanted 'Lee' to go along and keep his mother company on the trip. Before he left, he asked me to finish cooking the food and told everyone to stay and enjoy the brunch. He gave me a key and asked me to lock up after we left."

Realizing the time, "I want to thank you so much for coming," Emily said with sincerity. "I am so glad to know he had at least two friends who cared enough to come."

Burdee and Tuck looked quizzically at each other. Both started to talk at once.

"At least two friends?"

"He has oodles of friends!"

"You know that is the funniest thing," Burdee said. "The last I knew he and Fred had moved away but were still together. And no one I talked to knew he was sick!"

"I got the same reaction from people I called in Philly," Tuck added. "No one has seen hide nor hair of him but he kept in contact with cards and phone calls. No one had reason to think he would be here, dying."

Burdee reminded him, "He wanted to keep his life with Fred separate from his past, and maybe he was ashamed of his old lifestyle. He didn't let me visit, never came to visit me. I think he was afraid I would break his balls and reveal the sordid experiences we shared."

Looking at one and then the other Emily thought aloud; "It seems neither of you really knew him completely. He was very insistent that I call both of you and ask you each to bring the music he requested. I imagine he wasn't sure if either of you would come. That's probably why he had me call both of you. Originally, he didn't want anyone contacted and has shared very little family information. He only wanted to talk about his life as if giving a confession, like he was seeking forgiveness or understanding."

"Oh, that is so sad!" a teary Tuck blubbered. "Donna Summer's 'Last Dance,' he used to love dancing to that song!"

Burdee laughed. "I remember one night we went out dancing. He wore his keys hanging over his right back pocket. He shook his ass so much! Those keys clattered! Everybody was watching him shake his ass. Oh, I'm sorry, Miss Emily. I shouldn't have said that."

"A month ago, that would have offended me. Since I have met Lee, I have been subjected to some stories that would have un-curled my mother's hair, I'm not quite so sensitive today."

Putting an arm around Burdee's back, Emily offered. "It is getting late. and you two have traveled a distance. Why don't you go get a room at the motel down the road? Freshen up and come back tomorrow. I look forward to talking to both of you about Lee. I feel there is a reason he is taking so long to get the end of his story. Like he is building up to a grand finale, that's needs a great explanation. Once you check in, call back, leave your name, and phone number at the nurses' station in case of emergency. Things should be fine through the night, but you never know." Emily realized as she talked that she did have doubts as to whether he would make it through the night.

As the unlikely trio walked out to the parking lot something nagged in Emily's memory. Emily felt she had forgotten something. Mentally taking inventory, she had her sweater, glasses, carpetbag complete with umbrella. She could not figure out which mental thought was trying to get her attention. Trying to clear her head of the day's dark pervasive misgivings, she looked forward to a good night's rest. She found comfort knowing she would no longer have to bear the burden of Lee's demise by herself; his friends were here. He would not be alone.

It was a nagging thought, now she would not feel so badly at not fulfilling her desire to have Lee ready for her maker. He was not talking so she would not have to listen to any more of that nonsensical tripe. Hearing herself think those unkind remarks brought her back to the reality of the prejudices within her own soul; the many emotions his narratives often stirred within her bosom. She knew many times she wanted to mother him and tell him he was still loved. She was having a reaction to sharing him with these two male strangers. Lee was brash, vulgar, disreputable maybe; but he was vulnerable, and one of God's children.

Leaving the chatty old woman, who was so unlike the people they knew, Burdee and Tuck found the motel. Its adjoining restaurant, bar was surprisingly comfortable for being in Pennsylvania's "God's

Country." After notifying the nurses' station of their contact information they did just as Lee would have done in their situation, or any situation; they headed for the bar.

"We would have raised some hell and tore some new assholes if we had all been together. I mean if we both were running around with Lee at the time, same as him and me did in Philly," Tuck exclaimed.

"Tuck, I don't know about you and him, but we did raise some hell together. You know he never wanted to talk about his life in Philly. I don't know the wheres, whys and hows. What did happen that he left Philadelphia?" Burdee questioned.

"Well Burdee, I do know, the straw that broke that camel's back had to do with his lover Tim! That was a relationship he said many, many times that should have never started. He likened himself to a moth attracted to a flame. He couldn't give Tim up! He wouldn't give Tim up! He said they had many break-ups and reconciliations. Their final break-up was on a Wednesday afternoon.

"Lee had the day off. He was in town kicking around and called Tim to meet him after work for drinks. Tim told him he could not meet him; he would be working late. Impulsively, Lee decided to go visit an old friend, Eddie Peeples, he'd met while he was married. He liked the guy a lot but had not told him he was married when they first met. When the guy found out that he had not been truthful, he dropped him like a hot potato. They eventually became friends but never were intimate.

"He met Tim while he was home on a Christmas visit, from Florida. Although they met in a gay bar, Tim was involved with some girl in Florida and was going to get married. Lee felt it was his job to rescue Tim from making a terrible mistake. He just had to save the girl he did not know, would never meet, from a fate worse than death. Lee always felt guilty since he'd done the same thing to his wife. You did know he has been married?"

Burdee replied. "He mentioned it as a blip. He never talked about it – he didn't want to talk about any part of his Philadelphia life."

"When his wife found out he was gay she didn't have a problem with it." Tuck continued. "She was glad to be out on her own away from underneath her parents' control. He took her with him when he went to the gay bars. Apparently, many of the gay guys felt sorry for her. All gay men know what it is like to lose a potential lover. We all know what it feels like when someone you're interested in isn't that interested in you. I know you know what I mean!

"They lived in Southwest Philly and had taken jobs in the King of Prussia area. He decided he wanted to work in Center City and wanted rid of her. He pushed her out of the house they were buying. He convinced her it made sense for her to move. She didn't drive and could easily take a bus to where she worked. After treating his wife rotten, sorry to speak ill of the dead, I mean sickly? He even enlisted his wife's help trying to dissuade Tim from getting married.

"A few hot and heavy nights together, several long distances, and costly phone calls and Lee was in love! He and his 'still' wife talked Tim out of getting married. Mr. Wonderful told Lee he was in love with him! Over the phone from Florida!!

"Tim said he wanted to move back to Philly and live with Lee and asked him to fly to Florida and help him drive his car back to Pennsylvania. Lee borrowed the money from his friends; you know he could never manage money. When Tim got back to Philly, he did not have a job and didn't hurry finding a job. He was too busy reviving old friendships and buttering up to his aunt and uncle.

"Getting back on track, the old friend Lee went to visit that day, Eddie, couldn't wait for him to bring this new romance back to Philly. He made it his business to help Tim wile away the hours while Lee was working before Tim got a job. They spent a lot of time together and Lee never expected or thought there was anything going on between the two of them. He was always very trusting. During one of their many break-ups he discovered Eddie had been showing him where all the dirty bookstores and gay baths were. Now I ask you! What the fuck's up with that?"

"When Lee told me that part, I asked him, 'How the hell stupid could you have been? Why would you want someone like that? And have Eddie as a friend? I think not!' Well, yeah, Lee didn't know about their shenanigans then, they were not together when he found out. Moreover, Lee should have stayed broke up, the stupid faggot. Excuse me, I know you should not speak ill of the . . . yeah, he's just sick. Too much to drink! Anyways they hung out at each other's houses and ran around together. Eddie had a lover here and there... you know how that goes. ... The lover du jour and they often had a foursome for a dinner, an evening out, movies or the theatre, with Lee never thinking anything amiss.

"So that fateful Wednesday he went to his old friend's apartment.

"Unexpectedly?" asked Burdee.

"Yep: He rang the doorbell and the electric door lock buzzed and he opened the door and started up the stairs. As he's climbing the stairs Eddie opens his front door saying, "You're early!'

"The guy is obviously expecting someone. Someone who he's comfortable enough to greet only with a towel held close against his waist. Lee said, 'His face showed shocking surprise to see me.' It was evident to him that he was expecting someone for an intimate rendezvous, and not him. He was just out of the shower with what Lee thought was disappointment on his face. Before he even gets to the top of the stairs, Eddie starts explaining, 'I have plans. I really don't have time to entertain company right now.'

"Lee teased him, 'I can see someone must be coming over for a hot sex date.'

"'Oh, no!' Eddie says, 'I'm meeting a friend for drinks.'

"'Who are you meeting?' Lee asks.

"'Oh, you don't know him, just a straight guy from work.'

"'Well,' he says, 'Where are you meeting him?'

"'I don't know - he said he'd call and we'd discuss it.'

"'So, whoever was early was someone going along to have drinks with you and your straight friend?'

"Lowering his voice as if talking to a fellow conspirator, Tuck offered, "You know Lee was a good detective.

"Eddie asked him, 'Where did you find a parking space?'

"'Over on Lombard Street,' Lee told him, watching his face for a reaction.

"'So, what's new with you? Why aren't you at work? What brought you downtown?'

"The doorbell rings and Lee says, 'Aren't you going to answer the door?

"'Oh, was that my bell?'"

"'You know it was! And why aren't you answering it?" By now he thinks the guy must assume he's brain dead. Lee was sure something's going on.

"Well, I'm going to ignore it; it can't be my straight friend; because he doesn't know where I live! You're here, I have company. I'm not expecting anyone."

"You know you are so full of bullshit, answer the goddamned door or I will."

"Oh, I'll just look out the window and see who it is." Eddie's apartment faced the street so he went over to the front window. He opens the window, leans out, and waves his arms wildly in the air, resembling a helicopter trying to take off.

"Lee said it was a wonder he didn't fall out the damn window. He thought it looked like he was saying something to the person down on the street at his front door, but didn't want to be heard. Too curious for his own good Lee went to the next window. Opening it, he saw his lover starting to walk back up the street. He calls out, 'Tim!' Sure, as hell, it was his lover. He was too blown away to say anything to either one.

"He left Eddies stopping at a hardware store on the way home. When he got home, he changed the locks. He gathered all Tim's clothes and personal belongings and threw them into a pile in the backyard.

When Tim finally got home, Lee had the door locked and was in the yard with a garden hose wetting down all the things he had thrown there Now wouldn't you think he could realize it was time to put a period behind that relationship? No, not him!

Lee started to stalk Tim. He heard through 'friends' he had picked up with a Willy Blocum. He was told they were attending a gay Catholic church. On Sundays he would go and hide around the corner of the church and watch them coming and going. He started drinking too much, not paying his bills. His mother was in the Graduate Hospital again. He was working part time for the liquor control board and the old Five and Dime. Even so, he was having a hard time making ends meet.

"I used to tell him the reason he went home with so many strangers, was because he drank all his money. He didn't have enough money to buy heating oil. At least picking up someone with their own place gave him a warm bed to sleep in. He was hanging Christmas banners and decorations one evening at the Five & Dime when a young snot nose assistant manager made some remark to him about 'your kind are good at making things pretty.' He decided immediately he was going home with his mother when she was discharged from the hospital.

"Oh honey, he said he was suicidal. The decision to go home wasn't a snap thing. He had a close female friend at the Five & Dime. He called her and told her he was going to take an overdose of pills and liquor. He wanted someone to find him before he started to smell, and they wouldn't be able to make him look pretty. Always a drag queen! And he told her what he wanted to wear in his casket, and where to find whatever papers she would need.

Now see, that's the difference between me and other people. Had he called me, I would have said, YOU, stupid bitch! Quit being a drama queen! For once in your life, be a man, for Christ's sake!

Do you know how many years he put into that Tim guy? Too many! I know...a moth to a flame. But that's bullshit!!

'I never understood how it happened but Tim and his lover helped Lee move back to Lewistown.

He told me how they paraded all the drag dresses he acquired after his breakup with Tim one by one out the front door to his car to irritate the neighbors. They took all his stuff to Lewistown, unloaded it to storage. Then they drove the rental truck back to Philly, returned it, and even paid for it.

"Oh, that's right. The lover wouldn't go to Lewistown, so one of

Lee's friends, some Bartrow person, drove his car and Lee rode in the truck with Tim. He gave the Bartrow person his ID in case he was stopped.

"On the way to Lewistown, Tim told Lee how badly Willy treated him. Apparently, they did threesomes. Tim told him, 'He'll call me at work and tell me he was taking this hot number home for a threesome and that I should hurry home. By the time I get home, they already had sex and the guy was leaving.'

"The friend who drove his car kept his ID and tried to pass himself off as Lee for a quick minute. He was wanted for embezzling from a restaurant where he worked, Carmichaels on the Square. Lee never got his ID back and later found out that his two most prized possessions, a very old Wedgwood cup and saucer, and an old antique flow blue cup and saucer, were missing. They were last seen packed by Bartrow.

"You would think that is the end of the story, but no! Lee had a hard time adjusting to his parents' house and rules. He didn't have enough money to be on his own and he and his mother fought. Over simple shit. She complained he stayed up too late at night watching TV. He was using too much electricity and the furnace stayed on until he went upstairs to bed.

"He packed his clothes and ran back to Philly. He'd stopped paying the mortgage on the house, but they hadn't changed the locks yet. He had left an old folding sofa bed there and although there was no heat or lights, the water was still on. He hung there for a couple days before running back home.

"Another time he packed his stuff in cardboard boxes, took the train to Philly, and stayed with Tim and his lover. He said he was going to join the service, but he was past 35 and they would not take him. The arrangement didn't last, so he returned to Lewistown permanently.

"I always thought he was ashamed of screwing up so many good opportunities. He always landed jobs to pay the bills, owned a house, met some great men. He was good-looking, great personality. His only problem was could not get past Tim.

"That's the last part of his life I was in. That's when he withdrew and kept me in the shadows regarding most of what was going on in his life. Maybe you can tell me what happened."

Burdee was taken aback by what Tuck had told him. The person Tuck described didn't match the Lee he knew. "Well, I must say, I'm surprised! I don't know the man that you knew. Yes, he could be slutty!"

"Once a slut, always a slut" Tuck interjected as he slurped the cherry off the latest Manhattan the bartender gave him.

"Well if he was a slut, I was a whore." Burdee said. "He never whored around like I did. He was always Mother Superior. Not to say, he didn't have anonymous sex. The Lee I knew was never as masochistic as the Lee you knew. Quite the opposite!"

"Excuse me I couldn't help overhearing you talking about your friend. You are friends of Mr. Larue?"

"Excuse me but who the hell are you?" Tuck asked.

"Oh, I'm sorry, my name is Gary. Gary James, I work at Mountain View. I have worked with your friend occasionally. I just found it odd to hear you call him a slut."

"Well, he's our friend we're allowed to talk about him how we want. If he was here, he'd be saying worse things than that about us. Wouldn't he, Burdee?"

"I am sure he'd have something to say, that's for sure. But why are you sticking your nose in our conversation?"

"Because of your friend being a S-L-U-T." Gary gleefully said.

Getting up off his stool pulling his arm back to hit this sucker, Tuck said, "Maybe we shouldn't oughta talk ill of him, but damn if I'm going to let you talk bad about him!"

Backing away the man stammered, "Wait a minute, wait a minute! Don't you know what S.L.U.T. stands for? don't you know about your friend? How close were you?"

"We were the best of friends, had no secrets, so unless you want to pick your teeth up off the floor you better do some fancy talking and quick!" Tuck raged.

"S-L-U-T is an acronym some hospital staff use when talking about a hermaphrodite."

"What the hell are you talking about?" Burdee questioned.

"Your friend being a **S**ingle **L**onely **U**nwanted **T**ransgender!"

Temporarily speechless, they looked at each other for a few minutes not knowing what to say. "Man, you are so full of shit. You are wrong; you got someone mixed up with our friend." They said at the same time.

Gary quickly realized he had had too much to drink. He broke HIPPA confidentiality laws, and was risking getting the shit beat out of him. He quickly left muttering, "Yeah, probably right - sorry, bye."

"I know he's wrong!" Burdee said. "I would have known."

"How? Tuck asked. "Did you guys have sex?"

"Hell, no! Did you?" Burdee asserted.

Tuck pulled his head down into his neck like a turtle; popped it back up and out, and did a miniature, possessed neck twist and loudly announced, "Noooo - not my type. Well, surely you know guys he was with!" Tuck quizzed.

"Now I know you will have a fit when I tell you how we met. He better die, because he would never rest until I was dead, knowing I told you what I am about to tell you. We met at a roadside rest stop up on top of the seven mountains between Lewistown and State College known as Lollipop Park. It was in 1976 and he was living with his parents.

"I was up there one night and one of the regulars said, 'Hey there's a new guy coming up here that people are mistaking for you.'

"I asked, 'Yeah? What's his name?'

"John, one of the old regulars, said, 'I haven't met him yet but there is a resemblance. He's getting many of the Jones boys. Some of the guys are jealous. He's standoffish - he hasn't tried to meet Bob, Mike, me or anyone. Just keeps to himself with the occasional run to the bathroom to grab one before anyone else can.'

Taken back Tuck asked, "Excuse me, what were you doing at a truck stop and what is a Jones boy? Is there a Jones family lives close by, with sons?"

"Oops, that's right - you're from the city. Jones Boy refers to the drivers of the Jones Transport Trucking Company. Roadside rests have wooden freestanding outdoor shithouses. They are there so travelers, mostly truck drivers, can stop and go to the bathroom. Locals or travelers stop and have a rest break or a picnic. All the queens think the Jones Company hires the best-looking men for over-the-road driving. They work to get a hold of a Jones boy. Good-looking, clean, well endowed. You know how it goes, always a bragging contest. I had one this big. Someone had one this big. If you believed every story you heard you would think every truck driver had to lay it on the seat beside him so as not to get his feet entangled.

Gay guys would go there - occasionally during the day, but mostly at night - to pick up other guys who were mostly truck drivers. There were signals known by the gay guys. The truckers would turn their inside cabin lights on as if looking at their time charts, if they were interested. Sometimes the gay guys would walk up and down, along the road, smoking a cigarette. If a trucker was interested, he would light one up and puff back, almost like Indian smoke signals. It sounds silly now."

"But it worked?" Tuck queried?

"Right, like someone would be in charge of bringing china and stem wear. Someone else would bring linens and another Pina Coladas. Only the best of meats and fresh bakery bread; always baked potatoes with all the trimmings. Never dogs, burgers and cold salads for us! And you know we had classical music playing in the background. Dessert was with whoever you could hook up with.

No, Lee interacted like everyone else. I mean, like taking his turn grabbing the men as they came and went. Pardon the pun. He talked of giving head and admitted bending over sometimes, so I know he had sex there. Thinking about it I never remember him saying anything about topping someone."

Tuck chimed in, "You know I was thinking the same thing. We, the other drags and I, were always a little jealous of how good a drag he made. And while so many drags are masculine in bed, me included in case you're interested!"

Burdee questioned him, "Do you mean you think he could have screwed up sex organs?"

Tuck gave a loud harrumph, "Well, I never saw 'em. But I knew so many of the people he was with. Surely someone would have said something. Although, maybe not. When he used to work 13th and Locust in drag, picking up straight guys, he had this trick. To keep them from finding out he was guy, he'd wear a Kotex and say, "I'm having my period. You can screw me in the ass or I'll do head!"

CHAPTER THIRTY-SEVEN

EMILY HAD GONE TO BED WORRYING ABOUT not being able to connect something her mind nagged at her to remember. Jerked awake out of a fitful night's sleep, the restlessness ended, she felt reinvigorated. Her memory put together the elusive puzzle that bothered her reverie as she slept. Ripping the sleeping cap off her gray hair, she rushed to the bathroom to perform a shortened, quicker version of her morning abolitions. She now knew what she had to do if she only had the time to do it. With agility that belied her age, she moved through her apartment that morning with the speed of a person possessed. Her only concern was being too late.

Speaking aloud to her God she prayed, "Please God make me a servant of your work! If I have ever done your work, please, help me now. Please let me get there in time."

Stopping in the middle of putting on her shoes she called Mountain View. She demanded of the switchboard operator, "Put me through to the nurses' station!" As soon as she heard Central pick up, she asked, "Is Lee Larue still with us? Good. Listen closely. I want you to send someone back to his room to tell him what I am going to say to you. Write it down if you must. Repeat exactly what I say. Have it repeated and repeated! Maybe his eyelids will flutter as a sign he has heard.

"'You must hang on! Someone is coming to visit you.' Emily said. 'It is someone you will be glad has come and you will want to see them.'

"Yes, that is correct. Now may I speak to Nurse Rankin please?

"Yes, Nurse, Emily here. I need you to do something for me." Not sure her message would get to him, or Nurse Rankin would take her seriously, Emily hurried about getting herself out of the apartment and on her way to the hospital. Driving as fast as she ever had in her life the short trip seemed to take an eternity today. Again, she prayed to God to let her old car make it.

Anyone observing her as she pulled up to Mountain View would have thought she was running a marathon. This old woman with a cane ran through the lobby to the elevators and hurried to Lee's floor. As she got off the elevator, she saw an aide leave his room. Calling to Nurse Rankin over her shoulder, she literally ran down the hall and past the room. Hurrying she tried to catch up to the departing figure that had gone down the hall on the other side of the building. As she turned the corner, she was just in time to see a door close. Stopping at a door marked maintenance she yanked the door open. The person who entered the room was hurriedly removing a wig and peeling off a nursing uniform that had been put on over street clothes.

Edie turned around menacingly to face an out of breath Emily; "What do you want?"

"Just as I thought!" Emily exclaimed. "Why are you wearing a nursing assistant's uniform? And that wig! You don't work here. What is in this pitcher?"

Edie turned and quickly grabbed the pitcher she had put down and poured whatever had been in the vessel down the sink.

"If we had it tested, I am sure we would have found something in it that's been causing Lee to go downhill."

Hearing the last of Emily's accusation Nurse Rankin, having walked in on the conversation added, "And making your husband sleep more than usual!"

"It's just juice!" Edie squealed.

"You were right, Emily! Mr. Larue's insulin level is off the charts. Something you could easily hide in juice; High enough to push him completely over the edge."

Edie cried, "It's not fair - all those terrible things he said!"

"So, I am right! Quick, we have to get back to Lee and the Chief." Emily urged with concern

Nurse Rankin looked at Emily's retreating figure and thought, "The Chief? Never had Emily been concerned for the Chief."

Cornpopper had come to visit the Chief and Lee's two friends from out of town had arrived to visit with their friend. Several nurses were around the bed checking Lee's blood pressure and vital signs, shaking their heads. Rushing into the room, seeing the grim look on the nurses' faces, Emily saw them put Donna Summers' record on.

Through tearing eyes Tuck cried, "Oh, Miss Emily! We repeated what the nurse said to tell him, but he didn't react much. The comers of his mouth tried to move as if to say something, but nothing!"

"Quick, quick pull that curtain back." Emily cried out loudly. She tried to push the room divider curtains away from between the beds, calling to Lee, "Hang on Lee, hang on!"

Emily leaned over the dozing old man pleading, "Wake up Chief! Wake up!" She fervently prayed, dear god in Heaven, please let this miserable old soul have a clear moment of recollection, please.

Neither Cornpopper, nor anyone else knew what had come over Emily; she was acting like a wild woman!

Edie rushed in minus her nurse's clothes and wig and started pulling Emily away, shouting, "Get away from my husband!"

"Woman, get away from me! As God is my witness, I will hit you with all my might. I am trying to right a wrong here before a father loses his last chance to say good-bye to his son."

An audible gasp stunned the room. A frown crinkled Cornpopper's brow but lightened as he saw Edie's fill with rage.

"Chief, Chief, please help me! Do you recognize this locket?"

The Chief still unresponsive, Emily said to Edie, "Get me that picture of his wife and children that you put away."

"I am his wife!" Edie spit.

"Woman if you don't get me that picture, there's no telling what God is going to have to forgive me for."

Edie produced the picture and Cornpopper quickly remembered the Chief's attractive first wife. Looking at the picture caused a stir in the Chief; he started with his offbeat humor again. "The man called the undertaker and cried, 'Come over and bury my wife!'

"'But,' said the mortician, 'I buried your wife twenty-six years ago!'

"'I got married again,' sobbed the man."

"'Congratulations,' said the undertaker." The Chief started to cry.

"Chief, please! Try to think."

The Chief looked at the picture, then at Emily, his eyes tearing up and glazing over at the same time. Emily asked God's forgiveness and lightly slapped the Chief's cheek. "For God's sake man, please try to think back!"

Pulling the locket Lee gave her out of her blouse Emily asked, "Do you recognize this locket? Is this the locket your wife has on in this picture?"

"Bought it from England; youngest stole it when Edie and I married."

"What was his given name? What was name?"

"The youngest was Daaaa Doug... Douglas." Cornpopper offered.

Quickly moving and shoving furniture around Emily demanded. "Get him up on the side of the bed. Get his chair."

Cornpopper was putting the pieces together as he helped the Chief to his wheelchair.

All this time Donna Summer's song "Last dance, last chance for love" had been playing as his friends were weeping in the corner.

Emily rushed over to Lee's bed as Cornpopper helped the Chief to his chair. Edie retreated to a corner.

"Douglas, Douglas. Your father is here - right here!" Turning to the Chief she moved his chair as close as she could to his son's bedside.

"You didn't know Chief, but Edie chased your son away! She gave him that locket because she was tired of seeing you keep your dead wife's jewelry on her dresser. He didn't steal it. She also told him to take his mother's furniture and all the other things you thought he stole because she threatened to burn them as she burned the handmade cherry wardrobe her father made for her wedding gift that used to be in your dining room."

Emily took Lee's hand, "Your father is here. He loves you. He wants to tell you he loves you."

She took the dying man's hand and placed it in his father's. Turning her attention back to the old man, "We also believe she has been dosing his juice with Insulin to quiet him and we suspect she has done something similar to you."

"Edie?" the Chief stuttered.

"Yes, she figured out who he was when she heard our discussions. She didn't want you to find out who he was.

"But," the Chief stammered, "She told me shortly after she put me here that she received news he died."

"Who would want to know his kind is alive? Better dead than queer." Edie spit.

Although he had not seen his son in 26 years and sickness had ravaged the younger man's body, the Chief knew his son. At that moment, his blue eyes glowed the deep blue that his first wife fell in love with.

"All this time I thought he was dead, my youngest son."

"You may only have moments, Chief. Send him to God's mansion with your love!"

Trying to push himself as far up in his chair as he could, the Chief became very agitated and a hollow cry of anguish filled the room. "Son, I love you. I always have." He reached out to embrace the wan figure lying before him.

The chief took his long-lost son's pale almost lifeless hand and rubbed it against his cheek; sobbing, "I'm sorry, I'm sorry."

Lee's eyes opened wide and he looked up at the man holding his hand; maybe knowing as he drew his last breath, he wasn't alone, maybe he was loved. As his eyes fluttered, he opened his mouth as to speak. Instead the death rattle filled his throat. The Chief collapsed on top of his son. Other than the low playing record, the room was utterly quiet.

"See what you've done! You meddling old woman," Edie cried.

Emily lost control and pulled her arm back to hit Edie, just as Nurse Rankin stopped her. "Last chance, last chance for love" was gone as the needle lifted off the record.

Mountain View lost two patients that day. The Chief's heart gave out when he understood his youngest son had been alive all those years and may have died thinking his father didn't want him or love him.

CHAPTER THIRTY-EIGHT

CORNPOPPER LOOKED TO EMILY FOR explanation. When he had looked at the disease-ridden body earlier in the week, he thought he saw a resemblance of the youngest son. If only he had acted on his impulse then to tell the Chief about the man in the next bed bearing a resemblance to his son.

Nurse Rankin appeared with a security guard to remove Edie as Emily gathered her sweater and purse together and started to head home to collect her thoughts. Caught up in the moments of the men's deaths, she had forgotten momentarily about Tuck and Burdee. She went over to the sobbing men clinging to each other. "I am so sorry you didn't have time to talk to Douglas before he went."

"Douglas. Yes." Tuck murmured. "I could see him as a Douglas. I don't understand how I could know him all those years and not really have known him! When you think of it, how could we have been friends all those years and he not tell me his real name?"

"And what's more, why didn't he tell us he was . . .?"

Burdee stopped Tuck from going further uttering "unusual."

"I know he was blessed to have you Mrs. Anderson," Burdee said.

"Yes," Tuck added. "At least he wasn't alone at the end."

"What will you boys do now?" They looked at each other, each waiting for the answer from the other.

Looking lost, Burdee asked, "Well, surely there will be a service of some kind? Who will take care of it?"

"I expect," Emily offered, "that it would be up to Edie as next of kin!"

"I suppose we could call some of the people we know," Burdee suggested. "But it would take a while to contact them and ask for donations."

"Oh, honey, forget that! You know how those queens are. Once they find out you are dead, without a passing thought, all they think is, Less competition! And what about her costumes?" Just call and tell me where the reception is gonna be. And if there ain't no food, don't call! And as bad as he looks, he wouldn't want anyone eyeballing him - he looks too bad.

"Truth be told," Emily admitted, "He was very adamant in only wanting me to contact both of you. It was almost like you weren't friends, but only a means to an end."

"You mean that queen used us?" Tuck squealed.

"Oh, quiet down, Tuck. What's done is done." Burdee said. Continuing, he told Mrs. Anderson, "I'm going to stay at the motel for a day or two to see what plans are made for him. Would you please call me when you find out what they are?"

"Of course, I will. "Emily replied.

Tuck took Burdee's arm, "Come on girl, let's go celebrate his life. I'll tell you about Johnny Scarlett's funeral and what we did to honor her memory."

By the time Emily got home there was already a message on her machine letting her know that Edie, as next of kin, would not take responsibility for his arrangements. Worse yet the message let her know that the police had no evidence that Edie tried to poison anyone or do anything to her husband.

The day had been bad enough for Emily, but now to think that dreadful woman would not even see to Lee's burial... She had a hard time not thinking of Lee as Lee rather than Douglas. With an unusual lapse of decorum Emily, for the first time in her life, kicked her shoes off right where she stood and fell into her favorite chair. Hugging herself tightly, she silently wept. Emotionally exhausted she had fallen asleep, but as usual awoke with a plan of action and renewed strength.

"Good afternoon, Emily Anderson calling, may I be connected to the administrator's office please?" Well, this was easier than she thought

DANIEL F. POWELL

it would be. Since there was no family to take charge of the body all concerned were very happy for Emily to step up and take responsibility for the arrangements.

All of God's children deserve to have a Christian burial. Before she went to bed that night, she called her children to tell them she planned to use some of her meager savings to bury Lee/Douglas properly. She felt some remorse for using a little of what could be their inheritance but as her daughters told her, "It's your money, Mother! Do with it as you see fit."

She got out of bed the next morning feeling better than she had in weeks. She telephoned her pastor, Dr. Foley, saying she would not be in church tomorrow and explained why she was going to Lewistown. Someone else would teach her adult Sunday school class as she ministered in another way.

She called the motel and told Tuck and Burdee her plans and let them know she would be happy to see them at the service. Making a call to a childhood friend who was the wife of the black minister in Lewistown, she packed her bag and was off. Since Burdee was from Lewistown he took Tuck home with him to tear a path through the local bars

Katie Trueblood was a woman much like Emily, using the time God gave her to answer his call in her own way. Reverend Trueblood was a man of God. He didn't want to think he could ever find another woman like his first wife, but God sent him a little spitfire of a wife in Katie. He found Katie accepted his calling and fit right in, working with and for his congregation, making him proud to have such a great First Lady. Katie was always at your front door with hot food and herbal medicines when she heard you were ailing; in the hospital, she would visit with magazines. Before she left the invalid's room, any personal item you may have forgotten or be in need of would be provided.

After a death in the family, Mrs. Reverend Trueblood would organize the small group of women left in the church. They would march into action, making sure the bereaved had everything they needed - from cleaning the house and making arrangements for out of town visitors, to feeding the family. She was a resourceful, organized lady and always left you with hope and a prayer knowing all was taken care of.

Now Katie had a new mission! She had known Emily Anderson since childhood, although Emily was slightly older. Emily had always been perfect at everything. It might have been said she was a little jealous of Emily. Now was her chance to show Emily she had what it took. Emily needed her! She was going to do her best to help Emily lay *that* young man to rest the way he deserved.

When Emily arrived at the Truebloods' home she was greeted as a long-lost family member who had stayed away much too long. "Emily, it has been way too long! I don't think you have been back since Horace's installation!"

"Yes, you're right, Katie. It's been so long since I visited that I had almost forgotten about the lot where my grandparents were interred. I sat down for a nap and God showed me snow falling on the cemetery in a dream. When I woke up, I understood the message he was sending me."

Katie told Emily, "I called the cemetery association president and found out as long as you scatter the ashes on top of the ground, you don't need anything from them."

Settling in with a cup of chamomile tea, Katie asked, "Now how many people to we need to cook for?"

"None."

"No people?"

"There was only the stepmother and her family. She wants nothing to do with him; there are a couple of friends who came to the hospital. You may have a time understanding their ways, Katie."

Relaxing in the welcoming comfort of her childhood friend's home, Emily told Katie of her meeting and time with Lee/ Douglas. Trying to side-step some of the more colorful aspects, she shared some of the story she'd heard from the dearly departed. From a conversation with Cornpopper, she knew of no one who would be interested in attending the service.

"Well Mr. Trueblood will do the graveside service you talked of Emily, but he would be happy to have a service in the church first."

"No, Katie I think a graveside service will do just fine. If he had a loving family, I'm sure it would be different. But he didn't."

"I did ask the few we have to sing in the cemetery." Katie told Emily. "We have to celebrate his life somehow! Not **just** a somber prayer in a cemetery."

"Oh, Katie, that was so thoughtful of you - but it's not necessary"

"Well, you don't want him in some unknown county plot. And I think if he is all alone, we need to bang on heaven's door and let the angel Gabriel know he's coming."

That evening was spent on reminiscing about old times for the two ladies. They remembered Emily's grandmother Levinia who was a cook for the state prison warden. Every day the warden would send a big fancy car to drive her grandmother back and forth. No matter how bad the weather, the wardens' wife could not do without her Levinia. In addition to being a very good cook, she was queen of the pastry and sweets. She had a staff of 10 who helped with meal preparations. It was only Levinia whose hands dare make the luscious cream cakes and wonderful fruit pies for the warden and his guests. Before any entertaining was scheduled Levinia was consulted to make sure there was no conflict with her personal time. The warden's family could not entertain properly without their Levinia.

Katie's people ran the local neighborhood grocery store. Her family supplied the freshest greens and leanest meats to the local well-to-do. The children grew up in the business delivering boxes overflowing with the best of everything available to the gentry's kitchen via the back door.

Retiring late that evening, the next morning saw Emily rise with a few dark circles under her eyes. Reverend Trueblood drove them to the funeral home from where they would pick up the cremated remains the following morning. Emily had told Mr. Bellaire she would be in to pay the cremation costs.

As the clerk grabbed the receipt book an assistant came in and asked Emily, "Excuse me, Mrs. Anderson?"

"Yes," Emily responded.

"Would you please come into my office; I would like to speak with you." Emily looked at the Truebloods questioningly. The assistant said, "They can come also if you like." The small group was escorted into a richly appointed office decorated with expensive dark wood paneling, heavily brocaded furniture and beautiful pictures.

"Please have a seat, Mrs. Anderson. We needed to ask you to select the casket you would like for the deceased. We could go downstairs to the selection room but we do have everything featured here in pictures if it is all right with you?"

"No, this isn't necessary I am only buying direct cremation. I will pick up the ashes tomorrow and we have permission to scatter the ashes on my grandparents' lot."

"Yes, I understand. Mr. Bellaire apologizes for not being here himself to discuss this with you. He got called away on another emergency and asked me to talk to you. It seems this morning, quite early as a matter of fact, Mr. Bellaire received a call. He has informed me that someone has come forward to pay for a full service for your friend. They wired us a large retainer, more than we would need for a very elaborate service. You can really pick anything you want for the deceased."

My friend? Emily thought; for some reason that bothered her. She didn't know the man really. She only met him through her charity work. Yes, she heard more than she wanted to hear about his life. Yet, he was an enigma. She was willing to pay for a simple, very simple service, and now someone has come out of the woodwork and wants to pay for an elaborate burial.

"And who is this someone?"

"We are not at liberty to say. The instructions we received state, "Give Mrs. Anderson every consideration in anything she chooses to do or requests."

Katie turned to Emily and gushed, "That's wonderful Emily! It's *not like* your purse is so fat you can't shut it."

On top of being irritated by the remark regarding her "friend," now she was nonplussed by someone from behind a closed door giving her carte blanche for his arrangements. She had felt proud, pleased if you will, with herself that she had decided to take charge of the services. It was something she thought God would have wanted her to do. Something she wanted to do... But it has been wrested out of her hands. Standing up to leave, Emily said to the assistant, "I am truly sorry - I seem to have stepped on someone's toes. I find myself thinking I really should step out of the middle of this. Let the benevolent person know I apologize. They may make their own arrangements."

"Oh, Mrs. Anderson, it is I who must apologize." the assistant said. "I must have explained this badly to you. The party in question was able to reach us by phone and wire but can't be here to make the arrangements. He discovered from an acquaintance at Mountain View that Mrs. Powell had refused to take responsibility for the deceased."

"Deceased? He has a name. Can't you say his name? Must you say "the deceased"? Or "your friend"? We know he is dead. Talk about him by using his name, Mr. Powell, or Lee if it is easier." Emily burst into tears collapsing down into her chair.

"He liked his friends to call him Lee!"

Katie reached over and held her, as if soothing a child, cooing, "There, there, everything will be all right. Whatever is the matter, Emily? Aren't you glad someone does have enough regard for the man to pay for whatever you what done? However, **you** want to arrange his services?"

"He deserves better, not just charity from an unknown hand. You didn't know him. He had a heart and a soul. He was a good person; he was just off the path God chose for him," Emily sobbed.

Katie understood: Emily had not just done God's work, she had come to love him as a fellow human being, and loved him as we all should love each other. She truly loved this young man. She wanted to do for him, herself, out of love, as if he had been her own son.

"Emily, if this young man was your son, what would you do for him? Remember how you did for your husband; only the best for him."

"This is totally different! My husband was a man of the cloth for fifty years, he deserved the very best."

"In God's sight we are all equal. We are all given the opportunity to have the best life has to offer. No better. No less. We will be judged on our own merits, not on how we are laid to rest. Are you saying this young man is not as deserving as your husband when it comes to his funeral?"

Interrupting, the assistant said, "Mrs. Anderson, you do not have to do anything differently! You have the option of doing whatever you want. The gentleman who..."

"It was a man who contacted you?" Emily asked looking up sharply, stopping the lady mid-sentence.

"Yes, it was. He understands you are retired and doesn't want to strain you financially. He is a relative and can apparently afford to do this. Oh, I have gone and said too much! It is just that he has asked us to ask you, since he can't be here to carry on, since you came forward when you had no obligation to do so. He was very thankful you did. He is very glad someone did care about Mr. Powell."

With a shake of her head a weary Emily answered, "Very well. We shall make some plans."

To help Emily save money, two of the deacons from the church were going to dig the grave. That was one thing that changed that she was glad about. In the end a simple wooden casket and traditional blanket of flowers was decided upon. She also conceded to allow them to send a sedan, not a large, fancy limousine, to pick them up at the house for transportation.

The next morning promptly at ten o'clock the doorbell rang, a driver was waiting for them. Instead of going directly to the cemetery he took them to the funeral home. The driver explained he was told to bring them back to the funeral home for the closing of the casket. Emily felt like a trapped prisoner. She accepted the fact in her own mind that she had gotten very close to Lee/Douglas. It didn't change the fact it would have been less emotional for her to meet the casket at the cemetery.

A man dressed in a very traditional suit met them at the door. "Good morning Mrs. Anderson. I am Dean Bellaire. I apologize for not being here myself yesterday to explain things to you. How are you doing this morning?"

"Good morning. Well! Thank you! For an old lady my age, I did not expect to be present for the casket closing; I rather thought I would prefer to meet the casket at the cemetery."

"Yes. I did receive that information. Although I was also told by my assistant, she thought we should offer you the opportunity to say good-bye before we closed the casket. I understand you were very fond of Mr. Powell even though you are not related. If you want, we can escort you back to your car and we will go right to the cemetery. We will take care of matters here."

"Since I am here, we might as well take care of it together!"

"All right then, come this way please." The small party followed Mr. Bellaire to a side viewing room.

As they approached the casket Emily gasped, "My golly, the picture doesn't do it justice. It is beautiful wood." The simple blanket of roses Emily chose was above the casket. What grasped her attention more were the head and foot tributes. "Who is responsible for the beautiful flowers?" Emily questioned.

"The gentlemen who contacted us," Mr. Bellaire quietly replied.

The unknown person certainly had Emily curious. She walked up to the casket. Leaning forward, she gazed upon the man she had come to know as Lee. He had been prepared very nicely. They put a charcoal gray pinstripe suit on him and the traditional white shirt and black tie. They had filled out his face with excelsior, but you could still see the vestiges of his final illness. He looked older than his years, but had a handsome distinguished look about him in death.

She opened her purse looking for something and removed a lace handkerchief. Opening the crisp piece of linen, she took from it the locket Lee had given her. Replacing the handkerchief, she closed her purse, grasping the locket in her hand. Leaning into the casket she brushed Lee's cheek with the back of her fingers saying, *"Sleep well my child."*

Tears welling up in her eyes made her reopen her purse, forgetting what she meant to do, and reached again for her handkerchief. Having been given a private moment by the others, when they came back and saw her crying, they came forward comforting her and moved her back away from the body.

Mr. Bellaire at that moment slipped in and took the blanket from Lee's hands and covered his face. That quick the casket was locked and the seal pressurized. The curtains at the double side doors were slipped back to each side and his casket was rolled out under the veranda and placed in the hearse. Mr. Bellaire turned and guided the trio out to the opposite veranda and their car; Lowering her head to get in the car.

"Oh dear," Emily cried. "I wanted to place this locket of his mothers' with him!" And she started to cry harder.

It was a two-car procession that wound around the town square, down Main Street and on to Green Avenue. When they arrived at the cemetery, they found a large service waiting to start across the road in the old part. The black cemetery was laid out far back from the road behind the white peoples' cemetery. There were so many cars for the other funeral they had almost blocked the lane where Emily's group had to turn into. Whoever it was, there were many state and local police cars and fire equipment vehicles parked in and around the cemetery. "Oh, my heavenly days - all those official cars and fire units." Turning to her friends Emily cried, "Don't tell me that is the Chief's funeral! All that commotion for one ignorant, mean man. God forgive me I should not have thought that! He is one of God's children too."

"They may have numbers, but we have a joyful spirit," Katie boasted.

As their car stopped in the lane a little piece from her grandparent's graves, Emily saw a group of seven women by the canopy. As the cars stopped and the rear door of the slumber wagon opened the women broke into song:

> *"I come to the garden alone, while the dew is still on the roses.*
> *And the voice I hear falling on my ear, the son of God commands.*

And he walks with me. And he talks with me. And he tells me I am his own.
And the joys we shared as we tarried there, no other will ever know."

Emily hardly knew what they were singing; she was all too aware of the positioning of the casket. She recognized the Chief's old friend Cornpopper stepping out of the slumber wagon and helping with the deceased's remains. After the casket was placed on the catafalque, Mr. Bellaire opened her car door to escort her and Mrs. Trueblood to their chairs. Just as she stepped onto the artificial grass that was spread out for the service, another car pulled up.

Emily's two daughters rushed to their mother's side with exclamations, "Mother we had to come. You came to know this man and felt his pain. We had to be with you to help lighten your burden." Turning her attention to the two men with her daughters, "Ah, the prodigal son – Phillip, how good of you to come, we so seldom see you; and Gordon, faithful friend. So kind of you to accompany my lost sheep back to the fold."

Emily and her daughters took a seat as the two men filed in behind the ladies. Gordon whispered something into Philip's ear. Only Gordon heard Philip say, "No I haven't told her yet."

As Emily and her daughters took a seat Reverend Trueblood began. "Let not your heart be troubled: ye believe in God, believe also in me. In my Fathers' house are many mansions. ..."

No matter whose funeral she attended, Emily always welled up with emotion at hearing these verses. As Reverend Trueblood finished, a small van pulled up behind her daughters' car. Quickly clamoring out of both sides of the vehicle were members of her own church's choir. They formed a small double line and as they joined the others under the canopy around the lonely wood coffin and began singing,

"Precious Lord take my hand, Lead me on, Let me stand.
I am tired, I am weak, I am worn; Thru the storm,

thru the night, Lead me on to the light, Take my hand
precious Lord, Lead me home."

Emily was overcome with emotions. This was a song they sang for
her husband. And she was so proud that these people, from her own
church miles away, cared enough for her to come help her through
this day.

Reverend Trueblood continued. "We are gathered here today to
pray for the soul of the departed Douglas F. Powell. Although I did
not know him personally, he was known to our dear friend Emily
Anderson. Emily has made it her business to succor the very sick as they
get ready to cross over. She has told me she doesn't think this man had
many friends. Whether true or not I am proud to see those people who
cared enough to come and celebrate here today.

"As we are taught in John 12 Verse 47, And if any man hears my
words, and believe in me, I judge him not: for I came not to judge the
world, but to save the world.

"Emily lives her life by that verse, doing God's mission with the
mortally ill. Today she finds herself confused because she knows this
man was a sinner, as we all are, but he is one of God's children and she
must fight her own feelings and remember she is a servant of God. We
thank her for her work.

"Let us join together for the 23rd Psalm...

righteousness for his name's sake. Yea, though I walk
through the valley of the shadow of "The Lord is my
shepherd I shall not want. He maketh me to lie down
in green pastures: he leadeth me beside still waters. He
restoreth my soul. He leadeth me in the paths of death, I
will fear no evil: for thou art with me.

"Good people, we are here to celebrate this man's life. Not to
mourn. Emily is mourning, but I know she is happy that he has been
blessed and is now with our Father in Heaven.

"Let us rejoice and sing.

"Why should I feel discouraged, why should the shadows come, why should my heart be lonely, And Long for heaven and home, When Jesus is my portion?
My constant friend is he; His eye is on the sparrow, And I know he watches me; His eye is on the sparrow, And I know he watches me.

As Reverend Trueblood was closing the service he asked everyone to join in the Lords' Prayer.

Emily was surprised when she heard a strong male voice behind her, that she couldn't place, join in prayer.

The good gentleman closed with, "May God's benediction fall upon you through the hours of life, as sunshine falls upon the summer's opening flowers. But, should it be that crosses come to bring you naught but pain, remember God the gardener knows when the flowers need the rain."

"Thank you one and all for coming. If you will join us, we will have light refreshments in the church hall."

Emily bowed her head in silent prayer one more time, thanking God for all His blessings. She felt a presence and opened her eyes. Standing before her was a familiar looking stranger. He was a large man and wore a luxurious black coat. She stood up as the stranger reached out a hand and said with a twinkle in his blue eyes, "I do believe you must be Emily Anderson?"

"Yes, sir I am, but you certainly have the advantage. I do not know you. Looking at you, if I didn't know better, I would say I was talking to the man we just buried when he was in his better days. That being impossible you must be related."

"Mrs. Anderson, it is indeed an honor to meet you. Please sit down for a moment if you will. My name... is Douglas Powell. I was working my... ah... my musical variety act in Canada and didn't think I could arrange to be back this quickly. I am so glad to have been able to get here to say thank you in person for your interest."

At that moment the two friends who had been visiting at the hospital spotted the two talking. Squealing with glee they ran over and hugged and "Hollywood style" kissed the man in front of Emily.

Tuck screaming "Lee...Lee...we thought you looked too terrible to be you, even sick and all."

"But we have a few questions, Douglas," Burdee announced.

If Emily had not been sitting, she would have fallen over because she felt a weakening in her legs and a nervous clenching in her stomach.

"Hey guys, it is great to see you and it was really nice of you to come to my funeral. Pardon the irreverence, Mrs. Anderson."

Burdee observing the expensive coat announced, "That coat makes you look big as a bear."

"Jealousy doesn't become you now, any better than it used to, Burdee. Pull in your claws, remember where you are. Besides my lover - oops, sorry Mrs. Anderson - likes my teddy bear look. Listen - let me visit here a few minutes, guys, and then I will explain it all to you. Okay?"

Burdee and Tuck walked away talking excitedly, suggesting many scenarios for Douglas's mysterious appearance.

He turned to Emily, "You buried my fraternal twin Michael Charles Gilbert. My mother was very sick when we were born and my parents didn't want two more children to raise. My father suggested they 'get rid of' the baby that was named Charles because he wasn't what they considered normal. They decided to give him to her oldest brother Ben and his wife who lived in Paoli. They had lost their first child, stillborn - and were told they could never have more children. As it so often happens when couples are told they can't conceive and adopt, they later did have a child naturally.

"My parents kept it secret, not telling many people, and those who knew felt it was for the best for it to be kept a secret. My mother told me about Charles when she was a patient in The Graduate Hospital when I lived in Philly. She thought she was dying and wanted me to know the truth about my birth. When I lived in Philadelphia, friends complained I ignored them and wouldn't talk to them when I saw them in restaurants and clubs. Imagine their reaction when I explained I really did have a twin out there.

"I searched for him and found him. He was resentful of not having been raised by his birth family. He was treated very well and given a great education, the best of everything. Sadly, not too long after we met, my Uncle and his wife his were killed in a car accident in Europe. There wasn't a will in place; everything went to their biological son. My brother started to have mental health problems; he was never the same after their death. At that point he didn't want to bother with any of his birth family. My mother was always sickly and I really didn't want to give her more problems. We decided to keep our contacts just between us. Not speaking ill of the dead, but he had problems. He inherited some of our mother's emotional problems. When he lived with me in Philadelphia, I found out from people I would meet that he went from telling people he didn't know them to telling them that he was me."

"Did you know he had AIDS?" Emily queried.

"He didn't have AIDS! He had terminal cancer. He told my friends in Philadelphia he got it from Agent Orange when he was in Vietnam. Of course, he was never in the service. Our other brother was. I told him all about our family and everything I had done. When he visited me, he would want me to regale him with tales of my 'adventures,' with all the details.

"He took all the dramatic points of others' lives and wove them into a life for himself. I think it got so bad he lost touch with reality at times and didn't know anymore who he really was or what he had really done. When he visited me last year, he told me he was sick. We had a fight because he wanted sympathy and I told him he was still well enough to help around the apartment. He pulled a Sarah Bernhardt and ran away stealing AIDS medicine that belonged to a friend of mine. When he ended up in the hospital, they found AIDS medicine on his person, they thought he had AIDS. They asked him if he did, and he said 'yes'. Sarah Bernhardt all the way and always a martyr, they believed him. His cancer made him look like an AIDS patient. Who would think anyone would lie and say they had AIDS when they didn't? They didn't run tests, because to run tests would mean they were trying to treat him and he didn't want that. He wanted to die."

As taps were played across the road for the Chief, Emily asked, "Are you aware your father is being buried across the street."

"My father buried himself years ago."

"You and Charles have a very similar ability to sound snobby at times."

Laughing Douglas said, "I know. I think that might come from my father's side of the family."

When he laughed Emily could see the resemblance between him and the young mother she saw in the picture. "Oh, my Lord I almost forgot. God does work in mysterious ways." Opening her purse Emily retrieved the locket Lee had given her. "You must have this. Your brother gave it to me but it should be with you. Your father...."

"Yes, Charles took it with him when he left my house after that last visit in Philadelphia. Thank you so much. This has been so much for you to handle. If you don't mind though, I see out of the corner of my eye that the party across the street is breaking up. I would really like to put in an appearance before they all get away; the primary players are still there.

"I suppose you may be a little annoyed with my saying so, but it has been a pleasure meeting you even if it had to be this way. Thank you again for caring enough to do what you did. Don't feel too bad for Charles. He had a charmed life in some ways. Some ways he didn't. He could be very entertaining, and he really knew how to tell a story. You never knew where truth stopped and fiction began. You didn't know if you were hearing real experiences or tales of an unfulfilled fantasy. He liked to quote Rosalind Russell's autobiography title, 'Life is a banquet and so many poor bastards are starving.'"

With a quick hug and a peck on the cheek, he was off like a bear chasing an antelope. Emily turned around to see the Truebloods sitting wide eyed with a "Well, what do you know?" look on their faces. A bewildered Emily barely breathed out, "If that ain't nothing?"

Tuck rushed over, "Did I hear the Reverend say something about a little shin-dig and food at the church? Let's go. When he gets back, we won't let him go until we have all the questions answered."

Across the street heads turned when they heard ice crested snow crackling apart under footsteps. They looked to see who arrived late for the Chief's funeral; Edie's' knees weren't as strong as Emily's and she did fall backwards into her chair.

As Douglas approached the gathering there was a hushed murmur that rose audibly when they discovered the identity of the late arrival. Observers would later talk of the man who appeared, who turned out to be the youngest son of the Chief.

That was almost overshadowed by the news that the Chief and his first wife had another son who was buried that same day in a case of mistaken identity. Although not everything was said loudly, those within earshot heard the man tell Edie he was going to pursue his father's estate. His mother inherited money from one of her relatives which went solely to her; any remains were to go to her sons. The father had no money of his own and they had long spent his retirement money.

It sounded like Edie may end up back in a small non-descript apartment on the wrong side of the tracks; too bad for such a caring wife and lovely lady..

CPSIA information can be obtained
at www.ICGtesting.com
Printed in the USA
BVHW031624291119
565153BV00001B/14/P

9 781480 884229